Amelia Ann Blanford Edwards

My Brother's Wife

A Life-History

Amelia Ann Blanford Edwards

My Brother's Wife
A Life-History

ISBN/EAN: 9783337141523

Printed in Europe, USA, Canada, Australia, Japan

Cover: Foto ©Andreas Hilbeck / pixelio.de

More available books at **www.hansebooks.com**

MY BROTHER'S WIFE.

A Life-History.

BY

AMELIA B. EDWARDS,

AUTHOR OF

"BARBARA'S HISTORY," "THE LADDER OF LIFE," "HAND AND GLOVE," &c.

NEW YORK:

HARPER & BROTHERS, PUBLISHERS,

FRANKLIN SQUARE.

1865.

NOVELS BY AMELIA B. EDWARDS.

BARBARA'S HISTORY. 8vo, Paper, 75 cents.

THE LADDER OF LIFE. A Heart-History. 8vo, Paper, 50 cents.

MY BROTHER'S WIFE. A Life-History. 8vo, Paper, 50 cents.

From the New York Evening Post.

At this day, when so many indifferent namby-pamby novels are thrust upon the public—novels which it is a wearisome waste of time to read—we are quite sure that it is a kindly act to direct our readers' attention to such beautifully-written, and in many cases superior, works of fiction as are these by Miss Edwards.

From the London Times.

"Barbara's History" is a very graceful and charming book, with a well-managed story, clearly-cut characters, and sentiments expressed with an exquisite elocution. The dialogues especially sparkle with repartee. It is a book which the world will like, and which those who commence it will care to finish. This is high praise of a work of art, and so we intend it.

Sent by Mail, postage free, on receipt of the price.

PUBLISHED BY HARPER & BROTHERS, FRANKLIN SQUARE, NEW YORK.

MY BROTHER'S WIFE.

CHAPTER I.

HOME CHRONICLES.

I CAN scarcely believe that my task is real—that I am now guiding my pen along the first few sentences of my Life-History. It seems so strange a thing that any man (and myself above all men) should deliberately receive the whole world into his confidence—should take his own heart to pieces, as one might a passion-flower, and pluck it leaf from leaf, petal from petal, for every eye to gaze upon at will!

Stranger still is it that I should indite these pages in a foreign tongue—that I should, in the first instance, address myself to foreign readers. Yet not so strange, perhaps, when I reflect upon all the long past, and when I remember how dear and familiar is the English language to my lips and to my ears. It is the native tongue of many whom I have best loved in life. From my earliest childhood I have studied and spoken it. I could not write this book with satisfaction to myself in any other; and, be it well or ill done, it must go thus before all who read it.

My name is Paul Latour. I was born upon our estate in Burgundy, about two years after my father's marriage, and three years before the birth of my brother Théophile. I do not remember my father very distinctly, excepting as I saw him lying in his coffin, very pale and still, when they carried me to his chamber, that I might kiss him for the last time. His cheek was cold and sunken; he did not raise those heavy eyelids to gaze fondly upon me as was his wont; and I recollect that I sobbed bitterly without knowing why, unless it were in childish sympathy with the distress around me. Some other memories, vague and transient enough, seem now and then to flit before me—memories of a cordial voice and of a lofty brow—yet, when I strive to realize them, they fade away, and leave me doubting whether they be recollections or fragments of old dreams.

My mother was beautiful—nay, is still beautiful, though somewhat faded by the passage of events and years. According to my earliest impressions, she was tall, fair, and stately as a queen; and, when she spoke, the low tones of her voice were grave and sweet, like the cadence of our chapel bells down in the valley. I will not say that my mother's disposition was unloving; but it was cold—cold toward her husband, toward her servants, toward me. The touch of her white slender fingers was ever brief and unwilling; the expression of her large, calm blue eyes was serious, but frosty; her kisses, for me at least, were careless and infrequent. Théophile was ever her favorite child. She treated us in all respects precisely alike; she never accorded him any indulgence in which I was not an equal sharer; and yet I saw it, knew it, felt it from the first. That she thought her preference unjust, that she even resisted it to the utmost, I am fully certain; for I saw that also. I saw the effort as plainly as I saw the affection, and I wept away many an hour of the night-time thinking of it. No one ever knew how passionately I then loved my mother—how breathlessly I used to listen to her gentle speaking—how reverently and admiringly I used to look up to her beautiful, proud mouth, and to the rich folds of her golden hair! It was an idolatry—the idolatry which children often feel, and for which we are so little disposed to give them credit.

I once dreamt that I was with my mother in the library, and that she took me by the hand, and, looking into my face, said, "Paul, you are not my child." And I remember now, as if it were yesterday, how I woke up sobbing, and crept out of my little bed in the bright moonlight, and stole along the corridor; and how I crouched down at her chamber-door, listening to her breathing, and there dropped asleep. This it was which gave me the reputation of being a somnambulist; for, when they found me in the morning lying there, I would say nothing of what brought me.

I have already stated that Théophile was my mother's favorite; and when I look upward to the mirror near which I am now writing, I can not help acknowledging that her preference was sufficiently natural. My younger brother was tall and fair, like herself; noble-looking; full of spirit and enterprise; and as proud as if he were heir to all Burgundy. As regarded study, he was indolent; yet his abilities were great. He learnt rapidly, easily, brilliantly; and he relied upon this intellectual facility so much, that he frequently left himself more to do than any mind could accomplish in the time. The consequence was, that his knowledge was often superficial, and, still oftener, forgotten as soon as acquired. Besides this, Théophile met with universal indulgence, and from no one more than from our two instructors, M. le Curé, and Mr. Walsingham, our English tutor. He had so many excellent qualities—he was so affectionate — so affable. Though spoilt, he was light-hearted and enjoying. Though, perhaps, a little selfish, he could be profusely generous. Every creature on the estate loved him, down to the poorest *vigneron*. Such was his youth, and so he grew to manhood—willful, careless, in love with life, with pleasure, and with himself. Before he was twenty, Théophile was weary of the country. He was rich, for he would inherit all my mother's fortune, and his yearly allowance, even then, exceeded my modest rental by more than one third. So he left us, and launched himself, with all the heedless delight of youth, upon the brilliant dissipations of Parisian life. He had introductions, wealth, talent, personal advantages; and with many less recommendations than these one may become a wit, a man of fashion, and a *beau garçon*, amid the gay and glittering circles of the best Parisian society.

Must I now speak of myself? Alas! the subject is an ungrateful one; for I have but little to win the favor of strangers.

I am decidedly plain. I was plain from my childhood. My reflection in yonder mirror is that of a pale, dark, melancholy-looking man about eight-and-thirty years of age. I am not yet so old by more than six years; but I have suffered much both in mind and body. My infancy was sickly, and for many months I underwent constant pain from an injury done to my hip in falling from a cherry-tree, so that my countenance learned to wear an expression of settled discontent, which subsequent health has failed to dispel. I limp slightly when I walk— so slightly, I have been told, that it has more the effect of a peculiarity in my gait than a perceptible lameness. I am somewhat below the middle height; my habits are silent and reserved; I dislike much society; and I love to be alone for some hours in every day.

I carried this solitary habit almost to a passion in our old Burgundian chateau; and, as soon as I attained my majority, I proceeded to gratify it, though in a somewhat singular manner. Ever since I was sixteen years of age, I had occupied a wing of the chateau overlooking the garden. I can scarcely say that I occupied the whole of it, for only the ground floor was kept furnished. Here I had the rooms *en suite*, where no one but myself, or my valet, attempted to enter. The first of these was my library, the second my studio (for at that time I was fond of painting), the third my sleeping-room. The library I determined to improve, according to my own taste; and when I entered upon my twenty-first year, I carried my long-contemplated projects into effect.

I caused the windows, which opened upon a terrace leading down to the shrubberies, to be set in Gothic pointed frames, and fitted with stained glass in rich heraldic devices. I had the ceiling supported by arches of carved oak, like the Gothic ceiling of a church; and six spacious alcoves, sunk in the thick walls, contained my books. Between each alcove were panels carved with fruits, and foliage, and graceful arabesques, and hung with groups of arms, and antique coats of mail. Large crimson draperies fell in massive folds before the doors; a Turkey carpet of rich deep hues, like the wings of the peacock butterfly, covered the centre of the floor; several easy-chairs stood here and there; and a table covered with books, writing materials, reading desks, and spirit lamps of different sizes and constructions, occupied the middle of the room. In winter it was warmed by hot pipes concealed within the walls; and at night I used to light a silver lamp of graceful and antique design, which was suspended by chains from the middle of the ceiling, and the light from which streamed down through a globe of amethyst glass as through a painted window. But the most striking objects in my library were the twelve pillars which supported the roof, and which were placed about five feet distant from the walls, down each side of the apartment. These, during my father's lifetime, had consisted of gray marble; I replaced them by twelve colossal statues, carved in oak by a Flemish artist, representing the Apostles. There was something very stately and solemn about these lofty draped figures standing so silently around, especially by night. And night was the time I loved best—the time for thought —the time for study. I delighted in the quaint old literature of the Middle Ages; and it pleased me to fancy some analogy between the darkness of the silent hours before day-dawn, and that early period during which poetry and art groped onward, side by side, amid the gloom, looking with earnestness and hopefulness to the far-off rising of the sun. Then it was that I would take down the folios of long-forgotten writers from the dusty shelves, and read on and on during the quiet night, till I seemed to live back into those old times of emperors, and knights, and poets, who wandered, singing, from land to land, and whose very names have now almost faded out of the pages of history.

I made the early Romance languages my study; I gathered together the chivalric poetry of the Troubadours and the Trouvères; I studied all the varieties of the Provençal dialect, in French, Italian, and Spanish. The rude lovechants of the Emperor Frederick and his chancellor; the songs of the Jongleurs and the German Minnesingers; the old rhymes of King Arthur and his knights; the Romance of the Rose; the Castilian Romanceros; the early Spanish ballads; the Ossianic legends; the ancient chronicles of Froissart and of Stowe; the strange fantastic mysteries and miracle plays which preceded the drama throughout Europe; all "Niebelungen Lieds," "Ottfrieds," "Breviaries of Love," "Cancioneros," Lives of the Saints, "Versos de arte mayor," legends, serventes, canzones, or black-letter pamphlets, were my recreation and delight. Théophile's tastes were not mine. He scoffed at my worm-eaten volumes, at my old poetic lore, and at my church-like sanctuary. I loved the place dearly, for all that. It accorded with my taste for cathedral architecture, and for all that is sombre, solitary, and impressive.

Very different was the chamber opening from it, which I could enter by withdrawing a curtain, and which presented all the heterogeneous confusion of easels, draperies, lay-figures, casts, rusty arms, sketches, antique furniture, and color-boxes, which may generally be found in the atelier of an artist. Here it was my custom to spend several hours during each day, excepting when I took my sketch-book under my arm, and strolled away for all the long summer's morning, amid the shady hollows and rocky heights which extend for miles around that pleasant spot; or when I wandered, book in hand, along the banks of the neighboring river, or through the tangled pathways of the dark, silent forest.

At such times as these, looking round from some elevated point upon the massy woods; the green valleys; the sunny vineyards, with the *vignerons* singing at their work; the rivulets gliding like veins of silver ore along the pasture lands, or dashing in foamy cascades from precipice to precipice; the scattered villages and spires; the quaint slated turrets of our old hereditary chateau glistening in the sun, amid their environment of dark chestnut trees and stately poplars; the lofty mountains standing so solemnly and distantly around — at such times, I repeat, it surprised me that Théophile could relinquish a scene of such rare beauty, and a home so peaceful, for the glaring magnificence, the feverish amusements, and the hollow society of Paris.

Oh, the unspeakable beauty of sweet Burgundy, the vine-garden of France! Who can conceive of it without having beheld it? Who can so admire and love it as those who have been born in its bosom? We Burgundian Frenchmen cherish our native province as we would a beautiful bride, ever fresh, ever smiling, ever young! As the Swiss of his snowy Alps and his Alp-roses — as the Englishman of his wavy corn-fields — as the German of his broad feudal Rhine-river, so are we glad and proud of our mountains and our vine-lands. So do our hearts beat, and our eyes kindle, at the name of Burgundy!

It was my mother's pride and mine to keep up all the quaint old customs of our ancestry — to assemble our tenantry round the yule log, called in Burgundy *Suche* — to sing carols of the "Little Jesus" — to entertain the wandering piper — to attend the midnight mass, and carry the midnight tapers — to distribute the sugar-plums of Noel among the poor children — to preside at the supper of the Rossignon, and to order the festivities of the autumnal Vine-feast and the May pastimes — even as Gui de la Tour used in the olden time, when our family stood high in power and rank at the court of Burgundy.

My younger brother cared nothing for these old historical observances; and, save for a few days at the commencement of the shooting season, he seldom came down to visit us. He had accustomed himself now to the excitement of a great city; he found our home dull, and our pleasures *triste*. He was not at any time very fond of study; he soon became tired of sporting; and in less than a week he was ready to die from *ennui*. So his visits grew shorter and more infrequent, and we seldom saw him more than once in every year.

The last occasion upon which we all met together under the roof of our own home was for the celebration of his twenty-fifth birthday. For this once he had consented to leave Paris, although it was in the gay month of May, and to give us a week of his society, in honor of this quarter of a century of life which he was just completing. And he really came. So they rang the chapel bells as if for a wedding, and I rode out to meet him at the railway station. As we returned through the village, Pierre the blacksmith was nailing a white flag to the old sign-post in front of his door; and the school-children were all shouting at the road-side; and the old women were all peering at us from their cottage windows; and it was quite a triumphal entry, considering the limited resources of Latour-sur-Creil.

CHAPTER II.

A STAR RISES IN THE SKY.

It was during the first week in May that my cousin Adrienne arrived. Théophile had been at home about four days when my mother received the letter from England which announced her coming, and he made up his mind to remain a short time beyond his intended visit, just for the purpose of meeting her; for we were all somewhat curious to see Adrienne, on account of her foreign residence and education. Perhaps it will be as well if, in this place, I briefly sketch the outlines of her history.

My mother's maiden name was Lachapelle. She was the daughter of a gentleman of vast landed property, whose estates joined those of my father, and she had a younger brother named Adrien, an officer in the first regiment of Chasseurs, under Napoleon. The battle of Waterloo was fought—the peace ensued—Adrien returned home just in time to see my mother married, and then went over to England — to the very land against which his sword had been raised so long and so often. He fell in love with an English lady, married her, and made his home for life at a remote country-seat in the county of Devon. He never returned to France; and my grandfather died shortly after, without again beholding the face of his son. Time passed on, and my uncle sent us word that he was the father of a little girl, to be named after himself—Adrienne. From this time an unaccountable apathy seemed to take possession of him; his letters, never very frequent, became fewer and fewer, **and at last ceased** altogether. Then we heard that **his wife died, and,** shortly after, that he also was no more. My mother offered to receive and educate their little orphan, but her maternal relatives refused to part with her. She was adopted by her great-uncle, an old Devonshire esquire, who surrounded her with masters; lavished upon her every kind of indulgence; and placed her, child as she was, at the head of his household. Here she had remained until this very spring-time, when her guardian died suddenly, bequeathing to her the bulk of his riches in addition to her own fortune, and leaving her the entire control of her actions and her property. It was in consequence of this loss that Adrienne wrote to my mother, requesting permission to visit her father's sister, and saying that she could no longer endure to remain in a country which was, for her, the grave of all whom she had loved.

The letter was touchingly and charmingly worded, written in a large free hand, and bordered with deep black. I need scarcely say that my mother's reply was prompt, kind, and hospitable, or that we all awaited the arrival of our English cousin with some little impatience. Théophile, who could find little else to while away the hours, occupied the chief part of every day in wondering if she were pretty, and in casting up complicated rows of figures, in the vain endeavor to calculate the amount of her fortune on both sides of the Channel—which, however, he always threw aside when about half completed. My mother was very pale and silent, for she thought of the father and brother who had passed away. As for me, I fear I was hypocrite enough to affect a total indifference upon the subject of our visitor, and even to murmur audibly against the disturbance of our household quiet.

The day came at last—the day appointed by Adrienne in her second letter. The Paris and Strasburg line of railway does not traverse our part of Burgundy, and the nearest station is at Chalons, full eighteen miles away. We sent a carriage to meet her; and, as we could not tell by what train to expect her, we gave instructions to the servants to remain all day at the station until Mademoiselle Lachapelle should arrive. It was quite late in the evening before they returned. We were all sitting together at a large open window in the best reception-room, a lofty paneled chamber set round with antique mirrors and hung with amber damask, commanding a view of the high road and all the surrounding country. The dusk had closed in so thickly upon the landscape that we heard the quick rolling of the wheels long before the carriage drew near enough to be distinguished. On it came, faintly at first and louder by degrees, along the level road. We saw the flashing lamps between the lime-trees that stand for miles and miles on either side—we heard the cracking of the whip, and the hoarse cry of the postillion. Nearer it came and nearer. There was the throwing open of gates—the clattering

in upon the pavement of the court-yard—the sudden stoppage before the hall entrance.

"Diable!" said my brother, with a suppressed yawn; "I am glad that *la petite Anglaise* has come at last, for I am furiously hungry!"

In a moment the door was thrown open; "Mademoiselle Lachapelle!" was announced; and my mother, who had been striving, ever since we first heard the distant sound of wheels, to maintain her usual calm and dignified bearing, now stepped forward to the dark figure standing at the threshold, and saying, in a low voice, "My dear niece!" folded her in her arms, and imprinted a stately kiss upon her forehead.

Then my mother introduced us both by name to Adrienne, and led her straight away to her own apartments. All this took place so hurriedly, and the room was so dark, that we had not yet seen her face, or distinguished more of her voice than a few faltered sentences.

But, even then, I thought the voice was sweet!

They were a long time away—more than three quarters of an hour. Théophile rang for lights while we were waiting, and looked at his image in the glass, arranging the thick curls of his golden hair, and whistling dreamily to himself; while every now and then he would stride impatiently to and fro, murmuring against the delay, and exclaiming that he should be starved ere long. As for me, I drew a volume of Uhland's poetry from my pocket and tried to read; but my mind wandered from it, and I went over and looked out at the pale moon rising behind the poplars, and at the still, dark landscape, as it lay beyond the window like a framed picture. And sometimes, as I stood there, there came the swift whirring of a bat close before my face, and sometimes the intermitting passionate song of the far-off nightingales, amid the topmost branches of the trees.

Suddenly the door opened—they entered— the servant, who had been waiting outside for the purpose, stepped forward and announced that dinner was served—Théophile, as usual, gave his arm to my mother—I, confusedly and awkwardly, handed down our visitor, without even looking at or speaking to her—and thus, preceded by servants and lights, we descended the stairs and entered the dining-room.

But, when we were seated at table, I raised my eyes to her face and saw that she was beautiful. And now let me observe, if I were to describe her as she seemed to me that night, and for the few weeks following, I should use terms little short of extravagance. I had seen few women then, save the sunburnt peasants who labored with their husbands and brothers in our vineyards, and, on rare occasions, the daughters of some few and distant neighbors. Beauty and youth were too unfamiliar to me that I should judge of them very narrowly, and, to my eyes, Adrienne Lachapelle seemed radiant as an angel. In all my artist-dreams, in all that I had pictured to myself of the fair ladies of the songs of old, I had never imagined any thing so unspeakably fair. And yet I find it difficult to say in what her loveliness consisted. It was not in her eyes, though they were large, and soft, and blue, like my mother's; nor in her mouth, though it was delicately beautiful; nor in the contour of her head, graceful and self-poised, like that of the young Diana. It was not in her features, or her form, or in any one perfection you might name; but I think it lay, rather, in the sweet gentleness—gentle, yet animated—of her expression. Every thought and emotion that passed through her mind reflected itself upon her countenance, as the under-current of a streamlet breaks the sunshine into ripples on the surface. When she spoke, her color came and went with every earnest word. Mirthful as a child, the simplest jest would light her face with smiles—smiles not only of the lips, but of the eyes. A sweet, mournful poem, read aloud, would cover her cheeks with tears. She varied every moment, like an April day; and when she blushed, the faint crimson would suffuse her very brow, as a sunset on the Alps. But I am speaking of her now as I saw her after some days, not as I saw her on that brief evening; and, even so, how useless is my attempt to depict in words that which I can not make clear to my own thoughts! Nothing is more difficult than to describe a really beautiful countenance (especially if it be one we dearly love); for there is always, in real beauty, a something for which we find no equivalent in language—a something so refined, so evanescent, that all written description seems poor and clumsy in the comparison. Such was the beauty of Adrienne, and this it is which, as I first begin to speak of her, seems to embarrass and defy me.

The dinner was long and formal. Adrienne, in her black dress, bending down her head and scarcely partaking of any thing placed before her, replied lowly and by monosyllables to the few commonplaces which were from time to time addressed to her. My mother, still pale and sad, looked toward her at intervals, but spoke seldom. Even Théophile, after a few efforts at conversation, said no more, and applied himself wholly to the business of the table. Indeed, he was the only one among us to whom it was not almost a mockery; he enjoyed and partook of it as usual. For myself, I never once broke the silence, but sat there at the head of the board like one dreaming; mechanically performing my duties of host; gazing earnestly on the downcast face between me and my mother; and listening with suspended breath to every murmured word that proceeded from her lips.

This dinner-ceremony, so long, so silent, so constrained, came at last to a conclusion. We returned to the salon, whence, after a few moments, Adrienne, pleading the fatigue of her long journey, retired, accompanied by my mother, and, as far as the room door, by Théophile, who sprang forward to hold it open for them as they passed.

"What a wretched evening!" he exclaimed, returning and flinging himself upon a fauteuil near the window. "Mais n'est-ce-pas qu'elle est belle, cette petite cousine?"

What had he said that I should feel the hot blood rush up to my brow so angrily? What was there in his words that I could not answer them? Was it that he had spoken somewhat lightly, and that I, already, could not bear to hear it? I know not; but it seemed, at all events, to jar upon the pleasant harmony of my thoughts. I turned away, and was silent. Presently I also left the room, and went down into my library to read.

To read! Ah! no; I could not read that night. It was all in vain that I took up volume after volume of my favorite authors. Something seemed to interpose between their thoughts and mine—something whereby I was made restless, but not unhappy—something which prompted me at last to close the book, to withdraw the heavy folds that curtained out the night, and to stand there at the open casement, looking up to the sky and the stars.

The moonlight lay upon the turrets and the trees, and fell in patches, faintly colored by the stained glass, upon the floor beside me. The Apostles stood within, brown, shadowy, and gigantic. The silver lamp burned dimly. There was a magical stillness in the air—a holiness unutterable in the night-silence. It seemed to me as if all Nature were one vast cathedral, with blue arching roof—with a starry multitude of lamps, and with myself for a solitary worshiper. And in that supreme hour an impulse of infinite gratitude and awe came over my soul, and I thought of heaven, of truth, of life, of Adrienne.

I felt as one who reads the opening page of a strange, sweet poem, or as one who sits for the first time in a brilliant theatre. Beauty and grace are met on every side. The air is heavy with perfume. The orchestra gives forth a low intoxicating melody, and the hush of expectation is on every lip. His heart beats; his breath comes and goes; he trembles; his eyes are fixed upon the dark curtain which is so soon to rise, and the skirts of which are already fringed with the radiance beyond.

And was it not truly so? Was I not unfolding the poem in my heart—gazing upon that curtain? Was it not the first Act of my Life-Drama that was about to commence?

CHAPTER III.

THE FOUNTAIN OF ROSES.

About eight miles from Latour-sur-Creil, half way up a wooded mountain in the direction of Strasburg, there may be found a delicious little spring, quite shut in and hidden by trees and wild rose-bushes, which was christened by my mother La Fontaine aux Roses. It is somewhat difficult of access; for, after leaving the cultivated fields and vineyards that extend for about a quarter of a mile up the ascent, you find the road, which has been getting narrower and narrower all the way, diminish suddenly to a steep shingly footpath, wide enough for only one person at a time. Following this amid the thick green shade, you arrive at last, wearily enough, upon a little level platform cut sheer away, as it would seem, from the shelving rock, which here rises precipitously at the back, in overhanging blocks of rough dark granite. Facing you lies the continuation of your pathway, narrower, steeper, more unpromising than before; at the edge of the platform, the cliff (steep and bush-grown) seems to sink away beneath your very feet; to the left a tiny opening, or fissure in the rock, seems to indicate the track of some animal, looking too narrow for the passage of any thing larger than a goat. Nevertheless, try it. You will find it sufficiently wide to admit of your entrance. Once through the little straits, you are in a sort of natural vault, hollowed out of this same granite; treading softly upon a carpet of thick gray moss; making toward that day-opening at the end of the rough corridor, about forty yards in advance. When half way along, you pause and listen: it is the gush and gurgle of water that you hear echoing down the cool stillness of the granite walls; and, hastening on to the end with what speed you may, you there discover a little "heart of green," all set round with trees, and rock-cliffs, and wild wavy ferns; with a broad boundless landscape stretched out far and wide at one side, and, on the other, a fount of fresh bright water welling up through a bower of wild dog-roses from the inner depths of the rough mountain mass overhead. Springing, foaming, leaping forth—eddying down into a pebbly basin—flowing with a sudden calmness in and out the trees, and across the few square yards of grassy platform—winding, as it were, unconsciously toward the brow of the cliff—whirling over in swift madness, and falling, ever falling, from ledge to ledge, from steep to steep, all spray, hurry, and confusion, till at length it disappears among the forest trees down far below, and is seen no more—unless, indeed, it might be that smooth gliding rivulet which shows so silverly along the valley, and flows, miles away, into the current of yon broad river setting onward to the sea!

Exquisite *Fontaine aux Roses!* Was I not the first to penetrate thy fairy nook; to drink of thy waters; to press thine untrodden turf; to lie in the shadow of thy trees, gazing upon thy wild mountain flowers and feathery grasses, and listening dreamily to the sweet cadence of thy falling music? Chancing upon thee in one lonely walk some nine years past, did I not become the Columbus of thy vernal world? and may not I (as thy discoverer) be pardoned for dwelling, perchance too tediously, upon the praises of thy beauty? Hither, then, one genial afternoon in May, we came to show the view to my cousin Adrienne, and to picnic beside the fountain. She had been with us about a week; and by this time the first strangeness had worn away, and we had become, in all respects, better acquainted. We were charmed with Adrienne. Already she had fascinated us, as she fascinated every one through life, with her graceful kindness of manner; her deep feeling for truth and beauty; her airy wit and playful bearing. Susceptible alike to pleasure or sadness—sunny, yet variable—now childlike, enjoying—now womanly, tender—it was impossible to determine when, or in what mood, she seemed most winning. Hers was a nature wild, beautiful, capricious—a soul

"Where shadows dark and sunlight sheen
　Alternate come and go!"

On this sweet day of May how fair and seasonable she looked, like a delicate May flower, and how her bright laugh cheered the rugged mountain-path, and lapsed in with the water-song of the fountain! Théophile was in high spirits, looked handsome, flushed, excited. My mother unbent for once, and smiled, and conversed gayly. Even I, silent, distant, unsocial as I am, grew cheerful, even conversational, under the influence of that bright sky, that fountain nook, that magical presence!

We were very happy. We admired the view—we sat under the shadow of a mountain ash—we opened the basket of sandwiches which Théophile and I had carried alternately up the mountain—we cooled our Champagne bottles in the running stream, and chinked our glasses laughingly together—we made a wreath of oak-leaves, roses, and green berries, and placed it upon Adrienne's golden hair—we poured a libation of red wine into the dancing waters, and drank to the "flowery-kirtled naiad" of the fountain—we chatted—we jested—we sang—in short, we yielded up our whole hearts to the influence of the hour and the place, "giving no thought to the morrow."

"How pleasant it is," observed my mother, looking round with a contented smile, "to be assembled up here, on this beautiful day, where no one can interrupt or find us! Do you know, these trees—this landscape—this 'enameled sward,' as it is called by the romancists—nay, the very wine-glasses yonder, remind me irresistibly of the Decamerone?"

"I had often wondered," said Adrienne, suddenly, "who it was that originated that hackneyed simile, 'enameled sward;' but the other day I found it somewhere in the 'Purgatorio' of Dante. He calls it 'la verde smalto.' How pretty it is—in Italian!"

"How pretty any thing is in Italian!" exclaimed Théophile. "Why, a Neapolitan fisherman might swear at you for an hour, and you could almost fancy that he was addressing to you the choicest compliments—if you did not understand the language. I have heard them at it many a time in the Chiaja. Two of the fellows, with their scarlet caps and black curly beards, will stand face to face, leaning against the doors of their houses, or even lying lazily on the ground, and swear at each other in the most deliciously intonated liquid tones for hours together. It is one of their national amusements."

"How horrible! And perhaps one assassinates the other afterward!"

"By no means. That is quite a lady's notion! They are the greatest cowards imaginable. They quarrel, they glare upon each other, they swear to their heart's content, but they never come to blows. And these men's forefathers were the masters of the world! Alas! degenerate Italy, once the birthplace of heroes and the garden of Europe!"

"But it is a garden still!" cried Adrienne, warmly. "It has lost its Cæsars, but not its vineyards, its olive-groves, its fair Lombardian plains!"

"True, mademoiselle," I said, turning toward her and taking up the theme. "True, it is a garden, but a garden in ruins—a garden such as your English Shelley describes in the 'Sensitive Plant'—such as Hood pictures in his 'Haunted House.' Rarest exotics spring up side by side with the nettle and the deadly nightshade; the fountain is choked and moss-grown; the very sun-dial is broken, for what need is there to mark the progress of Time where Time finds nothing to record? There are statues also, defaced, neglected, lying in the grass; the present generation, plodding idly on, treads them deeper and deeper into the clay; the traveler, the stranger, alone reverences and re-erects them. They are the statues of Dante—of Petrarch—of Ariosto—of Tasso!"

"Do not omit my favorite Metastasio," said Adrienne, who listened while I spoke with a bright, earnest gaze peculiar to herself, and which I have never seen on any other countenance. "I so delight in his long musical periods, and, for the sake of his harmony, pardon the monotony of his plots. And pray do not forget that noble woman who lavished such exquisite verses on so worthless a husband—I mean Vittoria Colonna."

"It appears to me," observed my mother, quietly, "that your remarks are very partial. Pray, has Italy no modern poets and historians, no men of eminence whatever? Have you nothing to say for Manzoni—for Casti—for Pellico?"

"Not much," replied Adrienne, smiling. "'I Promissi Sposi' is tedious, and as for 'Gli Animali Parlanti,' it is very uninteresting; Gay's and La Fontaine's Fables are worth a thousand of it. Pellico's prison-narrative is perfection, and has, I suppose, become a classic in almost every language. I have not read his poetry."

"His poetry!" echoed Théophile. "Oh, defend me from his poetry! I once attempted to read his tragedy of 'Francesca de Rimini,' but I could get no farther than the end of the first act. It is a feeble imitation of Alfieri; and his long romanza, 'La Pia,' founded on a passage in Dante, is a weary performance, in I know not how many cantos. The original is four lines long, and one of the sweetest, saddest, briefest stories ever written in verse."

"I remember it," said Adrienne. "It is the tale of Madonna Pia. Her husband took her to a castle in the marshes of Volterra, and there watched her fade and die beneath the noxious influence of the *malaria* incidental to the swamps. A fearful vengeance!"

"Fearful indeed, and national; like the swearing," said Théophile. "The Italian is cruel and cowardly; or, rather, he *was* both, but now he is only the latter."

"But Italy has, within the last forty years, produced several lyric poets of considerable merit," I said, after a pause. "Do you know anything of Rosetti, Berchet, Leopardi?"

Adrienne shook her head, and I went on.

"Rosetti is a revolutionary poet, full of fire and military ardor. His songs relate chiefly to the Neapolitan disturbances of 1820 and 1837. There is one commencing 'O Cittadini all' armi!' (Oh, citizens, to arms!), and another 'L'Asilo e l'Arpa dell' Esilio' (The Home and the Harp of the Exile), both of which are admirable, and have the heart of a patriot beating in every line. He was exiled in consequence, and fled to England. Berchet, too, is well worthy your attention. His political romanzas are both novel and affecting."

"And Leopardi?" asked Adrienne. "Is he equally clever?"

"He has not written so much as either of the others, and the little which we have is, for the most part, fragmentary. But it is graceful, fresh, suggestive, like the ballad-poetry of Uhland and Müller. There is one little strophe of his which pleased me so much, and is so utterly Germanic in style and conception, that I translated it into English. I think I can remember it, and you shall tell me if you like it:

> "Parted from thy native bough,
> Whither, whither goest thou,
>   Leaflet frail?
> From the beech-tree where I grew
>   In the vale,
> From the woods all wet with dew,
> Lo! the wind hath torn me!
> O'er the mountain tops he blew,
>   And hither he hath borne me!
> With him wandering for aye,
>   Until he forsakes me,
> I, with many others, stray,
>   Heedless where he takes me.
> Where the leaf of laurel goes,
>   And the leaflet of the rose."

"That is delicious!" said Adrienne, her eyes filled with tears. "It is simple, yet how sweet! Without uttering it in words, it seems to suggest a feeling of Life and its shadowy Beyond. What is its title?"

"I call it 'The Leaf and the Breeze;' but the poet has only prefixed to it the inappropriate and modest word 'Imitazione.' It would make a beautiful song for music."

"Yes; but the composer must also be a poet. Mendelssohn should have done it, with his profound feeling and picturesque mannerism. I shall ask you for a copy of that poem—the original as well as the translation."

The sun was now sinking lower and lower on the horizon, and shining crimsonly through the belt of amber vapor that skirted the landscape all around. The air, too, grew somewhat chill upon that mountain height; and the birds, twittering softly, came wheeling round the trees and fluttering in among the leaves to their nests in the branches.

The conversation dropped, and we sat for some time gazing at the sunset. Then, as if by common consent, we looked into one another's faces, and rose up from our pleasant seat beneath the mountain ash. It had been a happy day; but the sweetest poem must end, and we felt that this had come to a conclusion.

So we bade farewell to *La Fontaine aux Roses*, and went down silently into the brown shadows of the valley.

CHAPTER IV.

DREAMING.

WE have an old French proverb which says "*Le bien vient en dormant.*" Better had it been written "*L'amour* vient en dormant," which it truly does. Love! why the very word hath some such slumberous spell in the mere sound of it! Doth it not come to us, for the most part, gradually, imperceptibly—as a dream to our sleeping? Nay, is it not a dream, a golden gossamer dream, transfiguring the shows of Earth, and clothing all Life as in a divine garment?

In the semblance of a dream it came to me; and I knew it not until the time arrived when I could no longer deny it, even to myself. I loved her. I loved her passionately. I loved her with all the force of a heart long silent and long solitary, and yet I did not discover it for many weeks. Be it not supposed, for this reason, that I loved suddenly. Ah! no. I had felt the joy at my heart, though I knew not whence it came. I had seen new gladness in life—in thought—in the world. My tongue had been loosened in speech, so that I sat no longer like a misanthrope among others, but, emboldened by her presence, learned to pour forth my thoughts, if not with eloquence, at least with that earnestness which befits a true man. And she had listened to me —listened with attention—with smiles—it might be, sometimes, with tears. Oh, blessed time when I loved and knew it not! Oh, still more blessed morning of early June when I first interpreted the sweet new secret of my heart! It happened thus:

I had risen early—earlier than was usual with me; for I awoke soon after day, and could not sleep again. Aimlessly, carelessly, with thoughts elsewhere busy, I strolled into my painting-room, and, taking my accustomed seat, leaned my head upon my hand, and gazed vacantly upon the half-finished picture that stood before me on the easel.

It was an interior—how well I remember it! —a church interior, lofty, pillared, gloomy with shadow and deep-stained oriels; empty, save a few scattered worshipers kneeling on the polished flags in the foreground; with vacant altar,

and long tenebrous aisles lighted dimly in the distance. An interior such as I delighted to imagine; for, as I have said, I had a true love and appreciation of cathedral architecture, especially of that order called the Flamboyant Gothic.

Thus thinking and looking, I resumed the palette and brushes close at hand, and began, as it were mechanically, to fill in the outline of a female figure kneeling before a confessional in the foreground. The confessional itself, with carved foliage and cherubim, and florid pediment and traceried lattice, stood, half hidden, in a dark angle of shadow; but I had so contrived that a single thread of light, falling through a partially opened door, should irradiate the face and head of the penitent almost like an emblematic glory.

On this head and face I worked, still absently, still with thoughts intent on other things. Strange, that the eye and the hand should toil on without the master-guidance of the mind! Stranger yet that the eye and the hand should, all unconsciously, respond to that inner working, and begin shaping forth the hidden thought upon the canvas, visibly realizing the invisible!

Suddenly I dropped the pencil—started—rose —returned, and looked long and earnestly, till the gathering tears blotted out and blurred the picture from my sight.

In that face I had painted the face of Adrienne!

I can not tell now how long I stood there gazing—gazing, or in what vague, unreflecting state of confused happiness I was; but, all at once, a sudden flush overspread my countenance—I trembled—I turned away from the picture—I paced rapidly up and down the room.

"Yes, Adrienne," I cried aloud, with passionate vehemence, "I love thee! I love thee!"

Oh happy secret, so welcome and so beautiful! And yet, even then, I seemed both to rejoice at and fear it!

The room felt close and oppressive. I could scarcely breathe.

I threw open the windows, and stepped out into the morning.

There was a warm soft air abroad, heavy to the sense, and somewhat obscuring the distant landscape. The turf sent up a pleasant odor of fresh earth. The sky was dull and gray. Every now and then a breath of fresh breeze came sweeping over the fields, bearing with it a perfume of sweet hay and May blossom, and shaking the bright drops from off the broad leaves of the chestnuts and acacias. The trees in the garden looked round and shadowy. The grass was full of tiny yellow flowers, and stretched out in one broad green and golden sweep down to the river bank. All was still and slumbrous in the dreamy atmosphere of the June morning.

Forth I went, restless—intoxicated, with a fountain of gladness welling up from my heart. Forth I went, across the long wet grass and into the shade of the tall trees. I looked back at the chateau, with its steep roof, its long ranges of small glittering windows, and its quaint pointed slate-roofed turrets. It was my chateau, the chateau of my fathers, and I thought in my heart how fair would life be were she the mistress of those gray old walls. To the left I saw her window, curtained and closed. I stretched out my arms as if embracing her, and again I said,

"I love thee, Adrienne! I love thee!"

I passed out of the wicket-gate and into the forest beyond. The sun came slowly out, and the birds sang in the boughs. There were wild strawberry-blossoms and violets under my feet —green leaves, and sunshine, and openings of blue sky overhead. A young lizard, feeble, emerald-hued, half-stupefied, lay in my path, and I stooped down and placed it on one side amid some high soft grasses; for my heart was full of love, even for the green lizard. Then the shade grew deeper. The clouds met, and melted into a shower, and I uncovered my head and looked up, and let the warm rain-drops splash heavily upon my brow. Then the sun came out again; and the birds rejoiced and shook their sleek plumage, and sang more merrily than before. And I went on, still on, amid the living stillness of the forest, with a new fire in my eye and a new freedom in my step, and with the same words of foolish exultation ever on my lips,

"I love thee! I love thee!"

Once I paused and asked myself, "Art thou beloved also?" But with the question came a doubt, and the heavens were darkened. Then I said, "Let me be happy, if it be only for this one day!" And I dismissed the question and the doubt, and went forward blindly rejoicing— rejoicing that I had seen, that I loved her— wishing that she might remain in Burgundy forever—drinking in hope and joy from every sight and sound: from the rustling of the leaves, from the song of the wood-birds, from the hum of the wild bees.

"Ah! con che affetto amore e fl ciel pregal,
Che fosse eterno el dolce soggiorno ;
Ma fu la speme al ver lunge assai !"

Dreaming, dreaming — consciously dreaming, and refusing to be awakened!

CHAPTER V.

WAKING.

THERE is a German tradition respecting a certain Saint Elizabeth of Marburg, who, in proof of her sanctity, hung out her washing to dry on a sunbeam. To this saint, by one of those strange contradictory impulses of our nature which sometimes contrast the saddest with the most ludicrous things, I involuntarily compared myself, as I sat silently apart in a dark corner of the salon some few evenings after my

* TRANS.—Ah! with what earnestness did I pray to Heaven and Love that so sweet a stay should be eternal; but my hopes were far from anticipating the truth!

ramble in the forest. Had I not trusted to an illusion as glittering, as beautiful, as unsubstantial ? Had I not hung my hopes on a sunbeam ?

Alas! it needed but a brief time to work this change—to steal the brightness from my dream and the hope from my heart.

Théophile loved her. I was convinced that he loved her. Had I not seen him walking beside her in the garden-paths in the evening of that day—that one happy day; and had it not chilled me even then, although I knew not why ? Since that time had not his attentions been redoubled? Was he not hovering round her at all hours? Sitting beside her at table ? Riding with her? Walking with her? Reading to her while she sat embroidering under the laburnums? Nay, is he not at this moment hanging over her, as she looks through the music lying loosely upon the piano, and allows her fingers to wander idly along the ivory keys? Is she not listening, with head half turned aside —listening to his low speaking, and thinking nothing of piano or music?

My mother is not present, and I am affecting to read by the waning twilight. They are quite at the farther end of the room, and they speak in that subdued tone which people's voices are so apt to assume in the dusky hour. I watch them jealously over the edge of my book. I can not hear any thing they say. I neither wish nor try to hear; but I can not help looking at them; and, though I turn resolutely to the window every now and then, I find myself, the very next minute, falling back into the old posture. I am very unhappy — very lonely! "Ah!" I think bitterly to myself, "if she could but know how I love her! if she could but judge between us, and choose the one who loves her best!"

Théophile is still bending over her—lower, lower! His yellow curls shine through the gloom. How handsome he is! There is a mirror near me (the room is paneled with mirrors), and I look up, with an angry pang, at my own sallow, sorrowful countenance. What! am I envious already? Envious as well as jealous? I feel the hot blood flush up to my face for very shame—I struggle resolutely with my own heart —I fix my eyes upon the book, but the letters waver, and grow distorted, and swim before them. Now I reproach myself. After all, it is I, and only I, who am to blame! Why, I loved her from the first. I loved her from that very night, five long weeks ago, when she first sat before my eyes, so pale, so silent, so beautiful, in that dining parlor below! Why did I not try to win her then, even then, and every succeeding day? Why did I leave the field open to another? I have education, I have heart, I have a wild latent poetry in my nature wherewith I might have won a woman's love as easily as with perfumed locks, and compliments, and a low flattering voice! Pshaw! am I a man, that I should have sat thus tamely by and lost the treasure without a single effort?

Would she not despise me now if she knew how I loved, how I loitered, how I suffered?

Thinking thus, I lash myself to fury. I feel an impulse upon me to utter my rage aloud—to pace violently up and down the room—to tear the book to pieces which I hold in my hand! But, for all this, I sit still and silent. I press my lips together, and clench my hands till the nails wound the palm. I become alternately hot and cold. I endure a martyrdom of envy, jealousy, and remorse; and still I sit watching them over the edge of my book, and still Théophile bends down to Adrienne till his yellow curls almost meet the soft braids of her lustrous hair!

All at once she touches the instrument again, and plays some few notes of a very simple, but a plaintive symphony. Théophile draws back and leans against the wall, listening. I breathe more freely now that the distance between them is greater. Presently the notes of the symphony become fewer and fainter, like the last drops of a shower—there is a moment of suspense—then her delicious voice, modulated to a low, clear under-tone, inexpressibly pathetic and sweet, sings this little ballad:

> "Oh, lady, thou art fair and free
> As are the heavens above thee!
> A student I, of low degree—
> What wouldst thou say if thou couldst see
> This heart, which dares to love thee?
>
> "Thou hast been told that rank and state
> Are gifts beyond all prizing,
> The poet singing at thy gate
> Were all too lowly for thy hate,
> Too poor for thy despising!
>
> "So proud, and yet so angel-sweet!
> I fall down and adore thee:
> And oh! whene'er we chance to meet,
> I stand back in the public street,
> And bare my head before thee.
>
> "'Tis said that thou wilt wedded be
> To some more noble lover,
> To-day the bells ring out for thee,
> To-morrow they will toll for me,
> When all my tears are over.
>
> "What radiant party passes by
> With plumes and pennons flying?
> Thy wedding train? Nay, then, will I
> Straight in thy path all prostrate lie—
> One look, love!—I am dying!"

The song is a simple song enough—a translation of a little German ballad—and yet it moves me deeply. Toward the last verse her voice grows lower and lower, with breaks and pauses, and at last trembles, fails, sobs forth despairingly—then ceases altogether.

When it is ended Théophile applauds, enraptured; and I sit speechless, feeling as if a sorrowful hand had been laid upon my heart. Perhaps it is the revulsion of feeling from wild rage to melancholy—perhaps it is that the little story conveyed in those simple verses touches a chord in my own breast—answers to a thought in my own mind. At all events, it utterly subdues and saddens me.

Once more Théophile bends down. By this time it has grown so dusk that his yellow locks are no longer visible. I still sit silently in the dark corner, affecting to read, and my tears fall slowly and heavily, one by one, upon the open pages.

CHAPTER VI.

THE END OF THE FIRST ACT.

"Wish me happiness, mon frère!" said Théophile, springing up from his chair, and advancing toward me with outstretched hands.

It was in my mother's breakfast parlor. She was sitting near the window, with her hands lying folded together on her lap, and some pens and paper spread upon the little work-table beside her. She turned her face slowly toward me as I entered. There was a faint flush on her cheeks. She looked agitated, but happy.

"Yes, Paul," she said, with a voice slightly tremulous, "to-day you must rejoice with us. Your brother is engaged to Adrienne."

So, then, it was over! I felt myself turn pale; but I was very calm.

"I have expected this, madame," I said. "It does not surprise me."

"Indeed! Well, it is not surprising. They are so suited to each other in every respect." And my mother looked up admiringly in my brother's face. "It is a most happy event!" she added, with a sigh.

"A most happy event, madame," I echoed.

"And so advantageous with regard to property. Adrienne is rich."

"A clear rent-roll of three hundred thousand francs per annum!" interrupted Théophile, joyously. "We shall be very rich. I mean to buy the Hauteville estate for our country residence. It is just announced for sale. Did you hear of it?"

I shook my head. I could not trust my voice to speak.

"Yes, it is announced at last—for two hundred and fifty thousand francs! It is a high price, but I am determined to have it, for it was formerly one of the possessions of our family. Besides, we shall, of course, live a great deal in Paris, and we can come down here every summer en retraite. Will it not be charming?"

"Charming, indeed."

Strange! the harsh, level tones of my voice, so cold, so mechanical, seemed scarcely to proceed from my own lips, but sounded to my ear as if they were uttered near me by some other speaker.

"It is really remarkable that the Hauteville property should be vacant so opportunely. Nothing could have happened better. And when we come down, to be so close to you! Why, it will be almost the same as living at home! We can have a path laid down through the shrubbery, and a gate of communication, and so run from one house to the other in a few moments."

"And I shall see you for many weeks in every year," said my mother, with the tears standing in her eyes.

"Weeks! nay, months, ma chère mère," said Théophile, kissing her hand. "I have so many plans—so many improvements in my head; and I shall superintend all the alterations myself. There is a moat there which I mean to have filled up; timber to be felled; conservatories and out-houses to build; stables to **repair. Oh!** it will need an army of workmen, and I must come down to see that every thing is carried out as I wish. I shall be here for a long time in the autumn. Besides, Adrienne is so fond of Burgundy!"

Plans—improvements—alterations! Alas! gentle lady, had I been thy choice, methinks there would have been less thought of thy wealth, and more, far more of thee!

I fancy that even my mother, with all her love for Théophile, and all her native coldness of disposition, felt this, for she turned the conversation.

"Adrienne is a charming demoiselle," she said. "I like the English system of education, it is so solid. She is not only accomplished, but amiable, polished, and thoroughly well-read."

"And so beautiful, mother! How she will be admired in Paris! We must take a mansion in the Chaussée d'Antin, and she shall have a fixed reception-evening in each week."

"Théophile is very happy, is he not?" said my mother, appealing directly to me for a reply. "It would have been impossible for him to have made a more eligible connection."

"Impossible, madame," I said, huskily.

"Your brother now receives from me an income of one hundred thousand francs yearly; but it is my intention henceforth to double that sum. They must not be too unequally matched in point of fortune. However, at my death, Théophile's property will be as large as that of his wife. But this is not to the purpose. We wished to ask you, Paul, if you would object to receive them here on their return from the wedding tour? The Hauteville chateau can not be got ready for them in time; and they might take the whole of the right wing without inconvenience to any of us; for you, although master here, occupy only a suite of three rooms."

"Be it so, madame," I replied, absently.

"Thank you. I will take care that none of our arrangements shall disturb you. The marriage, of course, must take place here. We ought to give a ball and fête upon the occasion."

"Certainly!" cried Théophile—"that is, if Paul permits it. There are many whom I should wish to ask from Paris, besides all the neighbors here. And we must have sports for the tenantry, and—"

"And Adrienne must be asked if she would not like to invite some English friends," interrupted my mother.

"Théophile!" said a voice from the garden. "Théophile!"

I started. My icy self-possession, hitherto so stoically preserved, threatened to give way at the sound of that sweet voice which called so familiarly upon his name. In one instant the full sense of my desolation rushed upon me. In that single word, revealing so much of love and home, I seemed to see all the extent of happiness which I had lost!

Théophile sprang to the window.

"I will bring her here," he cried, as he stepped out upon the terrace and flew to meet her.

I turned toward the door. I could not stay to see them return together.

"Madame," I said, articulating the words hoarsely and with difficulty, "Madame, this house, and all that it contains, is at your disposal, and—and at my brother's. Make any arrangements you think proper, but do not—do not take the trouble to consult me!"

There must have been a strange unusual something in my tone, or in the expression of my countenance, for my mother turned suddenly, looked at me, and half rose from her chair.

"Mon Dieu!" she said, hurriedly, "what is the matter?"

My hand was on the lock—I trembled in every limb—I heard their voices approaching—nay, I heard the very rustle of Adrienne's dress upon the terrace!

"Nothing, madame," I said, and closed the door.

Scarcely master of myself, I ran along the corridor and across the hall. My favorite hound, who had been lying near the door of the library, came bounding toward me; but I spurned him with my foot and passed on. In the library I paused and looked around with a kind of angry despair.

"Alas! ye books," I cried, "of what use are ye? Poets, philosophers, historians, what do you teach us? Can you give us peace or wisdom? Be ye accursed! Man in his savage state alone is happy!"

The curtain that led to the painting-room was drawn aside. Pacing up and down, backward and forward, raging in my strong passion like a caged panther, I went in.

These scenes of my former occupations seemed hateful to me. What was art, or science, or literature to me, now or henceforward? Tricks, phantasms, accursed phantasms, all!

A cast of the Medicean Venus stood in my path. I dashed it down with one blow of my hand, and trampled the smiling features into dust and fragments. The last work of my hands—the unfinished interior—stood yonder on the easel. I advanced toward it and extended a destructive hand—then I paused—stood still—dropped upon a seat before it, and covering my face with my hands, burst into an agony of tears. Adrienne's portrait! Adrienne's portrait, painted there by me a few short days ago, and now smiling toward me from the canvas! Oh, fair cousin, how dearly this heart loved thee!

I know not what burning visions, what desolate retrospections, what wild plans for the dim future passed through my mind as I sat there with my head bent down upon the easel, and my whole being convulsed by strong, deep sobs. I know not how long I even remained there, for I took no heed of time, or of the broad day beyond. I had arrived at one of those terrible epochs of man's existence, when the highway of life threads that solemn valley of the shadow of death—when to look back is misery; to look forward, despair—when the storm-clouds gather overhead, and thick darkness lies every where around; and the wayfarer pauses, trembling, and awaits his destiny. He is bewildered, reckless, helpless against others, helpless against himself and his own impulses. Evil from without, evil from within, combine to torture him. A word may destroy, a word may save him! Alas for him if, in that hour, there be none at hand to guide, to console, to pray for him!

My tears had ceased to flow—a struggling sob broke now and then from my lips—my head was still buried in my hands. Within, all was black misery. Without, the day bent toward the west, and the shadows lengthened in the level sunlight.

Hush!

The outer door was cautiously opened, and, after the lapse of a few moments, closed as cautiously. I heard it; but, as one might hear through sleep, without receiving any impression from the sound. Light footsteps crossed the library—paused at the second door—approached nearer and nearer; and still I heard without heeding. Then there was the rustling of silken garments at my side, and a hand was laid upon mine—a cold slender hand, whose touch roused me in a moment like an electric shock.

I sprang to my feet, grew hot and cold alternately, tried to speak, but could not. My mother looked marble-pale. Her eyes wandered from my face to the picture, and back again to me, with a mute mournful expression of tenderness and pity, such as I had never seen in that gaze before. There was no surprise in her countenance—no pride, no coldness, no austerity; but grief—grief only. For some minutes we stood thus face to face, with the picture between us, both silent.

"Paul," she said at length, very softly and sadly, "why didst thou conceal this?" My lips moved again, but uttered no sound.

She took my vacant seat, and pointed to a stool beside her. "Come," she said, "come, Paul, confide in me!"

My senses seemed bound up in ice, though my heart beat wildly. I neither spoke nor stirred.

"Speak to me, my son, speak to me! Thou sufferest—may I not weep with thee?"

She extended her arms to me. Her words, her look, her tone, went to my heart.

"Oh, my mother!" I cried, wildly, falling upon my knees before her, and hiding my face in her lap, "I love her! I love her!"

She folded her arms around me—she pressed her lips to my forehead, my burning head to her gentle bosom—she mingled her tears with mine—she breathed words of pity and consolation in my ears—she passed her hands over my hair, and called me her son—her dear son!

Yes, in that dark and bitter moment, I rested for the first time—oh, God! *for the first time!*—upon my mother's heart—received the first outpourings of my mother's love! Thanks be to Heaven, she saved me—I dare not think from what!

Let me not reveal the particulars of that first confidence. It is to me a sweet, almost a sacred thing. Sufficient if I say that the day declined lower and lower in the west; that the shadows widened and lengthened, and gradually overspread all the landscape; and that I still sat at my mother's feet, with her hands clasped in both mine, and her eyes looking down upon me with that light in them for which, as a child, I would have gladly died. At last I rose and looked out upon the gathering gloom of evening. The thought which had been lying silently at my heart for many hours must sooner or later be uttered.

"It is getting dark," I said, looking earnestly at her. "It is getting dark, my mother. I must go now."

She turned a shade paler, and her lips trembled. She understood me.

"You are right, my son," she said. "But will you go to-night?"

I made a mute gesture of assent. It was enough. She went into the library, rang for refreshments, and desired the attendance of a servant.

"Where wilt thou go?" she said, after a brief absence, during which she and Jeanne had prepared my valise. "In what direction?"

"I know not—care not."

"Thou wilt write to me? Good. What money hast thou?"

I opened my desk. It contained about thirty Napoleons, and some notes to the value of eight hundred francs. These I placed in my pocket-book, saying that they were enough. My mother shook her head, and laid her own purse upon the table before me.

"Take this," she said; "it contains a thousand francs. Nay! refuse a gift from thy mother! Take it—I entreat! It is well. Now go, my son, for it will soon be night. Heaven preserve and bless thee!"

We went round together to a door at the back, opening on a dark lane. Two horses and a groom were waiting. Not another soul was near, and all the house was silent. There we parted—there I received one more embrace—one last farewell word—and then I rode away into the gloom—into the unknown Future.

After galloping some distance, I reined in my horse and looked back. But it was too late. All was dark; the limes stood up between; I could not even trace the outline of my old turreted home. The veil had fallen between her life and mine. The first Act of the Drama was played out, and ended!

I put spurs to the horse—I flew madly forward, with the groom clattering at my heels. The eighteen miles were soon past; we reached the Chalons station; I flung the reins to Pierre, seized my valise, and, without even giving the faithful fellow a farewell glance, ran up the steps and stopped before the bureau.

"When does the next train go?"

"Directly, monsieur."

I threw a note on the counter.

"Where to, monsieur?"

"As far as it will take me."

The man passed me the change and the ticket; the bell rang; the engine came panting up, with its black train; I ran forward, leaped into the first carriage, and in another moment was moving on.

"Pray, monsieur," I said, turning to my nearest neighbor, "how far does this train go tonight?"

"To Strasburg."

CHAPTER VII.

STRASBURG.

A LONG drear night of perpetual traveling, broken by snatches of feverish sleep, which seemed scarcely sleep, but rather the distressful wanderings of a mind restless and over-wearied. The oil lamp flickered vaguely overhead, and cast an uncertain glimmer upon the forms and faces of my fellow-passengers, all of whom were profoundly sleeping. Without were clouds, and moonlight, and an ever-shifting panorama of the alternating flats, forests, vineyards, and steep mountains of South France, all gliding silently by, and looking ghostly in the moonshine. Every now and then there came a steep cutting, or a long black tunnel. Sometimes a sudden blaze of gas; a stop; a hurrying past of quick feet; a confusion of loud voices; passengers getting in and out; and the entrance of a guard, with imperative voice and blazing lantern, marked our arrival and brief pause at some station by the way. Then came the shrill whistle, and we flew on again; trees, mountains, villages, flitting past us as before, and ever the low continuous bass of our rushing progress sounding along the iron roadway.

Oh! a weary, weary night, checkered by fantastic dreams and wakings up to miserable realities—by heart-sickness—by sullen melancholy!

About three hours after midnight I fell into a dull, heavy sleep. It was gray morning when I awoke. So profound had been my slumber that I started; stared round at the sleepers; could remember nothing for some moments. My head ached; my lips were parched; my eyes were burning hot, and swollen from the tears of yesterday. Worse than all, an oppressive sense of misfortune seemed to weigh upon my chest, though what that misfortune was I could not at first remember. Alas! are there any who have never so suffered, slept, forgotten?

One by one my companions awoke also. Three of them were Germans, and they kept talking inaudibly among themselves. I fancied that I was an object of remark, and I shrank back into a corner and feigned to sleep. Grief makes us suspicious.

"How far are we from Strasburg?" asked some one near me.

"Look out," was the reply, "and you will see the cathedral spire."

In a few moments the guard came to collect our tickets, and before half an hour we had reached the end of our journey.

I alighted. The unfinished station was crowded with carpenters and masons; the yellow omnibuses from Kehl, with their German drivers, were ranged in long rows outside the doors; soldiers, hotel agents, porters, and passengers crowded the platform, the waiting-rooms, and the square beyond. All was noise, hurry, and confusion. Through these I made my way, as it were mechanically, for I felt nervous and bewildered. Without, the gray morning had dissolved into a slow continuous rain, and dingy vehicles were rattling swiftly to and fro. I emerged upon a line of quays, bordering a broad turbid river crossed by many bridges. In every direction were high, quaint houses, and shops with overhanging stories; and, straight before me, showing dimly through the driving rain, one sharp, delicate brown spire rose up into the gray sky, and I knew that it was the highest pinnacle in the world—the spire of Strasburg Cathedral.

Keeping my eyes fixed upon this, and following its direction, even when it was no longer in sight, I went across a wooden bridge and into the broad streets of the town. It was market-day, and the open places were all crowded with stalls and people. Here were soldiers, German and French; peasant-women from over the Rhine, with silver-embroidered caps or large black bows upon their heads; mountebanks vending cosmetics and articles of mock-jewelry; itinerant ballad-singers; fruit and cake sellers; purchasers and gazers of all ages and of two countries, hurrying, loitering, hither and thither in the rain, and protected by umbrellas of every color and shade. Past the Place Gutenberg I went, where stands the bronze statue of the First Printer, with his printing-press and types beside him—through a low vaulted passage, or arcade, with mean shops and stalls on either side—up a turning to the left, at the top of which rose the dark cathedral, a mountain of perfect architecture.

Near the entrance I paused, forgetful for the moment of every thing but wonder and admiration, and looked up at the gigantic mass above me—at the intricate network of arcades and buttresses—at the thin spire, delicate as an ivory carving, and towering up so far into the sky that one feels dizzy, though only looking at it from the pavement below—at the labyrinthine processions of carved figures over the arching doorways, where, as a French poet beautifully says,

"Stand the old stone saints in niches hoar;
Praying so softly—praying for the living."

Inside, the rich golden gloom that pervades the pillared aisles, and dims the lofty roof, awed and oppressed me. I felt wearied and ill. There was scarcely a living creature—scarcely the echo of a sound. I wandered on, and seated myself

B

upon a stone bench just in front of the singular organ, which, with its glowing arabesques, its gilding, and its long pendent, terminating in a painted carving of Christ riding upon a lion, looks more like a stupendous clock than any thing else, so fantastic is it, and perched up, as it were, so perilously in the very roof of the building.

Nowhere in the world is there so much superb stained glass as in this Cathedral of Strasburg. The whole interior is dark with beauty, steeped in an atmosphere of religious gloom. Here are windows dating from the early part of the thirteenth century, which "blush with the blood of queens and kings"—windows crowded with mailed champions, and bishops, and royal saints, robed in the most gorgeous contrasts of color—deep red, azure, and orange. To read in this dusk is impossible; and so magical is the effect, that persons standing a few paces off look dim and transfigured.

Leaving the cathedral, I passed a motley crowd assembled near the south entrance—beggars, market-women, soldiers, peasants, and fashionable visitors, all grouped together most republicanly, waiting to see the great clock strike at noon. Presently the brazen cock crew, and the whole paraphernalia of machinery were put in motion. Strange mixture of emblems, Christian and heathen, of grave science and puppet-show puerilities! I wandered into the street, with the rest of the spectators, as soon as the performance ended. It was still raining heavily.

"Hotel de Metz, monsieur!" said a dark man, who wore a badge suspended round his neck. "Hotel de Metz—quite near—good breakfasts—table d'hôte at five—will monsieur permit me to conduct him?"

I was worn out mentally and physically, so I followed him to a large white hotel near the station, and breakfasted alone at a little table in a window overlooking the street. I was weary of the noisy life and bustle of this frontier town, and longed to escape from it to some green peaceful place farther away—farther away.

The surging crowd went rolling on, in spite of the rain, ever moving, ever changing—the swell and hum of voices ascended from beneath—a brass band stationed itself before the house—some German University students, with spurs on their heels, and little crimson cloth caps on their heads, came clattering into the room, calling loudly for "bier und cigarren!" and were followed by three or four others wearing tri-colored caps—orange, white, and blue. Their frank, jovial voices, their peals of laughter, so full of young life and enjoyment, jarred painfully upon my present mood. I drew back into the curtained embrasure of the window, and debated with myself whither I should go next. To Switzerland, by way of Basle, or to Germany, by the Rhine? In my then wearied state of indifference, it mattered little which. An accident decided me.

"Let us dine together, boys!" said one of the noisiest among the students, striking his com-

panion on the shoulder. "Let us all dine here, or at the Rothes Haus, and then go to the theatre. There's to be a new play to-night!"

"I can not," said one of the crimson caps, moodily. "I must go back this afternoon to the old mill."

"To Heidelberg?"

The student nodded.

"Confoundedly dull place, that Heidelberg, is it not?"

"Oh, confoundedly! Nothing going on from one year's end to another."

"No amusements? No theatres? No gaming-rooms?"

"Nothing of the sort. It's so terribly out of the way, you know, that none but honeymoon-tourists and young ladies with sketch-books and camp-stools come near the place. The only fun we ever have is beering, boating, and dueling."

"Abominable!" "Intolerable!" chimed the rest, to the friendly music of the clinking glasses. Heidelberg!

Why not to Heidelberg, oh Paul Latour? To that ancient abode of learning in the Neckar Valley—to that low ruined fortress on the "shores of old Romance," whence the tide of life hath long since retreated into the great ocean which is eternal?

So to Heidelberg I went.

———◆———

CHAPTER VIII.

HEIDELBERG SCHLOSS.

It was already somewhat late in the morning when I drew aside my window-curtains at the Hotel Adler, expecting to look out upon the castle ruins, and saw instead the steep narrow road-way, with its high rock-wall, the small flint pavement, and the usual Continental gutter, now swollen by the rain, running swiftly and broadly down the centre of the street. Overhead, the sky was blue and sunny, with large snowy clouds floating across, one after another, like an army with white banners. A party of laughing girls went up toward the castle, riding upon donkeys, and then some pedestrian tourists; so I also hastened out, and proceeded to make my way up the toilsome ascent. The birds sang and darted about in the air; little children were playing upon door-steps; the poultry strutted up and down; and I passed two or three little knots of women and old men preparing plates of horn for combs—a trade much followed in Heidelberg.

Shall I describe the Castle of Heidelberg, that red old ruin, standing midway up a fir-wooded mountain, which is chapel, fortress, and palace in one? Alas! no. It has been done too well and too often. For such word-painting, oh reader, turn thee to the pages of that prose-poem which ascends from the shores of the New World like a steam of golden incense offered up to the glories of the Old. Those pages will tell unto thee, in such lordly language as befits the theme, of the triumphal gateway with its leaf-carved pillars, which was erected in one night by command of the Elector Frederick V., that his English bride might pass through it on the morrow, and which is still called, in remembrance of her, the Elizabethan Pforte, or Elizabeth's Portal—of the second gate, where the iron teeth of the portcullis yet threaten overhead—of the silver shield that was stolen from its place above the entrance by the French besiegers—of the two grotesque gigantic stone figures which stand, in the guise of armed warders, on either side—of the glorious façades of the Friedrichsbau and the Italian Rittersaal of Otto Henry, with their statues of knights and heroes, their cornices, entablatures, and rich mouldings, and blank open windows where the blue sky shines through—of the blasted tower and its leafy linden-trees waving on the top—of the canopied well of royal Charlemagne—of the tower of the library—of the deserted chapel, with its blue marble altar, and the paintings spared by the destroying lightning yet suspended, all faded and blackened, above the different shrines—of the armory, and the clock-tower, and the great tun, and of all the beauty and romance of that rare old building, which is, "next to the Alhambra of Granada, the most magnificent ruin of the Middle Ages."

All these did I see, and more besides; for I wandered in and out the ruins and the garden walks as I listed, thinking of many things. For the place was to me something more than a mere sight—than a fine ruin: it was a history —a poem—a prayer.

In this mood I sat for a long time upon the steps of a crumbling solitary tower, where a cherry-tree grows wild against the wall, and droops its fruit-clusters across the very path on which you tread. Hence I went down and wandered through the interior of the castle, seeing the tun and the wooden image of the jester; the dungeons, and the collection of old paintings.

But oh! the first sight of that view from the garden wall—the town beneath, with its slate-roofed University, its church spires, and its bridge — the shallow turbid Neckar eddying through the arches—the broad, level Rhine-valley, with its vineyards, and corn-fields, and flashes of the river here and there—the dark green Odenwald; and the dim, distant Hartz Mountains fading on the horizon, with the spire of Strasburg Minster showing up midway upon the plain! The immensity of the circuit bewildered and oppressed me, and I gazed so long and so earnestly that the bright sunlight dazzled me, and the near and the far were confounded together upon my sight.

"Eine schöne Aussicht, mein Herr!" (a fine prospect, sir!) said a pleasant voice close beside me.

I turned. A tall, fair young man, with an open book in his hand and a long German pipe at his lips, was standing at my elbow, with his arms resting upon the parapet. An almost indefinable something in his accent, in the fashion of his dress, in the free-falling curls of his light brown hair, and the frank cheerfulness of his address, told me at once that he was a foreigner. I glanced rapidly at the open book : it was Carlyle's "History of the French Revolution."

"Indeed, a most divine prospect," I replied in English. "One that might drive a painter to despair."

The young man colored.

"I suppose," he said, after a moment's hesitation, "that my countrymen never are to succeed in concealing their identity. During the two years that I have been here, I have studied the peculiarities of the language very earnestly, but I have not yet mastered what may be called its nationality. How did you know me to be an Englishman ?"

I pointed to the volume in his hand.

"Your accent told me something," said I, smiling, "and your book confirmed my suppositions. What do you think of Carlyle ?"

"Oh, he is magnificent!" exclaimed the Englishman, with some warmth. "A most original genius, and a very Titan in literature. He wields words like mountains, and hurls them, not at Heaven, but at 'idols' and 'mud-gods.'"

"His style is very eccentric."

"Granted ; but is it not vivid, earnest, passionate ? Does he not carry your sympathies forcibly along with him ?"

"That is true, especially with regard to his history. It lacks, perhaps, the majesty of Gibbon and the lofty grandeur of Macaulay, but it is history with a heart in it."

"And then, notwithstanding the severity of his principles and his hatred of 'shams,' what a deep well of love, and pity, and even of humor, lies buried down in the depths of his nature! Besides, what force and power in his language! It is as if his thoughts were cast in bronze."

"I perceive, sir," I said, with more cordiality than was usual to me when conversing with strangers, "that you are an enthusiast for books; but here is an epic that passes the art of the poet—a history more impressive than any which can be related by man. Surely there can be no second place on earth so beautiful as this !"

"If there be, I have not seen it," said the Englishman, "and I have traveled much. Dear old Heidelberg!" he continued, facing round to the castle, and leaning against the wall with his back toward the landscape ; "dear old Heidelberg! I know every nook, and cranny, and owl's-nest in its crumbling walls! Some of the happiest hours of my life have been spent here, reading my favorite books under the trees in the garden ; dreaming my favorite dreams in unfrequented corners of the ruins ; talking German metaphysics with my University friends, beside that little fountain bubbling up yonder in the sunlight. I believe that, with the one exception of the tun-keeper's, those silvered globe-mirrors in the court-yard have reflected no face so often as mine for the last two years. I have rooms down in the town, but I am scarcely ever there unless at night. I almost live up here; and a fine day, a quiet nook in the ruins, my pipe, and a book, are all that I require to be perfectly happy. You can't think how I love the place, or in what curious fancies and comparisons I delight to indulge respecting it. Standing up thus, so lordly and so battle-worn, and inclosing within its shattered walls these flower-beds and that fairy fountain, it often reminds me of some old disabled warrior with his grandchildren smiling on his knee. But night is the time for Heidelberg! Have you been up yet by moonlight?"

I said that I had only arrived at a late hour the evening before.

"Then I envy you the sensations of that first view by moonlight. You have not yet an idea of the beauty and poetry of the spot. The moon rises to-night about ten o'clock; come to my rooms, and I will accompany you. I know all the best points of view, and I shall be delighted to witness your enjoyment."

"A thousand thanks; but had you not better call for me? I am staying at the Hôtel Adler, half way up the hill. We can sup together before we start."

"As you please. This, too, is the month when the nightingales sing sweetest; and I promise you that you will hear such songs 'shaken from their little throats' to-night as you never heard before. By the way, who knows but we may even see the spectre-mass in the chapel of St. Udalrich!"

"What is that, pray?"

"Oh, one of our Heidelberg legends! We have plenty such."

"Delightful! you shall relate some of them to me by moonlight. How glad I am to have made your acquaintance!"

We were friends already; and the conversation thus begun lasted for more than two hours. We talked of paintings, and of our favorite books; of Goëthe, and Jean Paul, and of Uhland—of philosophy—of history—of the German and French character, and of many more things than I can now remember. Our tastes seemed to agree in most respects; or, when they differed, differed just sufficiently to lend an interest to discussion. Averse as I generally am to strangers, I was pleased with this young Englishman from the very first. His smile, his glance, the cheerful tones of his voice, impressed me favorably. He had read much, and his reading had been well chosen. That he was a good German, French, and Italian scholar I had already discovered; and the enthusiasm with which he spoke of places and of authors showed me that he possessed a warm imagination, and an almost boyish enjoyment of beauty and talent. In a word, he seemed to be good-natured, unaffected, and a gentleman. It was almost noon when we parted, renewing our engagement for the evening. My new acquaintance walked with me to the door of my hotel, and as we passed the restaurateur's in the castle gardens, we saw a party of English dining in the open air, one of whom exclaimed as we went by,

"Capital place, this Heidelberg! Magnificent old ruin; and the very best beer I have tasted since I left home!"

CHAPTER IX.

NORMAN SEABROOK.

I know not whether it was the heart-suffering through which I had passed that made me more susceptible to every kindly influence, but I have often been surprised when I recall how quickly that friendship was formed between Norman Seabrook and myself—that cordial and manly friendship which has ever since been one of the greatest joys and consolations of my life!

He had so true and just a feeling for poetry and art—he was so generous, so high-spirited, so warm of heart, so earnest of soul, that it would have needed a nature far colder and more ungrateful than mine to reject the golden gift.

Not that Norman Seabrook was faultless and a hero! Alas! no. Our age, reader, bringeth forth no heroes. He was simply a young man with a good heart, a liberal education, and a somewhat indolent and luxurious disposition. I never knew any one with so great a capacity for enjoyment. The sight of a pretty child, of a good picture, sculpture, or engraving, the far sounds of music, the summer sky, and the landscapes around Heidelberg, used to afford him the keenest sense of delight. He would dwell upon a passage from some favorite author with a gusto that I used positively to envy; tracking the idea through every possible gradation of meaning; discovering little hidden beauties of accentuation and phrasing, and seeming actually to taste the inner-sweetness of every deep and lovely thought. It was the same with paintings—the same with music—the same with riding, boating, or walking. He enjoyed every occupation to the uttermost, and with the careless glee of a school-boy. He seemed to drink in contentment with the very air, and I do not know that there was any one thing in which he took a greater pleasure than lying upon his back in the deep grass upon the river-banks, with a pipe in his mouth and a paper of chocolate *bonbons* in his pocket, looking up to the sky and the clouds, and suffering his imagination to stray unheeded through all the wild untrodden ways of thought.

"There are times," he used sometimes to say, "when the heart is more than usually open to impressions of beauty—when the form of a tree, the rustle of a leaf, the piping of a solitary bird, are sufficient to fill us with a vague and subtle feeling of delight which is more than half sadness, and for which no expression can be found in language. At such moments how beautiful is the world—how divine is life! What poetry is it only to feel the warm sun; to breathe the pleasant air; to lie in the quivering shadows of the trees, or the cool angle of some gray ruined wall, and to look up to the blue sky overhead with that unspoken longing of soul after the Infinite and the Far which our human nature loves to recognize as the stamp of its own strange immortality!"

In all this there was something of the dreamy mental self-indulgence peculiar to German theorists, and to that school of poetical philosophy which possesses so irresistible a fascination for those young men whose imaginations are warm, and whose experience of the realities of life has been but limited. Norman Seabrook would perhaps have been a nobler and more useful member of society had his intellectual training been less of the Sybarite than the Spartan—had Bacon, and Newton, and Locke been studied rather than Fichte, Swedenborg, and Shubert. He would have learned to seek after difficulties, that he might overcome them. As it was, he only searched for beauty, that he might worship it. He shrank instinctively from all that was harsh and unprepossessing; he attached himself, as unconsciously, to every thing that was agreeable. No one could say a kind word or perform a gracious action more pleasantly than he; but I must confess that, where a distasteful duty had to be accomplished, he would delay, neglect, and even avoid it, if he could. It was the weak point of his character—an amiable weakness, if you will, and one that was adorned by a thousand good and graceful qualities. It is often well for a man when he is either poor or proud, for the desire either of opulence or fame urges him on to play his part as a laborer in that field wherein it has been truly said that "to work is to worship." Unfortunately for Seabrook, he loved knowledge better than fame, and he owned a small independence which just sufficed, with economy, for the requirements of a bachelor.

"I love books," he said, "and I have wherewithal to purchase such as I love best. I am fond of travel and of Continental life, and I contrive to enjoy it. When I can not afford to rent rooms on the first story, I am content with the attic; if my purse be too low for the first class in the railway, I do not object to the second or the third. When I am too poor for either, I take my knapsack on my shoulders, my book in my hand, and walk. After all, this is the best traveling. You get a lift by the way from some peasants going to a fair or a wedding; you gather some grapes from the vineyard or some cherries from the road-side, to eat with the loaf in your pocket at noon; you go by the river-banks, and along the green meadows, and at the foot of steep precipices, which the fashionable travelers on the high road never dream of investigating; and at night you arrive at some little hamlet, with bells ringing and cows being driven out to the pasture after milking, where you sup at the rustic inn, and listen to the legends of the Rhine and the Black Forest, as they are told by mine host, over the pipe and the ale-jug, when the dusk gathers round, and the neighbors come dropping in on their way home from the harvest-fields."

Such was my new friend—a dreamer among men—a loiterer by the wayside on the great road of life and endeavor. In my lonely and meditative condition of mind, I attached myself to him with my whole soul, and his very faults were almost as virtues in my eyes. Disappointment had worked some evil already upon me; and, placing myself but little value upon ambition, how could I blame his indolence, and the carelessness of its advantages?

We met daily—we walked together—we read each other's favorite books, and studied side by side in the University library. We always supped and spent the evening together, either at my rooms or his; and sometimes we wandered up to the castle, or crossed the river to laugh away an hour or two among the students who frequent the Hirschgasse—a little, solitary white inn, about half a mile out of Heidelberg, where as many as four or five duels take place daily among these riotous children of philosophy. We also spent long afternoons upon the Neckar, taking it in turn to row, while one read aloud from the pages of some old poet or historian, till the pleasant dusk came gently over all, and the last brightness faded from the lofty tower of the Königstuhl. Then we would look upward to the pale moon, and, resting a while upon our oars, hear only the falling drops that splashed back from them into the river—the surging of the stream against the banks on either side—the melancholy cry of the heron among the reeds—or the lowing herds at the homesteads in the valley.

Oh, those calm, delicious evenings of warm June, when the stars came glowing through the tranquil depths of sky, and the sun went slowly down behind the mountains in the purple distance, like a monarch to his grave, clad in scarlet and gold!

It was on the morning following some such evening ramble that I lay at the foot of a clump of trees bordering the footpath called The Philosopher's Walk, about half way up the hill fronting the town. In my hand I carried a volume of Lamartine's "Méditations Poétiques;" the sultry air hung heavily upon the sense; scarce a blade of grass waved—scarce a leaf stirred—scarce a bee hummed near me. All was silent above, below, around. The faint murmur from the town came drowsily and at intervals. The very river lay sluggishly along the landscape, as if torpid beneath the sun. Gradually I fell into a dream—a waking dream, wherein the dim land of the past was wafted before me, and the poets of old days walked by in their singing-robes, serenely glorious. Suddenly a rapid step came along the path—a free, firm, careless step that I well knew, and my English friend, with his dog at his heels, had bounded almost past me before he was aware of my presence.

"Eureka!" he exclaimed, laughing, as he stopped short, and flung himself down beside me on the grass. "Found at last! Why, man, I have been looking for you in the ruins,

and down by the river, and in the library, and
had just given you up, when it struck me that
you might possibly have strolled in this direction. See! I called for you at the 'Adler,' and
finding these new arrivals upon your table, I
put them in my pocket, that you might have the
pleasure of reading them the sooner."

And he flung a couple of letters down before
me.

This one, so slenderly and accurately directed, was evidently from my mother; that, with
its rough, dashing superscription all blotted and
defaced, I recognized for the handwriting of
Théophile.

Alas! the dream-threads were broken, and
at the sight of those letters the chill remembrances of love, and home, and exile, and disappointment came back upon me, and broke the
brief reverie into which I had fallen. I took
the letters up, laid them down, took them up
again, turned pale and red by turns, and remained quite silent.

"Are they from your family in Burgundy?"
asked my friend.

I nodded.

"But won't you read them? Pray don't let
me be an interruption!"

I dreaded to open them; and yet how strange
it would seem were I not to do so! My mother's—no! I could not read that one yet! I
placed it reverently in my pocket-book, and
broke the seal of Théophile's letter. As I did
so, a vague shuddering dread ran through me,
and the paper fluttered in my fingers.

"Read it to me, mon ami!" I said, hoarsely,
turning away, and holding out the letter toward
him. "Read it to me; I am not well to-day."

He glanced at me, took it without a word,
and read it aloud.

"By the time that my dear Paul receives
this letter, his brother will be the happiest of
men and of husbands. Yes, mon frère, the contract is to be signed this evening by my dearest
Adrienne and myself, and to-morrow at midday
the ceremony which unites our lives forever will
take place. Every thing will be conducted as
quietly as possible. We shall have no fête except for the peasantry, and no company excepting that of Adrienne's maternal uncle from England—the brother to her late guardian. I am
very sorry that you will not be here to share
our happiness. I would have written to you
before this, to acquaint you with our wedding
arrangements, had not our mother prevented
me from time to time. It is a great pity that
you should have fancied to travel just at this
time; but you were always a contrary fellow,
and unlike the rest of the world, mon cher, so
we can but lament your sins of omission. To
tell you the truth, I fear lest Adrienne should
imagine that you are not favorable to our marriage, or that you do not like her, and have
gone away for the purpose. Seriously, it has
that appearance, and I am sorry for it, although
I know it can not be actually the case. I have
purchased the Hauteville property. The price
was high, and the house, I regret to say, is almost a ruin; but the repairs will be commenced
in a few days. There is a kiosque in the park,
which I mean to convert into a smoking-room.
I have given my Andalusian mare to Adrienne,
and bought a new bay riding-horse for my own
use. Adrienne looks charming on horseback
—quite an Amazon. Besides, the mare had
not fire enough in her to suit me. Our mother
is looking well, and these matrimonial prepara-
tions keep her constantly employed. That good
heart! it would have been almost worth while
to have married, had it been only for the sake
of seeing her so proud and happy. I wish you
could be here to-morrow for the ceremony; but
I know that you are too firmly wedded to your
old bookworm habits to care any thing for love
or marriage. Will you ever fall in love yourself, mon cher? The very question, as applied
to you, seems an absurdity—unless, indeed,
some fair Olimpia Morata were now living in
Heidelberg for your sake! Adieu, my dear
Paul. Take care of yourself, and let us see
you at home again when we return from our
wedding tour.

"Your attached brother,
"THEOPHILE LATOUR."

"A letter filled with good news!" exclaimed
Seabrook, gayly, as he concluded my brother's
epistle. "Come, you must describe this fair
bride to me—is she beautiful?"

"Most beautiful!"

"Amiable?"

"As an angel."

"And rich?"

I nodded.

"But this is not half a word-painting. What
hair has she? What eyes? Is she tall or
short? brunette or blonde? gay, grave, lively,
or severe? Now manifest your artist-skill, Latour, in enumerating me so glowing a catalogue
of your sister-in-law's charms, that, as the
knightly Troubadour, Geoffrey de Rudel, of the
fair Countess of Tripoli, I may become enam-
ored of her beauty, even without having once
beheld it!"

His unconscious levity jarred upon me. I
turned my head suddenly and looked him in
the face.

"Mon ami," I said, earnestly, and with all
the firmness I could muster, "do not ask me to
dwell upon this subject—to speak to you of this
lady. I—I can not."

He started; the letter dropped from his hand,
and he pressed my hand silently. We were
both silent for a long time, and I was the first
to speak.

"Tell me, Seabrook," I said, "who is, or
was, this fair Olimpia Morata whom my brother
mentions? Do you know any thing of her?"

"Yes; she was an Italian lady of much beauty and learning, married to a young German
doctor named Grunthler, who fell in love with
her at Ferrara, and fled with her to Augsburg

in 1518, to escape the persecutions of the Italian Church. Chased from Augsburg to Schweinfurt, from Schweinfurt to Hammelburgh, they settled at last in Heidelberg, under the protection of the Elector Palatine. Here Grunthler obtained the appointment of Professor of Physics to the University, and his wife delivered lectures upon the Greek, Latin, and French languages, and upon the paradoxes of Cicero. They were now perfectly happy; and the great beauty of Olimpia, as well as the fame of her acquirements, brought many listeners and gazers from far and near throughout all Germany. In 1555 she died, at the age of twenty-nine years. You may see her simple monument yonder, in the church-yard of St. Peter. Shall we stroll down into the town and look at it?"

"Not now, Seabrook, for I want to propose something to you. You have no particular motive in remaining at Heidelberg, have you?"

"You know that I am only loitering about here among the books of the University for my own amusement."

"Good. Would you object to go to Frankfurt?"

"To Frankfurt? Certainly not; but why do you wish to visit Frankfurt?"

"I only name Frankfurt because it is near. I care not where we go, if we but go somewhere; for I need change, amusement, relief from the monotony of thought. You are free —free as myself—let us get away, farther away, to Frankfurt, Darmstadt, Wiesbaden—any where you will!"

Once more he pressed my hand in his, for he understood me.

"To Frankfurt, then, and with what speed we may! When will you go? To-night?"

"Not to-night. Let us spend our last moonlight evening together among the ruins. I may never behold them again."

"And sup afterward with the University lads at the Hirschgasse! We must be merry for the nonce, for who knows when we shall again share their 'cakes and ale?'"

So that evening, when the crescent moon stood over the clock-tower like a silver sickle in a field of stars, we went up to the ruins, and heard the nightingales sing in Heidelberg for the last time.

Alas! for the last time!

Farewell, then, to thee, thou majestic monument of many centuries! Though I behold thee no more, yet keepest thou thy desolate state on the steep verge of the Jettenbuhl, and some of my greenest memories cling round thy crumbling walls, even as thine own ivy. This wintry sun which gleams in so coldly through my casement as I write, sleeps now upon thy grassy court-yard, thy fountain, and the maimed heroes of thy kingly Rittersaal; this chill air, which shakes the gaunt poplars yonder by the dull pond, stirs amid the branches of thy drooping willows, and rustles the last yellow leaves upon the lindens of thy Blasted Tower. The

people come and go amid thy solitudes—the river eddies far beneath—the town lies at thy foot. Thou art the same, and I alone am changed! Farewell to thee!

CHAPTER X.

THE MOONLIGHT SONATA.

FROM Heidelberg to Frankfurt we went in the misty morning, past the Sea of Rocks—past the dark leafy Odenwald—past the sunny Bergstrasse, and the little stagnant capital of the duchy of Hesse Darmstadt.

The sunny Bergstrasse! This "road of mountains," as the Germans poetically name it, is an undulating chain of hills, cultivated in fields, orchards, and vineyards up almost to the summits, and crowned, like Indian chiefs, with solemn plumes of the fir and pine. At the feet of these hills lie little white villages with heaven-pointing spires, and yellow corn-stacks, and pillars of blue smoke rising up into the "pageantry of mist" which hangs in fantastic billowy wreaths low down the sides of the mountains. Here, also, are fields of pink poppies, maize, wheat, and potatoes—wooded bluffs, and dark green hollows—steep ravines, and slopes of radiant green, and towers, and streamlets crossed by rude wooden bridges, and feeding cattle, and rustic gardens, and foaming mill-streams turning busy wheels, and yoked oxen bending their proud heads to the earth before the steady plow. A fairy fertile region—a land of corn and wine! And past here, with the beautiful Bergstrasse on our right, and the broad, sandy, flat Rhine-valley, with the river winding far away, and the summits of Mont Tonnerre and the Vosges Mountains dimly showing through the distance on the left, we went from feudal Heidelberg to the "ancient imperial free city" on the River Main, where Luther lived, and where Goëthe was born —that fair fine city of Frankfurt, where the houses are so white and high, and the public streets so broad and busy; where the shops are so gay and the women so fair, and where the slates on the roofs are shaped like fishes' scales.

It was a sultry sunny day, that first day of our arrival in Frankfurt; and when we returned to our hotel, after seeing the Römer, with its kingly portrait gallery, the public library near the Ober Main Thor, and the monument of the Emperor Günther von Schwartzburg in the old cathedral, we were too warm and too weary to do any thing but sit smoking beside the open window till summoned down by the pealing bell to that second and later meal which is provided in most German hotels for such foreign visitors as object to the national midday dinner.

Our apartment overlooked the broad Zeil, all thronged with carriages and promenaders, and looking like a Parisian boulevard without the trees. It was to me a new and cheerful scene. Here were elegant loungers, and travelers with the Guide-book in their hands, and sun-burnt peasant-women selling cherries by the roadside. Boyish soldiers of the town-guard, with their dull gray and green uniforms, and their round hats surmounted by bunches of cock's feathers, went sauntering by, arm in arm, clanking their spurs. Luxurious private carriages, belonging to the merchant-princes of the city, dashed past, raising the dust in clouds. Humble yellow calèches, indicative of hotel-stables, ambled along, filled with smiling and admiring tourists. Sometimes a red railway omnibus went by, with its two gaunt horses, and its bearded conductor, who pauses and rings a bell as he nears every hotel by the way; sometimes a dark, keen-looking Hebrew, from the neighborhood of the Judengasse, glided gravely through the crowd; and once a troop of glittering cavalry, with helm and breastplate flashing back the sunlight, rode down the street to ringing sounds of brazen music.

Pleasant to me, oh Frankfurt! are the recollections of thy wealth, and thy dignity, and thy free stateliness, as thou sittest on the banks of the Main River, fair and beautiful, like Dorothea by the brook-side in the Brown Mountain.

The table d'hôte of the Baierischer Hof was attended chiefly by English and French visitors, with a sprinkling of Germans and a small knot of Polish Jews, who congregated together at one extremity of the table, and talked loudly and unintelligibly during the whole period of the dinner. These gentlemen wore each a scrap of red ribbon at the button-hole, and were called by the waiters Lord Baron and Lord Count, notwithstanding that their jewelry looked somewhat questionable, and that their linen might have been washed with considerable advantage.

When the second course of that hopelessly incongruous ceremony, a German dinner, had just been removed, a gentleman came hastily into the room and took a seat which had been left vacant at the table just opposite my own. I say a gentleman, because, despite the poverty of his attire, there was an air of faded gentility about the appearance of the new-comer that seemed to entitle him to the appellation. He wore an old brown frock-coat, buttoned nearly to the throat, and trimmed with ragged braid across the breast; and in his black stock a small pearl brooch inclosing a lock of dark hair. He was very thin, and stooped much, and his hands were yellow and spare, like those of a sick man. His hair and mustache were thick and quite gray; and his face, as he looked up, bore that peculiar expression, so worn and so sorrowful, such as we see given to the martyrs in the old paintings by Van Eyck and Wilhelm of Cologne. It was a remarkable face — so remarkable that, after gazing upon it in silence for a few moments, I could not forbear observing it to my friend beside me. I should not have called him a plain man; on the contrary, his nose and mouth were somewhat delicately shaped; and yet the skin seemed drawn so tightly over every

feature that the cartilage of the nose showed whitely beneath, and the lips were shrunken so as partially to expose the teeth within, which were irregular, firm, and glittering. His forehead was particularly massive, and projected in two knots above the eyes, causing them to look deep-sunken and glowing, like a lurid fire in the depths of a dark cavern. Added to this, his whole complexion wore one dull, unhealthy sallow hue—his actions were nervous, trembling, and eager—the tones of his voice high and querulous—his glances rapid, furtive, and suspicious. I also noticed that he devoured the dishes, as they were placed before him, with a quick voracity that I felt shocked to witness.

"Look at our opposite neighbor," I whispered, softly; "can you not read a long story of privation and anxiety in that poor fellow's pallid countenance?"

Seabrook looked up. A sudden flash of surprise and recognition passed over his face.

"I know him," he said, in a low tone. "His name is Fletcher. He is an Englishman—a strange, eccentric creature, of wild and irregular habits, but a real genius."

"A genius—in what?"

"In music. He plays the organ and violin—composes the wildest and most wondrous laments, fantasias, and capricios that ear ever heard—lives the most restless, wretched life on earth—eats opium, and is killing himself inch by inch, day by day, in the pursuit of that fatal intoxication. I used to meet him constantly in Vienna, about a couple of years since, at the houses of two or three musical friends, and we became tolerably well acquainted. I will speak to him."

And he bent forward and addressed to him some brief words of ordinary civility. The musician looked up hastily. He seemed startled and confused.

"I—I beg your pardon," he said, nervously, "for not having observed you before. I hope you are quite well. It is a fine day, but they say we shall have rain. Have you been to the theatre much? This is a very bad dinner—red currant jelly with salmon—faugh! Do you like the German wines? Rudesheimer is the best. Have you been long here? I have been here two months; but I leave to-morrow. Going to Ems. How are our friends in Paris?"

My companion smiled and shook his head.

"It was not in Paris, but Vienna, that we used to meet, Mr. Fletcher," he said. "Don't you remember our choral evenings at Alexander Braün's, and our quartett parties in the Frederic-strasse, near St. Stephen's church?"

"True, true; but I have no memory now except for music. I hope you will forgive me. I remember you perfectly. You play the violoncello, and very well too. Those were pleasant meetings at Braün's. Do you recollect the evening that Chopin came in? He played splendidly that night. Do you know many people in Frankfurt? Plenty of music always going on. I have been conducting the band at the

Main-lust; but this will be my last evening. Will you come round and hear us?"

There was an anxious rapidity and incoherence in this man's conversation that was to me unaccountably distressing. His words and ideas came hurrying forth, one after the other, without connection or pause; and when he had ceased speaking, it seemed rather that he relapsed into some previous train of silent thought than that he waited for a reply.

"I should like to hear your music very much," said Seabrook, "and I am very sure my friend would also. Let me introduce you: Monsieur Latour—Mr. Fletcher."

He bowed, almost without looking at me, and went on.

"Do not expect too much. The band is only tolerable; but the Frankfurt Choral Society sing to-night. They will amuse you. Have you ever been to the Main-lust? It is an odd place. You sit under the trees and drink coffee while we play to you. Don't touch this calf's-head —it's intolerable. By the way, you have tasted sour-krout? Schröder is dead. You remember Schröder—he used to take the tenor in the quartetts. Are you lodging at this hotel? We can go down to the gardens together after dinner. It is now four, and at five we begin."

He relapsed into a dull silence, bent over his plate, and, when Seabrook again spoke to him, seemed not to hear.

Almost as silently, he conducted us, when the meal was over, to the concert-gardens called the Main-lust, just beyond the town. Here the most respectable of the citizens repair with their families, and, sitting beneath the leafy roof formed by the close-planted trees, have coffee and ices, and even suppers, in the grounds. The gentlemen amuse themselves with pistol and rifle shooting in a gallery set apart for that purpose, and there is a circular kiosque for the band. The ladies read and knit; the children sit by demurely, listening to the music and eating cakes; and the waiters glide about, silent and attentive, with little badges on their arms. A large hulk is moored beside the garden—for it abuts on the river, just in view of the city spires—and on this hulk a sort of arch is erected, all hung round with evergreens and colored lamps, and surmounted by a bust of Mozart. Desks are placed here for the singers, and it is all fenced round by trellis-work, and flowers, and Chinese lanterns, and gay flags and streamers. Here the Choral Society, some thirty gentlemen in all, assemble presently, and the evening passes pleasantly away between alternate vocal and instrumental pieces. They sing well, and their voices come richly to us from the river. Then it grows dusk, and the moon rises. The colored lamps are lit, and the light from them—blue, green, and red—falls, with a curious effect, upon the faces of the singers. Mr. Fletcher conducts in the orchestra, but we can not see him from where we sit beneath the close avenues. Well-dressed people promenade through the garden walks, and numbers of tiny pleasure-boats, filled

by young men and maidens, come stealing softly round the singers in the river—some with a twinkling lamp suspended at the prow, which casts a light upon the ripples of their progress. The bridge close by is likewise crowded with listeners; and the boys from the town, in their blue blouses, come climbing up the shrubby banks, with the true German love for that art which has been called "the poetry of sound."

Thus the cool hours glide; and, by-and-by, the gay company, the flitting pleasure-boats, the loiterers on the bridge, disperse their several ways, and the gardens are deserted. The singers mingle with their friends in the departing crowd; the musicians in the kiosque pack away their instruments; the waiters go round, extinguishing the lights and collecting the empty glasses. Mr. Fletcher joins us where we are waiting for him near the entrance, and we all go out together into the blank, silent streets. It begins to rain, and we hurry on in silence, past the Städel Museum, and the Allée facing the theatre, where stands the bronze statue of Goëthe, looking shadowy through the mist— pass the Rossmarkt, and into a narrow street opening on the Zeil, where our companion stops suddenly, and, pointing to a lighted doorway before which we have just arrived, says,

"Let us go in for an hour. It is early, and I always sup here. We have music and goose-pies. It is a sort of private club; and nearly all the band come. Have you any objection? Mendelssohn came in one night with Weigel and Hirt!"

We are only too delighted, and we follow him down a passage and to the door of an inner room, whence come the sounds of loud laughter, and chinking glasses, and snatches of gay songs. A porter, who touches his cap as we approach, sits by the entrance, and throws the door open. It is a room filled with tobacco-smoke, and the odors of beer and hot savory dishes. Around a long table in the centre sit some sixteen or eighteen dingy-looking, bearded men, busily occupied with the viands before them. Some are smoking during the intervals between the courses; some are arguing, telling tales, whispering confidentially together; some are reading the "Frankfurt Journal" while they eat. All is freedom, and enjoyment, and good-fellowship.

We sit down, almost without being observed, at the lower end of the table; and, being supplied with all that it affords, fall to work heartily. Fletcher is more taciturn than ever, and eats voraciously, like a dog, holding his head down, and helping himself to every thing that is near.

"Take no notice of him," whispers Seabrook, observing my surprise. "He is very eccentric, and you have not yet seen him to advantage. Wait till the supper is removed, and you will find him no longer the same man. He knew Beethoven, and his conversation is sometimes most interesting. We must contrive to lead to the subject in some way by-and-by."

The smoking, the talking, the eating still goes

on. Indeed, it would seem that the relays of dishes are never-ending, especially the favorite goose-pies of which we have been told. However, the supper does at last arrive at a conclusion—the table is cleared—tobacco, beer, wine, and cigars are laid before us—the chair is taken by a stout dark man in a green coat—the readers lay down their newspapers, and music and conversation become the order of the night.

"A song!" cries the president, in a powerful bass voice. "A song! I call upon Brenner for a song!"

Brenner, a fair young man with an amber beard, hereupon rises, amid general acclamation, and, seating himself at a piano, preludes cleverly for some minutes, and then glides, by an agreeable transition, into a graceful tenor song by Schubert. His voice is sweet, but not powerful; and he sings remarkably well. I learn from a gentleman opposite that he belongs to the summer theatre at Bockenheim, and takes the rôles of second tenor. Great applause and cries of "encore" prevent him from resuming his seat after he has concluded. Seabrook suggests "Adelaide"—it is repeated by several voices—the singer bows and smiles, and the song is sung.

"I know no music like Beethoven's, after all," says Seabrook, with a glance toward me and a little emphasis in his tone. "There is a power and passion in it which I find in no other; a deep, earnest under-current of poetry; an inner meaning; a universality of feeling and perception totally unlike others of his craft. I often think that if Beethoven had not been a musician, he would have been a great poet. Look at his bust—it is almost Homeric in its stern beauty. Those loose, thick locks; that large, eloquent mouth; that furrowed brow; those deep, thoughtful eyes—are they not the very types and outward revelations of the strong, wild nature of the man, and of his great warm heart?"

"You are right, sir," says Fletcher, turning suddenly toward us with kindling eyes. "And he put that heart into his music—that heart that was so torn and rejected by his fellow-men. What pictures of life and emotion are many of his symphonies and sonatas! How characteristically some of them are conducted! At first wailing and lonely, like a sorrowful voice in the night-silence; then agitated, broken, throbbing, like the yearnings of a full heart; then stormy, torrent-like, burning, as the billows of a tempest, which rage and leap, and then, all suddenly, subside away, while some aerial melody, like a charmed boat, comes gliding over the surface, bringing calm, and sunshine, and openings of blue sky, and airs from heaven!"

"You knew him personally, Fletcher," says the gentleman opposite, who has been lending an attentive ear to all that passes. "Can you not tell us something of himself?"

This speech is somewhat injudicious; for the musician is of a contrary temper, and dislikes talking "by desire." He pauses, looks discon-

certed, and, but for a well-timed observation from Seabrook, would probably have relapsed into his previous taciturnity

"His music," says my friend, "is his best biography. In it we have a record, intelligible enough to those whose sympathies are with him, of his joys, sorrows, and struggles—nay, even of certain incidents of his life, and of his politics, as in the case of the pastoral and heroic symphonies. From it we learn to read his every feeling; for, like himself, it is all tenderness, and impulse, and stormful energy."

"It is beautiful and terrible," says Fletcher, thoughtfully, "as his own nature. It is an incantation—a poem—a spiritual philosophy. Did I ever tell you how or why he composed the Moonlight Sonata?"

"Never," replies Seabrook, giving me a triumphant glance.

"It happened at Bonn. Of course you know that Bonn was his native place. He was born in a house in the Rheingasse; but when I first knew him, he was lodging in the upper part of a little mean shop near the Römerplatz. He was wretchedly poor just then; so poor that he never went out for a walk except at night, on account of the poverty of his appearance. However, he had a piano, pens, paper, ink, and a few books, and from these he contrived to extract some little happiness, despite his privations. At this time, you know, he had not the misfortune to be deaf. He could at least enjoy the harmony of his own compositions. Later in life he had not even that consolation. One winter's evening I called upon him, for I wanted him to take a walk, and afterward to sup with me. I found him sitting by the window in the moonlight without fire or candle, his head buried in his hands, and his whole frame trembling with cold; for it was freezing bitterly. I roused him, persuaded him to accompany me, urged him to shake off his despondency. He went; but he was very gloomy and hopeless that night, and refused to be comforted. 'I hate life and the world,' he said, passionately. 'I hate myself! No one understands or cares for me. I have genius, and I am treated as an outcast. I have heart, and none to love. I wish it were all over, and forever! I wish that I were lying peacefully at the bottom of the river yonder. I sometimes find it difficult to resist the temptation.' And he pointed to the Rhine, looking cold and bright in the moonlight. I made no reply; for it was useless to argue with Beethoven, so I allowed him to go on in the same strain, which he did, nor paused till we were returning through the town, when he subsided into a sullen silence. I did not care to interrupt him. Passing through some dark, narrow streets within the Coblentz gate, he paused suddenly. 'Hush!' he said. 'What sound is that?' I listened, and heard the feeble tones of what was evidently a very old piano, proceeding from some place close at hand. The performer was playing a plaintive movement in triple time, and, despite the worthlessness of the instrument, contrived to impart to it considerable tenderness of expression. Beethoven looked at me with sparkling eyes. 'It is from my symphony in F!' he said, eagerly. 'This is the house. Hark! how well it is played!' It was a little, mean dwelling, with a light shining through the chink of the shutters. We paused outside and listened. The player went on, and the two following movements were executed with the same fidelity—the same expression. In the middle of the finale there was a sudden break—a momentary silence—then the low sounds of sobbing. 'I can not go on,' said a female voice. 'I can not play any more to-night, Friedrich!' 'Why not, my sister?' asked her companion, gently. 'I scarcely know why, unless that it is so beautiful, and that it seems so utterly beyond my power to do justice to its perfection. Oh, what would I not give to go to-night to Cologne! There is a concert given at the Kaufhaus, and all kinds of beautiful music to be performed. It must be so nice to go to a concert!' 'Ah! my sister,' said the man, sighing, 'none but the rich can afford such happiness. It is useless to create regrets for ourselves where there can be no remedy. We can scarcely pay our rent now, so why dare even to think of what is unattainable?' 'You are right, Friedrich,' was her reply. 'And yet sometimes, when I am playing, I wish that for once in my life I might hear some really good music and fine performance. But it is of no use—of no use!' There was something very touching in the tone of these last words, and in the manner of their repetition. Beethoven looked at me. 'Let us go in,' he said, hurriedly. 'Go in!' I exclaimed. 'How can we go in? what can we go in for?' 'I will play to her,' he said, in the same excited tone. 'Here is feeling—genius—understanding. I will play to her, and she will appreciate it!' And before I could prevent him, his hand was upon the door. It was only latched, and instantly gave way; so I followed him through the dark passage to a half-opened door at the right of the entrance, which he pushed open and entered. It was a bare, comfortless apartment, with a small stove at one end, and scanty furniture. A pale young man was sitting by the table, making shoes; and near him, leaning sorrowfully upon an old-fashioned harpsichord, sat a young girl, with a profusion of light hair falling over her bent face. Both were cleanly but very poorly dressed, and both started and turned toward us as we entered. 'Pardon me,' said Beethoven, looking somewhat embarrassed. 'Pardon me—but—but I heard music, and I was tempted to enter. I am a musician.' The girl blushed, and the young man looked grave—somewhat annoyed. 'I—I also overheard something of what you said,' continued my friend. 'You wish to hear—that is, you would like—that is—shall I play to you?' There was something so odd, so whimsical, so brusque in the whole affair, and something so pleasant and eccentric in the very manner of the speaker, that the ice seemed broken in a moment, and all smiled involuntarily. 'Thank you,' said the shoemaker; 'but our harpsichord is wretched, and we have no music.' 'No music!' echoed my friend. 'How, then, does the fräulein—' He paused and colored up, for the girl looked round full at him, and in the dim, melancholy gaze of those clouded eyes he saw that she was blind. 'I—I entreat your pardon,' he stammered; 'but I had not perceived before. Then you play from ear?' 'Entirely.' 'And where do you hear the music, since you frequent no concerts?' 'I used to hear a lady practicing near us when we lived at Brühl two years ago. During the summer evenings her window was generally open, and I walked to and fro outside to listen to her.' 'And have you never heard any music?' 'None—excepting street-music.' She seemed shy, so Beethoven said no more, but seated himself quietly before the piano, and began to play. He had no sooner struck the first chord than I knew what would follow—how grand he would be that night! And I was not mistaken. Never, never, during all the years I knew him, did I hear him play as he then played to that blind girl and her brother! Never heard I such fire, such passionate tenderness, such infinite gradations of melody and modulation! He was inspired; and from the instant that his fingers began to wander along the keys, the very tones of the instrument seemed to grow sweeter and more equal. Breathless and entranced, we sat listening. The brother and sister were silent with wonder and rapture. The former laid aside his work; the latter, with her head bent slightly forward, and her hands pressed tightly over her breast, crouched down near the end of the harpsichord, as if fearful lest even the beating of her heart should break the flow of those magical sweet sounds. It was as if we were all bound in a strange dream, and only feared to wake. Suddenly the flame of the single candle wavered, sunk, flickered, and went out. Beethoven paused, and I threw open the shutters, admitting a flood of brilliant moonlight. The room was almost as light as before, and the illumination fell strongest on the piano and the player. But the chain of his ideas seemed to have been broken by the accident. His head drooped upon his breast—his hands rested upon his knees—he seemed absorbed in meditation. It was thus for some time. At length the young shoemaker rose, and approaching him eagerly, yet reverently—'Wonderful man!' he said, in a low tone, 'who and what are you?' Beethoven lifted his head and looked up at him vacantly, as if unconscious of the meaning of his words. He repeated the question. The composer smiled, as he only could smile, benevolently, indulgently, kingly. 'Listen!' he said, and played the opening bars of the symphony in F. A cry of delight and recognition burst from the lips of both, and exclaiming, 'Then you are Beethoven!' they covered his hands with tears and kisses. He rose to go, but we held him back with entreaties. 'Play to us once more

—only once more!' He suffered himself to be led back to the instrument. The moon shone brightly in through the curtainless window, and lit up his glorious rugged head and massive figure. 'I will improvise a sonata to the moonlight!' said he, half playfully. He looked up thoughtfully for a few moments to the sky and the stars — then his hands dropped upon the keys, and he began playing a low, sad, and infinitely lovely, trembling movement, which crept gently over the instrument with a sweet and level beauty, like the calm flow of moonlight over the dark earth. This delicious opening was followed by a wild, elfin, capricious passage in triple time—a sort of grotesque interlude, like a dance of sprites upon the midnight sward. Then came a swift *agitato finale*—a breathless, hurrying, trembling movement, descriptive of flight, and uncertainty, and vague impulsive terror, which carried us away upon its rushing wings, and left us at the last all emotion and wonder. 'Farewell to you,' said Beethoven, abruptly, pushing back his chair, and turning toward the door; 'farewell to you.' 'You will come again?' asked they in one breath. He paused, and looked compassionately, almost tenderly, at the face of the blind girl. 'Yes, yes,' he said, hurriedly, 'I will come again, and give the fraülein some lessons. Farewell; I will come soon again!' They followed us in a silence more eloquent than words, and stood at their door till we were out of sight and hearing. 'Let us make haste back,' said Beethoven, urging me on at a rapid pace. 'Let us make haste, that I may write out that sonata while I can yet remember it!' We did so, and he sat over it till long past the day-dawn. And this was the origin of that 'Moonlight Sonata' with which we are all so fondly acquainted."

The musician ceased speaking. There was a dead silence, for all had been intently listening.

"And did he afterward teach the blind girl?" asked some one, at length, from the farther end of the table.

Fletcher smiled sadly and shook his head.

"He never went again. When the excitement was past, the interest was gone also; and though doubtless they remembered and expected him week after week, he thought of them no more, excepting as his eyes chanced now and then to fall upon the pages of the 'Sonata.' Is not such the rule of life?"

Shortly after this the company began gradually to disperse, and by the time we rose to leave, nearly all were gone or going, with the exception of a knot of choice spirits at the upper end, who had made up their minds to herald in the daylight.

The rain was over now, and the night starry. As we passed the doors of the theatre, we saw the bill-stickers busily placarding the programmes for the following evening.

"Look here!" cried Seabrook. "There is to be a performance to-morrow night! 'Der Freischutz,' by all that's glorious! We must

go, Paul! See, THE ENGAGEMENT OF MADAME VOGELSANG, in letters half a foot long! Who is Madame Vogelsang? Does any body know?"

We both turned toward Fletcher for a reply. He had been conversing gayly but a moment before, yet now he stood still and silent. The light from the street-lamp fell full upon his face. He was very pale, and his lips quivered convulsively. He caught my arm as if for support, and I felt him trembling.

"*Mon Dieu!*" I cried, involuntarily. "You are ill!"

He shook his head—subdued his emotion by a strong effort—relinquished his hold upon my arm—drew his hat down upon his brow—and, without a word of reply, turned abruptly away, and dashed down a neighboring street. In a moment he was out of sight, and we were left standing together by the theatre door, in mute amazement.

"A most eccentric man!" exclaimed Seabrook, drawing a long breath, as we resumed our way. "I always fancied that he was half-cracked, and I do not suppose that drinking and opium-eating have done any service to his brains!"

CHAPTER XI.

CIRCE.

"I REALLY believe, Norman, that you, familiar as you are with the pleasures of cities, feel more anticipation and enjoyment this evening than I, who have not witnessed a theatrical performance more than thrice in my life!"

I was tempted to say this on seeing the buoyant exhilaration of his manner and countenance as he surveyed the house through his lorgnette, and gazed impatiently toward the drop-curtain.

"'Der Freischutz' is my favorite opera," he replied, smiling. "I enjoy the wild devilry of the legend; and, above all, I delight in the picturesque music of Weber. He has all the science of Spohr, and more than the sweetness of Rossini."

"The part of Caspar is immensely powerful."

"Immensely. I could listen to the drinking-song for a whole evening, and to the low, fitful music of the incantation scene, with its muttering thunders and grotesque imagery. I have often thought that the part of Zamiel might be made more striking by the performers in a dramatic point of view, for—"

My friend's criticism was arrested by the opening chords of the overture, and from this moment he became entirely absorbed in the progress of the performance. We occupied a small box near the stage, whence we could see the actors closely, but whence, also, we suffered under the disadvantage of witnessing somewhat too much of the "business" of the *coulisses*. This was particularly annoying to Seabrook, who, faithful to his love of complete enjoyment, regretted the lost illusion of the scenery.

"I prefer," said he, "to be for the time utterly deceived. I do not wish to see that Zamiel's nose is false, and that Caspar wears a wig. I would rather believe that yonder pale spectres have just arisen, shuddering, from the Tartarean gulfs, than watch them drinking beer at the sides, out of sight of the audience. There ought to be no side-seats in a theatre. There should not be, were I the architect."

Accompanied by such brief remarks on music and the stage, the piece went on. Like all German performances, it was conscientiously rendered. The band played as one instrument; the chorus sang as one man; but, with the exception of the *prima donna*, the principal performers were little beyond mediocrity. The scenery, too, was faded and worn — the dresses dingy—the house far from cleanly. Yet it was crowded—crowded from pit to gallery with earnest listeners—lit by close rows of eager upturned faces. Madame Vogelsang, it would seem, was the attraction to the good townspeople of Frankfurt — Madame Vogelsang, whose name had been placarded in letters half a foot long, and of whom Norman Seabrook had never heard.

And here let me pause for some moments, that I may briefly describe this woman as I then saw her for the first time.

Thérèse Vogelsang was already past the bloom of her first youth. She might then have been perhaps thirty, or thirty-two years of age, and, in place of the slight proportions of early beauty, her superb figure had attained all the majestic grace and fullness of a Juno's. She was somewhat above the middle height. Her head was noble; her arms were the whitest and loveliest I had ever beheld; her dark hair was gathered in abundant braids around her serene and stately brow. There was something very dignified in her look, her bearing, her walk, in the very movements of her hands; something statuesque in her repose, her action, her every attitude. But her face, her lovely face, with its dark, languishing brown eyes, so soft and dangerous — her mouth, so full and so alluring—her rounded cheeks, her small straight nose, her smile, like the siren-smile of Italian Circe —of all these I have not yet spoken—of these I weep to speak, even to think.

Woe is me that this pen should have to trace the record, oh songstress, of thy most fatal beauty!

Her voice, like her person, was full, voluptuous, infinitely sweet and powerful. Its luscious tones, alternately tender and commanding, had a thrilling and peculiar accent, which left what is in French called a *retentissement* in the hearts of her hearers. Her love-accents, so tremulously sustained and touching, seemed to vibrate in one's very soul — her tears, stage-tears though they were, moved the inmost sympathies of one's nature. Looking at her, you felt yourself in a dream; listening to her, you fancied yourself in Elysium.

I do not exaggerate her fascinations. Indeed, I describe them almost in the very words of my friend, and of many others who subsequently felt them.

"What a glorious woman!" exclaimed Seabrook more than once during the evening. "What a regnant head! There is something in her glance that seems almost to take my breath away! Did you ever see such eyes— such a smile? She looks just like some Phidian Venus warmed into life!"

And such, truly, was the character of her beauty; warm—life-like—sensual—the perfection of mortality. In strict accordance with the genius of Greek art, there was the uttermost refinement of personal loveliness; the luxurious repose which veils strong physical energy; the outer calm which half reveals the inner passion. One thing alone was wanting, and wanting that, I found all the rest blank and unalluring. Need I say that that one thing was Soul? Yes, from the very first, that flaw in the diamond, that dark stain upon the marble, was plain to me. I saw in her only the Mortal-Beautiful—perhaps the Sinful-Beautiful. I missed that spiritual glory which I have sought and worshiped during all the years of my life—which has shone out upon me from less beautiful, but dearer eyes—which, in God's heaven, lights the foreheads of the angels!

The opera progressed, amid the acclamations of the audience, to a conclusion, and at last the curtain fell. A tempest of applause burst forth from all parts of the house; the pit rose simultaneously; the name of "Vogelsang" was shouted enthusiastically by hundreds of voices—by none more rapturously and loudly than that of Norman Seabrook. After some delay the drop-curtain was moved aside—the hurricane redoubled—the vocalist once more stepped before the audience.

Her stage-costume was thrown aside, and she wore a robe of plain black velvet, which became her beauty and complexion ten times better than the former dress. Her cheek was flushed with pleasure—she smiled—she advanced to the footlights—she clasped her hands upon her breast, half deprecatingly, half joyfully—her eyes wandered round the house with an indescribably fascinating expression—she bent lower and lower —she gathered up the flowers that fell around her on every side, and pressed them alternately to her lips and to her heart.

How strange it was, but in the midst of that tumult, while every eye was directed to the stage —while Norman, flushed and excited, was leaning forward from the box, applauding frantically—while the very players in the orchestra were joining in the general *furore*, I was tempted, by some sudden and inexplicable impulse, to turn all at once and look round at the box-door behind us.

Not vainly — not vainly; for there, there, pressed closely against the little window in the door, and staring wildly forward at the smiling singer, I saw a ghastly face—a face distorted by passion and pale rage—the face of Fletcher!

For an instant I could not speak, so unexpected and strange was the apparition. Then a smothered exclamation broke from my lips—I seized my friend by the arm—I pointed to the door, and, even as I spoke, the face glided suddenly away and disappeared.

"Fletcher—the musician—look!"

It was all I could say.

"Where? what do you mean? Who?" asked Seabrook, impatiently.

I made no reply, but, rushing to the door, opened it and looked into the lobby. There was not a soul there. I listened; but the noise from the house would have drowned the sound of his footsteps, even had they then been echoing along the corridor.

One of the box-keepers was coming up the stairs. I ran to him, and asked if a gentleman —a pale, thin gentleman, had passed him on the way? No one had passed him, he was convinced. Was there a gentleman answering to my description in any private box on this tier? Not one.

"What is all this?" interrupted my friend, hastily. "What are you saying about Fletcher? Why did you run away just as the Vogelsang was before the curtain?"

"Fletcher was looking through our box door!"

"Nonsense! He is gone to Ems!"

"I swear I saw him; and looking terrible, glaring, almost unearthly!" Seabrook burst into a laugh.

"Pooh! my dear Paul," he said gayly, passing his arm through mine, and leading me back toward the box, "you will next fancy that you have seen a ghost! It was a delusion, and nothing else. Poor Fletcher is far enough from Frankfurt to-night, and at the dullest place in all Germany. I hate Ems—that is to say, I hate the people who go there. The spot itself is a paradise, but it is also a hospital. You see none but invalids and physicians wherever you go. No, no, you did not see Fletcher, take my word for it. Hark! they are beginning again. Let us go back and see the ballet."

CHAPTER XII.

AM DEN RHEIN.

We had not been longer than a fortnight in Frankfurt, when Seabrook came into my room one bright fresh morning, and, sitting down beside my bed—for I had not yet risen—said abruptly,

"Why do we remain here, Latour? We have seen all that is to be seen in this place. We have been to Homburgh and to Offenbach—we have visited all the stock-sights of the city—we know the Ariadne and the music by heart. I was up and out this morning while you were soundly sleeping, and in the fruit-market near the Römer I heard a peasant-girl singing a song that has well-nigh driven me frantic. 'Am den Rhein! am den Rhein!' Oh, delicious! Get up, *amigo*, and let us not lose a day!"

"In the name of common sense, Norman, what do you mean? Where do you want me to go?"

"Where should I, if not to the Rhine?"

His gay, enterprising nature swayed mine in many things by the mere force of its own joyousness; and now I yielded to the bent of his humor. Before midday we had arrived at Biberich, within sight of the turreted city of Mayence on the opposite bank, and in a few moments more had taken our places on board the "Königen," and were gliding swiftly and pleasantly over the broad-flowing waters of the Rhine River.

Gliding, ever gliding, with the warm summer's air around us, and the bright sunlight glittering up from the foaming river, and the pleasant sounds of voices, and of paddle-wheels, beating like a busy heart, and of humming insects, and faint murmurs from the banks on either side!

Now, one by one, we pass the rush-grown river-meadows, as they call these islands of the Rhine—Peters-meadow, and Ingelheimer-meadow, and Haller-meadow, facing the bare and lofty chateau of Johannisberg, with its viny slopes and its chapel spire. The cupolas of Mayence have by this time faded and sunk beneath the level distance—the green hills advance toward the stream on either side, like the wings of an army—the Taunus Mountains, far away, grow pale and cloud-like—through a dark gorge to the left comes the gentle tide of a tributary river, with houses, and an old collegiate church, and a ruined castle, all clustered at its mouth. This is the little Italian-founded town of Bingen; and the castle bears the name of Roman Drusus. Now the banks grow narrower, and the white and stately castle of Rheinstein, with its iron cresset suspended from the topmost tower, and its tiny chapel sheltering on a narrow ledge of rock just within shade of the battlements, stands up erect, like a warden-knight, guarding the curve of the river. This, says Seabrook, is the summer-schloss of the Prince of Prussia. It is now one hour past noon, and the sailors are busily suspending a canvas awning overhead. The waiters place long tables all the length of the upper deck, and, covering them speedily with relays of snow-white cloths, silver, and glittering glass, prepare every thing for our *al fresco* meal. Next comes the little ancient town of Bacharach, with its walls and towers, and its exquisite fragment of old red Gothic architecture, St. Werner's Chapel, lifted high above the town upon a rise of green hills. We now take our places at the table, beside some merry students, and opposite to an elderly Graff with a grizzly beard, and his pretty young wife by his side. The clatter of knives and plates commences; voices talk loudly all around in French, German, and English; the slender-necked amber Rhine-bottles start up in all directions; incongruous dishes, eel and sweet pudding, boiled beef and preserved cherries, smoked salmon and cheese, pass backward and forward, and succeed each other with bewildering rapidity; there is the noise of cork-drawing, conversation, and laughter; and a pale, sickly-looking youth, about sixteen years of age, takes his place beside the man at the wheel, and begins playing with no little skill and taste upon a curious instrument, like a gigantic accordion, which contains several rows of keys, and is so large that it rests upon the deck between his knees, like a violoncello.

Amid all this, we still glide on in the bright sunshine, amid the woody hills, the mouldering ruins, the nestling villages, and sunny vineyards of the fair Rhine-country.

Now come heights steeper and darker — the castle of Gutenfels, with the little hamlet of Caub low-lying at its foot, with towers and slated roofs—the gloomy turreted Pfalz rising abruptly from the middle of the river, like a stone ship at anchor — the green hills beyond all, the blue sky overhead, and the boat flying on, ever on, like a swallow on the wing.

Here is Oberwesel, with high round tower and embattled walls, and circuit of slate mountains, clothed with vines; and yonder black and beetling rock, all riven into crags, and surrounded at the base by a narrow ledge of winding pathway—what threatening cliff is that?

"Look! look!" cried Seabrook, "there comes the Lurleyberg — that bare, stern precipice to the right! That spot where the river falls and foams is the famous Whirlpool; farther off you see the beginning of the town of St. Goar! This is the loveliest spot upon the Rhine! Listen to the echo—it repeats twelve or fifteen times!"

Whereupon a man starts out of a little straw-thatched hut upon the opposite bank, and, just as we arrive in face of the rock, fires a sudden pistol-shot. We all start, and some of the ladies utter timid exclamations, for it would seem that a regular and rapid discharge of fire-arms is taking place around us, so loud, so steady, so continuous are the repetitions. By the time that the last faint report dies away, we are threading our way between the sister-towns of Goarhausen and St. Goar, and gazing up at the vast and far-stretching ruins of the red fortress of Rheinfels.

The fourteenth course of our Rhine-dinner has just been removed — strawberries, cheese, and sweet biscuits are placed before us—the gentlemen begin to order cigars, and the ladies rise from table and walk up and down the lower deck, or sit sketching and conversing in little knots at the farther side of the vessel. One of the merry students at my left volunteers to relate a legend. We order a fresh bottle of the ruddy Assmannshausen—all that are near gather eagerly round — the narrator fills his glass, looks round with an air of satisfaction, leans back in his seat, and commences, in his native German tongue, the following

Legend of the Lurleyberg.

"A very great many years ago, when these ruined castles were impregnable strong-holds in-habited by the old feudal barons — when every passing boat paid a tribute to the castellan—when the gnomes had not yet fled the mountains, the fairies the forest, nor the Lurley nymph her caves under the river, there lived in a little vine-grown cottage, hard by the Castle of the Katz, a pretty maiden named Ida Müller. Now Ida was the only child of the head huntsman to the Lord of Katzenelnbogen, and would inherit not only the cottage and garden, but two little fields down by the water; so, you see, she was rich as well as pretty; and, what was better than either, she was good. I need scarcely tell you that Ida had many lovers. All pretty girls have, especially when they are rich. Among these, the only two who seemed to have a chance of success were Otto Wolfsohn and Max Steigerwald. Otto was a small proprietor whose vineyards and cottage lay just at the opposite side of the river, close by the whirlpool called the Gewirr; Max was nothing but a poor artist, a sculptor in stone and wood, who lived in an old ruined tower, which has long since utterly crumbled away and disappeared, about half way between the towns of Oberwesel and St. Goar. Here he made his home and his workshop; and, although it must be acknowledged that he was exceedingly poor, he contrived to lead a very happy existence. He loved Ida and he loved art—he was ambitious, light-hearted, and in love — life he found pleasant—the future, he thought, could not fail to be as golden as he wished it — so he carved and sang from morning till night, and on Sundays attended mass at the chapel of St. Peter of Goarhausen, less, it is to be feared, through devotion than love, for there he saw Ida among the young girls near the altar—there he watched her fair head bent over her missal, and tried to separate the tones of her voice from the others in the sweet-chanted responses. Of course it happened, as it always did and does in love-stories, that Ida, with a woman's keen-sightedness, read the heart of the young sculptor, and contrived in some way to let him see that she preferred him and his poverty to Otto Wolfsohn, despite his lands and his riches. This knowledge only made Max ten times more industrious than before; and when, at length, his talent and his perseverance were rewarded by a great piece of good fortune, he went straight over to Müller's cottage at the castle-foot, and formally demanded the hand of his daughter. A great piece of good fortune, indeed! The Abbot of Kamp, having seen some of his efforts, had actually bidden him, Max Steigerwald, to carve an oaken image of the Blessed Mary, to stand over the great altar in the monastery chapel. Nor was this all; the best part was that the abbot had engaged to pay him the sum of thirty golden ducats on the very day of its completion. Thirty golden ducats! why, what marvelous things might be done with thirty golden ducats! A cottage might be rented—a field might be bought—a pair of silver ear-rings might be given to the bride! What more could the heart of man desire?

Thus pleaded the lover when he urged his suit in the ear of Meister Müller the huntsman.

"Now Meister Müller loved Ida dearly, but he loved money also, and it needed many arguments and persuasions to gain his consent to the betrothal! He would have preferred the wealthier and less amiable Otto for his son-in-law; and, even though he yielded, yielded unwillingly. But Ida cared little for Otto, and little for his wealth; still less for his scowling glances when he chanced now and then to meet her by the river-path, or the chapel-door, or in the market-place of Oberwesel. She loved and was loved; and so she trusted gayly to the future, like a bird to the summer-time.

"Meanwhile the winter came and went—the snow melted in the mountain-hollows — the spring-season filled the landscape with green leaves and flowers — the cuckoo was heard again in the meadows; and the sculptor worked on with ever-increasing energy, for the statue was now all but completed.

"I have said that Max Steigerwald lived in a tower by the river—a gray, dilapidated round tower, with long wavy grasses growing at the top, and swallows'-nests built in the crannies of the battlements. The upper part was utterly in ruin; so he made his home in the two lower rooms, and there, day after day, night after night, he toiled assiduously at his task, thinking of Ida; and often, as he carved on by lamp-light in the silent night-hours, he heard the siren-song of the Lurley wafted along by the wind from where she sat in the moonlight on the jutting base of the Lurleyberg, weaving garlands of the forget-me-not and the white water-lily. But at such times he would shudder, make the sign of the cross, and, fixing his eyes on the holy image, growing momentarily more and more beautiful beneath his busy fingers, breathe a pious prayer for protection against the spells of the pale maiden. Sometimes, too, he would fix his thoughts, instead, upon the gentle Ida, and upon the happy time that was daily drawing nearer, and he found this plan succeed quite as well as the other. Nevertheless, there were nights when he had a fearful struggle to overcome the temptation of obeying the melodious invitation conveyed in that unearthly canticle; for there is a sweet and evil power in the song of the Lurley which few human natures are strong enough to resist, and which, if they but yield to it, destroys not only the body, but the soul. So Max Steigerwald closed his ears to the spell, put his heart into his work, and was at last enabled to name the very day on which it might be conveyed to the monastery-chapel amid the walnut-trees of Kamp.

"It was late in the afternoon of a glowing day in May when the sculptor threw down his tools, and, gazing joyously upon the calm and lovely face of his statue, with its holy brow, its draped robes, and the slender gilded circlet of glory round its head, saw that the work of his hands was finished, and knew that it was beautiful.

"'Oh art! oh love!' he exclaimed, 'how happy ye have made me!'

"So happy, poor fellow, that he felt he must enjoy his gladness with her whose share in it had been so great! So he went forth into the evening sunset, and, giving one last backward glance at his beloved statue, closed and locked the door of his tower, and went along by the river-banks to the ferry of Goarhausen, by which he crossed over and went straight to the vine-grown cottage at the foot of the Katz, where Ida was seated spinning by the door, under the boughs of a yellow laburnum.

"They were so happy that evening, and had so much to dream and plan! The cottage was chosen; the field had but to be paid for, since it was already hired; the day for the wedding was even fixed; for would not Max be a rich man on the morrow, with his thirty golden ducats?

"The moon shone brightly on river and mountain that night as he went homeward along the meadows. His heart was full of love and gratitude. He could almost have danced for joy. He never had been so happy in his life, and the road seemed so short that he quite started to find himself at the door of his own tower.

"Now to see my beautiful Virgin again!" he said to himself, as he took out the key and prepared to enter.

"Strange! at the first touch of his hand, even before he could fix the key in the lock, the door gave way creaking, and rolled back a little on its hinges.

"An evil presentiment came over the sculptor: he paused—pressed his hand upon his beating heart — advanced, drew back, and finally flung the door wide open and went in.

"Alas! not vainly had he trembled and delayed! The moonlight shone in as a silver flood, illumining the interior of the room. Chair, table, working-bench, fireplace, all were clearly defined and bright as day; but the statue! the statue! the oaken Virgin, with her holy brow, and her divine smile, and her golden glory— where was she?

"Gone, stolen, lost, no one knew whither.

"He threw himself upon the ground — he wept—he raved; and at last, in a delirium of grief, ran wildly out of his tower, and down to the river-bank; for why live when statue, ducats, and bride were all reft from him in one brief and bitter moment?

"'Farewell, Ida!' he cried, lifting his hands to heaven, and gazing for the last time in the direction of her home.

"Suddenly he started—his lips trembled— the very power of motion seemed to desert him; for lo! a pale shadow—pale, but how lovely! glided like a moonbeam over the surface of the stream, midway between the two river-banks. There were white water-flowers twined in her hair and around her arms; her eyes were languishing and full of tenderness; her smile sweeter than the breath of the roses. She sang, and he listened:

"'Come hither, young mortal! come, taste of the wine
Divine!
Of the wine of a love so immortal as mine!
Come drink from my lips—be my lover, my guest!
Lay thy cheek to my cheek, and thy breast to my
breast!
Come hither to love, to elysium, to rest!'

"The sculptor heard the fatal song. His
breath came thick and fast—his cheek flushed
—his heart beat wildly. Nearer and nearer
floated the river-maid; sweeter and sweeter fell
those liquid tones; brighter and brighter grew
the vision of her beauty.

"'Come!' murmured the Lurley. 'Come
hither!'

"'Ida! Ida!' he cried, with desperate courage. 'Ida!'

"The shadow on the water seemed to wane
and tremble. The sculptor fell upon his knees.

"'Ave Maria,' he began, in the earnest tones
of one who prays for life or death. 'Ave Maria
beatissima—'

"Dimmer and dimmer grew the form of the
Lurley; her song died away into a low wailing
cry; she bent her head, shuddering, and sank
in one moment beneath the surface of the water.

"Max rose from his knees, but he beheld
only a chaplet of white lilies drifting on with
the current.

"Earnest and awe-struck he gazed for some
moments; and then, turning slowly away, went
onward in the moonlight, leaving river, and
tower, and Ida behind him, and disappeared
amid the shades of the forest.

"Many and strange were the rumors when it
was found that Max Steigerwald had disappeared, and that the oaken Virgin was gone
from her place in the old tower. Very indignant was the abbot of the monastery among the
walnut-trees of Kamp; very sad and broken-
hearted was the gentle Ida in her father's cottage at the foot of the Katz. Otto Wolfsohn
alone showed neither surprise, nor sorrow, nor
anger, but simply hastened to profit by the absence of his rival in the renewal of his former
suit. This time, however, he addressed himself less to Ida than to her father, wisely judging that his arguments and his wealth would be
more favorably received by him than by her.

"'Steigerwald is gone,' he said. 'Either he
is dead, or he has deserted and no longer de-
serves her. I love her. I am rich—I am
young. She will be happy, she will be prosper-
ous, she will be respected as my wife. If you
command, she will marry me.'

"And so Meister Müller commanded, and
Ida, despite her tears and her grief, was forced
to obey; entreating, however, that she might
yet be allowed one year of tarrying. But the
year passed away, and he came not; and the
day of her wedding dawned through the mists
of November.

"How pale she looked—how pale and how
joyless—more like a victim than a bride, as she
sat in her father's house, in the midst of the
guests, with the crown on her head, and the

silver arrow, for the last time, in her hair, awaiting the bridegroom.

"It was strange that Otto alone should be so
late in arriving! 'Let us go out, and see if he
be coming,' said one of the bride-maidens. So
they all went forth upon the river-bank; for you
will remember that Otto lived on the opposite
shore, just beyond the pool of the Gewirr. But
there was nothing in sight. Hold! what is
that? A boat putting off from the bank, about
half a mile up the river? Yes—at last? That
boat is Otto's; it is moored by his orchard-gate:
he will row himself down to the Katz! Welcome, bridegroom! Row swiftly and featly, for
Ida is waiting.

"Quite silently they stand, expecting and
watching. Hark! what strange sound is that?
The sound of music!—of what music? Of a
voice!—of what voice? How unlike any voice
that we have ever heard! How sweet, how
liquid, how enchanting!

"And see! what white form is that which
rises from the mists of the river?

"A shudder runs through the spectators.
'The Lurley!' they say, with tremulous lips.
The young men grasp each other by the hand
—the young maidens hide their faces in the bo-
soms of their mothers.

"Row, bridegroom! Row swiftly and featly,
and heed not the danger.

"Horror! he drops the oars—he listens—he
extends his arms to her—he stands up in the
boat, and, as if impelled by some invisible power, drifts rapidly toward her.

"One sudden, fearful cry bursts from every lip:
"'The whirlpool! the whirlpool!'

"Alas! too late. The Lurley ever beckons
—the boat ever follows. It nears the fatal circle; it rocks and strains, like a panting steed;
it flies madly round and round, and is sucked
down, down, down into the foaming gulf!

"Who is this that bursts through the crowd,
with flushed cheek and hair wildly flying, crying,
'Make way! I will save him!'—who plunges
headlong into the stream—who strikes out for
the whirlpool, and boldly breasts the strength of
the current?

"Max Steigerwald, the sculptor.

"Swim on, brave sculptor—swim swiftly and
featly; thy rival is sinking!

"On he went, with his fair gallant head lifted
above the waters—on to the spot where the Lurley had sank, and where Otto had followed.

"Now he pauses, as it were, on the brink
of the whirlpool; now he dashes forward with
fresh strength, and dives down to the depths of
the Gewirr.

"There was an interval of suspense—breathless, agonizing suspense. Can he ever return
to us? Hah! what is that? Now blessed be
Heaven and all the saints in the calendar, 'tis
the fair gallant head coming back once more
over the waters—and not alone! See! he bears
a dark form in his arms! Welcome, brave
sculptor! Swim swiftly and featly—but a yard
or two farther, and thou art safe on the shore.

C

"Now he waxes faint and weary—has no one a rope? No! 'tis not needed; he strikes out once—twice—thrice; he staggers forward, and, with his burden, falls heavily to the ground.

"They rush toward him—they carry him up the bank, and lay his head on Ida's breast. But Otto! Where is Otto, and what is this dark form which has been borne, with such peril, to the shore?

"By heaven! the oaken Virgin, with her holy brow, and her divine smile, and the golden circlet, somewhat dimmed and water-worn, around her meek head.

"The mystery is great—almost insoluble.

"Slowly the sculptor revives, and opens his eyes upon the loved bosom of Ida. He can explain nothing, save that he has traveled and studied, and wrought a second and a lovelier statue, which he had brought this very day to the monastery at Kamp, and sold for thrice the sum before agreed upon—that he has returned richer and wiser, to make Ida his bride—that he beheld the danger of Otto, and sought only to save him—that he dived—that he clasped a form at the bottom of the waters—that he seized and upbore, and saved it, nor knew all the time but that he was saving his rival.

"Two things only are certain—that Otto is drowned, and the Virgin discovered.

"'But how came she in the depths of the Gewirr?' asks Meister Müller, the huntsman.

"This is a question to which no one can reply; and Max, going over to the image, raises it from the ground, and clasps it to his breast with all the joy of a father who recovers the child of his affection.

"A sudden exclamation escapes the lips of the by-standers—they snatch the image from his grasp:

"'See! see! what words are these cut on the back of the figure?'

"Simply these:

"'OTTO WOLFSOHN. A TOKEN OF REVENGE.'

"So it was thus. Yielding to the impulse of a base vengeance, he had sought to destroy the fair statue, and with it the prosperity and happiness of his rival. Fortunately, all was without success; and on the afternoon of that very day on which Otto was to have wedded the fair Ida, Max Steigerwald stood with her before the altar rails of the little chapel of St. Peter, and received her for his wife. I will venture to say that no happier or fonder pair ever occupied that place before or since.

"And this is my LEGEND OF THE LURLEY-BERG."

This night we sleep at Coblentz; and, as the dusk draws on, I retire to my chamber, for I am weary, and long to be alone.

A waiter has lit candles and drawn the curtains closely. The room, too, is warm and oppressive. I extinguish the lights, draw aside the muslin draperies, throw up the sash, and lean out into the quiet night.

Fronting my window flows the King-river, broadly and silently, reflecting the lights which shine down at regular intervals from the lamps along the bridge of boats which connects Coblentz with the opposite bank. Beyond the river, standing up darkly and boldly upon their steep rock-base, spread the fortress-ranges of the citadel of Ehrenbreitstein. Far hills and forests close in the landscape round. Every where there are lights gleaming—lights on board the steamers moored along the quay—lights in the windows of the hotel of the Cheval Blanc, on the other side of the river—lights here and there along the shore, which stream out redly, and waver on the current. A vaporous mist is now rising from the water, and a late steam-boat comes panting up with a crimson lamp at her prow, discharging her bewildered passengers in the darkness. Now the city grows more silent, and a droschky rattling along the pavement sounds noisily. Presently some Prussian soldiers, with their brazen helmets glittering in the lamp-light, go singing past the window, for they have just strolled out of a neighboring wine-shop. Then the town clocks chime, and the notes of a solitary trumpet ring out faintly and clearly from the fortress. Soon the night grows darker, and the mist upon the river whiter and heavier. Some rain begins to fall, and I close my casement with a sigh.

Alas! to-night the sorrow lies heavily at my heart, and I can not shake it off. For many hours I toss restlessly upon my bed, and it is gray dawn before I sleep.

CHAPTER XIII.

ROUGE ET NOIR.

"AND is it possible, Seabrook, that you do not admire this place? It seems to me almost a paradise!"

It was evening-time. We were sitting together on the verge of one of those precipitous wooded hills which inclose the little watering-place of Ems on every side. Far below us extended the public gardens; the avenues of chestnut-trees and lindens; the Kurhaus, with its white façade stretching beside the water; the long, irregular row of hotels and lodging-houses which constitute the town. Calmly and brightly, glassing the green shadows of the hills and the white clouds overhead, flowed the Lahn River, child of the Rhine. Crowds of gay company were promenading along the banks, strolling up and down the light-roofed suspension bridge, lingering round the band in the garden-pavilion, or eating ices under the trees.

Along the winding road at the foot of the mountains there passed sometimes an open carriage; sometimes a troop of donkeys, accompanied by their liveried drivers with blue blouses and red-trimmed caps; sometimes a little band of peasants singing together, and laden with fruits and vegetables for the market. Now an artist trudged wearily by with sketch-book and folio, returning from his diurnal labor. Now a single horse came wading up the very middle of the shallow river, towing a barge.

Below was life and animation — above and around us, infinite quiescence. And through all the landscape, winding and glistening away, with villages, and churches, and raftered farm-houses nestled here and there along its banks, and boats moored under willows, and evening bathers in among the rushes, and little foaming weirs, and water-mills, and knots of white and amber lilies nodding with its current, lay the river, shut in by mountains and hills, with the soft fleecy haze of the coming night spreading slowly over all.

Seabrook looked up smiling.

"I never said that I did not admire the place," he replied; "I only told you that it was monotonous; that it was peopled by pale-faced invalids, and ruined gamblers, and fashionable physicians; and that I detested it heartily. You are walking, perhaps, in the gardens; you see an elegant couple sitting together in an arbor, and you please yourself with fancying some little love-romance. Ten to one, on drawing nearer, but that the gentleman, who seemed to you to be gently pressing the fair hand of the object of his affections, is feeling her pulse all the time, and that she is just drawing forth her purse to tender him his fee! The doctors hold their *séances* in the open air, and consult with their patients to the accompaniment of the band. You wander in the vicinity of the Kurhaus, and every person you meet carries a colored glass tumbler or a silver goblet in one hand. These are on their way to the springs. All the world is ill or getting better; drinks the waters or bathes in them; diets rigidly at the table d'hôte; takes exercise in an invalid chair, and sees a favorite physician at least once in every day. Defend me, oh Common Sense, from all such humbug!".

"But if the people are really ill, and come hither in search of health . . . ." I urged, gravely.

"No such thing!" interrupted my friend, with an impatient gesture. "Not the tenth part of them ail any thing at all. It is the fashion to be ill here—*voilà tout!* People make acquaintances at the springs, and through their medical attendants. They condole with each other, and sickness forms the staple resource of all their conversation. Without something is the matter with you, you can get no sympathy, no society; if you are an invalid, you have every chance of spending your three months very pleasantly. A liver complaint is a sure introduction, and you find a galloping consumption an immediate passport to the best circles."

We went down by a winding path, crossed the suspension bridge, and mingled with the promenaders in the gardens. We saw Fletcher in the kiosque, conducting the band; but he was occupied with the music, and did not recognize us among the by-standers. Like the rest, he wore a heavy brass helmet and a fantastic uniform; and I know not whether it was the effect of illness or of his unusual costume, but he seemed to me paler, sterner, and more haggard than ever.

They were playing a selection from the "Euryanthe" of Weber when we arrived, and as soon as the last chord was struck, we made our way up to his desk and addressed him.

He started, held out his hand, drew it back, held it out again, and shook ours nervously.

"How do you do?" said he, in his old quick, incoherent way. "This is quite a surprise. Have you been on the Rhine? Ems is a gay place. Where do you live? Have you been long here? The waters are very bitter."

"We only arrived this morning," replied Seabrook, "and we are staying for the present at the Hotel d'Angleterre."

"Very dear hotel. What do you say to our band? Wretched set this year. The King of Würtemberg is in the gardens to-night. Are you from Frankfurt direct, or did you stay at Coblentz? This is pretty scenery. Fond of ruins? I am not. The Rhine is greatly overrated. So is Goëthe. Have you been down to the springs? It's like going into a vault. See that dark man yonder — Mazzini. He's talking to the Princess Von Hohenhausen. Plenty of celebrities. Of course you've seen the Conversation Haus?"

In conversing with Fletcher, I always made it a rule to reply to the last thing said, since it was hopeless to think of disentangling the parti-colored threads of his wandering ideas; so I told him that I was at present such a stranger as not to know where the Conversation Haus was to be found—nay, I was even ignorant of what its purport and uses might be.

"It's a part of the Kursaal. A set of showy rooms—café, ballroom, and gaming-rooms. It all belongs to the Grand-Duke. Seventy and eighty thousand florins are lost there annually by play. We call the hazard-tables the duke's treasury. He also lets lodgings at the Alte Kurhaus. Quite a commercial prince. Poor as a mouse. Hush! We have to play now. Last piece. We'll go to the rooms when it is over."

We went down again, and waited for him at the back of the kiosque while the band performed Mendelssohn's "Wedding March" from the "Midsummer Night's Dream." By the time that it was over, the gay company had almost deserted the gardens; the shades of evening had closed in and darkened all the landscape; some stars were out in the clear sky; and a flood of warm light glowed from the windows of the Conversation Haus. Then the musician rejoined us, and we followed him to the rooms. He had laid aside his helmet and braided coat, and as he walked along with his hat in his hand, letting the cool breeze play upon his brow, I fancied that the thick gray hair looked somewhat thinned, and the careworn brow more deeply furrowed than when we parted with him at Frankfurt a few weeks before. Besides this, his conversation seemed more disjointed and wandering. He frequently paused in the middle of a sentence—sometimes in the middle of a word. Often he spoke as if in reply to his own thoughts; and still oftener, as though his mind were occupied on other matters, and his tongue a mere mechanical agent uttering commonplace observations, with which his powers of reflection were totally unconnected.

At the door of the Kursaal we found knots of visitors talking and smoking; little bands of promenaders from the gardens strolling up and down the colonnade; and in the empty ball-room several gentlemen reading the newspapers of the day.

"But where are the gaming-tables?" asked my friend.

The musician pointed to an open door at the farther end of the apartment, through which several persons were passing and repassing, and whence a busy hum, accompanied by an occasional clicking noise, was distinctly audible.

We entered. The atmosphere was warm and oppressive; the blaze of gas intolerable; the crowd of lookers-on so great that for several minutes we could get no farther than the door. All were thronging round one long table which almost filled the room, and no one spoke save in low whispers. Presently a slight movement arose near us. A gentleman came out, and Fletcher took advantage of the moment to make a way for us to the front rank next the table.

The players only were sitting. They were of all ages and both sexes. Some of them had pieces of card, which they pricked occasionally with a pin, according to the progress of the game. Many had little piles of gold and silver, rouleaux sealed at either end, and packets of yellow Prussian notes lying beside them. All looked serious and interested; but there were none of those violent emotions of which we read in books depicted in their countenances. They won and lost with the best-bred composure, and the stakes upon the table varied from half a dollar to twenty gold pieces at a time. Four elderly, respectable-looking men, occupying raised seats at the centre of the table, were the bank-company. One of these dealt the cards, the others paid and received the money. Each pack of cards, as soon as it had been once dealt, was thrown into a well sunk in the table, just in front of the dealer.

The scene was utterly new to me. I looked round from face to face with untiring curiosity, and saw the gold changing hands without in the least comprehending the laws of the game. Opposite to me sat an old lady, very highly rouged, and decked in artificial flowers and false jewelry. She had a cunning eye, and on her lips a fixed smile. I observed that she always won. Next to her a sallow boy leaned forward upon both elbows, now and then hazarding a ten-franc piece which he drew from his waistcoat pocket. Farther on, a dark handsome man and his wife sat side by side, drawing their stakes from a heap of money between them, and adding to their store with every venture. Just at my elbow I noticed a young and well-dressed woman, who watched the cards with affected indifference, putting down a florin every time, and losing invariably. Others there were whose fortune seemed to fluctuate, but none in whom those fluctuations produced any visible emotion.

I could not help remarking this to my friend. He smiled.

"Your observation," he said, "proves to me that you have never before visited a place of the kind. It is only in novels that ruined gamblers rush wildly from the tables, with distraction in their faces. Here a man will lose his last florin with a smile which looks, at least, sufficiently natural. Your real *habitué* is perfect master of his countenance, and would scorn to betray himself even to a gesture. In fact, he rather seeks to reverse the ordinary course of matters; for he smiles when he loses, and looks indifferent when he wins."

"And what game are they now playing?"

"Rouge-et-noir. Will you hazard a thaler or two?"

"Not I. In the first place, gambling possesses no attraction for me; and, in the second, I can not even fathom the rules by which they play. They all seem to me to do the same thing, and yet how different are the results to each person! What is the reason that—"

"Hush!" interrupted Seabrook, plucking me by the arm and speaking in a hurried whisper. "Look there! My life on it, but this man's a gambler!"

I turned, and saw Fletcher in the act of lifting a couple of silver dollars from the table. His cheek was flushed, and his eager eye fixed upon the dealer. The old lady opposite staked two gold pieces, and won. A half smile flitted over his lips—he replaced his two dollars on the board—the color proved favorable, and his little capital was instantly doubled. Again he tried, and again he was successful. The next time he ventured all, and with the same result.

Seabrook and I exchanged glances, but we were too much concerned to speak. We stood by, silently observing him; and he, evidently, had lost every recollection of our presence.

Presently a seat became vacant just where he stood. He slipped into it mechanically, as it were; exchanged a glance of recognition with a gentleman sitting on his left, and went on playing.

For a long time we remained there, watching him. His success was not invariable, for he lost once or twice; but he was, on the whole, a considerable winner. At length the weary sameness of the scene, the hot glare, the oppressive silence, and the still more oppressive atmosphere, fatigued and annoyed me. I made a sign to Seabrook, and he followed me from the room; but, as I went, I cast a last glance at the musician, and I saw that his two dollars had by this time multiplied to thirty or forty, among which gleamed some five or six yellow Friedrichs-d'or.

Quite silently we went out arm in arm through the empty ballroom, along the deserted garden-walks, and out upon the bridge, where the white moonlight slept upon the river, and where one or two romantic couples were yet loitering to and fro.

Seabrook was the first to speak.

"Upon my soul," said he, gravely, "I am very sorry for what we have seen to-night—the more so, as I believe this infatuation to be a recent thing."

"Recent!" I echoed. "On the contrary, I should say that it had been the practice of years. See how haggard, how nervous, how absent the man is; and what more likely to make him so than the gaming-table? Depend upon it, he is well known at all the Brunnen in Germany!"

My companion shook his head.

"I have seen more of life than you, Paul," said he, "and have studied the 'dimensions, senses, passions, and affections' of mankind more attentively. I repeat that Fletcher has not long been a gambler—nay, more, he is still in his novitiate. Did you not see how his hand shook when he took up his first gains from the table? How his cheek flushed as he proceeded? How terrified he looked when he thought the 'luck' was turning? How, when he was winning, he staked all that he had previously won, without reserving a single piece to carry on the war in case of loss? No habitual player would do this. No habitual player would watch the successful competitors as he does, staking upon their colors, and trusting to their good fortune rather than his own. No, no, mon ami! A true gambler has strong nerve, impassive features, self-reliance, and a 'theory' of his own respecting chances, numbers, and colors. Fletcher has none of this; and I dare wager a hundred Napoleons that his initiation into the mysteries of rouge-et-noir has dated solely from the period of his arrival at Ems."

"But are there no means by which we can save him?"

Seabrook shook his head again.

"I fear not," he replied, sadly. "He is nervous, excitable, irritable to the last degree. Besides, what amount of resolution or self-denial can you expect from a confirmed opium-eater? His power of control over his own inclinations is already gone—his nervous system is shattered—his mental and physical energy utterly weakened and broken down. The case, I fear, is hopeless; but we must see more of it before we pass judgment. Let us come here again to-morrow evening, and watch the progress of the disease—for a disease it unquestionably is. After all, what is gaming but a kind of opium-eating? And who shall say which of the two is the more fatal intoxication?"

CHAPTER XIV.

ALSATIA.

We remained for more than three weeks at Ems, notwithstanding the prejudices of my friend, and passed them very pleasantly. We sketched, rode, read, and made long pedestrian excursions to the Lindenbach Valley, the Castle of Marksburg, and the Convent of Arnstein. We also visited the iron-works of Hohenrain, and the silver-smelting furnace in the neighboring vale, and spent many happy hours following the windings of the Lahn, or boating up to that romantic point where the little troubled river glides peacefully into the broad embraces of the Rhine.

During this time we had repeatedly entered the Conversation Haus at hours when the music was not going forward, and seldom without finding Fletcher in the gaming-rooms. It was plain that he had become a confirmed player. He had his appointed seat at the table; his nod of recognition from the croupier; his mute greeting from one or two who, like himself, were punctual in their attendance. He had also acquired a certain command of feature which he did not at first possess; yet such was the constitutional nervousness of his temperament, that, despite all his care, it was still betrayed now and then in the eager intensity of his gaze, and in the tremulous lip and hand. An attentive observation of his play and the variations of his luck assured me that in the long run he was no inconsiderable loser. What he gained one night he lost, and more than lost, the next; and at those very moments when Fortune seemed more than usually kind toward him, the most signal reverse was certain to be at hand.

I do not say that he ever hazarded largely, or that he lost to any great amount; but I saw enough to convince me that his limited resources could not long withstand the impoverishment consequent upon drains so exhausting and so incessant as these. I also noticed, with a feeling of regretful pity which I can not express, that each day only added to the ghastly pallor of complexion and the unnatural brilliancy of eye which stamps the opium-eater—that his tone of mind grew more absent, more unsettled, more purposeless and disjointed—that his gray hair, once so thick, became thinned, and hung about his neck and brow in long, uncut, neglected locks. Sometimes, when we met him in the grounds, he would pointedly avoid us; sometimes maintain an obstinate silence after the first greetings were exchanged; sometimes pour forth a string of wandering phrases with a kind of voluble indifference that was infinitely painful to witness. Once or twice, when we encountered him in the rooms or under the colonnade, he did not even recognize us; and he seldom or never recollected either of our names. I have stood for hours together behind his chair, and watched the changes of his fortune, without his ever dreaming that I was there.

I found myself much interested in the fate of this eccentric man — more interested than Seabrook, who had known him longer. I knew that he was blindly traveling toward ruin, and the same fascination which impels us to watch a rider whose horse has taken fright, or a shipwreck, or any fatal and inevitable misfortune, impelled me, as it were, to track the course of this infatuation. I felt that I must be at hand to count the steps of his descent—to watch it from day to day, from depth to depth; and, when matters came to the worst, to be enabled, at the right moment, to step forward and save him from absolute destruction.

"It is his only chance of amendment," I replied, when rallied by Seabrook on my devotion to the gaming-tables. "When all is lost I will say to him, 'Here is gold for thy necessities, but not for thy vices. Promise me to play no more.' If he have a spark of honor and good faith remaining, he will be cured."

But my friend only shook his head, and sighed, and went off to play at billiards with some young men whom he knew in the town, and among whom he passed away those hours which I spent in the Conversation Haus.

One evening I missed him from his accustomed place. I scarcely knew whether to be pleased or alarmed at this unusual absence; but, at all events, I felt an inward uneasiness that caused me to direct my steps to the gardens at an earlier hour the next night.

The music of the band came pleasantly through the trees as I entered the gate, and I made my way at once to the pavilion.

A stranger was conducting in his place—he was not there. A cold sensation crept over me.

"He has lost every thing," I said to myself. "He was in despair—perhaps he has committed suicide. And I! Alas! I had hoped to save him!"

This fear was too much for me. I sat down upon a vacant bench, and leaned my head against a tree. Presently the music ceased. I rose up and went over, with the intention of asking some of the players; I hesitated; and while I hesitated, the leader gave the signal, and they recommenced. I returned to my seat in an agitation for which I could not account, and of which I felt ashamed, even to myself.

"What's Hecuba to me, or I to Hecuba?" I muttered. "Doubtless the man is safe; and, at all events, the fault is not mine."

Selfish reasoning, and hollow as selfish, for it availed me nothing; and when I at last summoned resolution, and asked the conductor after my new acquaintance, I felt as nervous as before.

"The Herr Fletcher," replied the young man, politely, "is not well. For some days he has been indisposed, and for the last two he has been confined to his apartment."

"Will you oblige me with his address?"

He penciled it on the back of an old letter, and handed it to me.

"Thanks. And his illness?"

The musician shrugged his shoulders.

"Really, mein Herr, I have not the least notion."

I touched my hat, turned away, and, glancing at the address written on the letter, threaded the garden paths as rapidly as I could, and went out into the town.

Holländischer Hof! I did not remember to have seen any hotel or lodging-house of that name since my arrival at Ems. I went up to a waiter standing upon the steps of the Hotel de Russie, and inquired of him if he knew it; but he only stared at the paper with an insolent air, and bade me ask the donkey-drivers over the way.

Rudely as the advice was meant, I acted upon it, and was directed to an obscure quarter of the town, lying down by the river side, near the bridge of boats, where the watermen colonized.

It was a wretched spot—wet, unpaven, and dirty. There were children, pigs, poultry, and donkeys wandering, uncared for, through the narrow lanes. Large heaps of refuse lay before each door. The voices of women quarreling were loud within; men leaned, smoking, from the upper windows; and all the atmosphere around was tainted and heavy. At the farthest extremity of this Alsatia I found the mean inn dignified by the name of the Holländischer Hof.

He was crouching over a small stove in a comfortless garret, wrapped in a blanket taken from the bed, and shivering piteously. He looked very pale and ill, and had not shaved for three or four days. His hands, too, as he held them toward the open door of the stove, seemed almost transparent. I could not have believed that I should see so startling a change after so brief an absence.

When I tapped upon his door he made no answer—when I entered the room he neither turned nor spoke — when I stood beside him, and uttered a few simple words of apology and condolence, he only looked up with a listless, weary air, and sighed heavily.

"I am indeed sorry to find you thus, Mr. Fletcher. I feared that you were ill when I saw a stranger conducting the band, and so I took the liberty of calling to—to inquire if you were better."

He stared dreamily into the fire, but remained silent.

"You have some medical advice, I trust?"

He moaned and shook his head.

I looked round the room for a chair, and, seeing only an old deal box beside the window, I dragged it over to the fire, and sat down opposite to him.

"I consider that it is absolutely necessary for you to have proper attendance, Mr. Fletcher. You must permit a friend of mine—a man highly distinguished by his professional skill — to call upon you. I know that he will gladly oblige me in so small a matter."

Heaven forgive me! I had not a friend, or even an acquaintance, in all Ems, except Norman Seabrook. But any eminent physician would suit the character; and I consoled myself by arguing that it was, after all, but a figure of speech.

As the musician still said nothing, I went on.

"My friend shall see you this very evening—and—and I think—that is, I suppose it probable, that he will order you wine—generous living—perhaps expensive medicines."

He looked up hastily.

"No—no," he said, in a low, hurried tone, "no—I am well—better. No physician—no physician!"

"Pardon me, but it is necessary. I assure you that you are more unwell than you suppose. I will go at once in search of my friend; and, in the mean time—in case you should require any thing—pray excuse me—I shall call again to-morrow. Good evening—good evening!"

And I hastened from the room, down the dark staircase, with its balustrade of greasy rope, and out into the lanes below, leaving a couple of gold pieces upon the table at his side.

Once more outside the house, I shuddered, and thrust my hand into the breast of my coat, for I had touched his at parting, and that clammy chill, like the chill of death, seemed yet to cling against the palm.

What a den! what a neighborhood! I strode rapidly along the slippery lanes in the direction of the Hauptstrass, in the hope of reaching the gardens before all the company had departed, and of finding there some one of those medical gentlemen whom I had learned to recognize by sight during my brief sojourn. Every thing seemed to impede my way. The watermen were returning to their homes for the night; the donkey-drivers, with their weary beasts, were thronging along on their way to such wretched stabling as the place afforded; a broken-down cart, with a gaping crowd around, blocked up the pathway. Added to this, it was getting dark, and some rain began to fall.

When I felt the first drops of the shower, I knew that my last chance was gone, and my fears proved to be correct; for when I reached the gardens, the gay company had all dispersed, and the musicians were just in the act of hastening away with their instrument-cases in their hands. One of these I stopped.

"Pardon, monsieur; but can you direct me to a physician?"

"A physician! Indeed no, mein Herr—not I."

And, shaking my hand roughly from his sleeve, the man endeavored to pass on.

"One moment, I beseech you," I continued, nothing daunted, as I again seized him by the arm. "It is for Mr. Fletcher—he whom you know. He is very ill. Pray help me to find a physician!"

The name of Fletcher instantly produced the desired effect. He paused—looked at me—hesitated—and, finally, summoning one of his companions, exchanged with him some sentences

in a kind of rough patois German which I could not understand. After a few moments, the newcomer turned to me with an air of respectful civility, saying,

"If the Herr Graff will be so good as to follow me, I will conduct him to the apartments of a famous physician close at hand."

He led the way, I followed, and the man whom I had first addressed turned swiftly off in another direction.

Suffice it here that we found the gentleman, that I introduced myself to him, stated the particulars of the case, furnished him with the address, and had the satisfaction of seeing him depart.

CHAPTER XV.

A MIDNIGHT VIGIL.

SOMETIMES together, sometimes separately, sometimes in the company of the physician, we visited Fletcher at his miserable lodging at least once in every day. We had found him too weak and ill to be removed; but he had now a nurse, and all such comforts as his condition required. He was, indeed, very ill. Intense mental anxiety acting upon a nervous constitution, which was already sufficiently undermined by the long and unremitting use of opium, had ended in a low fever, which day by day was assuming a more malignant character.

One morning we found him moaning and tossing upon his bed, and quite delirious. The nurse said that he had been thus since a little past midnight. It was a painful spectacle; and we stood silently by the fire, looking at him, till the physician arrived. This gentleman was stout and tall, with a lion-like face, and green eyes, and a profusion of rings and chains, and a mass of rough, shaggy hair, like a mane.

He was late to-day, and came up stairs very quickly and softly, stopping short upon the threshold as he saw the condition of the patient. He then took his place beside the bed, and saying that he had expected this change, laid his hand upon the hot brow, and counted the leaping pulse.

After a few moments he shook the mane very gravely, and laid poor Fletcher's hand gently down upon the coverlid.

"Brain fever," he said, very distinctly and slowly. "Brain fe—ver!"

We looked each other in the face without speaking. The physician rose, and imparted some directions to the nurse—scrawled a hasty prescription—bowed, and moved toward the door.

"But there is hope?" cried Seabrook, in a low, quick voice. "There is hope?"

The physician paused, glanced keenly from me to the patient, and back again, and looked uncomfortable.

"Well—really," he said, hesitatingly, "I—I— The gentleman is your friend, perhaps, monsieur" (turning to me)—"a—a relation?"

I made a gesture of dissent, and Seabrook said impatiently,

"Mr. Fletcher is comparatively a stranger to both of us, sir. Pray give your unreserved opinion. Is he in much danger?"

He appeared relieved by this, but still hesitated.

"Brain fever," he remarked, "frequently proves fatal; and, again, many persons recover from it. The—the patient is not strong; but delicate persons often go through sickness better than more robust subjects. We must, however, remember that opium is, in itself, a slow poison."

"But your reply, sir! your reply!" urged my friend. "Is there hope?"

The physician was now at the door, with one foot down upon the first stair.

"I—I fear—that is to say—at least— No, gentlemen. I regret to say—none."

And once more shaking his head, so that the mane swayed like a pendulum from side to side, he bowed, coughed apologetically, and made his way down as quickly and softly as he came up.

It was quite late in the evening when I next saw him. I had left Seabrook writing letters; the night was dark and wet; the low lanes by the river were ankle-deep in mire; scarce a soul was abroad; and the hungry dogs were fighting over the bones upon the dunghills. There was noise of revelry and loud laughter in the public room of the Holländischer Hof, and as I hurried through the dark passage and up the narrow stairs, I heard fragments of a popular Rhine-wine song and chorus, and inhaled a fog of coarse tobacco-smoke.

It was strange; but, as I advanced, the sound, instead of lessening, became louder. I paused at the foot of the last flight, and listened attentively.

Yes—beyond a doubt. It grows more distinct with every step I take. The words are those by Mathias Claudius, which I know so well; the voice—ah! the voice in which they are chanted! I shudder— I pause— I hasten forward—I push open the door. Alas!

> "On the Rhine, on the Rhine,
> There grows the vine!
> Bless'd be the Rhine!"

He is sitting up in his bed, wild and haggard; and, as I enter, chants these lines with a ghastly mirth more shocking than tears or ravings. The fire has gone out; the candle burns dimly; the nurse is absent. All is gloomy, comfortless, and chill.

Shuddering, I take my seat beside him; but he never notices my presence, and still goes on singing:

> "From the banks down below,
> Up the mountains they grow,
> And yield us the wine!
> This wine of the Rhine!"

He has thrown off the covering, and flings his arms up wildly above his head as he finishes the verse. I twine mine around him, soothe him with gentle words, and induce him, for a few

moments, to lie down.

omitted to shut the door
with its accompanimen
swells loud below, and
our ears.

He starts up, laughin;
not laugh in that way!
with a hoarse, frantic
me shudder:

> "With the leav
> Let us gayl
> Each beake
> Drink it men
> And all Euro}
> To equal th
> This wine o

I go over and shut
—listens eagerly—lool
nothing, moans softly :
himself to and fro, as if

Once more I induce l
keeps muttering absentl
shivers piteously. I pi
and coats, and a woman
side the door. I chafe
I place the candle on o
see the light; and, as l
that he may sleep. I
and mutters, and from
ments of the song yet e

"Faster!" he says
that he is conducting
you are all too slow—
What! here already!
London. Frankfort!
not stay here! Away!
you! Hark! what is t
Wine and cards! 'S
Rejoice in the vine!'
Margaret? Poor Mar
are, poor Margaret!
garet — like your moth
in her shroud, poor M
Where is Frank? Fra
resa! Ah! I remembe
yourself before me? I
poor—"

His voice grew fai
thickly and heavily—hi
ed twice or thrice, and

His slumber lasted,
hours. At first he see
and tossed restlessly up
my hand the while with
sociating with it some v
tection. By-and-by he
relaxed; his head fell
quick, moaning respir
have fancied that he wa

Thus the dreary nigl
in the inn-parlor break
ing, into the streets.
loudly below. The pr
vails within and witho
sadly in this and the r
still the sick man slee
comes not.

By-and-by he wakes. I am not apprised of this by any movement of his, but, on turning round, find his eyes fixed earnestly upon me. Something peculiar in the expression of his face —something strange in the depths of his eyes, causes me to bend down suddenly toward him, and call him by his name.

"Is that you, sir?" he says faintly, and with some difficulty of articulation. "Is that you? You're very good to me, sir."

The delirium is gone; but there is now a look upon his face which fills me with more dread than that of mere insanity.

"Do you feel better now?" I ask him. "Are you in pain?"

"No, sir. No pain—but a—a numbness seems to be taking me. I—I think I'm going —this time—sir."

I strive to reassure him—to smile—to shake him by the hand; but mine trembles so that even he feels it, and the words die away upon my lips. He asks for water, and, when he has it, closes his eyes, and so lies for several minutes quite still and silent. Presently he looks up and speaks again, and this time I notice that his speech is more labored than before.

"I feel it coming. This—numbness—this —I—I have no one to ask—but—but you, sir. Will—will you—"

"I will do any thing for you," I exclaim, with warmth. "I meant to offer, in—in case—"

He understands me, and looks grateful, but for some minutes seems unable to enunciate. The hand which I hold in mine appears momentarily to grow colder, and large drops of perspiration gather upon his brow and upper lip. Again I bid him speak, for, alas! there is no time to lose now.

"I—I have a daughter, sir—a daughter—Margaret—in—Brussels—a school—write—"

"I will go to her!" I say, quickly. "Give me her address. What do you wish me to say to her? Have you any property?"

"No — money — spent — gambled — poor—school—Brussels."

"Yes, I know! But where? what street?"

"Rue Leopold, No. 24 — Madame — Von Placts—"

"Enough. Have you any thing else to tell me? Any message to Margaret? Any other person you wish me to see?"

I speak this earnestly and loudly, for his sense of hearing seems to grow dull, and a gray, gray tint is stealing down gradually over his face.

"Protect—warn—protect—"

"I will protect her!" I say, fervently. "I will protect her!"

He stares up at me with a beseeching expression, and strives to rise. I lift him in my arms; but he can scarcely breathe, and his dumb efforts at articulation are fearful to witness. Then the pupils of his eyes dilate preternaturally; his lips move; his features assume a look of intense anxiety, almost of rage or hatred; the gray shadow creeps down, down, and overspreads all his countenance; he falls heavily back, quivers once all over, and is then quite still.

He has fallen upon my arm, and for some time I dread to move it, lest I should disturb his last moments. However, he lies there so motionless that I need not fear his waking; so in a few minutes I withdraw it, and, taking the candle over to the bedside, stand there looking down upon the dead face.

What untold tale was hidden there? What strange tragedy of wrongs, and bitter hatreds, and fond loves, would go down unrecorded to the grave, and be buried in the outworn heart of this poor human sufferer? What hand was destined to unclasp the Book of the Past, and read therein the Chronicle of his Life-history?

I knew not; but in that solemn hour I felt a strange awe and exultation upon me, as if, in the great duty which I had undertaken, an Era had begun for me, and a new blessing had dawned upon my path.

CHAPTER XVI.

"OH SWEET, PALE MARGARET!"

"Rue de Leopold, No. 24—Madame von Placts!"

I had arrived in Brussels late the night before, and, over-wearied by the long journey from Cologne, had slept till the shops were opened and the foot-passengers all stirring in the busy streets around me. I woke with these words upon my lips—could think of nothing else during my hasty breakfast; and, immediately after, hurried forth in quest of the school and my young ward, self-constituted guardian that I was.

Strange, how this one event had changed the whole tone and tenor of my mind; how it had braced my weary nerves; reawakened my interest in things; occupied my thoughts with pleasant images, and given a purpose and an impulse to my daily life! I was always dreaming of this child which the poor musician had confided to me on his dying bed; wondering whether she was fair or dark, playful or sedate; hoping that her eyes might be blue, like those of Adrienne; and forming conjectures as to her age, size, disposition, and talents; for to none of these did I possess the slightest clew. I amused myself by rehearsing in my own mind all that I should say to her when we met; I accustomed myself, in idea, to the name of "Father," which I thought would sound sweeter than that of "Guardian" from her infant lips. I framed the wildest impossibilities. I was to devote myself entirely to her; to educate her in all that I deemed fittest for her improvement, and to grow wiser myself in the gentle task. She was to console me for my disappointment; to be the comfort and pride of my old age; the inheritress of my fortunes; the adopted daughter of my heart.

Nay, I had even thought of legally investing her with the name of our family!

From the moment that we had consigned the remains of poor Fletcher to the little burying-place beyond Ems, I had found it impossible to restrain my impatience, and had hurried along the glorious Rhine-scenery lying between Coblentz and Bonn without even a wish to linger by the way. From Bonn to Cologne, from Cologne to Brussels, had been the rapid journey of a day; and not even the persuasions of my friend, who remained obstinately at the City of the Three Kings, could induce me to defer my farther progress for a few hours. Perhaps, were I to search my own motives narrowly, I should be forced to acknowledge that his very determination to explore the antiquities of Cologne bore some share in the urgency of my desire to proceed. I wished to present myself alone to the little orphan, and I could not endure to share that first interview even with Norman Seabrook. There was to me an importance in our newly established relation to each other, a sacredness in the grief that I was to unfold to her, which admitted of no publicity; besides, I had built such a fairy château en Espagne upon the affection which she was to give me, that I felt jealous lest I should not be the first and only one whom she would learn to love.

"Rue de Leopold, No. 24 — Madame von Plaets!"

The road was not long, although I thought it so in my impatience; but I had to ask my way several times; to traverse streets and squares utterly strange to me; to turn back twice or thrice when I had taken a wrong turning, or been misdirected. Besides, it was market-day, and the open places were all thronged with stalls and country people, and many whom I had addressed could not comprehend either my French or German, but had replied to me in their unintelligible Flemish dialect. Then the novelty of the architecture, so different to any thing that I had previously seen, bewildered and distracted me. A regiment of Belgian Chasseurs, with their dark uniforms, and curious round hats surmounted by plumes of cock's feathers, defiled along the very street which I was about to cross, and kept me waiting, as it seemed to me, full a quarter of an hour. I was waylaid and followed by importunate guides and commissionaires — in short, every possible aggravation and delay seemed to combine against me.

At length I found the Rue de Leopold, a little street running at the back of the theatre, consisting of shops, hotels, and private houses. Walking slowly down the centre, and looking from side to side alternately, I came to No. 24. It was a large white house standing back from the street, with an outer wall, and heavy wooden gates, decorated with two ponderous knockers. Within were long close rows of jalousied windows; the topmost branches of one or two lofty lime-trees; and, on the coping, in letters a foot long, the words "Pensionnat des Demoiselles."

How my heart beat as I lifted the heavy knocker—as I asked for Madame von Plaets—as I heard that she was within, and followed the hobbling old concierge across the court-yard to the steps of the mansion, where I was met by a staid footman in a sober livery, and by him preceded to a spacious drawing-room opening upon a garden.

"Madame will be with monsieur directly."

Directly! It seemed an age to me. I sat down — rose — sat down again — examined the pictures upon the walls — the books lying upon the table—the visiting-cards in the filigree basket — the little figures of Dresden china on the shelves of the inlaid cabinet. Surely those were the sounds of music! I listened attentively, and heard a chorus of female voices, supported by the deep undertones of an organ. Doubtless we were in the neighborhood of some church; and yet it was not the hour for service.

It certainly appeared to come from the direction of the garden! I went over and opened the window. This time I could not be mistaken, for I heard the very words and recognized the very notes of a choral movement by Marcello.

The garden was spacious, but gloomy — surrounded by a high wall, overgrown by ivy and green moss, planted here and there with tall dark poplars, and laid out in formal walks and parterres. There was a broken statue of the Piping Faun, and a weed-grown sun-dial in among the trees; and, at the farther end, partially screened by a lofty laurel hedge, a small white edifice, apparently of recent date, pierced by a row of long and narrow windows, and surmounted by a glazed cupola.

Now, beyond a doubt, it was from that very building that the sounds proceeded.

Did Madame von Plaets, then, keep a private chapel for her pupils, or did the garden communicate with some other house or street behind the confines of that laurel hedge?

My curiosity was powerfully excited. I went out upon the terrace, and down into the garden, making my way cautiously along the paths till I turned the corner of the hedge, and found myself before the entrance to the building, when I stole forward into the shadow of the doorway, and gazed on the scene within.

It was one large and lofty hall, with bare white walls and matted floor, and rows of plain deal benches ranged down all the centre, like the seats in a church or a concert-room. On these benches sat some fifty or sixty female scholars, varying in age from six to twenty. Each held an open music-book in her hand, and all were singing to the accompaniment of an organ which stood at the upper end of the hall, and was played by a young girl dressed entirely in black. About half way down, adding to the church-like appearance of the place, stood a little pulpit-like oaken desk, behind which a stout, fair, and florid lady of middle age was seated, as if presiding over the assembly.

It was a curious scene, and for me an interesting one; for I stood there scanning those rows of fair young faces, and striving **vainly to** guess which was the one I sought.

Suddenly the lady-president, glancing in the direction of the door, fixed her eyes upon me with a startled expression, rose from behind her desk with an air of immense dignity, and came rustling toward me in her silken robes.

I felt that I was looked upon as an intruder, and as she advanced I gradually retreated.

"Monsieur is desirous of speaking to me?" she asked, with a stately salutation.

I was not particularly desirous of speaking to her; but I knew not what answer to make, so I bowed profoundly.

"Then monsieur will have the goodness to step this way."

She laid a pointed emphasis on "this," and preceded me along the walks, up to the terrace, and back into the saloon which I had lately left. She then indicated a chair with a languid gesture of her fat white hand, and sank, as if exhausted, upon a spacious fauteuil.

"And now," she said, turning to me and bowing somewhat more graciously, "and now, perhaps, monsieur will have the politeness to speak."

"Madame von Plaets, I presume?"

Another bow.

"I am the bearer of some painful intelligence to one of your pupils, Miss Margaret Fletcher. Her father is no more. I attended upon him in his last moments, at Ems, where he intrusted me with the care and guardianship of his daughter."

Madame looked concerned, and shook her fair head gravely.

"I am very sorry," she said, two or three times over; "I am very sorry." Then, as if suddenly remembering my words, "Mademoiselle is not my pupil," she added. "She is my musical gouvernante."

"Your musical gouvernante, madame!" I exclaimed. "I—I had expected to—to find her quite a child!"

There must have been something very blank and discomfited about the expression of my face, for the Flemish lady smiled outright, and saying, "Monsieur shall judge for himself," rang a silver hand-bell, and desired the attendance of Mademoiselle Marguerite.

So, then, all my predetermined speeches, my fairy plans, my pleasant dreams of education, guidance, and voluntary paternity, were vanished—my *châteaux en Espagne* had turned to "airy nothings," and I found myself the guardian of a musical gouvernante, as old, and perhaps older, than myself! But for the sad cause of my journey, I should have recognized something almost ludicrous in the situation.

She entered—a pale, slight girl about seventeen or eighteen years of age, with fair straight brow and downcast eyes, and her hands folded meekly together, like the picture of the Virgin Mary in the old German paintings. Her smooth brown hair was banded closely round her head; she wore a plain dress of some black material,

and a small white collar round her throat, so that I recognized her at once for the organist whom I had seen from my ambush in the garden.

"A gentleman to visit you, mademoiselle Marguerite," said madame, condescendingly.

The little gouvernante blushed and courtesied, and stole one timid glance toward me from beneath her long eyelashes, but made no reply.

"You can be seated, Mademoiselle Marguerite."

From the manner in which this was conceded, it was evident that madame deemed it a distinguishing mark of favor.

"This gentleman comes from abroad—from Germany, mademoiselle. He has seen monsieur your father, and will himself relate to you the melancholy details. Hélas! mais c'est dommage, monsieur. Ça me déchire le cœur!"

And madame sighed, and pressed her laced pocket-handkerchief to her eyes, and tried to weep, but could not.

"I beg a thousand pardons, Madame von Plaets," I said, rising hurriedly, "but I should prefer to speak with this young lady in private; the nature of my communication demands it. Have you any unoccupied room to which we might be permitted to retire?"

"Mais—c'est juste—mais—les convenances," stammered the mistress of the house, half rising and hesitating.

"The customs of society, madame, suffer a young lady to be alone for a few moments with her guardian."

"Monsieur is a young guardian," said madame, looking greatly disappointed, and moving slowly toward the door. "But—since it is wished—on this one occasion—I will retire."

She bowed again, very haughtily; I returned the salutation; and, after lingering for a minute with her hand on the lock, she finally left the room.

As for the little gouvernante, she had risen and sat down again a dozen times during this brief colloquy; but, now that madame was actually gone, she resumed her seat, and remained quite still and silent, revealing nothing of her previous agitation save by the trembling of her hands, which she strove to press firmly together.

I was troubled how to begin, and sat looking at her in silence for some moments. At last I spoke.

"I am the unwilling bearer of some painful intelligence, Mademoiselle Margaret," I said, gravely.

A startled glance from the downcast eyes—a closer clasping of the hands—a quickening of the fluttered breath—that was all.

"I—I was your father's friend at Ems. He desired me to visit you—to protect you—to inform you of—of his illness."

"My father has been ill!"

It was the first time she had spoken—the first time she had looked me steadily in the face; and, despite my anxiety and pity, I could not avoid remarking how sweet was the voice and how beautiful were the large brown eyes.

"Very ill. More ill than you imagine. Can you bear to be told how ill he has been?"

I said this very earnestly, looking at her sorrowfully the while, as in the hope that the expression of my face and the tone of my voice would speak my story for me.

She turned very pale—even her lips grew white; but she answered firmly, "I can bear it."

The task was too painful. I thrust back my chair, and took one or two hurried turns about the room. Then I stopped suddenly before her, and taking her hand,

"Margaret," I said, "I am your guardian—your guardian and protector for life. It was your father's wish that I should be so. Do you understand me?"

No reply—no glance—no movement.

"I am your guardian, Margaret, because—because you have no other."

The little hand that felt so cold in mine was hastily withdrawn.

"No other!" she repeated, in an inward shuddering tone. "No other!"

She rose up, pale and horror-struck, and moved slowly away, as if in dread of me and of my tidings. There were no tears upon her face, though mine were falling fast.

"No other!"

Suddenly both voice and strength seemed to fail her. She paused, wavered, caught wildly at my outstretched hand, and fell fainting into my arms.

CHAPTER XVII.

CLOUD-SHADOWS.

Norman Seabrook to Paul Latour.

"Hotel de Rubens, Antwerp, July 2d, 18—.

"EBBENE, *amico mio!* So thou hast even taken unto thyself apartments at Brussels, and a ward of seventeen with 'a face of saintlike purity!' By my faith, friend Paul, you improve. I can remember but a very short time since when the name of woman was never heard to escape those ascetic lips, and when to remain longer than seven days in any one locality was intolerable to your philosophership. But all is changed now, I perceive: a pair of 'large, earnest brown eyes' have been sufficient to charm even you into the paths of sentiment and sighs; and you must allow me to interpret your fine speeches about 'the duties which you have taken upon yourself,' etc., etc., according to my own reading. Ha! 'thou blushest, Antony!'

"I arrived in this place five days ago, and I have not yet thought about when I shall leave it. 'Tis a glorious old mediæval city, Paul, and not a moment passes that I do not wish you were here to enjoy it with me. The most glorious cathedral—a Musée of incalculable wealth—the quaintest old Bourse you ever saw; and a style of florid architecture every where abounding that absolutely feasts the eye with beauty. I never saw any thing like the house of Rubens. It is one wreath of fruits, and flowers, and rarest scroll-works—a perfect bower in stone. What an idea of magnificence that man had! What a princely splendid life he contrived to lead—embassador, chamberlain, secretary of the privy council, knight, and artist! Was ever painter so rich and so honored? Will ever painter be so again? They have his palette, and an old leather chair in which he sat while painting, preserved in the Musée.

"Talking of the Musée, I have seen a picture in it which I shall never forget, and which, if I could but describe it worthily, would, I think, induce you to take the rail and come down for a day or two—that is, if the sight of your English friend would not be sufficiently attractive. It is a small crucifixion by Van Dyck—to me a most affecting and remarkable picture. You see the cross standing up, as it were, alone against the leaden sky. There is nothing above or around but darkness, and one or two points of flinty rock peep up from below, giving an idea of the altitude and loneliness of the mountain. The evening shades are gathering; the sun is retreating behind a bank of slaty clouds, and the Savior of mankind looks upward into that heaven to which he seems so near, and from which his term of banishment is almost ended. The face is filled with a divine yet beautiful agony; the extremities assume the blue hues of death, and harmonize in a masterly manner with the tones of the background. All is solitary, silent, and awful. Do come, Paul, if it be only to see this picture. It is worth a pilgrimage. There is a copy of it in the church of St. Jacques; but the original is the gem.

"I have taken an immense fancy to the Musée. It is a noble building, and is surrounded by a quiet bit of garden, full of fine old trees, 'with seats beneath the shade,' and tablets inscribed to the memory of eminent artists set in the walls. The bust of Rubens stands over the entrance. Somehow the genius of a great man seems to reign forever in the place of his birth, and to hallow all the atmosphere around with something of his individual majesty. I have found this particularly the case with Frankfurt and Antwerp. Both cities appear like reflections of the minds of Goëthe and Rubens, and are, to me, as inseparable from the men as the men from their works. You will understand what I mean, though I write 'words—mere words.' Surely there is a something about Stratford-upon-Avon that is different to any other town by any other river in any other part of England.

"I spent yesterday at Ghent, and paid a hasty visit to the cathedral of St. Bavon, and the famous old belfry surmounted by the Golden Dragon, where I saw the great bell named Roland, with its Flemish inscription, mentioned, as you must remember, by the poet Longfellow:

" ' Then the bell of Ghent responded, o'er lagoon and dike of sand,

" I am Roland! I am Roland! there is victory in the land!' "

" His dragonship, by the way, is delightfully ugly, and suffers at present under the personal disadvantage of a broken queue. I could not resist the whim of taking up a bit of chalk lying on the top of the tower, and writing these words along the remains of that appendage—'This tale to be continued.' Forgive the poverty of the pun.

" There is a large establishment here for Beguine nuns which I much wished to see, but time forbade. These excellent women half people the dead streets of the city; soldiers and priests seem to make up the rest of the population. The grass grows in the public squares; the sluggish canals, with their waters 'thick and slab,' lie like torpid snakes along the thoroughfares; dogs go by dragging carts, and queer wagons rumble past, like boats upon wheels; there are little images of the Virgin and Child stuck up under tiny penthouses at the corners of all the streets; and down by the bridges and the water-stairs you see women scrubbing their bright brass kettles and peeling vegetables. I never beheld a more dreary place. I hear it is one of the most demoralized in Europe.

" Leaving the town in what they are pleased to call a 'vigilante' (!) on my way to the railway, we had to cross several of the canal bridges. At one of them my driver stopped while a barge passed through; for on these occasions the bridge has to be drawn up, so small a distance is there between the surface of the water and the planking above. I was amused at the primitive manner in which the toll was collected here. Two men in red woolen shirts drag the boat through the narrow straits; another man appears at the window of the toll-house, which overhangs the canal. He holds a fishing-rod in his hand, with an old sabot attached to the line. This he drops down to the level of the steersman's nose, and draws it up again, like Peter's fish, with a piece of money in its mouth.

" On the whole, I like Belgium, it is so undisguisedly stupid. I like its flat, strange scenery—its mouldering old cities—its population of dark priests and silent nuns. How ugly the women are! I have not seen a pretty face since I have been in the country. ' Formosis Bruga puellis,' saith a very respectable proverb of the Middle Ages. It may be; but I have not yet been to Bruges.

" I wished you had remained a few days with me at Cologne. There is a private gallery there, the property of Mr. Van der Weyer, which is worth half the national collections in Europe, and which you, as an artist and a man of taste, should by no means have omitted. Some of the finest specimens of the early German school, the works of Wilhelm of Cologne, Stephen his pupil, Hans Memling, Van Eyck, etc., adorn these walls with 'riches fineless;' and as for the maturer painters of a later age, which possess for me far greater charms, you can not conceive of a more exquisite selection. There is a Guido, an upturned head of Christ, full of the deepest poetry of feeling; a glorious Rembrandt—'Simon in the Temple;' and another equally grand, a portrait of a man dressed in a sort of Russian costume, with cloak, and furs, and heavy leathern boots, but with an Oriental turban on his head. The table near him is laden with 'barbaric gold and pearl;' a rich gloom hangs over all; and points of brilliant light falling here and there only serve to heighten the depths of shade beyond. I saw there a spirited 'Head of a Cavalier,' by Rubens, and a group of his own family; a fine Salvator, 'Cain after the Death of Abel;' a delicious 'Virgin and Child,' by Titian, all life and sweetness; and oh! such a calm and golden Cuyp. It is a landscape scene, Paul. A woman seated on a mule is led over the brow of a hill by a man in a red jacket. The far country lies behind, all liquefied and transparent in the sunny evening air. The blue mountains fade upon the horizon, and the towers of a distant chateau lift their peaks to the red clouds far away. Besides, there is a 'Forest-pool' by Ruysdale, with the trees standing silently around in that light of

" 'Clear obscure,
So softly dark, so darkly pure,
Which follows the decline of day,
Ere twilight melts beneath the moon away.'

And I must not forget a Velasquez—one of the most effective that I have seen. It is a portrait of Don Carlos, a youth whose long fair hair falls down upon his lustrous armor. He leans on a gorgeous mace all blazing with jewels; a dog stands at his side; and behind them are the gates of a palace by the sea. It is a model of high art in portraiture, and one laments that the coloring should be so faded.

" But, if I proceed at this rate, you will think that I am sending you a *catalogue raisonnée*, or else that I am qualifying myself to be an author of guide-books.

" I often think of poor Fletcher and his melancholy ending. There was a man utterly self-destroyed — self-sacrificed. I have sometimes fancied that a great care was weighing upon his mind, and was the secret source of all his errors. It might have been anxiety for his daughter. And to think of his having a daughter! I never even dreamt that he had had a wife. By the way, do you remember that little brooch he used to wear? I often wondered whose hair he could so value, and you would smile to hear some of the romantic tales which I was pleased to hang thereby. Perhaps, after all, it was his wife's.

" You must come and see me. I shall be here, I dare say, for a fortnight or three weeks longer, for I have still so much to see in the way of churches and private galleries. Really one might spend a year in Antwerp and still leave something unvisited. Suppose you come next Saturday, and stay for a few days with me on the banks of what Goldsmith calls 'the lazy

Schelde?' I name Saturday, because there is to be a grand fête on Sunday at the cathedral, and a procession headed by the archbishop.

"'I want you to make me a little sketch of Miss Fletcher's head, that I may know in what this 'saintly purity' consists. Is it in expression or feature? I should imagine the former, since you tell me that she is not beautiful. It is probable that I shall find my way to Brussels on leaving here; but perhaps I may go first to Bruges. I am very curious to visit that old city. In the mean time, I should like to see what your fair ward is like, and I hope, for the sake of our friendship, that I may be enabled to write beneath her portrait that old line of Chaucer's which you, as a Frenchman, I dare say, have not read—

"'Si douset est la Margarete!'

What a long letter I have written! N'importe, I know that you will read it all, mon ami, and that, were it twice the length, you would not deem it a trouble. 'Farewell, Monsieur Traveler.' I drink your health in a glass of admirable Curaçoa. Yours ever,

"NORMAN SEABROOK."

From the Same to the Same.

"July 4th, 18—

"DEAR OLD BOY,—This is good news! I did not really think that you would come, although I asked you. Start by the first train in the morning, and I will meet you at the station. Huzza!   N. S."

It was late in the evening, and getting quite dusk, when I parted from my friend upon the platform of the Antwerp railway station. I had passed two pleasant days with him, of which the greater portion had been spent in the Musée and the cathedral; and I could not help feeling a movement of regret as the guard closed the door, and the train began slowly to glide past the outskirts of the city.

The carriages were dimly lighted from the roof; the view without was flat, obscure, and ghostly. I turned wearily from the level marshlands, and the dull lines of poplars that seemed to travel past the windows, toward my fellow-passengers. These were three in number—a stout, jovial-looking priest, with broad-brimmed hat and long black robe, and a railway rug folded comfortably over his knees; a young officer of Chasseurs, sound asleep, with the fragment of a cigar between his lips; and a lady superbly dressed in a robe of violet-colored satin, and a cloak of velvet and rich sables, who sat precisely opposite to me, and kept her veil down closely over her face.

There was something in the attitude of this lady—in the shape of her hands, one of which was ungloved and glittering with diamonds—in the very style and splendor of her attire, that attracted my attention strangely. Having once looked at her, I could not remove my eyes, and I sat there vainly striving to penetrate the folds of lace that concealed her features.

Presently the evening mists rose thicker and the air grew damp. I raised the glass on my side, and the priest raised his at the other. The steam then gathered slowly on the panes; the night became quite dark, and the faint oil-lamp seemed to burn brighter by the contrast; the priest threw aside his rug; the officer muttered restlessly in his sleep; I removed my hat—in short, the atmosphere of the carriage was tropical.

Surely the heat must soon compel her to uplift that veil!

She takes a scent-bottle from her reticule—she loosens the cloak around her throat—at last, yes, at last, she throws up the veil!

Madame Vogelsang!

An unaccountable thrill ran through me at the sight of her, and I sank back, shuddering, in my seat. What was she to me that I should feel this presaging weight upon my heart?

Nothing; and yet . . . . . I drew my breath with difficulty, and closed my eyes that they might not look upon her.

The train flew on, and to me the journey seemed to endure for hours, although I knew how short the distance was, and how swift our speed. Then came Brussels, and at the first slackening of our pace I threw open the door, leaped out upon the platform, and never once glanced back.

Who shall say that it was not a presentiment?

CHAPTER XVIII.

"SUMMER HALCYON DAYS."

SOME three or four weeks went by, and Brussels arrived at the height of its summer glory. There were evening concerts in the park; public balls at the Café Vauxhall; shoals of carriages and equestrians on the Boulevards, and in the Allée Verte, during the day; and, above all, operatic performances at the theatre in the Place de la Monnaie, with Madame Vogelsang as the star of the season.

I partook of very few of these amusements, and divided my time between study, exercise, and the society of my ward. I had taken a couple of rooms in the neighborhood of the park, within sight of the green trees and the great basin, and here established for myself an humble imitation of my beautiful library at Latour-sur-Creil. During the mornings I wrote, and read, and walked if the weather permitted; in the afternoons I called upon Margaret, and either took her out for a little stroll, or read aloud to her from the pages of some favorite French or German writer; at night I studied again till late, and sometimes spent an hour in the park, listening to the band. It was a very quiet life, but a happy one; not the less happy, perhaps, for being tinctured here and there with some few shadows and regrets.

As I had felt and conjectured from the first —ay, from that very moment of that woful midnight—I had found peace and consolation in the new and solemn duty which I then assumed. To have the care of a life — of a life so young, and innocent, and fair! — this was indeed a high and holy trust, and I grew stronger in the mere effort to fulfill it. There was, however, one difficulty ever present to my mind. I, who had so easily built up a pleasant future for my child-ward and myself, could now determine on no fitting course of life for this grave and timid girl of seventeen. To suffer her to continue as I found her, a lonely and ill-paid musical gouvernante in a school, was out of the question. Indeed, I had already done much to soften the harsher points of her position. She had now a private sitting-room; leisure for study; and, owing to a pecuniary arrangement into which I entered with Madame von Plaets, enjoyed a far greater amount of respect and consideration than any teacher had ever before received at the hands of that majestic lady. For the present this answered well enough; but I could not reside in Brussels ad infinitum, and Margaret must not occupy a subordinate position for any longer period than was necessary for the completion of my plans. The subject was most perplexing, and cost me many hours of reflection every day. Yet I found it impossible to arrive at any definite conclusion.

Could I but have taken her to Burgundy, and placed her under the care of my mother—but I could not yet endure to think of the Hauteville grounds, which opened into mine, and of the near vicinity of Théophile and his bride. True, I might send or leave her there, and again depart upon my aimless travels; but was she not my ward, and I her guardian? Was it not my duty to remain with her, to console her, to guide her studies, and watch over every dawning impulse of her heart? How dull and solitary she would be, alone with my stately mother in that remote chateau, with its environment of old forests; how lonely I should be to leave her there, and go forth for the second time!

It was a step not to be thought of — at least for the present. A time might arrive when old griefs and old impressions would fade and wear away; when I might learn to look upon Adrienne without regret, and upon Théophile without envy; when to return to Burgundy would once more be a pleasure unalloyed by pain, and Margaret might rejoice to call that antique house her home.

And so I put it off day by day, and the summer weeks went on. She was singularly placid and silent for her age—the more so, perhaps, on account of her isolated position, and the sorrow which had lately fallen upon her — yet she thought much, and felt deeply. Her nature was so reserved, her inner world so far removed from all vain or idle scrutiny, that her ideas and feelings became known to me only by chance, and at rare intervals. I have spent hours reading the story of her calm eyes and serious brow, and striving to look through them upon the workings of her heart. She would often sit by with drooping head, and hands busy over some piece of delicate embroidery, suffering me to carry on the conversation unaided, and seldom uttering even a comment or an interrogation. Then again, at times, thoughts of such fresh purity and beauty would fall from her lips as caused me frequently to look round upon her with sudden admiration and delight, the more so because she was ever totally unconscious of the sweetness of her own sayings.

Every glimpse that I obtained into that fair soul revealed only grace and innocence, and these revelations were but the more precious for being so unpremeditated and infrequent.

Oh, this pleasant study of a young life! I had read many books, and was learned in many philosophies and languages, but in this first living volume that had been opened for me I read a wise and simple poem such as I had never dreamed before. It would be vain for me to attempt an analysis of all the peace and consolation which I learned from the perusal of that book's gentle pages. Slowly and earnestly I read, and observed, and commented upon them, and day by day rejoiced more heartily and gratefully that the care of them had been committed to my keeping. Yes, it was my duty now to win the confidence and affection of this lonely girl—it was my duty to shield her from sorrow, and to preserve in all their stainless purity the virgin tablets of her heart. Father, brother, friend, all these I must be to her, and all these, oh Beneficent Sustainer, did I not pray to Thee to make me?

The task, the responsibility, the anxiety was overwhelming, and Heaven knows with what humility and strong endeavor I armed myself to execute it worthily.

The more I understood, the more I respected and loved her. There was a something in her presence that seemed to hush my voice, as in the presence of a superior nature. Frequently I likened her mind to some Parian sanctuary peopled with pious, and chaste, and lovely images, and dedicated to the service of the gods; sometimes I compared it to a smooth lake whose translucent waters are dark only because they are deep, and beneath which grow fairest water-plants and flowers, such as the upper earth can not match for sweetness.

Scarcely a week had elapsed since my arrival in Brussels when I recognized the necessity of establishing some link of thought and action between Margaret and myself—some link that should induce a community of aim and a reciprocity of ideas between our minds. It was even necessary to the acquirement of her confidence; for how could the innocent familiarity which belonged to our relative position ever be attained by formal visits and conversations governed by restraint? To this end I began instructing her in drawing. Like all persons of high musical ability, she showed a remarkable aptitude for art, and progressed rapidly—so rapidly that in less than a month she had mastered the difficulties of the simple outline, and began studying from the round object. I must here observe that Margaret had a little **favorite** pupil in the school, a pale and sickly child, **with** large dark eyes and ordinary features, stunted in growth, but precocious in mind, and who loved her with a passionate devotion that reminded me of my own feelings toward my mother when I was myself a **child.** This little girl was her constant companion, the sharer of her studies, the partaker of all her simple pleasures, her walks, her rooms, her books. Little Clemence was too shy, and strange, and silent to inspire me **at** first with any great interest; but I willingly **taught** her all that I taught to Margaret, and in time grew almost fond of my earnest scholar. She was scarcely like a child in her tone of mind; she had none of the prattle and ingenuous confidence of youth. Her very amusements were odd and fantastic, and unlike all those which are suitable to childhood. I have known her sit silently in a corner for long hours at a time, inventing grotesque patterns in colored papers, or drawing maps of imaginary countries with bays and promontories, and strange outlandish names marked here and there. With Clemence for our companion, we passed many a pleasant evening hour, and enjoyed many a sunny walk together. With what delight I attended the sales of antique *bijouterie* and *objets d'art*, and found out quaint shops in the close dark streets of the mediæval quarter of the city, seeking models for her pencil! How I triumphed when I succeeded in bringing to her some graceful vase, or classic statuette, or fragment of old foliated cornice, making her little salon into the semblance of an artist's studio! And then what long rural wanderings we had in the neighborhood of Laken, and in the forest of Soignies, searching for ferns and leaves, and sketching moss-grown trunks of fallen trees, and telling fairy-stories to Clemence by the way!

A happy, happy time, and calm as dreamless sleep!

CHAPTER XIX.

A CABINET COUNCIL.

It is a bright and joyous morning during the first week of August. The boxes of mignonette in my windows send up a fragrant odor; the trees are nodding in the sunshine; my bird in his painted cage is almost wild with joy, and darts from perch to perch in the pauses of his song; pleasant sounds of children's voices, and cries of itinerant florists and chocolate vendors are heard outside, with now and then the passing wheels of some early vigilantes going to meet the first train at the station.

I am seated beside the open casement in my slippers and robe de chambre, reading and breakfasting. My book (Thiers's History of the Consulate and Empire") lies before me in a convenient position; my toast and coffee stand at my right hand; sometimes I look out upon a troop of passing cavalry, or **a** party of country milkmaids, with their graceful cans of glittering brass upon their heads. **In** short, I am just now exceedingly comfortable, very much interested, and have made **up my** mind to a morning of quiet study.

A tap at my chamber **door.**

I want no interruptions; **so I** affect **not to hear** it, and go on with my **book.**

· **A second** tap, very much louder than the first —a tap that insists upon being heard!

"Go to—Algeria!" I mutter sulkily **between my teeth,** and then, without removing my **eyes** from the page—"Come in!"

The door flies open—a rapid foot treads **the** floor—a friendly hand falls heavily upon **my shoulder, and a** frank voice cries cheerily,

"**Hail** to thee, worthy Timon!"

"Norman Seabrook! dear old fellow, is it really you? **How** glad—how very glad I am! When **did you come?** Where have you **put** up? Why **did you** not write and let me meet you? **Sit down and have** some breakfast! Well, this is a **pleasure!**"

And in an incoherent rapture of delight and surprise I shake him vehemently by both hands, force him into a chair, ring for fresh coffee, kick Thiers's "History of the Consulate," etc., to the farther corner of the room, shake hands again, and so on for some ten minutes at the least.

Presently we subside over our breakfast and sit talking eagerly. He has so much to tell and I so little, that I soon drop my share of the conversation, and leave him to speak of all that he has seen since we parted, uninterrupted save now and then by an interrogation or a brief remark. Besides, it is such a pleasure to see him once again, that I prefer to sit listening to his voice and looking at his cordial face.

More than five weeks have elapsed since we parted, and during that time he has visited all that in Belgium is worthy the notice of the historian, the art-student, and the archæologist. He has been to Ghent, Antwerp, Bruges, Louvain, Mechlin, Tournay, etc., and is all the browner for his traveling. He has seen every thing and been into all kinds of places; has journeyed from town to town in a lazy canal-boat; has jolted along the paven country roads in a peasant's wagon; has trudged on foot and on horseback; lodged at hotels, and farm-houses, and roadside inns; frequented theatres, churches, gaming-rooms, picture-galleries, markets, guinguettes, reviews, law-courts, and religious ceremonials. Life in all its phases, art in all its stages, he has observed, studied, and enjoyed. For five weeks he has done wonders, and nothing has escaped his quick eye, his ready wit, and his genial temper.

"And so," I say at length, "Brussels is all that you have left to see! How long do you propose to remain with me?"

"To remain with you, *amico!* Why, you are not going to establish yourself here for the term of your natural life! I had thought to stay here for some three weeks, perhaps, till you should have disposed of your interesting charge in some convenient and appropriate asylum, and then I hoped, and hope, that we shall on together 'to fresh woods and pastures new!' Why not to Paris? It is the most *insouciante* and delicious place on earth, and I must fain confess, with Madame de Staël, that it is my vulnerable side. Besides, you are a Frenchman, and have never visited the fairy capital of your native country! I tell you, Paul, 'tis absolutely a duty!"

I shake my head and look grave.

"Indeed, Seabrook," I say, tracing a pattern on the tea-tray with my spoon, "indeed, I find myself in a very delicate, I may say, a very difficult position. Miss Fletcher, you see, is not the child I had supposed; she—she is young, accomplished, interesting—Hem! interesting to me on account of her poor father, and—and—"

Here Seabrook bursts out laughing, and I pause disconcerted.

"Go on, old boy," says my friend, biting his lips to smother his risible inclinations. "Go on. You were speaking of the difficulties of your situation, and of the charms which *la belle Marguerite* inherits from—her father!"

"No jesting, I beg. The subject is a serious one, and I entered into it that I might be benefited by your advice, not mocked by your unseasonable pleasantries."

And hereupon I am so very grave and dignified that Seabrook holds out his hand and begs my pardon earnestly. So I continue.

"That she shall not remain in her present position I have quite determined, and I have many reasons why I should not wish to place her with my mother in Burgundy. She has no friends with whom I could even leave her as a boarder. Were she a child, or one of our own sex, the thing would be sufficiently easy; as it is, I know not what on earth to do!"

"Put her into a good school—not as a teacher, but as a pupil. You can make as many arrangements for her comfort and indulgence as you please, and you would be providing her with a respectable home," says Seabrook, decisively.

"*Eh bien!* that would, perhaps, be as wise a course as any. Yet I do not much fancy placing her in a school. I do not fancy the restraint, the discipline, the want of friends and society to which she must be subject; and—"

"And, most thoughtful guardian, you do not fancy the separation! *La belle Marguerite* at school, *l'aimable Paul en voyage—quelle idée affreuse!*"

"Really, Seabrook," I exclaim, rising angrily, and pacing to and fro about the room, "if you mean this for a jest, it is neither appropriate nor generous. I asked your advice; and if you can give me no better than this, we had better drop the subject."

Seabrook leans back in his chair and looks after me with a quiet smile, so full of good-humor and friendliness that I already more than half forgive him.

"Now listen to me, Paul," he says, firmly, "and I will give you the best piece of advice in the world."

"Well?"

"The girl is virtuous, amiable, clever, is she not?"

"Eminently so."

"Good-looking?"

"I think so. You might not."

"*Bien!* Now my advice is this: put her into a first-rate finishing school, and there leave her for a couple of years while you and I go together through France, and Italy, and 'tawny Spain.' Then come home and take her down to Burgundy, where you can portion her off to some worthy husband, 'an' it so please you.' Depend upon it, I counsel you wisely, *amico*. What, silent?"

"It needs consideration, Seabrook."

"Consider as long as you please, Paul. You will arrive at my opinion. And now let us talk of something else. What is there to be seen in this town?"

"There is the cathedral of St. Gudule — the Hotel de Ville—some private galleries—the arcades—the theatre, and the park."

"Well, to-day I am in the mood for neither pictures nor churches. Let us stroll out for a while under the park trees. It is fearfully warm here!"

So, arm in arm, we go forth together, and mingle with the tide of visitors who promenade, read, embroider, and converse in that most pleasant and fashionable resort of morning idlers. There are children floating their tiny crafts on the basin; schools demurely pacing the less crowded alleys; elderly financiers devouring the morning papers; aristocratic youths, with elaborate waistcoats, eating ices within the precincts of Velloni's; sentimental couples seated in the grottoes down in the hollows; groups of ladies and gentlemen discussing last evening's soirée, and soldiers playing dominoes on the benches. The spectacle is animated and amusing, and the weather brilliant. Seabrook is in high spirits, and sees and enjoys all.

"*Voilà!*" he says. "Do you see that lady with a face like the queen of spades, and her three *passé* daughters all dressed in red, like elderly flamingoes? I know them by sight, and have seen them in all the capitals of Europe, and they never can get husbands—it's impossible! Who is that saffron-colored little man with the wooden leg and the white mustache? But I forget—you know nobody. What a pretty girl that is with the lavender bonnet; and, by Jove! there's a handsome fellow—no—not there—here—just in front of you! Stay, he'll turn presently. What a pair of shoulders! I'd bet you a five-franc piece that that man's English!"

He points to a gentleman walking a few paces in advance—a tall, well-made man, about six feet in height, with a profusion of curling light hair, an easy bearing, and that indescribable air of self-possession that stamps good breeding. His back is turned to me; his head bent toward the ground, as if in thought; his hands buried in the pockets of his paletot.

My heart beats, though I know not why. He turns aside to watch some children at play upon the grass, and for one instant I catch sight of that beautiful and familiar profile.

"Heavens!" I cry, pausing suddenly and seizing my companion by the arm, "it is my brother Théophile!"

CHAPTER XX.

FACES OLD AND NEW.

"THÉOPHILE! Théophile, *mon frère!*"

I am close beside him now, with my hand upon his arm.

"How! Paul in Brussels! I thought you still in Heidelberg. But this is delightful! Have you seen much, my brother? Are you well?"

"Quite well, Théophile. Quite well—and you?"

He looks so handsome and florid, and withal so happy, that I have no need to ask the question. This he tells me, laughing, and drawing my arm through his, is, in a few moments, chatting as freely and carelessly as when we were last together.

Seabrook, I may observe, has walked away and left us to our recognition undisturbed.

Of course my brother's first words are of the subject most distressing to my ears.

"I am the happiest husband," says he, "in France! I possess in Adrienne the very model of a wife. She receives visitors with the best air possible, is the belle of every soirée to which we are invited, and certainly dresses with a taste that is beyond all praise! Besides, she has the sweetest of tempers. I assure you, Paul, we have not differed since our day of betrothal! Truly I believe that we were destined for each other."

"And about Hauteville? Do the repairs progress?"

"*A merveille.* Do you remember that little wood, scarcely five acres in extent, that lies to the right of the chateau, about half a mile from the house?"

"Yes. You mean that copse adjoining your domain?"

"*C'est ça.* I have bought it, *mon ami,* and am about to inclose it in my grounds. Laid out with winding paths and planted with wild flowers, it will form a charming promenade. It is my intention to place rustic seats here and there, and a little temple in the centre, dedicated to Love. The idea is good, is it not? As for the chateau, the repairs take longer than we thought. There are now twenty-five workmen employed upon it; but, even so, we do not expect that it will be habitable before November, and that is too dreary a season for the country. So we propose to remain here for the summer, and then pass our winter in Paris.

Adrienne has never been to Paris. Have you been long in Brussels?"

"About five or six weeks."

"Really! Is it tolerably full this year? Do you know any one?"

"Only my English friend with whom I became acquainted in Germany. As for the company, I believe that Brussels is very gay this season; but I never go into society, so do not take me for an authority."

"You must come and see Adrienne."

"I—I shall be most happy."

"Come directly. We are not far from the hotel, and I have nothing to do. She will be enchanted to see you. Stay! I forgot. I came out to see after a carriage. We must buy or hire one, and I believe there are very good carriage-makers here. Can you direct me to one?"

"Recollect, Théophile, how little I know of such things. I could scarcely tell a cabriolet from a barouche if I saw it. There stands my friend Seabrook; let me bring him here and introduce you. He can aid you, I dare say, as to the choice and fashion of your purchase."

"Excellent."

So I signal to Seabrook where he stands beside the basin, and make the two known to each other. We then leave the park and stroll along the Rue Royale, seeking a coachbuilder's.

Suddenly Théophile pauses in front of a large white house, with the words "Hotel de France" inscribed along the front.

"This is where we are staying," he says, turning to me. "Adrienne is within, and alone. Do go in and see her; it will be a charity. Monsieur Seabrook will, perhaps, kindly remain with me. Pray go up, Paul, if it be only for a quarter of an hour."

"Not now—not now," I exclaim, nervously. "As we return, Théophile."

"And shall I tell Adrienne that our brother passed the door, and knew that she was there *triste* and alone? Bah! enter, Paul, and amuse her with some stories of thy travels."

Thus urged, I yield, for Théophile is accustomed to rule every thing just as he wishes; so I enter the lofty door and ask for Madame Latour.

Madame Latour! How strange a name for Adrienne Lachapelle!

"Monsieur will have the goodness to mount to No. 5, *au premier,*" says the waiter, bowing.

Arrived at the door, I pause and examine my own heart before I knock. Adrienne is within—Adrienne whom I loved, and from whose beauty I fled despairing! Does not my heart beat or my hand tremble? Is there no flush upon my brow—no fluttering of my breath—no sign or evidence of that love which exiled and tortured me, and cast the darkness of night upon the morning of my life? I am almost angry with myself that there is none of this. I can not believe that the passion has burnt out—that I tread the ashes of a dead love—that Adrienne is no more to me than a pure, and lofty, and admirable woman, and *my brother's wife!* It

seems, then, that mine was a boy's fantasy—a—
Hark! a footstep on the stairs! I start, knock
hurriedly, and, before she has time to answer,
open the door.

"Madame Latour!" It is all that I can say.

"My brother Paul!"

She had laid her book aside and risen as I
entered. How beautiful — how radiant — how
fair! I was not agitated; yet a strange feeling, like shame, tied my tongue, and I could
scarce articulate the words of common compli-
ment that were required by the moment as I
bowed over that delicate small hand, and touched
it lightly with my lips.

"I had no idea of meeting you in Brussels,
mon beau frère. Are you here en route, or for
the season?"

"I scarcely know yet, madame. Circumstances will decide for me."

"Pray be seated. Have you met my husband?"

Her husband! The word jarred upon my
nerves painfully, and I replied by a gesture of
assent.

"How delighted he must have been to meet
you! And he missed you so much when you
left Burgundy."

"I can scarcely imagine that possible, madame, since you remained," I said, forcing a
smile.

She looked up hastily and fixed her eyes full
upon me. Mine fell beneath their gaze, but not
before I had seen her color change, and a troubled expression flit across her face. Perhaps my
mother— Ah, no! my mother would never
have betrayed me!

"Where is Théophile?" asked Adrienne,
changing the conversation, and affecting to
glance along the columns of the morning paper.

"I left him with an English friend of mine
—Mr. Seabrook. They are gone to purchase a
carriage in the town."

"I have heard of Mr. Seabrook—that is, I
have read of him in your letters. My husband
gives me all his letters" (a pause). "Stay!
here is our arrival published among the list of
'distinguished visitors.' Listen. 'Arrived at
the Hotel de France, Monsieur and Madame
Théophile Latour, of Latour-sur-Creil and
Hauteville, Burgundy.' They have given us
the honor of your estate in addition to our own,
mon beau frère. How amusing!"

"I dare say you will think me very much
hors du monde, madame, but I confess that an
announcement such as this would annoy me
very particularly. I should not wish all the
idlers of a city or a watering-place to 'know
the secret of my whereabout;' and it seems to
me that the half of a man's self-sovereignty is
gone when his privacy of action is wrested from
him by a miserable newsmonger in search of a
paragraph."

"There is some justice in what you say," replied Adrienne. "But, at the same time, these
announcements are useful. They bring friends
and acquaintances together who must otherwise

have trusted to chance for their meeting. Take
our own case to-day for an instance. Had you
not encountered your brother, the journal would
have informed you not only of our presence,
but of our address. But who is this?"

"Monsieur le Marquis de Courtrai!" said
the waiter, throwing open the door, and, with
great ceremony, ushering in a little, withered
old gentleman, dressed in the extreme of youth-
ful fashion, who advanced with a profusion of
bows and smiles.

He was one of Monsieur Théophile's oldest
Parisian friends—had known the cher garçon for
years—had been, indeed, the cher garçon's cha-
peron on many occasions when he first left Burgundy. He had seen the announcement of
their arrival in this morning's journal, and had
hastened to be the first to welcome Monsieur
Théophile and his charming lady to Brussels.
He was charmed, proud, enchanted to make the
acquaintance of madame; and he hoped that he
might become the happy means of introducing
her to the agrémens of the city. In all respects
wherein madame would condescend to make
him useful, he was her slave.

All this was said with an air of antiquated
gallantry, and in a strain of high-flown compli-
ment that I found particularly repulsive. Adrienne, however, received him with perfect toler-
ance and good breeding, and requested him to
be seated and await the return of Théophile;
whereat the marquis pressed his hand upon his
laced shirt-front, and declared himself penetrated.

"Permit me," said Adrienne, glancing toward me with a half-suppressed smile. "Monsieur Latour—my husband's eldest brother."

The marquis bowed again, showed his false
teeth, ran his jeweled fingers gracefully through
the ringlets of his wig, and took a pinch of snuff
from the depths of an enameled box glittering
with diamonds.

"What have we to see in Brussels, Monsieur
le Marquis?" inquired Adrienne; "and what
families are staying here at present?"

Monsieur le Marquis begged to assure madame that Brussels was just now in perfection.
The Prince and Princess of Saxe Hohenhausen
had been here for more than three weeks already; the Grand-Duke of Zollenstrasse was
expected daily at Laken; the Baron and Bar-
oness de Montaignevert were at the Hotel de
Bellevue, and the Comte de Millefleurs at the
Hotel de la Regence. Besides these, the Earl
of Silvermere and family had just driven up to
the doors of the Bellevue, and it was rumored
that a venerable and distinguished duke, to
whom the near vicinity of Waterloo could be
suggestive only of the proudest reminiscences,
might shortly be expected on a visit to the royal
palace. As for amusements, madame might
repose upon his assurances that she could not
be triste or gênée in Brussels. He would make
it his proudest duty to enliven the leisure hours
of Théophile and his most beautiful and accomplished lady. There was an instrumental con-

cert every evening at Velloni's, in the park—exhibitions, soirées, fancy and court balls without number; and at the opera, three evenings in the week, a celebrated singer—Madame Vogelsang—with a ravishing voice—*a femme superbe*—a Juno, in fact, and quite the *furore* at Brussels.

"Monsieur le Marquis is an enthusiast, I perceive," said Adrienne, smiling.

Monsieur le Marquis ogled himself in an adjoining mirror, and simperingly avowed himself the slave of beauty. It had been his *faiblesse*, he said, as long as he could remember; and, judging from his general appearance, and from the variety of ingenious fictions to which he was indebted for his hair, teeth, complexion, and figure, one might reasonably conjecture that the personal recollections of M. le Marquis extended over a considerable period of time.

At this moment the door opened, and Théophile entered alone.

"I could not persuade your friend to return with me, Paul," he said. Then, perceiving his visitor—"Monsieur de Courtrai, this is an honor which I had not expected. I will not ask after your health, for I see that you are well and young as ever."

There was a slight shade of sarcasm mingled with the respect and courtesy of my brother's welcome, which would have been observed only by those who knew him intimately. Adrienne instantly entered into it.

"Monsieur le Marquis," said she, with a fascinating glance and smile, "has been entertaining us with all the news of Brussels—the visitors, the society, and the theatre. The time has flown since his arrival."

"Monsieur le Marquis is famed for his judgment in all matters of fashionable interest, *ma chère*," said Théophile, with another inclination to that gentleman—"and for his brilliant powers of conversation."

"Now, positively, it is too much," remonstrated the peer, having recourse again to the enameled snuff-box. "I vow, Latour, that you make me blush—absolutely blush!" And he would have covered his face with his embroidered handkerchief, only that he dared not, for private and important reasons. "I was speaking," he continued, "of the Vogelsang."

"And who is 'the Vogelsang?'" asked Théophile.

"The Vogelsang, *mon garçon*, is the divinity of the Place de la Monnaie—the radiant star of the Belgian opera. She comes to us from Vienna and Frankfurt, where every one is *ravi*—even as we are in Brussels. You must see her immediately, and madame also. I have a little *loge* which is entirely at your disposal, and in which I shall be charmed to see so distinguished a lady as madame!"

This polite offer is, after a brief hesitation, accepted with many acknowledgments for the following evening, and presently the Marquis de Courtrai takes his leave as ceremoniously as an embassador, and drives away from the hotel in a purple chariot drawn by four horses, with a footman behind carrying a bouquet in his button-hole.

"Who is that absurd little old gentleman?" asks Adrienne, as soon as he has left the room.

"This absurd little old gentleman, my love," replies Théophile, with an air of superb gravity, "is Polydore Emmanuel Hippolyte de Courtrai, Marquis de Courtrai, Comte de Sauterelles, and Chevalier of the most noble Italian order of Santo Polichinello—a very great man, I assure you, and one whose genealogy dates from the reign of Clovis the Second."

"Not his genealogy, Théophile," I exclaim. "You surely mean himself!"

It is true, then, that I love her no longer! So surprised, nay, I might almost say, so troubled am I by this discovery, that I wander away restlessly out of the city and spend some hours amid the lanes and fields of Ixelles. Returning toward evening, I bend my steps in the direction of the Rue de Leopold, where Margaret has been expecting me these four hours past.

Oh, gentle Margaret! why is it that my troubles grow lighter as I arrive within sight of the roof which shelters thee, and whence comes this sweet and chastened feeling which, at the thought of thy fair image, streams down upon my heart like the pale radiance of the evening star?

CHAPTER XXI.

THE HEART'S MISGIVINGS.

"MONSIEUR will find Ma'm'selle Marguerite in the little salon," said Elise, courtesying.

Elise was the pretty *fille-de-chambre*, and the "little salon" I have already mentioned as that which had been assigned to Margaret for her private sitting-room and studio.

She was not there, however, and I even fancied that I had heard her flying footsteps on the stairs. She had never shunned me before, and the suspicion for one moment vexed me. Then I smiled.

"Some woman's vanity," I murmured to myself. "Some ribbon or collar to be adjusted! Childish *petite Marguerite!*"

I could not help finding something pleasant in this explanation, and, musing over it, sat down and looked around me.

The tokens of her presence were scattered every where about; the very atmosphere of the room, heavy as it was with the perfume of acacia-flowers and verbena, seemed to retain somewhat of herself. On yonder chair were laid her gloves and shawl; here, on the chimney-piece, her open book; upon the table, beside the window, her pencils and drawing-paper, and that little bronze Apollo which I had given to her only yesterday. Her fingers, perhaps, have but just left the ivory keys of the piano; this mirror, perchance, has but a moment since reflected back the semblance of her features!

and chaste of prison-stories, and one meet for a gentle maiden's studying. Her drawing—what criticisms can I make upon it before her arrival? As yet the outline is barely sketched, and—

Why, what is this? A tear-drop yet undried and blistering on the paper! Another on the table close beside it! Tears! tears from my gentle Margaret's eyes—those eyes which I had fondly hoped would never weep again, unless for joy!

This explained the mystery of her flight and subsequent delay. I paced to and fro, and to and fro, in my agitation and dismay. What could have occurred? Why had I not come before? Would she never arrive?

I was on the point, at last, of ringing the bell for Elise, when the door opened and she entered, pale, silent, downward-looking.

I went over and took her hands in mine. There were the traces of weeping in her white lips and cheeks, and red eyelids. She trembled too, and her hands were burning.

"Margaret," I said, looking down earnestly upon her, "Margaret, you are not well."

"I am well," she answered, in a low voice.

"Your hands are feverish — you tremble. What is the matter?"

"Nothing is the matter."

She tried to move away, but I detained her.

"Nay, stand here in the light, Margaret, and let me look at you. You have been weeping!"

She shook her head, but I repeated it.

"Yes, Margaret, you have been weeping. That forced smile can not deceive me. Look here!"

And, leading her to the table, I pointed to the tear-drop on the paper. She turned aside from my grave scrutiny, and, looking upon the floor—

"I can not help thinking sometimes of—of my father," she murmured, hesitatingly.

"You are evading the question, Margaret," I said, sternly. "Is it possible that you can stoop to an equivocation?"

She remained silent, and kept her eyes fixed upon the ground.

"Can you look me in the face, Margaret, and say again that you were weeping for your father? If you do, I will believe you."

No reply.

"Tell me that it was true, Margaret, and I will entreat your pardon!" She looked up at me, paler than before.

"It was false," she said, firmly, but with a quivering lip.

I drew a chair close beside her, and once more took her hand between both of mine.

"Margaret, dear Margaret," I said, gently,

"Have any of the servants or pupils displeased you?"

"None."

"What is it, then? Some one must have hurt the feelings of my little Margaret."

"Oh, no one! no one! Every one is too good to me — better, better than I deserve a thousand times—you, monsieur, most of all!"

She says this with a burst of eager vehemence, and, snatching her hand away from mine, covers her face and falls into a passion of tears.

In doing this I see a ring upon her finger—a plain hair ring, which I have never observed there before! A new and startling doubt flits across my mind, and strikes me with a sudden anguish such as I never thought to feel again.

"Margaret, look up!" I cried, seizing that hand and forcing it from her face. "What ring is that? Whence came it? Answer me truly, for I *will* know!"

She shuddered, glanced upward for an instant, and replied in a trembling voice, "I can not tell you."

"You shall tell me, Margaret. Remember who I am!"

The fury of my tone, so far from intimidating, seemed to give her resolution. She looked up calmly and steadily in my face, folded her hands together, and said,

"I will not."

The sight of her pale courage subdued me—my voice faltered.

"For your father's sake, Margaret! for your father's sake!"

The tears gathered in her beautiful eyes, and rolled slowly down her cheeks.

"Not for my father's sake," she answered, softly.

"Oh, Margaret, what is this terrible secret which you are concealing? Tell it to me, Margaret — if not for his sake, tell it for mine — for my sake, Margaret!"

She clasped her hands imploringly, and laid her head down upon the table, sobbing bitterly.

"Oh, forgive me," she said, "forgive me! Do not ask me—give me time—oh, what shall I do? what shall I do?"

Her sorrow tore my heart. I went over to her, and laid my hand upon her shoulder.

"Nay, then, child," I said, falteringly, "keep thy secret. It must needs be innocent, like thee. I will be content, and ask no more."

I took her head between my hands, pressed a kiss upon her hot brow, and left the room without one backward glance.

I do not wish to remember the agony of mind which I endured that night, or the torturing pity which, in spite of all, I could not help feeling for her. Till many hours past midnight, I paced the opposite side of the street in which she lived, watching the pale light from her window, and, when that was extinguished, finding some consolation in the thought that she slept peacefully.

Oh, gentle Margaret, hadst thou but heard the measured echo of my steps! Hadst thou but known the prayers which thy silence wrung from these lips, as I passed to and fro in the moonlight, like some phantom of the night!

CHAPTER XXII.

"UPON A SUNSHINY HOLIDAY."

THREE days without seeing her—three weary solitary days! It was the first time that I had so remained away, and I could bear it no longer.

Perhaps she, too, had been lonely and unhappy. This last thought decided me, and I went.

The day was resplendently fine; a cool breath of purer air came from the westward, and the white buildings and streets of the town glared painfully in the sunlight. The driver of a little open vehicle held up his whip invitingly to me as I went along. He was a good-tempered, red-faced, jovial-looking fellow, with a bunch of clover-blossoms in his button-hole. The carriage, too, appeared clean and new, and the horse wore a green bough upon his shaggy head, to keep off the predatory flies.

I paused and hesitated.

"Suppose," I said to myself, "that I took her and the little Clemence for a country holiday, and trusted to time and opportunity for an explanation of the past! Suppose, if it be only for a day, that I endeavor to enjoy the pleasant Now, and banish the Hereafter!"

The driver held up his whip again. I thought of Margaret's pale cheeks, of quiet lanes, and woods, and wayside flowers, and, replying to his signal by a smile, jumped in, and directed him to drive to the Rue de Leopold.

To reach there, to alight, to make my way rapidly across the court-yard, and up to the door of her little studio, occupied but a few rapid moments; to open the door softly and by degrees, to enter unperceived and steal up to the back of her chair as she bent low over her drawing, to stand there silently watching the touches of her pencil, and the coming and going of her breath, all this was more difficult and more delightful, and took longer to accomplish.

She was still at work upon the bronze Apollo, not much farther advanced, I noticed sadly, than when I last approached that table and looked down upon the outline. She had been, perhaps, too sorrowful to proceed, and I fancied, though I could see but a very small portion of her cheek, that she looked even paler than was usual with her. Poor Margaret! I felt so grieved for her grief, that I almost forgot my own distress at being excluded from her confidence.

So! that arm a little longer and more elevated—yes! As if she had heard my thought outspoken, her careful pencil corrected, and retouched, and traveled on. A haughtier curl, Margaret, to that imperial lip—more freedom in the backward falling locks—more power to the hand that grasps the bow! Ah! she effaces it with bread, and tries again. No! less effective, if any thing, than before. One more trial—now a light firm outline, and a steady perusal of the copy! Quietly, my pupil; no haste—no excitement—no—

"Admirable! The very inspiration of the Sun-god!"

Margaret suppresses a scream, drops the pencil from her fingers, and falls back, trembling and blushing, into her seat.

"How you have alarmed me, monsieur!" she exclaims, pressing her hands upon her heart. It leaps so wildly that I can almost see it beating there against her side.

"I did not intend to startle you, Margaret, thus suddenly. The words escaped me unawares. I had been watching you for many minutes, and had observed the previous failures; so you see, when the success was achieved, I forgot myself, and could not control the expression of my pleasure. But I am not here to-day to praise, or blame, or play the drawing-master; I have come to take you for a holiday this lovely morning—a holiday in the country."

"A holiday in the country—how delicious!"

She looked up at me with that grateful expression of quiet satisfaction to which I was accustomed from her, and began hastily to put away her drawing. How her hands trembled as she did so, and how the quick blushes kept rising and fading at every word! Never before had I seen her so fluttered and agitated; but then, to be sure, never before had I so startled and surprised her.

"Now, Margaret, depêche-toi, call hither the little Clemence, and I will wait while you make ready. I charge you not to outwear my patience with any 'silken dalliance in the wardrobe,' for our carriage waits below."

Whether it were the unwonted luxury of the drive and the rejoicing aspect of the summer morning, or whether it arose from the apparent cheerfulness and ease of my own manner, I can not tell, but the timidity with which she at first received me vanished quite away before an hour had elapsed. Indeed, I do not remember ever to have known Margaret more childishly happy. The general placidity and reserve of her character seemed to yield to the influence of that glowing sky, as the snow-drift melts and dances, sparkling, in the sunlight.

She rose up in the carriage to look round at the level harvest-fields and the distant city spires—she alighted ere she had well-nigh traveled a couple of miles, to fill her lap with honeysuckle and wild convolvuli from the roadside—she clapped her hands with delight at the sight of a small white butterfly, and imitated in her sweet low voice the prolonged shake of the nightingales that peopled the shadowy planta-tions of poplars and dark pines. As for Clem-ence, sitting by silently in a corner of the car-riage, she was by far the graver and sedater of the two.

For my part, I encouraged her mood by an assumption of unembarrassed kindness, which cost me, at the first, a strong effort, but which merged, ere long, into a sentiment of real satis-faction. Her smiles reassured me. I felt that to be thus innocently gay, her secret, if she had one, must be pure and maidenly; and presently the very remembrance of it seemed fading from my mind.

Toward noon we reached a small town, and, staying at the door of the solitary hotel, bade the driver look to his horses, ordered an early dinner from the smiling landlady, and wandered out on foot to stroll in the forest.

It was not what I should understand by the name of a forest, accustomed as I was to the old umbrageous labyrinths of mossy trees that skirted the horizon round about my fair Bur-gundian home; it was rather a few level acres, regularly planted with the slender fir and pine, and affording a pleasant promenade for students and young lovers.

Here Clemence seemed to wake from her si-lent apathy, and ran in and out the trees, seek-ing, with Margaret, for wild strawberries and "purple dewberries" in the long grass and tan-gled underwood. Yet, even in this search, the child was unlike other children, and pursued it with a quiet industry and a grave composed de-meanor that contrasted oddly with the innocent gayety of her older companion. She laughed but seldom, and then softly to herself, as if laughter were a thing to be subdued and con-quered. Even when she ran, it was utterly without the buoyant precipitation and careless eagerness of infancy. She was a strange child, and my attention became more and more drawn to her with every time I saw her.

Thus they amused themselves gathering wild fruits and acorns, and finding the brown pine-cones that lay scattered here and there beneath the trees, while I wandered near, keeping them in sight, and indulging myself in "fancies wild and sweet." Growing weary after a while, they sat down to rest at the foot of an alder that overhung a deep clear pool toward the skirts of the forest, and here, as it was not yet time to return, the child besought me to tell her a fairy-story.

"A fairy-story, little one! but what if I know none?"

Clemence shook her little dark head, and fixed her eyes full upon me. "I am sure you know one," she said, seriously. "Margaret says you do."

"I never told Margaret a fairy-story," I re-joined, laughing. "How should she know that I can do it?"

Margaret blushed and laughed too, and said she thought that monsieur could do it, if he liked—just to please Clemence!

"Well, then, I must try; but, as I know of none, I must even invent one for the purpose. You must give me some few minutes to consid-er, and—stay! I have it; but it is not a fairy-tale, Clemence."

"Oh, no matter, if it is pretty. What is its name?"

"I hardly know. Suppose we call it 'The Angel and the Wanderer!'"

"I like that name very much."

She crept up closer to Margaret, and laid her head down upon her shoulder. Sitting thus, with her pale cheek half turned away, her large dark eyes bent downward in listening expecta-tion, and her little slender figure curled up, as it were, beneath the folds of Margaret's shawl, she looked so sallow and elfin that one might almost have taken her for Goëthe's Mignon in person. After gazing at the pair for a moment as they sat thus in quaint companionship, I be-gan my story.

The Angel and the Wanderer.

"There was an Angel hovering over a great city by night.

"It was so dark, and the mist so thick, that the church spires looked like shadowy figures pointing heavenward, and the tall masts of ships along the river like the lances and pennons of a hostile armament.

"Scarce a footstep echoed along the wet pavements; scarce a shop threw its broad light out into the deserted streets. It was late; the cold wind rushed moaning on its way, and the rain came heavily down, blurring the pale light of the flickering gas-lamps.

"Still the Angel flew on, though the rain spared not his white wings; for he was a good Angel, and it was his mission to watch over the hearts of young children; to protect them from evil thoughts and angry impulses; and to bring pleasant dreams to the slumbers of those who had been good, and truthful, and obedient all the day.

"Presently he passed within sight of a small court-yard, at the end of which stood a large white house, with all its windows lighted; and he paused in his flight, for he saw a figure crouched up against the wall, just within the shadow of the archway that opened into the court-yard from the street.

"It was a poor little Italian image-vendor, with his tray of plaster figures laid beside him. His eyes were closed, his black hair fell in long damp locks over his face, and the tears with which he had cried himself asleep were yet wet upon his cheeks. One cold hand was sheltered in the breast of his jacket, and the other had fallen listlessly on the ground. The Angel bent low and dropped a tear upon the little hand, it was so wasted!

"He was weary, and sleepy, and hungry. He had not sold one image all that day, and he was dreaming of his cruel master, and of the heavy punishment that awaited him. But the Angel pressed his lips upon the pale forehead, and folded his wings around the shrinking form, and the bad dreams fled away, and he slept peacefully.

"Still he was chilled and weak for need of bread, and the Angel's heart of mercy was troubled. He looked up at the great house; its bright windows were crossed and recrossed by the shadows of the dancers, and the sounds of music and laughter were loud within.

"'Alas!' said the Angel, 'they are too happy to heed me!'

"Hark! there were footsteps coming quickly along the street! It was a wealthy old citizen hastening home from a card-party. He had lost money at the game, and he was out of temper with the weather and with himself. The Angel flew out of the passage and clung to him.

"'Help!' he cried. 'Help for the cold and the hungry!'

"The citizen shuddered, and drew the collar of his coat closer round his neck.

"'How the wind whistles into one's ears!' muttered he, and passed by.

"So the Angel flew back, and strove to warm his little charge by breathing on his cold lips and eyelids; but in vain. They grew colder and colder, and still the music and dancing in the great house went merrily on.

"Another passenger!

"It was a poor needle-woman returning from her day's labor—a good, earnest woman, thinking of her children at home, and never hearing the gentle voice of the appealing Angel.

"'Help! help!' he sighed. 'Shelter and food! shelter and food!'

"'What a thick, raw mist!' said the poor needle-woman. ''Tis like a cloud before one! Maybe, though, 'tis the long day's work that makes my eyes weak.'

"But it was the two white wings that she saw fluttering in her path, only she did not know it; and even the sacred tears that he wept down upon her face she mistook for rain-drops borne upon the wind, and so passed by.

"Still the Angel watched and waited, and still the music and dancing in the great house went merrily on.

"The sleeper moaned and feebly murmured 'Mother!'

"He was dreaming—dreaming of his far home beside the blue sea—that home where the shadows of the vine-leaves round the porch flickered on the floor in the bright sunshine—where his gentle mother sat spinning on the threshold, and his little brothers played with shells and sea-weeds at her feet, and all the days were happy.

"Then the Angel flew up to the windows of the great house, and looked in, and saw a party of merry children dancing gayly together, and a group of elder persons sitting by, and watching them with smiles. The chandeliers were shining overhead; the room rang with young voices; the floor echoed the quick touches of their light feet. The Angel clasped his hands in despair.

"'Help! help! before it is too late!'

"And he dashed himself against the window, and filled the air with his cries.

"'Listen to the rain,' said an old white-headed gentleman, who was standing close by with two or three others. 'Hear how it beats upon the panes!'

"'Ay, and to the wind,' replied one near him, taking a pinch of snuff from a jeweled box. 'It howls like a human voice. Bad weather, my lord, for the shipping.'

"And they spoke of it, and noticed it no more.

"So the Angel went back, and took the outcast in his arms, and pressed him to his divine heart. But the little cheek still grew colder and colder, and the faint breath fell more faintly—and an hour went by.

"Then a carriage with bright lamps and pawing horses drove up and waited before the archway; then another and another, till presently there was a long row of them waiting in the street. And very soon the door of the house was opened, and, amid the blaze of lights and gleaming of many faces, a gentleman and lady, with three little children, appeared upon the steps.

"But this time the Angel was silent, and just as they came forward he unwound his loving arms from round the boy, and stood apart.

"'Eh! what is this?' cries the gentleman, starting back as his foot touches the figure crouching by the wall. 'A boy asleep!'

"The servant snatched a lamp from the carriage—more gentlemen came crowding round—they tried in vain to rouse him as he lay. The first gentleman stooped down and held the light to his face. It was very white. He took the cold hand in his, and it dropped heavily as he released it.

"'Great heaven!' cried he, looking round upon the rest, 'the child is dead!'

"Then the Angel, weeping and invisible, spread his white wings, and, with a long sad wail, soared up into the night, far from the archway and the wondering throng around it. Onward he went, and onward, till the lights all faded away, and the site of the great city lay dark and indistinct beneath his feet. And presently there was a sound of rushing wings behind him, and another Angel, bright and beautiful as the morning, overtook him, and said,

"'Whence comes my sorrowful brother?'

"'I come,' said the Angel, 'from the great city. I have seen men in their blind selfishness reject the voice of pity, and I have seen a little child die from cold and hunger. Therefore am I sorrowful, and the decrees of our Master are dark before me.'

"'Dost thou question the justice of Providence?'

"'Alas!' replied the Angel, 'I question it not; but I can not understand the death and the suffering.'

"'Look upon me,' said the radiant Stranger; 'look upon me, and doubt no more. I was the soul of that little child!'

"So, hand in hand, and rejoicing together, they ascended through the mists and clouds of earth to that far space where the stars shine night and day."

The story ended, we returned to the inn. Some rare ferns, a tiny oak no bigger than a rose-tree, some feathers fallen from the wing of the golden pheasant, and a profusion of blue and yellow field-flowers, were among the treasures with which Margaret and Clemence returned laden to the Lion d'Or, and which they stored away in the carriage as it stood, horseless and driverless, awaiting us before the door. Then with what ceremony we sat down to our merry feast—how politely I placed my ward at the head of the table, and Clemence at my right hand—how gravely I apologized for my morning costume, and for the absence of a white waistcoat! How we jested and laughed, and drank each other's health in the frothing Champagne, and praised the fresh country fare, the vegetable soup, the fowls, the omelettes, the pastry, and the rosy apples! With what reluctance we rose at last, and resumed our homeward journey along the paven country road, just as the shadows began to lengthen toward the east, and the evening light to glint between the trees on either side!

How quaint and soothing it is, this monotonous and fertile Belgian landscape! For leagues and leagues it lies sleeping all around, rich in produce as a garden, level as a desert. Here and there nods a formal plantation of willows and beeches, and the evening breeze flows over wide luxuriant crops of barley, flax, and feathery oats, with long stripes of potatoes and other vegetables in between, and not a fence or hedgerow any where in sight. Sometimes we meet a lazy wagon on the road, or a group of market-women coming homeward from the town; sometimes we arrive at a broad and many-bridged canal, whose course, hidden till this moment by the lofty corn, is revealed to us only by the gliding sails of some boat topping the yellow grain, like a ship sailing upon land. Now and then we pass a white farm-house with tiled roof and trim garden, and perhaps a bower made all of ivy, and cut into points or battlements by the skillful gardener. Next comes a quiet town, with its high belfry and red-brick cathedral towering up above the plain; and perchance we hear the pleasant bells chime sadly and sweetly from turret to turret as we travel by. On all sides are wind-mills and feeding cattle, and long paved roads with never a curve or a hill-rise to break their arrowy perspective—a land of peace and plenty.

I bade our coachman drive slowly, for we enjoyed the almost conventual stillness of the hour. Somehow a change had fallen upon our mood since we had turned our faces homeward. A softer and more chastened sentiment seemed to be inspired by the scene. Clemence slept wearily in a corner; Margaret sat beside me lost in reverie. Both were alike absorbed and silent.

Then the faint far lights of Brussels drew nearer; carriages and market-carts became more frequent on the road; and presently a few houses scattered on either side, a solitary gas-lamp, and some bills placarded on a hoarding, warned us that our holiday was fast approaching its conclusion.

Just now we arrived near a little bridge crossing a narrow canal, and lit on one side by a single lamp. Beneath the lamp, with his arms resting on the parapet and his head bent down, a man stood looking at the water. There was nothing remarkable in his appearance, yet the involuntary start and catching of the breath with which Margaret leaned forward as we came in sight of him attracted my attention.

We were moving very slowly at the time—up hill, in fact, toward the bridge, and our horse was tired. I looked earnestly into her face, but she did not heed me. Her eyes were fixed upon the stranger, and her cheeks were pale.

Suddenly he looked up, and shaded his eyes with his hand as the sound of our approach drew nearer. It was too dark, and we were too distant from him to see any thing of his features; but, as if the action were convincing and she knew him, Margaret sank back in the carriage, and avoided my gaze by looking steadfastly down upon the floor.

At the same instant he turned rapidly away, and dived down a small street opening to the left. When we had crossed the bridge and reached this opening he was out of sight.

"Margaret," I said, sternly, "what man is that?"

"I know not," she replied, faintly, and with averted head.

I said no more—urged her no farther—but leaned back sadly in my place. This time no reproaches found their way to my lips—no tears betrayed the pressure at my heart. The iron had entered into my soul, and I was silent.

CHAPTER XXIII.

THE DIAMOND BRACELET.

"By my faith, Seabrook, I can not help it. Granted, 'tis a weakness, a folly, yet I can not help it. So young, so gentle, so false! Now, before Heaven, I feel as if a star had fallen from the skies when I remember how she is deceiving me!"

Seabrook whistled dismally—thrust his hands deep into his pockets, and walked over to the window.

"And she looks innocent! Would you believe that one could lie and play the traitress with a face so fair? Ah! I forget; you have not seen how fair—how fair she is!"

> "Be she fairer than the day,
> Or the flow'ry meads in May,
> If she be not so to me,
> What care I how fair she be?"

sang my friend, with a shrug of his shoulders.
"Seabrook, you have no feeling!"

"Paul, you have no common sense!"

He came and drew a seat close beside mine.

"Confess, now," said he, with his old kindly manner, half sad, half sarcastic, "confess, now, that our wise and faithful guardian has played a very foolish part! Is it not natural enough to suppose that a girl of seventeen has a lover, and that she has been too shy to confess it? Was it not absurd of the most potent, grave, and reverend seignior Paul to play Dr. Bartolo to his fair ward, while some gallant Almaviva was all the while lying *perdu* in the inmost recesses of her heart? Pshaw! man, swallow the nauseous draught with as good a grace as you can muster, and finish your part according to the good old stage-fashion, by forgiving and blessing the young couple as soon as you find it useless to do otherwise."

"And then sing a trio to cement our eternal union!" I said, forcing a smile.

He laughed, poured out a glass of wine, and nodded my health.

"Hush! do you hear?" said he, suddenly, pointing toward the window and listening attentively. "What music is that?"

"'Tis the band in the park. They give an instrumental concert every evening at Velloni's."

"A concert every evening! To think that I have been a week in Brussels, and not have known that before! Let us go instantly."

"I have no heart for such amusements, Seabrook."

"Heart! nonsense, *mon ami*; 'tis the very medicine to minister to a mind diseased! I prescribe—nay, I entreat it, Paul. Will you refuse me?"

I yield, as ever, to his gay sovereignty, and we are loitering, ere long, amid the throng of coffee-drinking and ice-eating loungers who frequent the space of sward and trees surrounding the celebrated restaurateur's. Seabrook is charmed with the music, with the company, with the gay and pleasant scene. The lights, the voices, the hurrying waiters, all serve to exhilarate him—to depress me. Amusement, to one of his joyous temperament, is food and life; to one saddened and harassed, like myself, by disappointment and doubt, is utterly intolerable. I take the opportunity, after some twenty minutes of uneasy endurance, to plead a headache, and escape by myself out into the public avenues of the park beyond.

It is not yet quite deserted in the principal walk and around the central basin, so I turn aside into the dark quiet alleys at the back of the restaurant's, where the music comes to me softly through the trees, and the dark night reigns unbroken, save by a gas-lamp at rare intervals.

Here the stars twinkle down between the roofing leaves, and, in the gloom and stillness of the place, my shattered nerves are soothed to somewhat like repose. I strive to think with calmness of the past and future—to arm myself for a dispassionate judgment and a generous line of action. It is hard to do this, nevertheless; and in the magnitude of the effort I discover the extent of the weakness. Whether to consult her happiness in preference to every other consideration—whether selfishly to use my power as her guardian, and—

Alas! alas! that our sternest foe should lie ambushed in our own weak hearts, and that the most brilliant of our victories should ever be the saddest humiliation of our lives!

The night deepened, and still I walked to and fro, to and fro, lost in a train of thought that absorbed my every faculty, and from which I was at length aroused by the sound of voices in a neighboring alley.

I will scarcely say "aroused," for, though I heard their footsteps on the gravel, and their very words as they passed now and then close beside me, with only the green hedge between us, I gave no heed to their vicinity, and attached no meaning to their speech. Nay, more, the words were English; yet, such was the strange, abstracted condition of my mind, I did not even remark that they were uttered in a foreign tongue. They fell upon my ear, but without finding their way to my mind; they were familiar to my sense, and my thoughts were at the time so earnestly engaged that I was content to hear them without asking whence they came. It has frequently occurred to me since, how singular an instance of preoccupation of mind was this, and how forcible a question of inner-duality it might suggest to the psychological student.

The voices were two—a man's and a woman's. The latter, somehow, appeared not wholly unfamiliar to me, and the murmuring sadness of their tones chimed in with my own melancholy.

Suddenly a something, which was more a shock than a suspicion, flashed over me. The woman was speaking.

"He doubts me," she said, and it seemed that she was weeping. "He doubts me. I am most unhappy!"

Margaret's voice! Oh, heaven, Margaret's voice!

"It is unfortunate," replied her companion, "but—"

They passed, and his words grew inaudible in distance. I was neither grieved nor enraged—only powerless, breathless, overwhelmed.

Presently they returned, and the man was still speaking.

"Avow nothing," he said, as if in continuation; "you know my position, and the necessity we have for strict concealment. I am well aware how firm my little Margaret can be, the more especially—"

Again the voice died away.

The blood rushed to my head and boiled in every vein; I felt as if an iron band were tightened round my brow; I uttered a cry like the cry of some fierce animal; I spurned the dull earth madly with my heel, and struggled for very breath.

On all sides disappointment, concealment,

deceit! Had I not one friend whom I could esteem and trust? Was there not one hand unarmed against me? Chilled in my childish affections—supplanted (and by *whom* supplanted?) in my manhood's first passion—wronged by this young creature whom I would have given fortune and energies to serve—to whom I would have devoted the cares and tenderness of a life —to whom I had resolved (Heaven knows with what unselfish purity of thought!) to supply the lost home-ties and work out my trust with holiness of purpose—for whom I was prepared, even this very night, to relinquish every personal and sordid hope, even as a father would relinquish for a child—Say, was I not tried almost beyond the bounds of patient faith? To feel a momentary resentment was not surely inexcusable—to doubt all love and fair seeming not utterly unjustifiable?

I felt that I must see this man—this lover-face to face. I must look into his eyes, and see him quail before me.

The impulse was obeyed as soon as felt. I ran with the speed of a madman down the dark pathway. It branched away to the right. I found myself getting farther and farther from the outlet which I sought. I retraced my steps —again went wrong—again doubled back, and at length reached the spot where, but a few short moments before, they had been walking together.

It was a long walk quite over-roofed by trees, and opening at one end upon the Rue Ducale—a long, straight, open walk, and not a soul in sight!

They had taken alarm at the sound of my footsteps—perhaps at the involuntary cry that had escaped my lips, and were gone!

Baffled, yet calmed by the disappointment, I sank exhausted upon a stone bench under some trees, and, after a brief interval of rest, rose up and went out at the gateway which terminated the path. The audience were pouring from Velloni's as I passed, and, by some strange impulse, I stood and watched for Seabrook.

It was never my disposition to seek society when grief was weighing on me, but this night I seemed to long for the sight of a face in which I might still see truth and friendship—for the pressure of a hand that had never played me false. The fever of anguish was past—the hour of the human weakness was come; and though, probably, I should not betray what I had suffered by look or word, I should not feel alone.

Presently he came. I stepped forward, placed my arm through his, and said simply,

"I was waiting for you."

"I would have left sooner had I known that," said my friend, with a smile. "Is your head better?"

I nodded.

"And what do you propose doing? It is yet early, and the music to which I have been listening is so good that it has only served to make me wish for more. What say you to dropping into the Opera House for an hour, just to hear a

song from the Vogelsang? She plays to-night in Norma. We shall be in time for the last act."

"Go where you please—I will accompany you."

The theatre was crowded when we arrived. We were warned at the entrance that no seats were to be had, and we took up our standing at the back amid a crowd of others similarly circumstanced.

The act had begun before we arrived; the Vogelsang was already on the stage, and every breath was hushed throughout the house.

Great as she had been when first I saw her, she was far greater now. Through all the gradations of stormy passion, jealousy, fury, despair, and agonized humility, she passed with a skill which was more than skill—which was reality.

"*Per Bacco!*" whispered Seabrook to me, "this woman gives me an oppression on the chest! What power—what instinct!"

Instinct—ay! that was the word. It was not intellect, for intellect is cold, and calm, and lofty. It was the fierce and fearful beauty of the panther, grand in its instincts, terrible in its rage!

I shuddered. Strange that, from the moment when I beheld her on the Frankfurt stage, I should have ever felt this creeping aversion, and that the third time it should be more strongly marked than even at the first!

The last scene—that tremendous scene where the despairing priestess wrestles for forgiveness with her father—came to an end. There was a dead silence for a moment; the audience drew a long breath of relief; then came that deafening shout of unanimous wonder and delight to which she was so well accustomed. She is called—she comes; the bouquets are showered round her; something heavy—something that glitters as it falls, is flung from a stage-box, and lights just at her feet. It is a bracelet—a gorgeous bracelet scintillating with diamonds! She lifts it gracefully, and, bending low in the direction whence it came, clasps it upon her arm.

In an instant every eye is turned upon that box; for a moment the liberal giver eclipses the songstress; even I, who am occupied with heavy thoughts, am influenced by the general impulse, and rise in my place to look upon—upon whom?

Upon my brother Théophile!

"*Ma foi*, Paul," said Seabrook, shrugging his shoulders and glancing toward me with a peculiar expression, "your brother must have a remarkable appreciation of talent, and more money than he well knows how to employ!"

Vexed, bewildered, uneasy, I made no reply, but hastened nervously through the crowded lobby, and bade farewell to my companion at the doors of the theatre.

Alas! there are times when the foreshadowings of evil, vaporous and undefined, rise up over the soul like the night-mists over the meadow-land, obscuring not only the landmarks of earth, but dimming even the star-guides of heaven. At such periods we find our only safety in solitude and prayer.

CHAPTER XXIV.

A PACKET OF LETTERS.

Théophile to Paul.

"Hotel de France, Aug. 30th, 18—.

"WHAT an age it is since we have met, *mon cher frère!* I vow that I begin to forget your very features. Twice have I called at your apartments, and twice have I been told that you were out; a statement which, at the risk of offending you, I must confess that I did not, on both occasions, entirely credit. Were it not that I have seen your friend, Mr. Seabrook, twice or thrice lately, I should not even know that you are living and well. I am glad that you chanced to introduce me to this Englishman. I find him pleasant and obliging, and an excellent judge of all that relates to the stable and the studio. He has kindly advised me in the purchase of some horses and paintings, which I think you will like, if you only come to see them.

"I have discovered many of my Parisian acquaintances here—people of whom you have never heard, and whose names would not interest you—and find myself, agreeably enough, in the centre of a *petite société très distinguée,* of which Adrienne is the reigning sovereign. We have determined upon giving a *soirée* on the 15th of next month, and are now issuing the cards of invitation. I know that it will be a trial to your patience, my philosophic brother, but I insist that, for this once, you make your appearance among us. I request it as a mark of respect to my wife. It is her first reception, and I am sure that I shall not find you obdurate. But you will come before then, *n'est ce pas?* I inclose Adrienne's card for the 15th instant. Write a reply such as you know I desire. Adieu, *vaurien! A toi,*   T. L.

"P.S.—*Apropos* of horses, I want to buy some at the great sale which they advertise at Malines, and I find my treasury somewhat poorer than I had anticipated. Could you lend me five thousand francs for a day or two?"

Norman Seabrook to Paul Latour.

"August 30th, 18—.

"It is past midnight. All is still in the house. I can not sleep. Thoughts and sensations which are not, perhaps, wholly strange, but which have presented themselves dimly and rarely to my mind, are now busy within me, and I write to you.

"Your anxiety, your vexation, the solitude which you have maintained for many days—seeing no face but mine—some words spoken by you this morning, have impressed me with a melancholy akin to your own.

"'I have none to love,' you said, 'and nothing to accomplish.'

"*None to love and nothing to accomplish.* Alas! I also, my friend, I have none to love and nothing to accomplish. In that sentence you epigrammatized my history.

"I do not know that I have ever felt so deeply on this subject as to-night. It seems to me that I am halting on the road of life; leaning on my staff, and calmly scanning the backward pastures and the forward waste. How fair and profitless a Past! how blank a Future! I fancied myself a pilgrim *sans souci*—a butterfly tasting the flowers by the wayside without a toil or a sorrow. I have shaken off the dream to-night, and I find that I fill no place among men. I am a drone in the hive.

"You know my affairs as well as I know them myself. You know that it is my pleasure to be a bird of passage, lighting here and there, and resting nowhere. You know that I have a small independence, just sufficient to keep me out of debt, and supply my few necessities. You know all this, Paul. Well, at this hour, I feel that a man without ties, without aim, without profession, is morally an offender against society and against Providence. I have head—I have education; yet of what avail are they to me? Will my knowledge of poetry and philosophy make me a poet or a philosopher? Can Plato teach me the law, or Homer qualify me for the profession of arms? My travels have not elevated me into a Humboldt. My amateur chemistry has brought me no nearer to the science of a Liebig or a Dalton.

"I have heart. Although I have, as yet, lived without loving, I am sensible of a capacity for love in my own nature. But dare I think of love? Dare I dream of wife and fireside, I who am without resources? Of what use am I in the world? In what path of human endeavor could I hope to earn bread for my children, were I so unfortunate as to possess any?

"Oh, the life of a man without ties, without home, without labor, is a want and a bitterness. I taste it now for the first time. 'Tis true that I may forget it to-morrow, and for many to-morrows, but I feel that it must come again and again, and that at last it will abide with me evermore.

"Would that I could begin to study even now! Would that I had something to work for and to love!

"As it is, I fear that I could not devote myself to any profession without some powerful incentive. My powers of mind are various, but not tenacious. I want not perseverance, but constancy. The proposition looks like a paradox, yet it is not one. Whatever I attempt, I attempt earnestly, and with my whole soul. My studies are interrupted by no self-indulgence. I devote myself to my subject night and day till I arrive at a certain proficiency. There I stop. My curiosity is satisfied. Other objects present themselves, about which I am equally desirous of knowledge. I throw aside the palette for the crucible, the violin for the microscope, the instruments of the mathematician for the wild reveries of the mental philosopher. I am 'everything by turns, and nothing long.'

"I despise myself to-night, for to-night, Paul, I see myself in my true colors. I stand face to face with my own spirit.

"There is something awful in it, Paul—something weird and terrible in thus summoning one's self to judgment. I feel as if I had looked in a mirror and seen a strange face there—a face unlike that to which mine eyes were accustomed daily, but which bore a certain palpable and dread resemblance that convinced me of its identity!

"Tell me, have you never known moments such as this, when the veil of custom seems to be rent suddenly before your eyes; when life and the world stand revealed in their true colors; and when the shows of things are for a few seconds stripped of the semblance of realities? Have you never been aroused by these brief revelations from the hollow seemings of every-day life? Have you never indulged them, as I now indulge them—forgotten them, as I to-morrow shall forget them?

"I have opened my window upon the outer night. It is so still that not a breath stirs the flame of the candle by which I write, and the brazen statue of St. Michael on the slender spire of the Hotel de Ville glitters close by in the moonlight. Surely there is something in the unruffled calm of Nature that overawes our little anxieties and doubts; the sight of these housetops and steeples, with the deep sky and the clustering stars above them, seems to have imparted some quiet to my mind. Perhaps I could sleep now. Good-night.

"NORMAN SEABROOK."

Margaret Fletcher to Paul Latour.

"Aug. 30th, 18—.

"So many days have elapsed since I last saw my father's friend, that I no longer dare to enumerate them. Some withered ferns and grasses on my table remind me of the time that has gone by since he gathered them for me in the little wood of ——; my unfinished drawing has long awaited the corrections of the master. In vain I ask myself if he can have left Brussels? if he be suffering? if I have displeased him? Whatever be the cause, truth were better than this intolerable suspense, and the truth I entreat from him, though it be conveyed but in a single word. Oh, if you are vexed with me, what shall I say or do to make you forgive me? If I have seemed ungrateful to you, believe, monsieur, that appearances alone are against me, and that my heart is unconscious of a thought that might be construed into a sin against my benefactor.

"I fear that I do wrong to write to you, yet how can I help it? You will not be angry with me, will you, Monsieur Latour? You will pardon the trouble and annoyance that I occasion you, for I am so unhappy. MARGARET."

CHAPTER XXV.

A LITTLE SCENE OUT OF THE DRAMA.

SCENE.—MARGARET'S *Studio. She is reading near the window, but lays aside the book when*

I enter, and seems both pleased and agitated. CLEMENCE *is not present.*

PAUL (*advancing and taking her by the hand*). Well, Margaret, are you glad to see me?

MARG. Oh, very glad, Monsieur Latour! I —I thought you had forgotten me.

PAUL (*archly*). Forgotten you, eh? But I think you were determined not to be forgotten, *petite* Marguerite!

MARG. (*blushing*). Do not speak of that, monsieur, I—I entreat you. I am—I am, indeed, quite ashamed that—

PAUL (*very earnestly and gravely*). That you should be sufficiently interested in one whom you call your "father's friend" to care to see him again! Is that it, Margaret; and did you really wish me to think you utterly impenetrable and hard-hearted?

MARG. Oh, not that! You—I am sure you know what I mean?

PAUL. I think I do, Margaret. Indeed, it is seldom that I am pained or perplexed by the ambiguity of words, for there is always more conveyed by the tone in which they are uttered and the glance by which they are accompanied. It is only the ambiguity of action that grieves and troubles me. Concealments, falsehoods, double-dealings, preconcerted plans of deception, these are the things that cut me to the soul; and sooner than be subjected to them from the hands of those whom I trust and love, I would go away, like the Athenian Timon, and live in a desert!

MARG. Monsieur!

PAUL (*in an excited tone*). I never loved any thing yet that it did not bring me sorrow and suffering—never! And to think that you too, Margaret—you who are so young and so secluded—you whom I thought so innocent, so docile, so affectionate—to think that *you* should plot and plan against me, as if I were a blind puppet to be bandied about from hand to hand, and thrown aside at last if occasion warrant! It destroys my faith in human-kind!

MARG. (*turning very pale and striving to speak firmly*). You wrong me, sir. I am no hypocrite.

PAUL. No hypocrite! Why, did you not stand there and blush, and smile, and speak fair words just now, and do I not know how false your heart is to me all the while? Do you not weep tears of which I never know the cause? Receive gifts (*pointing to the ring upon her finger*) from lovers whose names I never learn? Make evening assignations in the park (*she starts*) with men of whom I have never heard? Hah! you are silent, Margaret: you tremble; you can say nothing!

MARG. (*with effort*). I could say much, but I dare not.

PAUL. What! do you fear me?

MARG. Indeed, no; but—but—Alas! what would I not give now for liberty to speak!

PAUL. Then you confess that there is a secret?

MARG. (*hesitatingly*). Yes, there is a secret

You know there is, monsieur; why do you compel me to say so?

PAUL. And the ring?

MARG. (*bursting into tears and kissing it passionately*). The ring was my mother's — my dear mother's!

PAUL. Can this be true, Margaret? Why not have said that long ago, when I first asked you? How did you get it? How long has it been in your possession? Why ever have made a mystery about it?

MARG. Do not ask me; I can not tell you more; I have said too much already — more than I promised.

PAUL. Tell me, at least, who met you in the park?

MARGARET *looks down and shakes her head.*

PAUL (*trying to speak calmly and conciliatingly*). Listen to me, Margaret. I was in the park that night — in the next walk, and divided from you only by a hedge. I heard you speaking — speaking, I am convinced, of me. You agreed with your lover to deceive me. He called you his — his little Margaret. I heard all this.

MARG. (*anxiously*). No more than this?

PAUL. No more. Alas! you are relieved that I did hear no more! Do not seek to evade me farther; confide in me, Margaret — acknowledge this lover, and I will pardon all. Nay, I will serve you, I will serve him, I will do what a father would do (what your father would have done) to make your happiness. Speak!

MARG. (*weeping*). All that I can say is that I do not deserve your goodness! Only trust me for a little while; do not quite hate me; I am tied by — by a fatal promise, and I can not speak! Only trust me, monsieur — only trust me!

PAUL (*after a brief silence*). Well, I will trust you, Margaret; but beware, beware! Concealment is the cloak of Wrong, and your lover would scarcely impose this task of secrecy upon you save for some deep and doubtful reason. I almost question whether I am fulfilling my duties in thus yielding and trusting to you: it should be my place to sift his character and his motives; but let it be so, Margaret. Your face and voice have again overcome me. Promise me, at least, that you will take no decisive step — that — that you will not hear of marriage without —

MARG. (*smiling through her tears*). Be assured of that, monsieur. I shall certainly not elope with him, or — or marry — without *your* permission. (*Bell rings.*) Hark! that is madame's bell! The class is assembling, and I must go now.

PAUL. Trifler! that smile half reassures me. Must you go?

MARG. Directly, monsieur.

PAUL. *Au revoir*, then, Margaret!

MARG. *Au revoir!* [*Exit different ways.*

CLOSE OF THE SCENE.

CHAPTER XXVI.

THE SHADOWS DARKEN INTO FORM.

I WAS unwilling to go, but I went. The night was glorious — one of those dark, warm September nights, when the sky is thick with stars and there is no moon.

Long before I reached the house (for I should observe that my brother had engaged a furnished mansion for the season), I found the street blocked up by vehicles and bright with carriage-lamps. An awning reached from the door to the curb-stone — there were lights in every window — sounds of music dimly heard from without — passing shadows on the blinds — powdered servants in the hall, and pages in waiting stationed on the stairs announcing names and titles — statues, and figures of armed knights, and vases of rare flowers on the landings — stands of arms and trophies of broad antlers in the hall — vistas of brilliant rooms and galleries opening all around, and thronged with company.

It was the first time that I had crossed the threshold of my brother's house since his removal, and for a moment I stood still, gazing with surprise at the profuse elegance of all around me, and overpowered by that old feeling of nervous embarrassment which has been, through life, one of my most serious annoyances, and which is the usual penalty incurred by the student for the luxury of retirement. It was, however, too late to retreat; my name had already traveled before me, and as I reached the entrance to the first drawing-room, it was announced for the fourth time. At the extremity of the third apartment I found Adrienne, surrounded by a little court, receiving, conversing, resplendent with jewels and beauty, and looking like a queen, so lofty and so fair.

"Welcome, thrice welcome, *mon beau frère*," she said, with her bright smile, as I approached. "Take this seat beside mine, and let us talk together for a while. It is long since we have met, and you look pale to-night. Not ill, I trust? Monsieur de Saint Saturnin, will you favor me by relinquishing this seat in favor of my husband's brother? A thousand thanks. You will pardon me for troubling you?"

Monsieur de Saint Saturnin, a red-faced youth with an embroidered shirt-front and a blue silk waistcoat, bowed, rose with an affectation of immense alacrity, and mingled with the crowd.

I took the vacant seat, and she continued:

"It is really kind of you to come to-night, for I know that you take no pleasure in society. Have you seen Théophile? No? Why, he was here but a moment since, and — Ah! there he stands, almost under the central chandelier. He is conversing with two gentlemen — one, that is, the one in black, is M. d'Ermenonville, professor of Oriental languages to the College Royal of St. Egbert; the other is General Smithson, an American celebrity. This little gentleman with a diamond star upon his breast is a Neapolitan prince; and that handsome man with the long hair, just passing by, is Felicien David, the musician. I must endeavor to amuse you, and tell you who the people are, *mon frère*."

"You are very good, madame."

"Do not call me madame, I entreat of you. Let me be your sister in name as well as in reality. Here we have a Russian grandee and his wife—what a regalia she wears! and that small, quick-featured man with the glasses is Scribe the dramatist. He is leaning on the arm of a man equally famous—perhaps you guess who he is by his complexion and African cast of features—Alexander Dumas. Do you know, *mon frère*, a large assembly such as this reminds me of a menagerie."

"With a remarkable show of lions," I added.

"Ah!" said she, with a half sigh, "is it to be compared with our summer picnic at the Fountain of Roses?"

At this moment there was a universal silence at the farther end of the apartment; a few plaintive notes were heard upon a piano; and the rich, magical tones of a voice that sounded strangely familiar to my ears began the opening movement of an Italian cavatina.

"Hush!" said Adrienne, placing her finger on her lip. "Madame Vogelsang is about to sing."

"Madame Vogelsang, the actress?"

"Yes; we have engaged her for the evening, and Kiallmark as her accompanyist. Oh, listen—how delicious!"

It was odd how the very name and voice of that woman seemed to overshadow and depress me. I fell into a profound reverie, from which I was roused by the murmurs of applause, and by a hand laid suddenly upon my arm. It was Norman Seabrook.

"I have spoken to you twice, Paul," said he, "and have stood before your very face for three or four minutes, paying my respects to madame, and you never observed me. I was not aware that music produced such an effect upon you before. Did she not sing gloriously?"

"I must confess," I replied, smiling, "that I was lost in thought, and heard nothing of it whatever."

Adrienne was at this moment surrounded by her visitors, and busily engaged in conversation. I rose, passed my arm through Seabrook's, and proposed to make the tour of the rooms in search of Théophile, with whom I had not yet spoken.

"Your brother," said he, "has an absolute genius for mustering his forces. He would make a great general. By the way, have you seen that pair of Vanderveldes which he bought the other day, or the silver shield chased by Benvenuto Cellini?"

"Neither."

"Nor the case of fossil zoophytes?"

"No."

"Nor the Cabinet de Lecture?"

"I never even heard of all these things. What do you mean?"

"I mean that Monsieur Théophile possesses what you never will possess—a genius for society. He is desirous of filling his rooms with all available rank and talent, and he takes care to provide that which may render his house agreeable. Here are paintings and articles of *virtù* for the connoisseur; natural curiosities for the learned; books and engravings for those who like them; and the best music, the best society, and the best ices in Brussels for each and for all."

"You amaze me, for Théophile himself is neither connoisseur, bookworm, nor natural philosopher!"

"I did not say that he was; I only observed that he had a rare tact in society. There are people who refine upon this tact till it becomes a science."

At this moment our conversation was interrupted by a tall lady with a long waist, a long neck, and a long nose. She looked like a stork with a turban on, and had a young and somewhat pretty girl upon her arm.

"Ah! Mr. Seabrook," she said, languidly, "is it really you? One finds you every where. Emma, my precious love, you remember Mr. Seabrook?"

The young lady bowed, and her mamma continued.

"I think the occasion of our last meeting was at Cardinal Mezzotinto's, during the Roman Carnival. You went as—as—let me see, as Robinson Crusoe—such an odd costume! Charming *soirée*, this. Quite new people, too. Provincial landowners from the wilds of Burgundy, I am given to understand. Really a well-contrived evening. We came to-night with the Hospodar of Moldavia and his wife. Delightful family. Greek extraction. His highness is the most fascinating creature! So talented! So eccentric! Eats a pound of uncooked steak for his dinner every day, to keep up his stamina. But I am detaining you with my prattle, and you are, perhaps, engaged in conversation with your friend. Addio! My darling angel, wish Mr. Seabrook good-evening!"

"What a terrible woman!" I exclaimed, when we were out of hearing.

"Terrible species, but common," replied Seabrook, laconically. "*Order*—Aristocratic. *Generic character*—Detestable. *Locality*—Unexceptionable. *Habits*—Gregarious. *Family*—The Bores."

"I am glad, at all events," I said, laughing, "to find that the species is not dangerous."

"Not dangerous, my dear fellow! On the contrary, it belongs to a genus of the most unparalleled ferocity, especially when providing for its young. The *heir*, indeed, is its natural prey. Stay, here is a man I know, who fancies himself a poet of the highest order. Quite a character. He once held a capital situation in the Foreign Office, but found it too prosaic for what he calls his 'wild poetic nature,' and so relinquished it. I fear that his circumstances are wretched now, poor fellow! How are you, Mr. **Staines**! Been long in Brussels?"

"Scarce three sad, sultry days, my worthy friend," replied the poet, who wore blue glasses and long hair, and who, as I presently discovered, spoke always in blank verse.

"Rather a brilliant party here, is it not?" asked Seabrook, with an air of determined commonplace cheerfulness.

"These glitt'ring halls are lit for me in vain," rejoined the other, misanthropically. "To ears in love with cataract and storm; to eyes that gaze unshrinkingly on fate; to souls uplifted o'er the flat inane, cleaving the realms of thought and poet-lore, all revelry is stale—all music harsh!"

"Just so, just so," said my companion, smiling. "I see that we are of the same opinion. A glass of brandy and water, and a good cigar at a friend's fireside, is worth all this sort of display. Exactly my own idea, Staines. *Au revoir!*"

The poet looked after us with a lofty pity that was utterly ludicrous; and we made our way, as well as we could, through the crowd, which was momentarily increasing, toward the reading-room, or, as Théophile had chosen to designate it, the Cabinet de Lecture.

It was a pretty little Gothic room, lined with book-shelves, and furnished with costly volumes, but was, if possible, even more crowded than the larger apartments. The heat, too, was intolerable.

"*Diable!*" exclaimed Seabrook, "we shall die here if we remain long, *amico mio!* Suppose we go and have a peep at the conservatory. I have not yet seen it, and your brother told me yesterday that the fittings, flowers, and tropical plants had cost a little fortune. *Allons!*"

This was more easily said than done. The Cabinet de Lecture was situated at the extremity of the fourth and last reception-room, and the conservatory at the end of the entrance-hall down stairs. We had consequently to thread our way back throughout the entire suite, and, as the apartments were now quite filled, the task was by no means one of great facility. It gave us, however, a better opportunity of observing the general features of the entertainment.

Many of the guests were English, but the greater number belonged to the Continental nations. Now we pass a knot of Parisian wits and dramatists—now a group of artists discussing the merits of the Vanderveldes—now a clique of politicians occupied with the last new ministry. Here the swarthy features of an Ottoman dignitary, surmounted by the scarlet fez, contrast with the delicate beauty of some reigning belle, who glides along with her train of slaves around her. There we see a handsome and popular ecclesiastic discoursing honeyed righteousness to a circle of admiring ladies. Now and then we light upon some tender couple whispering together in the embrasure of a curtained window, and every where we are amused by the scraps of conversation that meet our ear in passing.

"A terrible state of affairs, I assure you. The quotation of gold is lower than it has been in the memory of any man living—population increases—the value of labor diminishes—our commerce is on the decline—our coasts unprotected—our navy and army almost disorganized—in short, sir, the country is going to ruin, and I see no hope for the government or the people unless the military are immediately re-enforced and—"

"Stewed down with port wine and sugar. It is the finest thing in the world. I have tried it myself for the last four years, and find it an unfailing remedy."

"And did you really come on purpose to see me, Charles?"

"You, and you only, my angel! You know that I live but in your smiles, and that your glance alone has power to reduce me to—"

"A heavy oily liquid, obtained from a double sulpho-carbonate of ethyle and potash, acted upon by diluted sulphuric or hydrochloric acid. Indeed, a most interesting experiment."

"Possibly so; but I acknowledge that the present cabinet inspires me with little confidence. Russell is too indolent for the duties of Premier, and Palmerston—"

"Has the loveliest legs and ankles you ever beheld! They skim along the stage, my boy, like—like—"

"The *Ficus Indica*, or banyan-tree, abounding chiefly in the vicinity of the Circar Mountains. It covers with its trunks a sufficient space to shelter a regiment of cavalry, and looks, when one is in the midst of it, like a thick grove or wood. You find the best account in Rumf's 'Herbarium Amboinense.'"

Through this Babel we gradually worked our way, exchanging a gesture of recognition with Adrienne as we passed by, and receiving an elaborate salutation from Polydore Emmanuel Hippolyte, Marquis de Courtrai, whose appearance did honor to the consummate skill of his valet, his tailor, his jeweler, and his wig-maker. He formed one of a phalanx of contemporary exquisites as boyish and fascinating as himself, all of whom were so resplendent with crosses, cordons, and stars as to elicit from Seabrook a doubt as to whether the Milky Way had not unexpectedly dropped in.

At length we reached the stairs (up which the fresh arrivals were still pouring, although it was now within half an hour of midnight), and in a few moments more were threading the cool dark passage leading from the entrance-hall to the conservatories. This passage was quite deserted; the hum and movement of the world beyond became hushed, and involuntarily we dropped our voices to a whisper. Then we passed through a doorway of painted glass that opened without a sound, and entered the warm and heavy atmosphere respired by the cactus and the palm. The roof was garlanded with creeping plants, whose large pendulous blossoms, like fairy pavilions, white, amber, and lilac, hung low above our heads. Fragrant magnolias, orange-trees with their round yellow fruits, delicate orchids, and all rare exotic plants, were marshaled on every side. Deep tanks of tepid water, gleaming with gold and silver fish, and supporting the languid leaves and flowers of strange aquatic vegetation, were sunk at either extremity; and marble statues of stern and rigid beauty, holding amethyst-hued lamps in their cold grasp, stood here and there, lighting the silent scene with a subdued and uncertain lustre. High and fantastic, like the grand, shadowy superstitions of an Orient clime, rose in the midst the luxuriant native of the tropics—the bamboo; the bread-tree, with its dark shining leaves and amber fruit; the sandal-wood-tree; the gigantic rhododendron, laden with white blossoms; the slender sugar-cane; the lofty cocoa-tree; the graceful palm; the royal cactus.

All was silent, strange, oppressive. Our very footsteps gave no echo on the soft matting where they rested.

Quite silently we passed from end to end, indulging our own thoughts. Then we reached the curtained arch that led to the next division of the conservatories. It had always been Théophile's taste, as well as mine, to substitute draperies for doors wherever it might be practicable. I did it in my own rooms at home, and here it seemed more than ever Eastern and appropriate.

I looked at my friend, as if asking silently whether he would go on. He nodded. My hand was already on the damask folds, when I drew back suddenly.

"Hush!" I said, in a low whisper. "I hear voices within!"

He smiled. "Some lovers, perhaps," he returned, in the same tone. "Let us go back. It would be a pity to interrupt them!"

And he passed his arm through mine. But there was some fascination in the faint tones which I had heard—some indefinable fascination, which ran through me like an electric touch, and chained my feet to the spot.

"Come away," said Seabrook, impatiently, "or I go without you. I have no wish to play the eavesdropper."

"Go, then," I rejoined, hoarsely. "Go. I must remain here."

"What is the matter? Are you ill?"

"Listen!"

The voices were dulled by the heavy damask intervening, yet not so dulled but that the words came through distinctly.

"All men are flatterers, and I believe none of them—not even you, monsieur, despite that imploring look! Have you not a wife whom you adore?"

"If I have a wife, it does not follow that I adore her! We men marry for wealth and position, but we reserve our hearts for beauty. Your logic is not sound, charming Thérèse!"

"Madame is beautiful. What woman could be more so?"

"Yourself! Nay, I swear by those glorious eyes that you are a million times more lovely

E

than the fair, soulless doll whom I call wife! Compare yourself with her, Siren, and confess that it is so!"

"I will confess nothing."

"—Except that you love me!"

"Vain man!"

"Not vain, for I deserve all that you can give in return for my devotion. Am I not your slave—literally your slave? Is there any thing which you could ask and I refuse? Is it not my pride to deck you with jewels that a queen might envy—with shawls that a caliph would not disdain? Is not my wealth, my heart, my life at your disposal?"

"And you really love me?"

"I never loved till now!"

"Then I suppose I must believe you. But I have not yet thanked you for the gift you sent me yesterday. It was so splendid, and chosen with such exquisite taste! I do not know that I have ever seen a vehicle so elegant."

"I hope to see you drive past my house in it; it will then look ten times more elegant."

"Not with my horses! They are too large for such a fairy chariot. How exquisitely a pair of cream-colored ponies would become it!"

"You shall have them to-morrow."

"No, no. I will not suffer you to—"

"I shall send them to you, and you will accept them. Promise me that you will accept them!"

"I can refuse you nothing!"

"Loveliest, queenliest of women! Say that word once again—just once! Oh, Thérèse! Thérèse! thy beauty intoxicates me!"

My hand was on the curtain, but Seabrook grasped me by the wrist and forcibly detained me.

"Let me go," I said, in a voice that trembled with deep passion. "Let me go!"

"Madman! what would you do?"

"Confront them!"

"To what end? To make an enemy of your brother—to exclude yourself from his house—to place an insuperable barrier between yourself and every means of useful action that intimacy and observation might afford you? Desist. You know not yet what you may be enabled to do. The first person to be remembered is his wife. She must not know this."

"Poor Adrienne!"

"Come away, come away! We can best serve her by remaining calm and keeping our heads clear. Come away from this place!"

The recollection of Adrienne had subdued me, and I submitted like a child to the influence of his graver and more temperate judgment. The fresher air of the outer passage seemed to cool the fever in my blood. We passed hastily through the crowded hall, past the long lines of carriages; and out into the quiet streets where not a footstep echoed on the lonely pavement, and where the innocent stars were still shining out of the depths of upper sky

"Like sweet thoughts in a dream."

This, then, was the secret of that long aversion, hitherto so inexplicable to myself—that aversion dating from the first moment that I had seen her upon the stage at Frankfurt—which I had felt so strong within me when I encountered her on the railway as I returned from Antwerp—which had affected me so powerfully but a few nights since in the Opera House of Brussels! Mysterious promptings of the heart—inexplicable repulsions and affinities, who shall presume to deny or to define them?

Oh, my brother, my brother, that thou shouldst do such evil!

Absorbed in these thoughts, and wholly occupied by my own distress of mind, I had taken no heed of external circumstances, and I started when Seabrook pressed my arm suddenly, and, pointing to a shadowy form gliding along by the houses at the opposite side of the street, said, in a quick whisper,

"Do you see that man yonder? He has dogged our steps ever since we left your brother's house."

"Pshaw! you fancy it. What could be his motive? We are two to one."

"I know nothing but the fact. See! if he approaches a lamp, how he turns aside to avoid the light!"

My curiosity became roused. We quickened our steps—we loitered—we made unnecessary detours. Still his pace altered with ours, and followed us wherever we went. We were watched, beyond the shadow of a doubt.

Suddenly we changed our tactics, faced round, and stood still. The spy stood still likewise.

Seabrook laughed and rubbed his hands gleefully. The affair, in his eyes, had already assumed the character of an adventure.

"Let us turn the tables," he whispered, "and follow him!"

We accordingly advanced rapidly toward our pursuer. Seen dimly in the angle where he stood, he seemed to pause irresolutely for a moment—even to take one forward step, as if with the intention of meeting us—then turned and walked very swiftly down the street.

It was our place to follow now, and this we did with so much determination, that the walk merged presently into a run, and away we went through the dark, silent thoroughfare, pursuers and pursued, as fast as our flying feet would carry us.

Up one street, down another, across the market-place, in and out a labyrinth of narrow winding alleys and crooked passages—it was evident that he knew the intricacies of the old town by heart. Presently my breath began to fail, and my head to grow giddy. I staggered—I stopped suddenly—I could go no farther.

"Keep on, Seabrook," I gasped, leaning back heavily in the shelter of a doorway. "Keep on. I will wait here for you."

Agile and unwearied as a greyhound, he sprang forward even more rapidly than before. In a few moments, however, he returned reluctantly and slowly. The brief delay occasioned by my stoppage had favored the escape of the spy. When Seabrook turned the corner he was already out of sight, and beyond this point several streets and courts branched off, amid which it would have been useless to pursue the search.

The game, for once, had outsped the huntsmen, and we were left to find our way back to the upper town as best we might, wearied out with the chase, and marveling together over the events of the evening.

CHAPTER XXVII.

"THE ROAD TO RUIN."

"How, Théophile! and thus early?"

"Myself. Hardly hoped to find you awake, mon frère. Have not been to bed all night myself. Not worth while, you will say, when I tell you that I was out till past three o'clock this morning. Society is a Maelstrom. Once in, you can never get out of it, and are whirled on faster and faster, till—"

"Till it swallows you up altogether!"

"Very true—very true. But I am not yet ingulfed. By the way, you left us very early, Paul, the night of our soirée."

"Yes, I left early, and without having spoken to you once. How did you leave madame?"

"I really do not know. She was asleep when I left home."

"You have come to breakfast with me, Théophile?"

"No, thank you. I have no appetite this morning. The fact is, I—I came to ask you if you had another five thousand which you don't particularly want just now. My remittances will arrive to-morrow or next day, when you shall be repaid instantly."

All this was spoken rapidly and nervously; and I observed that he stood before the glass arranging his cravat, and avoiding my eyes as much as possible.

"Another five thousand!" I echoed, pushing back my chair, and fixing a searching glance upon his face. "Another five thousand! What can you want with such large and frequent sums?"

"I want nothing, my dear fellow," he returned, with a forced laugh. "The affair concerns my tradesmen! I have bought largely, pictures, statues, plants—"

"For the conservatory," I interrupted.

"Just so—for the conservatory," he continued, with the slightest possible shade of embarrassment in his tone. "And the soirée was an immense expense. Besides, there have been ornaments for my wife, horses, carriages, hotel bills. Really, I dread to think of what we have spent already!"

"It must cost you a great deal for horses, carriages, and jewelry," I remarked, dryly.

Théophile flushed crimson up to the roots of his hair, and looked at me very earnestly. Seeing, however, that I maintained a perfect composure, he drew a long breath and resumed, though with a more constrained and anxious manner than before,

"Yes, we find the 'season' costs money; but we are rich, *mon frère*, and we may as well use our wealth in moderation. But, to return to my first question—have you the five thousand francs to spare me this morning? I could ask Adrienne, for no doubt she has as much by her; but one doesn't like to borrow from one's wife."

"Why not? You but need to tell her how much you require, and for what you require it, and she loves you so much that I am sure that she would give it on the instant."

"Ah! yes—of course; but women do not understand these things; and— But, if you do not wish to oblige me, I have no wish to press you. I should have thought my credit good with my own brother."

"It is not that, Théophile," I replied, very calmly. "You should be welcome to the money if I had it; but I assure you I have not more than, if so much as, half that sum in my desk."

He colored up again, but this time it was with disappointment.

"You shall have two thousand francs, if they be of any use to you," I said, after a few minutes' pause, during which he had been pacing to and fro between the table and the window. "Surely that will suffice till you receive money."

"Thank you," he replied, somewhat stiffly. "I accept your kindness; and I hope to return all that I owe you before the week is out."

"You need not be so proud about it, Théophile. I would come to you if I wanted money to-morrow, and not deem myself under so very heavy an obligation when you had lent it. How proceed the repairs at Hauteville?"

My brother blushed again. It was strange how often he blushed this morning; but then, as a boy, his handsome, ingenuous face had always betrayed every transient emotion that flitted through his mind.

"Hauteville? Oh, tolerably, I believe. That is, I—I do not think they are doing much at present. Burgundy is a dull place."

"You did not think so when you first purchased the estate."

"True; but—but Adrienne has seen more of the world since then, and cares less for retirement. I may not keep Hauteville, after all."

"You amaze me! And our mother—?"

"Would, perhaps, be a little disappointed; but then she would soon be reconciled to the change. Besides, although I have talked of it, we may not give it up, you know."

"I earnestly hope not, Théophile," I replied, gravely. "You are our mother's darling, and you hold much of her happiness in your power. Going already? Stay, you must not forget your money. Here are the notes."

He crushed the papers into his pocket-book, wished me a hasty good-day, and protesting vehemently against the trouble I took in seeing him to the door, sprang into his carriage and drove away.

Returning slowly and sadly to my room, I find a paper lying near the door—a little open note, on which a few words are written in a delicate female hand. So few are they, that, as I lift it from the ground, I read them at a glance —indeed, almost before I am aware of it.

"Why have you not been to-day, *mon chéri*? I have expected you since noon, and it is now past midnight. Meet me in the *foyer* at eleven o'clock to-morrow evening, and return with me to sup. I can not ask you sooner, for we have a rehearsal during the day. Bring me some money; my *modiste* wearies me with importunities. Ever thy THÉRÈSE."

The letter bore the date of the previous day.

There were two entrances to the *foyer*—the one leading from the public part of the theatre, the other opening into the street. Through this outer door (which, properly speaking, should be called the stage entrance) the actors, musicians, officials, and certain privileged *habitués* passed to their various destinations behind the scenes; and hither, accordingly, I repaired about twenty minutes before the time appointed, for I judged that it was by this door my brother would come to the place of meeting.

It was a little side entrance opening into a dull back street, and lighted by a powerful jet of gas. Just within the threshold I saw a young man sitting sleeping at a desk, with some papers and the fragments of a frugal supper lying before him. Hence a second door, which was occasionally opened by passers to and fro, revealed glimpses of a whitewashed, dreary-looking bricked passage, also lighted by gas, and offering but few temptations as a means of transit.

Outside this place I paced slowly and methodically until he should arrive, only pausing at times to listen anxiously to the sound of distant wheels, or loitering now and then to glance at the clock above the head of the sleeper at the desk.

Watching and waiting—watching and waiting—what a weary task it was, and how every minute seemed the length of ten!

Yet I was not quite alone in my promenade, for on the opposite side of the street, sometimes pacing backward and forward, sometimes pausing and leaning against the wall, I saw a second loiterer. There were no gas-lamps in the street, and the night was so intensely dark that I could distinguish nothing clearly; but his appearance seemed that of a man in the middle station of life—perhaps even a grade poorer. He was waiting, most likely, for his wife or sister—some ill-paid *coryphée* or chorus-singer. A wretched life! Somehow, despite my own cares and all that I had to make me anxious, my thoughts, having been once diverted into this channel, continued to flow there, and I found myself inventing a sequence of contingent probabilities—picturing his home, his children, the meagre furniture, the scanty meal to which they returned at night after the glare and weariness of the evening's performance. Thinking thus, I forgot the presence of the very man of whom I was thinking, and was only recalled to my original purpose by the sudden driving up and stoppage of a hackney-carriage at the stage door.

I sprang to the spot; a gentleman leaped out of the vehicle, and in an instant Théophile and I were face to face.

"Stay, my brother, stay! I know all—I found the letter—I am here to try and save you! Remember your wife—remember Adrienne!"

The light from the open doorway fell full upon his face. He stood quite still—his color came and went—his lips quivered—his whole attitude and countenance expressed the struggle of many feelings.

"You are ruining yourself, Théophile! I have known something of this for several days, but I abstained from speaking until now. Oh, that I may not be too late!"

Still silent—still down-looking—still red and pale alternately.

"Not only for your fortune, but for your reputation, your happiness, your peace of mind, which are all in danger, I implore you to reflect!"

"I but act as others act," he said, in a suppressed tone. "Why should it be a greater crime in me than in them?"

An elegant close-carriage, with blazing lamps and prancing horses, drove up as he was speaking, and stopped before the door. The man at the desk woke up suddenly; the second door leading to the brick passage was flung open; a cry of "Madame Vogelsang's carriage!" was repeated by many voices, and several persons came hastening out, surrounding and escorting a lady whose features were almost concealed beneath the hood of a velvet opera-cloak, and who was leaning upon the arm of a repulsive-looking man with a profusion of red whiskers and mustaches.

A flash of anger passed over Théophile's features at this sight, and he took a forward step. I caught him by the arm.

"Stay! It is a madness!" I cried. "You know not what you do!"

"It is a madness," he rejoined, furiously, as he shook off my grasp like a roused lion. "It is a madness and my fate. Let me go!"

In another moment he had saluted her, and, bestowing a haughty stare upon the red-whiskered escort, had offered his arm, handed her into the carriage, stepped in after her, and driven rapidly away.

As for me, I stood like a statue—frozen and motionless. Then my eyes fell upon the gentleman whose services had been superseded, and who yet remained standing upon the pavement where she had left him. His countenance was contracted into an expression of malignity and baffled shame, and his head was yet turned in the direction by which the carriage had disappeared. Presently the features relaxed—a sneering smile writhed on his lips—he ran his jeweled fingers lightly through his hair, and sauntered into the office, whistling softly. Then the clerk resumed his seat at the desk; the other loiterers, with the other gentlemen, retired back whence they came, and in a few seconds all was silent and empty as before.

A strange feeling of curiosity came over me—a feeling that I must learn the name of this man whose presence inspired Théophile with such open discourtesy and anger. I stepped forward, entered the room, and civilly asked the question.

The clerk smiled and looked surprised.

"His name is Lemaire—Monsieur Alphonse Lemaire."

"And his station?"

"He is the manager of this theatre."

I thanked him and turned toward the door. There was a pale face peering eagerly in and suddenly withdrawn—a pale face that gave me a sudden shock for which I was unable to account, and which for a moment struck me with a sensation like that of fear, as if I had seen a wraith—or, rather, as if I had beheld it before under some strange and terrible circumstances that I could not remember. Perhaps in a bad dream—who could tell?

During a few seconds I stood still, with my eyes fixed upon the door, expecting every instant to see it return. Suddenly a suspicion flashed upon me. I thought of the loiterer upon the opposite footway—of the spy of a few nights since! It was plain that I was watched, and constantly. I uttered a hasty exclamation, flew to the door, and gazed eagerly up and down the street.

The man whom I sought was no longer keeping watch on the other side. He had crossed over, and was waiting in the shadow close against the wall, some few yards from the spot where I stood.

CHAPTER XXVIII.

THE ARROW IS FITTED TO THE BOW.

He made no attempt to elude me this time, but, to my surprise, stepped forward to meet me, and was the first to speak.

"I beg your pardon, sir," he said, quietly, touching his hat the while, "but might I ask the favor of a few minutes' conversation with you?"

"I was about to make the same request. Pray speak."

"You will allow me to put a few questions to you, sir?"

"Yes, on condition that I may afterward use the same privilege."

"Agreed."

We had been standing, half defyingly, face to face, but upon the conclusion of this brief treaty we involuntarily dropped side by side, and commenced walking leisurely to and fro in the shadow of the silent street. It was so dark

that I could not see his features very distinctly,
but they looked commonplace enough, and I
could distinguish nothing of the expression and
character that had struck me so forcibly only a
few moments since.

He recommenced.

"In the first place, then, were you not present at a *soirée* given in the Rue ——— on the 15th
evening of the present month?"

"I was."

"Are you acquainted with the giver of that
soirée?"

"Yes."

"Was that he with whom you were speaking
to-night, just as Madame Vogelsang was coming
out?"

"Why do you ask me these questions?"

"That is my business. Answer them, and I
will answer yours. Such was our bargain."

"I will not answer the last till I know your
motive for inquiring."

"Very well; then I will pass on to another."

There was something brief and matter-of-fact
in his manner that did not altogether displease
me, but I felt disposed to be equally brief and
decisive with him. Every now and again I
strove to see his face more plainly, and sought,
by turning suddenly at times, to catch any return of the expression seen at first, but in vain.
I observed, too, although he spoke with perfect
fluency and propriety, that his pronunciation was
slightly grating and peculiar, as if bearing traces
of a foreign origin.

He went on.

"You are aware that Madame Vogelsang
was present at that *soirée*, on the 15th?"

"Yes—I heard her sing."

"Did it appear to you that there was any
thing remarkable in her conduct that evening?"

"You must speak more clearly. I do not
understand what you mean by 'any thing remarkable.'"

"To be plain, then, any thing light—any
thing wanton?"

After a momentary hesitation, I replied in
the affirmative.

"Will you have the goodness to relate the
circumstances to me?"

"Certainly not."

"You are afraid of implicating yourself?"

This was spoken somewhat harshly and satirically; but I took no notice of it, and replied
more calmly than ever.

"For myself, I fear nothing; but I have neither the right nor the inclination to betray the
errors of others."

"Good; I perceive that you are cautious.
One more question, however: Was this conduct
(which you admit to have observed) open and
unconcealed—visible to all eyes, or only to your
own?"

"I believe it to be known only to myself and
to a friend who happened to be with me at the
time."

"The same with whom you left the house
that night?"

"—When you followed us? Yes."

"True; when I followed you, and you hunted me. But let that pass; I want to know all
that you saw."

"I have already refused to tell it to you."

"At least tell me who this *preux chevalier*
may be upon whom the chaste Thérèse bestows
her favors, 'secret, sweet, and stolen!' Is it not
he with whom you were speaking by yonder
door some ten or twenty minutes since?"

There was something more than harshness,
brevity, or satire in the voice now. There was
a deep inner vibration, as if of some vital string.
I was startled. Might I not already have said
too much? Might I not be on the brink of betraying Théophile to a deadly foe? Suppose
that this man were a— I shuddered.

"I will reply to no more of your questions,"
I said, hurriedly. "I am sorry that I have answered any. Who and what are you? By
what right do you hang upon my footsteps?
Why do you waylay, and spy, and follow after
me? You were watching me the other night—
you watched me to-night. What is your purpose? How do I or my movements concern
you? Are you a *mouchard?*"

The word *mouchard*, so offensive in a Frenchman's ears, seemed neither to sting nor annoy
him. Indeed, I almost doubt whether he even
observed it, for he still sauntered on beside me
in the same unmoved, meditative manner, with
his head a little bent and his eyes fixed on the
ground. He never once looked up as I uttered
this passionate rush of words, and was silent for
several minutes after I had ceased speaking.

At length he replied, yet so musingly that it
seemed less a reply than an answering to his
own thoughts.

"I expected this," he said. "It is natural
that you should feel angry and suspicious. I
was not such a fool as to think you would be
cross-questioned in this fashion. I only did it
to try you."

"To try me?"

"Ay. Suppose now that I knew, if not all,
at least the greater part of the information I
have been asking from you—what then?"

"What then? Why, you are content, I suppose, and can have no farther occasion for interrogating me," I replied, stiffly; for I saw in this
supposition only a trap for the disclosure of all
that I had refused to tell.

"Not so; I still require your aid and confidence. Suppose now—for the sake of argument—that I know precisely in what position
you stand to the giver of that *soirée?*"

I started and was silent. My companion
gave a short dry chuckle, as if enjoying my
perplexity, and went on:

"Suppose I know that you and he are brothers—that you are both from Burgundy—that he
is lately married?"

"Supposing that you do," I retorted, impatiently, "you are no wiser than half the tradespeople and visitors in Brussels. It is no more
than you might have learnt from servants with

less than half the trouble you have taken to watch me!"

"Precisely so," he replied, in the same tone of quiet self-possession and authority; "precisely so. It is just what I *have* learnt from servants and tradesmen, and it was not to ascertain those facts at all that I have taken upon myself the office of your shadow. What I require from you is your confidence and co-operation, and a detailed account of all that you know respecting the *liaison* between your brother and Madame Vogelsang the singer. This I have determined to obtain. I have waited and watched for an opportunity of speaking alone with you. The other night you were, as you just stated, in the company of a friend. I followed you in the hope that you would part with him somewhere, and end your walk alone; on the contrary, you both turned round and pursued me. Of course I ran for it. What I had to say was for you alone, and I did not choose to be questioned. To-night every thing has happened well. I have even seen your meeting with your brother — heard your expostulations — seen him drive away with her side by side — in short, gained ample confirmation of my suspicions and the current rumor. Still I have occasion for you. There has been much done with which I am unacquainted, and which you must tell me. There is much to be done wherein you must assist me. You see that it is my wish to be frank with you. Be the same with me.

Frank indeed! Despite the anxiety with which this strange dialogue inspired me, I could scarcely forbear a smile at these words. A peculiar sort of frankness, where he preserved the strictest incognito himself, and exacted the fullest confidence from me!

Finding that I replied not, he spoke again.

"Tell me all that you noted between them on the night of the *soirée*."

"Between whom?"

"Your brother and the singer."

"I never said that there was a *liaison* between them. What right have you to suppose it is he? You know that he is married — married to a woman whom he loves."

"Of course you say so at first; but you forget what I saw and heard in this very street to-night."

I was dumb.

"Besides which," he continued, "I have watched her, too, and I have watched her house. I have seen him go in and out at strange hours — I have marked the increasing splendor in which she lives — I have seen the chariot and the cream-colored ponies which he sent to her, and I know from whom they were purchased. More than this, I know that he is plunging blindly into ruin, and that he is already in debt and in difficulties. With all these things I am more fully acquainted than yourself."

There was, to me, something almost appalling in this man's cool, dispassionate *resumé* of all that touched me most nearly. I recoiled from his narrative of patient, business-like espial, which, like a dissecting-knife, laid open the anatomy of that infected spot which I would have given half my fortune to keep secret!

Tortured by an anxiety which had become almost desperate, I suddenly stood quite still, seized him forcibly by the arm, and, stooping down to the level of his face, for he was somewhat shorter than myself, said fiercely,

"Who and what are you? Speak, or, by the fiend, I shall do you some mischief!"

He first made an attempt to disengage himself from my grasp, and then, finding the effort useless, looked up at me composedly and said,

"What am I? Why, a man like yourself, to be sure."

"Why do you pry after my brother, and what are his courses to you? Who are you?"

"Let me go first, and I will tell you."

"No, by heaven, you shall not escape me this time! Till you speak you are my prisoner."

"Just as you please. I do not open my lips again till I am free."

He was perfectly calm and undismayed as he said this, and, looking steadily forward at the angle of a building close at hand, seemed utterly unconscious of my presence, my threats, or my hold upon his arms. For several minutes we stood thus. Talus himself could not have been more impassible. I might as well have tried to intimidate the brazen figure on the belfry of the Hotel de Ville. I saw that it was vain for us to stand here like two statues, so I released him sullenly, and waited for his explanation.

He laughed again—the same dry chuckle as before. At the farthest extremity of the street, where it opened into the broad thoroughfare leading to the front of the theatre, there stood a solitary lamp. To this he pointed, and beneath it he stopped.

"Look at me," said he, removing his hat and smiling grimly. "Look at me well. Now, who do you suppose I am?"

His face was pale, and, though it gave me the impression of belonging to a younger man than I had previously supposed, was deeply furrowed around the mouth and eyes. The forehead was knotted, care-lined, somewhat contracted at the temples, and prominent over the eyes; his hair was thick, and sprinkled prematurely with gray. He wore neither beard nor mustache, and stooped in the shoulders like an aged man. At the utmost, as I guessed, he could not be much past thirty, and yet his aspect was withered, neglected, trouble-worn.

I looked at him with a painful interest. There was something in the face which I almost pitied —something not wholly strange to me, as it seemed. Where had I seen that singular expression before? I could not solve it; I sighed —I shook my head.

"I can not imagine who you are," I replied, "but I seem to have seen you before — somewhere—some time long ago—in a dream."

"No, you haven't," he said, shortly, replacing

his hat and leaning back against the lamp-post. "I've seen and watched you these several days past, but we have never been face to face with each other before this minute."

There was another brief pause. He seemed reluctant to speak, and drew his breath quickly once or twice, as if in the effort to say something which it annoyed him to reveal. Then, turning suddenly toward me and looking up, as if to mark the effect of his words upon my countenance, he said,

"*I am the husband of Madame Vogelsang.*"

Had a thunderbolt fallen at my feet, I could scarcely have been more dismayed. I staggered back a step, and stared at him blankly. The husband of Madame Vogelsang! And Théophile? A confused dread of vengeance—exposure—shame, swept over me, and paralyzed my very powers of speech and breathing.

He looked at me for some time in silence; then, with a somewhat gentler mien, "Well," he said, "does that surprise you? Have you nothing to say? Why, who else should I be, to take so much trouble about the matter?"

"And you are the Herr Vogelsang?"

"Eh? ah! yes—I am the Herr Vogelsang. It is an honorable title to bear, is it not? Don't you envy me my wife—my charming, chaste, devoted Thérèse?"

Again the deep, bitter, vibrating tone that had struck me so before. It made me cold at heart to hear it now.

"Alas! Théophile!" I exclaimed, involuntarily.

He turned sharply and looked at me again.

"I mean no harm to him," he said, harshly and quickly. "I should not have spoken to you, or told you what I have, if that were my intention. I know the character of that woman too thoroughly to need any explanation of how the affair began. She entangled him—seduced him—preys upon him now, like a beautiful vampire. He is not to blame. I wish to save him, if it can be done."

I could scarcely believe my ears for wonder and joy at hearing this. An inexpressible sense of relief came over me, and I breathed again more freely. My countenance must have expressed something of this, for my companion's voice assumed a less austere accent, and his communications became more unreserved.

"I married her," said he, gloomily, "when I was little more than a boy. Her father had been my father's oldest friend, and although she was a year or two my senior, the match had been agreed upon from our childhood upward. I never cared for her; but the thing seemed so certain, so inevitable, and I had heard it discussed for so many years, that I never thought to oppose it, even in a dream. Every year she grew more beautiful, yet every year I conceived a greater distaste for her. I told my father this, and he entreated me, with tears, to banish such feelings and ideas forever from my mind. His oldest friend, and her father, he said, had been consoled on his death-bed by the prospect of this union. The old promises had been renewed in that solemn moment. It was as a favor, nay, as a right, that he demanded from me the fulfillment of an engagement entered upon in my name while I was yet an infant. I loved my father. I yielded. I married her. From that day I date the degradation of my judgment—the abnegation of my manhood's royalty. We were poor, and she was a public singer—an actress—a faithless wife—a—well, no matter—we have been parted many years. She, beautiful and infamous, revels in luxury and applause. I, laden with dishonor, poor, comfortless, and unhappy, lead a wretched, wandering, aimless, homeless life, without a hope for the future or a regret for the past."

There was an inexpressible melancholy in the tone in which this was said—a tone so sad and so subdued that I was tempted to hazard a few words of sympathy and consolation.

He laughed—a bitter, sardonic laugh—and shook his head haughtily.

"I want no pity," he said. "All I seek is justice, and justice I will have. How pleasant it is when justice and vengeance are one!"

"Vengeance!" I repeated.

"Yes, vengeance. Now listen to me. When my wife (how well it sounds—my wife!) first fled from my roof, she robbed me—robbed me not only of money and jewels, but of the title-deeds of a small property to which I had succeeded in establishing some claim after a protracted litigation. This was about two months before the last and final hearing of my cause in the law-courts of Vienna. No one knew whither she had fled with her paramour; every search was useless, and my cause was lost for want of the necessary documents. For years I never heard even the echo of her name. She was as completely lost to the world as if the ground had opened beneath her feet and ingulfed her. About six months since she emerged from her seclusion, and reappeared upon the Viennese stage. I was in England at the time, and knew nothing of it. She created a *furore*—went from Vienna to Munich—from Munich to Berlin—Dresden—Frankfort. I heard it all by the merest chance. I traveled from England to Vienna with the speed of an avenger. I found no difficulty in proving her identity, for there were many there who had seen and known her both then and now. My first step was to lodge an accusation against her for the abstraction of papers and other valuables; my next to follow her from place to place (always finding myself, by some luckless chance, a day, or, perhaps, only a few hours, too late), and at last to discover her here, in this town of Brussels, in my power—in my power, whenever I choose to exercise it!"

"How can she be in your power, even now?"

"I do not speak without reason, sir," said he, impatiently. Then, as if correcting himself, "I have that with me which, once produced, will compel her to leave this place and return forthwith to Vienna—an injunction from the government—an injunction which she, as an Austrian subject, can not choose but obey—which can call her from the stage before the eyes of the audience, if I so please; and for the enforcement of which, if she resist it, I can claim the aid of the Belgian authorities. Now do you comprehend me? Now do you see how I can aid you, and save your brother from utter ruin?"

I held out my hand to him in the impulse of my gratitude; but he appeared not to notice it, and I allowed it to drop unheeded by my side.

"Still I can not understand why you should have sought me, or have cared to interfere between my brother and this woman," I said, inquiringly.

He looked down and bit his lip.

"The question is natural," he said, at length. "But I scarcely like to answer it. The confession is an ugly one. Yet it must out. I hated her," he continued, very swiftly and passionately, "before I married her. But, once wed, once surrounded by the hourly fascinations of her presence, once master of all her loveliness, I—I was fool enough to—"

"To love her!" I exclaimed.

"Ay," he muttered, sullenly, changing at once from the excited tone in which he had just spoken, "ay—to love her! Curses on me that I should have ever loved a thing so vile! Curses on me that I should love her still, and take a dainty vengeance in wresting her from her handsome lover—her handsome lover with the white hands and the curling hair! Pshaw! this is sheer folly. But my plan and my motive—yes, this is what you seek to know; that is why I have sought you, confided in you, plagued you with this dull story. Listen. My vengeance would be no vengeance if it did not part them utterly. I could not accomplish this without your aid, and to do it is your interest as well as mine. Do you understand me?"

"Not quite. I know what you mean, but I do not see how we can prevent the continuation of their intercourse. I fear that he would follow her. He is mad. He confessed to me to-night that it was his 'fate.'"

"Precisely. Then all that we have to do is to strike the blow suddenly; to keep him in ignorance till it is over, and never to let him know what has become of her."

"Impossible! He sees her daily."

"To contrive his absence for a day, or even two days, must be your share of the scheme. I will undertake to achieve the rest. On his return he shall find her gone. The manager must be bought—the officials must be bought; complete secrecy—secrecy at any price, must be secured. To judge from that manager's face to-night, I should say that it would not be difficult to enlist him in our service."

"I see it all. Nothing could be better. When shall it be done? Let us lose no time."

I was excited, flushed, and spoke rapidly.

"No, no," said he, quietly, "not yet. Let us wait a while, till we have matured our scheme together, and laid the train surely. Besides, I would rather your mind were familiarized with it, and your nerves steadied to the task first. One false step would lose all."

"But, in the mean time, this thing is going on. Théophile is being ruined, and your wife—"

"My wife, sir," he interrupted, "may go on as she will till the moment of retribution comes; and as for your brother, a few days more or less can not either save or beggar him. A vengeance such as mine can wait—is the sweeter for delay."

I submitted, but I sighed as I submitted.

"And now," said he, "we have said enough for to-night. It grows late, and I already see a gray tint in the sky, which looks like coming day. If you will meet me again to-morrow night, we can consult afresh. What say you to Le Roi Fainéant of Ixelles, at ten o'clock in the evening? It is a quiet little out-of-the-way inn and brasserie, about a couple of miles out of town. We shall be safe and undisturbed enough there!"

"As you please; but why at night, and so far?"

"Can you ask why? Ah! I forget that you are no conspirator. Well, then, do you not see that I must keep myself concealed? That if she knew of my presence all our plot would be endangered? I have not dared to venture in any place where I should be likely to encounter her. I have scarcely stirred out, save at night, or dared to take exercise, save in the country suburbs, ever since my arrival in Brussels. A stab, to fulfill its errand, must fall suddenly and in the dark. Good-night to you, sir."

He touched his hat as when he first spoke to me, turned away suddenly from my side, and, almost before I could tell in which direction he had vanished, plunged into the shadow and disappeared.

For some time I remained standing where he had left me, stupefied by the crowd of thoughts and emotions which his language and presence had aroused within me. His pale, care-worn face; his strange story; the espial which he had exercised over me; the plot which he had unfolded; the peculiar influence with which he had swayed me during the interview, all combined to trouble, to excite, to oppress me. I felt myself, as it were, a tool in his hands. His face and voice haunted me. I could not forget the expression of his features as he watched me from the doorway when I had entered the little office inside the stage entrance of the theatre. The whole thing seemed to me like a dream, or rather the dream of a dream, for I could not rid myself of the impression that I had seen him before, at some sad and remote time or other. Himself seemed to me almost as a phantom. I tried to remember that I ought to feel gratitude—joy —relief from what I had learnt and undertaken. I almost hated myself for the unutterable melancholy that had fallen upon me the instant he was gone from my side, and for the hopeless, dreary feeling with which I contemplated the future. It was as if I felt the spell of some approaching danger; and ever, as I threaded the solitary streets leading to my home in the gray morning, I murmured to myself,

"Oh that it were to be done to-morrow! Oh that it were to be done to-morrow!"

CHAPTER XXIX.

THE SKY DARKENS BEFORE THE STORM.

I CALLED on Adrienne the next morning, and found Seabrook there before me. She was leaning back in a *fauteuil* with a book lying open upon a small table close at hand. He was bending over some geraniums in the window, and looked up, as I entered the room, with a troubled expression upon his face, such as I had seldom seen there before.

Adrienne observed my glance, and smiled somewhat sadly.

"I have been undertaking the graceless office of adviser to your friend," she said, after the customary salutations were over. "I think it is almost his duty to employ his education and talents in the exercise of some honorable pursuit."

"Then, madame," I replied, "you should advise me likewise, for I find myself in precisely the same position."

"Not so; you have estates to cultivate—dependents whose happiness must rest, in a great measure, upon your treatment—wealth which it is your task to employ worthily. All these things may be sufficient for a rich scholar who loves his library, his old home, and his 'paternal acres' better than the civil warfare of professional life. Such is not the case with your friend. He confesses that his resources are insufficient for his requirements. He would fain be the possessor of some few hundred volumes of poetry, history, and romance. He enjoys refined society, and would wish occasionally to be the entertainer as well as the entertained. It would please him now and then to purchase a painting by some favorite artist; and he could love a faithful horse, or three or four sagacious dogs. if it were in his power to become their master."

"A very pretty picture of the beau ideal of a wealthy connoisseur," I replied. "It reminds one of Beckford and Horace Walpole, or of that luxurious desire of Gray's, who wished that he could lie all day upon a sofa, reading eternal new novels of Crebillon and Marivaux!"

She smiled again, and shook her head playfully.

"You misapprehend me," she said. "It would distress me to hear Mr. Seabrook aspire only to the position of a 'wealthy connoisseur.' You speak of a life thus devoted—I of a leisure. He must earn the privileges of taste and liberality before he can enjoy them."

"Am I then to understand that Seabrook contemplates entering upon the study of a profession?" I asked, incredulously.

He blushed and laughed. "The die is not yet cast," he said, with an assumption of *badinage* that seemed hardly natural, "but I really contemplate such a step, and have contemplated it for some weeks. When a man passes five-and-twenty, he finds a blank in his life that needs to be filled up by some grim word, such as 'physician,' 'lawyer,' or 'statesman.' It is my turn now, I suppose; and Seabrook, the idler *sans souci*, the picture-loving, adventure-seeking, all-enjoying rambler, the scorner of carriage-tourists, and the sworn foe of all cicerones, guides, and *valets de place*, is about to subside into a respectable member of society, with a brass plate on his door, and (if the gods permit) an interesting little account at his banker's!"

"Here is a change, indeed! Have I not heard you say of poverty that it was the only wealth—of riches, that you pitied those who are burdened with the care of them—of books, that in the liberty of reading in the great free libraries of Paris, London, and Berlin, you commanded the finest collections in the world—of picture-galleries, that you enjoyed them, and that their owner could do no more? Oh, shame! you are seceding from your own tenets!"

"An honorable retreat, Paul—not a flight!"

"Then you acknowledge that there has been a combat—a combat wherein madame is the victress."

"On the contrary," retorted Adrienne, vivaciously, "it has, I fear, too nearly resembled that celebrated battle of Bologna of which Guicciardini relates that it 'was a victory obtained without a combat!' Mr. Seabrook was the first to enter upon the subject, and I believe that the opinion which I ventured to express was precisely that which he most wished to hear."

"Jesting apart," I replied, "I am heartily pleased to know this. To what profession do you think of turning your attention?"

"I can not say that I have yet arrived at any decision," said he, with an assumption of profound gravity. "It lies at present between the Church, the law, finance, and the study of medicine. Indeed, I am hourly expecting the arrival of deputations from each of these professions, soliciting me to confer immortality upon their respective bodies; and until I have considered the advantages and disadvantages attendant upon all, I can not definitively state whether it is to be the Archbishopric of Canterbury, the Woolsack, the Chancellorship of the Exchequer, or the presidency of some distinguished medical society."

Thus conversing, mingling jest with earnest, some time passed by, and I was just about to take my leave, when the stoppage of a carriage beneath the windows, and a man's voice on the stairs, told us that Théophile had returned home from his morning drive.

Up he came, bounding over three or four steps at a time, and entered the drawing-room by storm. His face was flushed; he carried some cards in his hand, and the very air with which he threw them down at Adrienne's feet was that of a man nearly beside himself with excitement.

"*Voici, voici, ma femme!*" he exclaimed.

"Here is some life, here is some amusement, here is some variety at last! A *bal masqué*, *Dieu merci!* and one patronized, authorized, originated by all the best people in Brussels! The king lends his name—the nobility and visitors subscribe—it is every thing that is private, select, and extravagant! I have taken a dozen tickets directly, and it is expected that all will be sold before evening. Oh, *comme c'est delicieuse!*"

Involuntarily I glanced at Adrienne to see how she would relish this proposition and the tone in which it was conveyed; but her eyes were fixed upon the ground, and I could not read the most transient emotion in the composed immobility of her face.

"Here are tickets for you both," continued Théophile, boisterously, as he forced the cards into Seabrook's hand and mine. "We will make a merry party—we will invent costumes—we will have a glorious night of it!"

He began walking to and fro in his wild mood, and his words came thick and fast, like those of a man whose tongue has been loosed by wine.

"You, Adrienne, you shall go as Marie Antoinette; she was blonde and belle, like you! Marie Antoinette!—no, no—that would be an evil omen. Let it be Marie Stuart!"

"Just as bad," interrupted Seabrook. "She was beheaded."

"Joan of Arc, then!"

"Joan of Arc was burnt," remarked Adrienne, forcing a smile. "You are resolved that mine shall be a tragic part, Théophile."

"*Diable!*" exclaimed my brother, looking round with an odd, wandering stare. "Why do these fatal names come into my head? We mean to be merry—we mean to forget every thing but pleasure—we want no evil omens! Be Pallas, or Helen, or the Virgin Mary—they were not beheaded, or burnt, or guillotined, were they? Ha! ha! Let us enjoy it in prospect! *Vive le bal masqué!*"

"But you have not yet told us where it is to take place," said I, addressing him for the first time.

"Where? Why, where should it be held, unless in the ballroom of the Opera? We shall have the entire orchestra for our band, and it will be the best ball of the whole season! What characters shall we take? What will you be, Seabrook? What will you be, Paul?" Then, not waiting for any reply, "I have thought of hundreds for myself," he continued, "but I can't decide. What say you to Robespierre—Charles the Twelfth—Philip de Comines—Dante—the Man with the Iron Mask—Shakspeare—the Count of Monte Christo—Sir Philip Sidney—the Knave of Hearts—Rob Roy—Masaniello—Napoleon Bonaparte—Polichinello—Richard the Third—Erasmus—Bluebeard! Ha! ha! What a medley! Enough for all to choose from!"

"And when does it take place!" asked Adrienne, with a sigh.

"To-morrow week—the 16th of October?"

"But shall we be in Brussels, Théophile! Were we not to start for Burgundy in three or four days?"

"What folly! Would you think of missing the ball for that? We can go to Burgundy a week later—or we need not go at all!"

"Not go at all, Théophile?" cried Adrienne, rising and fixing a searching glance upon his face. "What do you mean?"

"Bah, Adrienne! How you take every thing seriously! Let us be happy while we can! I *will* go to the ball—I swear it! And so will you, *ma femme:* I shall insist—*mon Dieu!* I shall insist. Courtrai is to be a steward," he continued, falling back into the reckless strain he had pursued before, "and De l'Orme master of the ceremonies. They wanted me to be a steward, but I would not; no, no, I was resolved to be merry—to be free! free! free!"

And again he laughed aloud, and still he kept striding backward and forward—backward and forward—like a prisoner in a dungeon.

Quite silently I rose and left the room. I could not bear to see it. There was something ghastly in his wild mirth, and I dared not give way to the displeasure which it roused within me.

As I passed down the staircase, a hand falling lightly on my arm caused me to turn. It was Adrienne.

Pale as marble—breathless—with one finger pressed on her lips, she opened a door upon the landing, and, with her hand still resting on my sleeve, led me in and closed it softly.

For some moments we were both silent; then, in a voice that went to my heart, so measured, so low, so unnaturally calm it was, she spoke to me.

"You are his brother, Monsieur Paul. You have known him longer and better than I. You know all his faults. Tell me what this is."

I looked down and shook my head in silence.

"Strange things have taken place of late, Monsieur Paul," she continued, still firmly. "He has not been the same man since we arrived in Brussels. He has anxieties, debts, associates of whom I know nothing. Immense expenses have been incurred—timber, and even land, has been parted with. Do you know any thing of this?"

Again the same mute reply. What other could I give her?

"He—he has sold some farms of mine in England," she said, and her voice wavered slightly. "His lawyer was with him every day last week. There is some fatal propensity—some—some infatuation at work, I am convinced. The other night he came home as day was dawning, and in the morning I found a pack of cards scattered upon the floor of his dressing-closet. He—he gambles."

"No, no," I exclaimed, eagerly, "there I am certain you do him an injustice. However weak and thoughtless he may be, Théophile, I am assured, could never be a gambler!"

"He is a gambler," she said, in a rapid and

more excited tone, "he is a gambler. I know it, for I heard him call the names of the cards and colors in his sleep. But let that pass; let him gamble—let him ruin himself and me—let us be beggars, pensioners, outcasts—every thing, in the name of heaven, so that our hearts be not estranged from each other! I could endure every thing but neglect; I could be happy under every privation save that of my husband's confidence! Why did we ever come here! Why was I ever born? He loves me no longer! he loves me no longer!"

All her pride and strength was broken now, and, bending her face down upon her hands, she sobbed convulsively.

"Alas! madame," I said, sorrowfully, "what can I do? This is a sad sight for me. I know that he loves you still—I would stake my life upon it! Shall I speak to him?"

She dashed her tears aside with a haughty gesture of the hand, rose to her full height, and looked at me with a sort of proud anger in her eyes that blinded mine, as if I had been guilty of some deep offense, and could not lift them in her presence.

"Speak to him, sir!" she cried; "speak to him! Have I fallen so low that even you insult me now? Think you that I need an intercessor? that I must plead for mercy? that I am about to kneel down at my husband's feet, and pray for his kind glances? No—it is too much!"

Standing there in her lofty scorn, upbraiding me with her flashing eyes, and curling lip, and flushed, disdainful brow, she looks almost more than woman; then suddenly gives way and weeps again, and entreats my pardon, sobbingly and through her tears.

It is her grief, she says, that makes her unjust; she has been thinking of it, and fretting over it, by day and night, for many weeks, till her brain and her heart ache, and her very voice grows strange to her own ears. I must forgive her! I will—will I not? She is but a weak girl; she knows not what to do, or where to turn; she wants help—advice—comfort. She is broken-hearted, and she longs to die!

All this is said at intervals, with a face buried in the cushions of a sofa, and a form trembling from head to foot.

How am I to help—comfort—advise a grief like this! What can I say or do, with the solution of the dark secret hidden in my breast, and the knowledge of a blacker sin than even she dreams of pressing down, like the weight of an iron hand, upon my heart? My only resource is in vague, general terms of sympathy—in reiterated assurances of her husband's affections—in suggestions that his new pursuit, far from being a fixed passion, could only be considered in the light of a passing folly—in promises that I would endeavor to keep him in my sight as much as possible, and, by every indirect means in my power, hasten his return to Burgundy.

Uncertain and unsatisfactory as they are, these assurances serve in some degree to calm the impetuosity of her mood. Presently the excess of agitation subsides, and by-and-by a low occasional sob is all that I hear.

Thus at length I leave her, and, pausing with suspended breath outside the door, hear the voices of Théophile and Norman Seabrook yet conversing in the drawing-room. It seems that they are still discussing the subject of the ball, for the words "costume—feathers—grotesque," accompanied by a prolonged peal of laughter, come distinctly to my ear, and jar upon it painfully.

And so I turn away, and hasten down into the street unnoticed.

I am to meet Vogelsang to-night at the little inn of Ixelles, and I hope much from the interview. It must be done quickly—it must be done quickly!

CHAPTER XXX.

THE EVENTS OF A WEEK.

A FEW words will suffice to relate all that took place during the week which intervened between the last chapter and the next. It was a weary time, occupied by delays—disappointments—doubts—daily-increasing apprehensions.

Adrienne was in the right—Théophile gambled. Vogelsang had discovered it long since, and on the evening of the very day that Adrienne confided her fears to me, the intelligence received its final confirmation from the lips of my associate. Nay, worse even than this, Hauteville—Hauteville, which had been purchased in the morning-time of his happiness, and which was to have descended as an integral portion of the Latour property from generation to generation, was publicly advertised for sale in all the Belgian and French newspapers!

He might have been saved—he might have been saved even now, had I but succeeded in rousing Vogelsang to immediate action. Alas! some unaccountable torpor seemed to possess him. Whether from the fear of failure, the reluctance to face his wife, or a refinement upon his vengeance which delighted in holding the sword suspended above her head, I can not tell, but every day he deferred the execution of our project—every day I lost hope and courage—every day plunged Théophile deeper and deeper into sin.

Twice I saw Adrienne, but only upon the last occasion did I find myself alone with her. I had no favorable intelligence for her—no consolation which could afford her the faintest hope for the future. She had read the announcement respecting Hauteville, and was even more unhappy than before. Théophile had refused to give her any explanation of his affairs—had spoken to her with harshness and impetuosity—had absented himself as much as possible from home, and now seldom met her, even at meals. In society alone they appeared together as before, and in the face of the world maintained the semblance of that sacred confidence which existed no longer.

All this Adrienne told me with a heart-anguish which only made my own trouble too heavy for endurance. I could do nothing to alleviate her misery, and I found the interview so painful that I had not the courage to repeat it.

As for my other friends, I saw Margaret twice or thrice, and Seabrook even less frequently. He was much occupied now in making arrangements for commencing the study of the law, and was frequently absent upon visits to Antwerp, where he had consultations upon the subject with an English solicitor resident in that city. Somehow a check had fallen upon our intercourse of late—a check, but not a coolness. We loved each other as heartily as ever, but we met less frequently, and our traveling projects were all given up and forgotten. Perhaps the fault lay with myself, after all. I think it did. There were events and anxieties which I dared not reveal to him; I had appointments which I could not explain—schemes in which he could be admitted to no part. Perfect friendship and perfect confidence are one. Where there is a lack of the one, the other droops like a flower in the shade.

Thus matters stood till within two days of the *bal masqué* from which Théophile anticipated so much enjoyment. Then Vogelsang told me that he had opened his negotiations with the manager of the theatre, and had purchased his promise of silence with a fee of two thousand francs, which I was to pay. Lemaire agreed to conduct a similar treaty with the subordinates, and all was at last *en train* for the speedy accomplishment of our plot. Still no day was absolutely fixed, and though I felt that the first step was taken, I yet chafed impatiently at the delay, and urged for speed—speed—speed!

So the 16th of October came round, and nothing decisive had been done.

CHAPTER XXXI.

THE MASKED BALL.

MORE from the desire of affording an escort to Adrienne during the evening than from any curiosity with which the scene itself could inspire me, I consented to accompany my brother and his wife to the masked ball. She went with the vague hope that her presence might preserve him from the temptations of the card-tables, which, as the announcements told, were to be prepared in the king's retiring-rooms. I, because I felt convinced that Théophile would take his own course, and leave her to the companionship of whatever acquaintance he might chance to meet. Seabrook, too, was absent upon one of his Antwerp excursions. Probably, had he been near at hand, I might have excused myself, for I felt but little in the mood for this carnival folly.

From Théophile's residence to the Opera House we traveled in unbroken silence. Two hearts out of three, at least, were too heavy for speech; and even my brother, leaning back moodily in a corner of the carriage, was grave and absorbed.

It was a dark, windy night, and sudden gusts of rain came dashing against the windows. The street was full of vehicles moving along in two lines, and all toward the same spot. Going onward thus slowly, with the lights from the shops and the glare of the surrounding carriage-lamps flashing in upon us every now and then, revealing our pale, sad faces and fantastic dresses to each others' eyes, we seemed more like a party of mourners than a company of masks on their way to a ball, and I could scarcely divest myself of the idea that we formed part of some grotesque, yet awful funereal procession.

As we neared the theatre door, our progress became more and more difficult, and at last we stopped altogether. The carriages were "setting down," it appeared, about a hundred yards in advance, and we were not likely to reach our destination for a quarter of an hour or twenty minutes at the least. Théophile muttered an impatient curse, and, after looking angrily from the window for several minutes, flung himself back, as before, and played with his sword-knot.

He wore the rich and elaborate costume of Prince Charles Edward the Pretender, and looked, in his ruffles and velvets, the very type of Scotland's chivalric darling. Sitting there, with his plumed hat resting on his knees, his fair hair hanging in natural curls almost to his collar, his breast covered with jewels, and his hands with rings, I thought I had never seen him so handsome. Adrienne could be persuaded to wear nothing more conspicuous than a white satin domino, embroidered with silver flowers; and a similar costume made in plain black silk furnished me with the only incognito I cared to assume.

Gradually we advanced, a few steps at a time, and soon there remained but one carriage between ourselves and the door. Adrienne sighed. Théophile stirred uneasily in his corner.

"Why do you sigh, Adrienne?" he asked, roughly. "We shall be released in another minute."

"That is why I sigh, Théophile," answered his wife. They were the first words that had been spoken since we started.

"How! Do you not like the ball? Are you dissatisfied with your dress—which, I confess, might have been more elegant?"

"I like the dress as well as any other, Théophile, but I care nothing for the ball."

"She cares nothing for the ball! Bah! all women are contrary. If you care nothing for the ball, madame, pray why have you taken the trouble to come to it?"

This was spoken even more harshly than before, but with an effort, as if he were endeavoring to be out of temper. Finding that she remained silent, he repeated the question.

"Why have you taken the trouble to come?"

"Because you are here, Théophile."

He coughed, and looked aside out of the window. Presently he began again.

"If one goes to a masked ball, it should, at least, be with the intention of enjoyment. I insist upon your trying to be amused to-night."

"I will try," she replied, and her voice faltered.

At this moment the carriage in advance of us drove away, and we moved on opposite the lighted entrance with awning and carpeted pavement, and crowds of maskers thronging in the hall.

Théophile suddenly flung off his assumption of ill-humor.

"Adrienne!" he exclaimed, with emotion, "you are an angel!"

He seized her hand and kissed it warmly. At that instant the servant flung open the door; my brother leaped out and assisted his wife from the carriage; we passed rapidly through a double row of eager, curious faces, and in another moment had entered the hall, presented our cards, and made our way up the broad staircase to the ballroom beyond.

A strange scene, truly, but more confused and less imposing than I had anticipated. Only a dense crowd of richly-costumed persons walking, standing, conversing, and scarce any space to spare for those who were disposed for dancing. Many characters held their masks in their hands, or wore them hanging loosely from the belt or wrist; and the whole assemblage seemed to me more a vehicle for the display of taste, and an opportunity of conversation, than a bal masqué, such as I had often read and heard about in history and romance.

A stream of promenaders was circulating slowly round the room, and into this train we involuntarily fell; Théophile and Adrienne in advance, I following in their wake. One of the first persons we encountered was M. le Marquis de Courtrai, laboriously scented, powdered, and rouged, and carefully made into the likeness of Louis Quatorze, "to whom," as he smilingly averred, "he flattered himself that he bore some humble resemblance."

Finding Adrienne retain the arm of Théophile, M. le Marquis fell presently into the rear, and honored me with his conversation.

He began by assuring me that the first requisite in society was the possession of the grand air, and that the grand air was precisely the point upon which the youths of the present day were most deficient. He next proceeded to inform me that there were many fine women in that very ballroom who were languishing, absolutely languishing for him (M. le Marquis); and he accompanied that interesting announcement with a variety of piquante and alluring details. From thence he diverged into a resumé of his bonnes fortunes, past and present, and (as I made a good listener, and never opened my lips in reply, which would, indeed, have been rather difficult, seeing that I heard without comprehending one half of what he said) he enlarged upon this theme with considerable complacency and eloquence. Finding, however, that my attention was neuter rather than passive, and becoming, perhaps, dimly aware that my mind was occupied with other thoughts, M. le Marquis at length thought fit to drop the subject of his conquests, and to indulge in a few observations on the persons and things around him.

"The Hospodar is looking remarkably well to-night. You did not see him? Heavens, how droll! He passed us on the instant in the costume of a bashaw, with his eldest son carrying the tails before him. A pretty girl to the left, in that Circassian dress. Charming back and shoulders—charming! A good arm, too, and a nicely-turned ankle. Scarcely plump enough, I think. Eh? A nice girl, though—a very nice girl." (M. le Marquis had an agreeable way of dissecting the perfections of a lady, as if he were a butcher, and of commending them afterward, as if he were a cook.) "Here is Madame la Baronne de Vallonvert, looking hideous in the costume of la Reine Elizabeth! Mon Dieu! that woman is positively too fat! Ah! Madame la Baronne, this is a veritable pleasure! Always charming, always récherché, Madame la Baronne. I find your costume delicious. By the way, M. Latour, I think that we have the history of perfide Albion at the ball to-night. I myself have seen three Henry the Eighths, four Richard the Thirds, two Princes Noirs, and more than one Oliver Cromwell. Ah! ah! Do you see that woman yonder in the costume of Norma, with the wreath and sickle, and the classic drapery? Mark her fine figure—her graceful head—her neck—her arms—her pose! She wears her mask, yet can you not tell who she is?"

I looked, started, doubted, shook my head.

"Mon Dieu! Not know the Vogelsang, even though her face be masked! My good garçon, have you no eyes—no senses? There is not such another woman in Brussels. She is glorious—magnificent—superb! Your brother, I fancy, would not need to look twice—eh? Comment! do you not comprehend? Why, the world does say—"

And Monsieur le Marquis elevated his eyebrows, shrugged his shoulders, took a pinch of snuff with the grand air of Louis Quatorze, and subsided into a significant silence.

Just at this juncture Théophile conducted Adrienne to a seat. Monsieur le Marquis abruptly quitted my side, and flew to the back of her chair, where he took up his stand in the attitude of her devoted slave. Théophile dived away into the crowd and disappeared; and I, in compliance with my sister-in-law's request, strolled on idly amid the throng, silent and observing, feeling my mind agreeably diverted, for a brief space, by the novelty and richness of the scene around me.

There was a band playing at the farther end of the room, where an area had been cleared for dancing. Hither I made my way by slow degrees, and found the space surrounded by admiring spectators. A party of twelve persons, habited in the picturesque fashion of the reign of Louis XI., were going through the stately and solemn figures of certain antique traditionary dances of that early period, to the accompaniment of quaint music, as intricate and grave as the windings of the dances themselves. Becoming interested in these obsolete measures, I stood gazing for a considerable time, till I found that a vast crowd had gathered behind me, and that I was standing in the front rank of a phalanx of spectators, many of whom had mounted upon benches and seats, and even upon the pedestals of the columns which skirted the room.

It was a matter of no little difficulty to retreat from this position; but, on consulting my watch, I found that I had left Adrienne more than two hours, and I doubted not that she was by this time completely wearied of the conversation of Monsieur de Courtrai. I therefore worked myself gradually out of the press, and had just emerged into a part of the room which was comparatively clear, when I came suddenly face to face with the masked Norma, and received a smart blow on the ankle from the sword of her companion, a tall man wrapped in a long Spanish cloak reaching almost to his feet, and whose head and face were shrouded in a broad *sombrero*, with heavy black plumes.

They seemed to be in haste; but the gentleman, though nearly put, turned to apologize.

"A thousand pardons, monsieur," he said. "I did not observe that my rapier was in your way."

It was the voice of Théophile!

For a moment I stood still—then sighed heavily, and went upon my way. Of course it would be so. I might have guessed it before. He came to this ball for the purpose of meeting her—had most probably presented her with the admission!

Yet I was pleased that he should have assumed a second disguise. That, at least, testified to some little regard for the opinions of the world—averted somewhat of the notoriety of his intrigue—argued some lingering respect for his wife.

I found Adrienne where I had left her, and the marquis was so obliging as to relinquish his post on my return. She was less sad than usual, and the gay scene amused her. The kiss, too, which Théophile had imprinted upon her hand in the carriage, had revived her drooping spirits.

"Perhaps," she said, hopefully, "his mania for extravagance is on the wane. You were the good prophet who foretold it, *mon beau frère!* It was, after all, but a whim; and if it be over, and that he was pleased by the indulgence of it, I shall not remember whether it were or were not an expensive or a dangerous one."

"Indeed, madame, I hope that it may be so."

"Do not say it with such a grave air, M. Paul. I feel assured that it is so; and the assurance makes me, ah! so happy. To-morrow I will persuade him to withdraw Hauteville from the market, and we will go down together to dear old Burgundy before a week be over. How pleased your mother will be to see us, will she not, M. Paul? And the servants, and the dogs —ah! yes, even the dogs. Poor Hector! he will not forget me."

Fond child! how slender an act of grace sufficed to fill that trusting little heart with gratitude, forgiveness, love—ay, even to overflowing.

Conversing thus—she full of garrulous hope and anticipation, I silent and dispirited—two more hours passed away, and the rooms began, though almost imperceptibly as yet, to grow thinned of their brilliant company. It was ten o'clock when we first arrived, and it is now two. Adrienne suggests that we should look for Théophile, and return home as speedily as may be, for the hour grows late; so we rise and make the tour of the *salons*.

Abundance of princes, kings, knights, cavaliers, Highlanders, historical celebrities, Romans, Hamlets, Mephistopheles, Polichinellos, harlequins, debardeurs, jesters, peasants, officers, Persians, and Spanish noblemen we met, but never the beautiful and glittering Charles Edward whom we seek, or that dark Hidalgo with the sable plumes, for whom I keep an eager watch by the way.

Adrienne grows nervous.

"Perhaps," she whispers, falteringly, "perhaps he—he may be in the card-rooms!"

I pity the little hand lying upon my arm, for I see it contract, as if with a sudden spasm, at this thought. But we go.

The card-rooms are almost deserted. Only two tables are occupied, and those by some elderly gentlemen in plain dominoes, whose masks are laid aside, and whose faces look earnest and business-like over whist and picquet.

It is a relief to find that he is not here. We must have overlooked or missed him down stairs, after all. Let us go back and search again.

So we go back and search again, threading our way through all parts of the ballroom, passing in and out the pillars, peering eagerly into the recesses of the windows and behind the draperies of the curtains. Thus another hour passes. It is three o'clock, and Théophile is not found!

Poor Adrienne! Every limb is trembling now. She takes off her mask; the room, she says, is so warm she can scarcely breathe; yet she stands at this moment in the current of cool air from the door! Her face is deadly white, and I can feel her heart beat against my arm.

He must have gone home. Can he be ill? Has any accident happened? That idea is terrible, and I can not prevent her from asking one or two persons near whom we are standing if they have seen her husband, or if any gentleman has been taken ill. They only stare, smile, or remain silent, and one shrugs his shoulders and mutters, "Poor thing!" half pityingly, from behind his visor.

I now suggest that the best thing she can do is to return home. If he be unwell she will find him there. At all events, it is plain that he is no longer here. He may have sought her, all this time, as anxiously as we have sought him, and is, perhaps, now waiting for her at home.

"To be sure! Why did I not think of that before? Oh, that is it, I feel convinced! Thank you, thank you, brother Paul! Do not let us lose a moment. Where is my carriage? Oh, let us go—pray let us go directly!"

So we go down hastily, and Madame Latour's carriage is called. I have some difficulty in finding her cloak, which we had left in the care of an attendant, and there are so many carriages filed along the pavement that it is a long time before ours can reach the door.

All these delays are torture to Adrienne, and she stamps her white-slippered foot upon the marble flooring in the impetuosity of her haste.

At last the vehicle draws up. "Madame Latour's carriage stops the way!" is shouted by three or four voices at once. We rush forward; the door is opened, and I hand her in.

"Pray come with me, Paul," she entreats, forgetting, in her anxiety, the forms of address which we have always so scrupulously observed.

I obey. My foot is on the step, my hand upon the door, when I am seized roughly by the arm and dragged forcibly back.

"Stop!" whispers a hoarse voice in my ear—"stop! All is lost; we are betrayed; they are gone!"

The form is that of a gray friar—the face is masked—the voice is the voice of Vogelsang!

"Lost—gone! What do you mean?"

"They have eloped together—from this very spot—two hours ago. We must follow them at any risk. Oh, I will have blood for this before I have done with her!"

There is a savage energy in the tone with which he utters these words that appalls me. Adrienne calls to me from the carriage; I plead a flurried excuse, shut the door, direct the coachman to drive home, and so the vehicle rolls away, with her pale face looking back at me from the window.

"Well," I exclaim, turning round upon my associate, "what is to be done? What next?"

"What next?" he says, fiercely. "What next? VENGEANCE AND PURSUIT."

CHAPTER XXXII.

THE FIRST CLEW.

I FOLLOWED him to a little dingy cabaret in the next street—a place of mean resort, with every shutter closed, and a pale light streaming from the open door upon the wet pavement. A man and woman were drinking at the counter, and a sleepy garçon in shirt sleeves and slippers ushered us into the parlor at the back, now deserted, but bearing evidence of recent company. The sanded floor was strewn with fragments of broken glasses, corks, and ends of cigars; the tables were smeared with wine; a hazy atmosphere of tobacco hung about the room like a fog; and the clock pointed to half past three.

Vogelsang called for a half bottle of *eau-de-vie*, poured it out into a tumbler, and drank half at a draught. In doing so, he threw back his friar's hood, and I saw that his brow was covered with blood, and that his face and lips were deathly pallid.

"You are wounded!" I exclaimed. "Let me go for a surgeon!"

"No—no," he replied; "it is nothing. I fell. I am a little faint. In a few minutes I shall be the same as ever."

He sat down and leaned his head back against the wall, looking ghastly. Trembling with eagerness to know more, I yet abstained from speech or movement, and stood watching him. I could hear my own heart beating as I did so, and I remember noticing at the time (with a sort of painfully acute susceptibility to every sound, however trifling) that it went so much faster than the ticking of the clock.

Presently he seemed to revive, and came over feebly to the fireplace. His hands shook like those of an aged man as he held them to the blaze, and he stared vacantly before him.

"Now tell me," I cried, impatiently, "tell me all! Where are they? Quick—quick!"

"Gone," he said, moodily, and without changing his position. "Gone!"

"I know it; but where?"

"Ay—where?" he repeated. "Where? That's the question."

There was a strange, dead apathy in his manner, totally different to the furious impetuosity with which he had stopped me at the doors of the theatre a few minutes previously.

"And have you no idea of the route they have taken?"

He shook his head silently.

"Nor of the way in which they travel?"

The same reply.

"But we must pursue them—we must discover them—we must part them!"

"Ay," he replied, "we must—we must."

"Instantly."

He stared up at me for a moment, then dropped his head again, and seemed to watch the embers, moaning softly to himself.

I resolved to rouse him.

"Up!" I said, authoritatively, "up and be doing! The hours are going fast, and every minute sees them a mile farther. We have to discover every thing for ourselves. I will bring a cab, and we will go round to both railway stations. Perhaps something may be done that way. I trust to energy for every thing."

My voice, my gestures seemed to animate him. He sat erect, and made an effort as if to collect his wandering thoughts.

"You are right," he said, at length, and more firmly—"you are right. Let me have a basin of water and a towel, and bid them bring me some bread, for I am faint. I have lost blood, and have eaten nothing since noonday."

I did as he desired, and assisted him to wash the stains from his face and clothing, and to throw aside the friar's mantle which he wore outside his dress. He then ate a small crust, and both looked and felt better.

"Now I am ready," he said. "Let us go."

There was not a vehicle in sight. I went round to the theatre, and the few that stood there were engaged by maskers; for the ball was not yet over, and I could hear the music going on merrily as I passed by.

Down two more streets in the rain and darkness, and still without success—back again past the theatre a second time, and on in the direction of the old town, where I met an empty vigilante rolling slowly along, and hired it with difficulty, for the driver was tired, and his hours of work were over.

I found Vogelsang better than when I left him; but he had bound a red scarf round his head, which made him look whiter than ever by the contrast, and he leaned heavily upon my arm as he got in.

"To the Antwerp line, *cocher*, and as fast as you can make your horses go!"

On, still on, but very slowly, for the weary beasts are scarcely equal to even that short journey, and the driver is nearly asleep on the box. On—on—till it seems that we shall never arrive there.

Again I urge my companion to tell me more. "How did you learn their flight? Where did you get that blow?"

"One question at a time. As to their flight, I saw them leave the rooms together. I had been at their heels the whole evening in my friar's cowl; I followed them to the cloak-room, and saw him hurry her into the carriage; she dropped this note as she went: listen: '*To-night you will be prepared for escape. I will have all in readiness. We can leave the rooms about midnight, and before suspicion is roused we shall be beyond the reach of discovery.—T. L.*' I only paused to pick this paper up—to read it once, and then I followed the sound of their carriage-wheels with the speed of an Indian. Suddenly my foot slipped; I fell; my head came sharply against the curbstone: I remember no more till I recovered my senses about half an hour since, lying on my face in a dark, solitary street, with not a soul in sight. On striving to rise and walk, I found myself giddy and confused, and my face wet, but whether with rain or blood I knew not. Then I remembered what had happened, and my first impulse was to find you, to pursue them, to be revenged! I did find you, for just as I came up you were leading the lady to her carriage. You know the rest."

"And do you still feel equal to the pursuit? Had you not better see a surgeon, and take some brief rest before we go farther?"

"Rest! No—not if I die upon the journey!"

His old courage and determination speaks out again now in voice and bearing, and when we reach the station he is the first to alight.

The doors are all fast closed, but there is a light burning in the windows of one of the lower rooms, and we knock lustily and repeatedly.

We are not heard; all is perfectly still within; the station seems deserted.

Again we knock, and are just going away disappointed, when a door is opened suddenly, and a man in a dressing-gown and slippers looks out, and asks us angrily what we do there at such an hour.

"We want to know when the last train left? Has there been one since midnight? Does monsieur remember to have seen a fair gentleman and a dark lady (both very handsome) together on the platform? Did they take tickets, and can he remember for what place?"

The station-master thunders forth an artillery of abuse. There has not been a departure since ten minutes before eleven. We must know that. We are *mauvais sujets*. To the devil with the dark gentleman and the fair lady, and with all impertinents!

Thus rebuffed, we turn away and resume our places in the cab, desiring the coachman to drive to the Ligne du Midi, or South Railway. To this he gives at first a positive refusal; but, being bribed by promise of a triple fare, consents at last to go on, though at a slower pace than ever.

At the South Railway the outer gates are closed; not a light is any where visible—not a sound is audible. The coachman thinks that there is no train between midnight and six o'clock P.M., and declines to drive us any farther. In vain I expostulate—entreat—threaten —urge the importance of our business and the illness of my companion. Jehu is inflexible. His horses are of more importance to him than any man's business, and to knock them up would grieve him more than any man's illness. He has driven us as far as he had agreed; he must be paid and dismissed. In short, he dismisses himself.

So we are compelled to alight in the thick close mist of the early morning, and, taking shelter under an archway, hear the vigilante rumble lazily away.

"What shall we do now?" asks Vogelsang, peevishly. "I feel as if I had no power to think or act; it is this cursed blow that has done it. What shall we do?"

"The first thing is, obviously, to get another coach," I replied. "The second, to find by which road they have left Brussels."

"But how? How?"

"There are thirteen gates to the city, are there not?"

"Yes."

"Then we must go from gate to gate till we find through which they passed. And now for the coach!"

I set off upon the same search as before, and this time with readier success, for in a few moments we are once more seated side by side, and driving in the direction of the Porte de Halle.

At the Porte de Halle we meet only with disappointment. No carriages have passed that way since midnight; but there have been four market-carts, which came from the country, and one traveler on horseback.

"Which, then, is the nearest gate from this?"

"I hardly know, monsieur; I should think the Porte d'Anderlecht."

"Allons! to the Porte d'Anderlecht."

Again the blinds are drawn up, and we dash forward between the gray lines of trees that skirt the Boulevard. It still rains, and the morning dawns slowly. Vogelsang leans back with a groan, and presses his hands upon his aching brow.

"You must take the lead now in every thing," he says, moodily. "I am as helpless as a child."

At the Porte d'Anderlecht we find the gates shut, and have to wait for several minutes before any one makes his appearance. Then a soldier comes out yawning, and proceeds to unlock them. We put the same questions to him. Has a carriage passed this gate since midnight—a carriage with a lady and gentleman inside?"

He knows nothing of any carriage. He is only just come on duty. Shall he call Jean-Simon? Jean-Simon, it appears, is his comrade yonder, sitting sleeping heavily by the fire. We see him through the open doorway, and we see how hard it is to rouse him. At length he stumbles forward not half awakened, and listens to my interrogations with a glazed, heavy eye, and a half-opened mouth.

"Has a carriage passed through this gate since midnight?"

"A carriage, monsieur?"

"Yes, yes—a carriage. You know what a carriage means?"

"Yes, monsieur. I—I think a carriage did go through. But I'm not sure. It might have been a chaise—or a wagon. I was very sleepy at the time."

"Nay, nay, Jean-Simon," cries a shrill voice from within, "a carriage did go by about—let me see, about one o'clock of the morning."

"Ay—she knows," says Jean-Simon, pointing over his shoulder toward the gate-house. "It was a carriage, of course. She knows."

"And in which direction did it go? To or from the town?"

"From town, I think, monsieur. At least, I'm not certain; but I think it was from town."

"From town, Jean-Simon," says the shrill voice, confirmatively.

"Did you see who was in it?"

"No, monsieur—that is, I won't be sure. There was a gentleman, I think."

"And a lady? Try to recollect—was there not a lady also?"

"Truly, monsieur, I can't tell. I don't think there was a lady. I was very sleepy just then."

"Holy Virgin, Jean-Simon!" screams the shrill voice, impatiently, "there was a lady—a lady with a velvet cloak and a veil, leaning back as if she did not wish us to see her. You must recollect the lady!"

"Ay, she knows," says Jean-Simon, contentedly. "There was a lady, of course—and a gentleman—and a carriage. I saw them all.

Of course I did. It's all true, messieurs. She knows."

"Where does this road lead to?"

"To Halle—Enghien—Tournay."

"And the nearest poste aux chevaux?"

"Plait-il?"

"Where is the nearest place that I can hire a carriage and post-horses to follow after them?"

Here our driver interposes. He knows of a post-master's close at hand, whose horses are excellent. I direct him to take us there forthwith, and away we go again between the lines of gray trees, growing distincter now in the increasing daylight.

All were asleep at the post-house, and ten minutes more, at the least, were lost in knocking before we succeeded in rousing a soul. Then a half-dressed ostler came down—then two more, and presently they were putting the horses to a post-chaise in the yard.

And now, for the first time since we started, I remember Adrienne and her distress. What must she be suffering? What thinks she of my sudden refusal to accompany her—of my subsequent absence?

But this is not the time for reflection. I must act, and that quickly, for the carriage is being prepared, and I am going on what may prove a long journey. I tear a couple of leaves from my pocket-book, and scrawl a hasty note on each. One is to Seabrook, entreating him to break this matter kindly to Adrienne, and telling him, in three words, the cause and object of my departure. The other is to Adrienne, commending Margaret to her care during my absence, and referring her to Seabrook for all other information. This done, I fold and address them.

"Is there any man here who will faithfully deliver these letters for ten francs?"

The three ostlers each start forward and offer themselves.

"Nay, I can choose but one. Do any of you know how to read?"

There is but one out of the three who can do this, so him I choose, and have the satisfaction of seeing him go, with the letters in his hand, just as we step into the chaise and drive off.

Once more away! Away through the narrow streets—along the Boulevard—out through the Porte d'Anderlecht—now giving passage to a succession of market-carts and pedestrian peasants, bound for the markets of the city. Away through the scattered villas, and brick-fields, and market-gardens that sprinkle the outskirts, and on to the flat green country, all dim and faded through the falling rain!

CHAPTER XXXIII.

THE CHASE GOES ON.

THE gray dawn gives place to the dull day. The travelers are few, and go trudging through the rain and mud, with discontented faces.

Now and then we whirl past some little cart or wagon, spattering the horses, and sometimes the driver, with our rapid wheels, and dash on before he has time to utter the indignant remonstrance which rises to his lips.

Always on—on, and so fast! The formal lines of poplars and pollards seem to rise up beside the windows as we go, and to glide out of sight, like ghostly sentinels going through an exercise. Now a gate—now a fallow-field, with the idle plows lying in the furrows—now a little farm-house—a bridge—a canal, all dimpled with the rain—a plantation—a party of country-girls in cloaks and hoods, all become for a moment visible, and the next are left far behind.

See! yonder lamp-post by the roadside marks the first toll-barrier, and tells us that we have journeyed one league. Only one league! Why, we seem to have been two hours at least upon the road; yet, on consulting the watch, we find it scarcely twenty minutes. We might pay the tolls to the post-boy to avoid delay, but we must stop and speak with the toll-keeper.

"Ho! Has there been a carriage past here this morning before dawn—a carriage containing a gentleman and lady?"

The gate-keeper is an old man. He shades his eyes with his hand, peers up at us from beneath his shaggy brows, and says, tremulously,

"You must speak louder. I am rather hard of hearing."

I repeat the question like a stentor, and a flash of intelligence crosses his face.

"Oh, ay—ay. There was a carriage, to be sure. A dark green chariot, with four bays. You must ride fast if ye would catch 'em!"

On again—faster and faster! The post-boy shall have a double fee for his speed. The trees seem to fly—the people on the road stand still, and look after us in wonder.

"Cheer up," I say to my companion, "cheer up! we are on their track most surely, and we will take four horses at the next post-house. We shall overtake them after all!"

Vogelsang groans and points to his head.

"You are in great pain? Well, we can stop at the first town, and have the wound dressed."

"No, not for a second. They will pause somewhere to rest. Our only chance is in perpetual traveling."

He is so resolute on this point, and there is so much reason in his argument, that I know not how to refute it. So, after a brief expostulation, I yield, and we are again silent.

Another lamp-post marks another league. Here toll-house and post-house are one, and while we change horses, I put the usual questions, and receive the same answers. A carriage has been up about five hours ago (it is now nearly eight o'clock A.M.), and took a relay of four horses. "The four horses, indeed," says the groom, "are now in the stable, feeding."

"And the post-boys who drove them—where are they?"

The groom points to two men who are hastily donning their jackets and buckling on their spurs inside the stable door.

"They are now preparing to drive, monsieur."

They are instantly called and questioned, and their replies confirm every thing. The carriage contained a lady and a gentleman. The lady kept her veil down, and leaned far back all the time; but they saw her hands and her fine rings. The gentleman had light hair, and paid them with gold, as if the ten-franc pieces were nothing but cents. They went like lightning. Holy St. Francis, what a hurry they were in!

"Eh bien! To your saddles! Five francs apiece for you if we clear the next two leagues in twenty minutes!" My urgent tones and gestures seemed to lend some meaning to the chase, for the grinning ostlers look and laugh among themselves, and I overhear one of them mutter, "C'est sa femme, peut-être!"

Useless to chafe at the boorish jest! I affect not to observe it, and again we are on the road —faster and faster!

Thus on and on for hour after hour, till mind and limbs grow weary from the lack of sleep. At noon the sky clears, and the sun comes out, and we reach the old fortified city of Mons, with its grand steeple and surrounding ditches. Here we purchase bread and wine, and partake of it as we go; and presently we have left the busy streets and squares, and are traveling along by the bleaching-grounds and coal-districts that lie beyond.

Were farther traces needed, we gather plenty on our way. Every where they are about five hours before us; sometimes a little more or less. They are remembered at toll-house and post-house all along the road. In many instances we are driven by their very post-boys, and these we examine eagerly. It is curious how all their stories tally. The lady was always veiled and leaning back; the gentleman always scattering gold with a careless hand. At one town the lady had a glass of milk. The gentleman sometimes smoked. The carriage was their own. They seemed to care nothing for money, but every thing for speed.

On and on! Vogelsang, despite his suffering, sustains the fatigue better than I had expected, and sleeps at intervals.

In the afternoon, at a small post-house, we find their carriage. The rough, paved Belgian roads have split the wheels in every direction, and hence they were compelled to travel in a hired vehicle. In a moment I spring out and search it eagerly. Here is Théophile's morocco cigar-case under one of the cushions, and a bag containing a few biscuits. The cigar-case is a prize, and I secure it.

Now the town of St. Ghislain, black, flat, dreary. The roads are thick with coal-dust; the cottages mean and many; the tall chimneys casting forth clouds of smoke. Then come hamlets, trees, and canals again, gliding like a phantasmagoria—then Quievrain.

At Quievrain we reach the limits of Belgium, and are vexatiously hindered by the authorities of the customs. Our passports are not quite *en régle*—we are subjected to a tedious interrogatory — are compelled to procure *visas* in the town, and are not suffered to pass the frontier till after a delay of nearly three hours. At the custom-house we still pursue our inquiries, and are referred to the *chef de bureau's* office, where an old gentleman with a white beard and an eyeglass asks our business.

"We are anxious to overtake a lady and gentleman who passed the frontier this morning. We have reason to believe that it was by this road they went, and we want to know for what place they are bound."

The old gentleman mends a pen slowly, and coughs twice or thrice, as if to gain time.

"And what may be your object in following these persons? Have they committed any offense?"

"None for which I am bound to account to you. It is enough that we are in the utmost haste, and that we beg you to be quick, as we have already been delayed three hours."

"What are the names of the parties?"

"Thérèse Vogelsang and Théophile Latour."

"And yours?"

We hand him our passports in reply, which he examines carefully.

"Which of you is Heinrich Vogelsang?"

My companion steps forward and says it is he.

"Are you the husband of Thérèse Vogelsang?"

"I am."

Here the old gentleman smiles cunningly to himself, and tries the nib of his pen upon his thumb nail. He then turns to me.

"And you are Paul Latour, of Burgundy, French subject?"

"Yes."

"What relation are you to Théophile Latour?"

"His elder brother."

"Hum! And your elder brother, sir, and *your* wife, sir, passed this barrier this morning?"

"So we believe."

The old gentleman opens a large book, wipes his eyeglass carefully, and, pointing with a fat fore finger, begins carefully examining the pages from bottom to top, as if he were reading Hebrew. This goes on for so long that we begin to despair. At last he stops suddenly.

"Hem!" (he has a bad cough, this old gentleman.) "Hem! '*Passed this day, between the hours of one and two* P.M., *Thérèse Vogelsang—vocalist—Austrian subject. Going to Paris from Brussels.*' Is that the lady, sir?"

"Yes—yes," says Vogelsang, hurriedly. "It is she! Let us go directly; we have no time to lose!"

"Stay," says the old gentleman, calmly, "you have not heard all. What did you say was the name of the other party?"

"Théophile Latour."

"No, that is not the name."

"Not the name?"

"No."

"What is it, then?"

"*Alphonse Lemaire — proprietaire — French subject.*"

Vogelsang and I look involuntarily at each other. The old gentleman is watching us, and reads the meaning of the glance as plainly as if the thought had been spoken.

"Then it is an assumed name," he says, with a keen look. "Alphonse Lemaire is really Théophile Latour! *Bien.*"

And he makes an entry beside the former name, with a gleam of the old cunning smile hovering round the corners of his mouth; then shuts the large book with a sudden bang; bows politely, and asks if he can be of any farther service. Of course not; we have heard enough, and may pursue our journey as we will.

So we pass out into a sort of waiting-room beyond, and consult together. We have now lost four hours. When we first started we were five behind. Five and four make nine. What chance have we of overtaking them upon the road now, being nine hours after them? The swiftest horses that ever ran could not accomplish it. Better take the rail, and push on for Paris direct. Most probably it is the very thing they did themselves!

So we decide upon this course, and dismiss the post-chaise.

Fortunately, there will be a train in about half an hour. We spend the intervening time in accomplishing a hasty ablution, and in procuring a little refreshment, for we shall be traveling all night.

Then the train comes up; we take our places, and are once more forward in pursuit.

We are in France now—on the Great North Railway—on the road to Paris; and so the feverish day passes to its close.

It is night — dark, lonely night, with the misting rain beginning to fall again, and the wearisome rushing sound of our progress dinning in our ears.

Utterly overcome by long watching and excitement, I find my ideas wander and my eyelids grow heavy. Troubled dreams, which mock reality, weave themselves in with the web of my thoughts, and I wake with a start from visions wherein Théophile, Vogelsang, Adrienne, Seabrook, and Thérèse are mingled in hideous confusion.

Every now and then a sudden stoppage — a flashing light—a passing view of a station and passengers—the entrance of fresh travelers and the departure of others, or the abrupt voice of a guard calling upon us to show our tickets—the starting off again — the monotonous rushing sound—the blurred picture of a dark wet night —dreams—waking up—complete forgetfulness once more—this over and over, with alternate slumberings and moanings from my restless fellow-traveler, who tosses his arms wildly in his

sleep, and, dreaming or waking, is ever muttering to himself.

Once in the dark night I wake up entirely,
and fall to thinking over all this strange adventure. Théophile eloped with Thérèse—Thérèse
the wife of this man beside me—Adrienne deserted! Strangest of all that Théophile should
take the name of the man Lemaire for his incognito! Done to mislead us, of course. But
we are not to be so misled. From this theme
my thoughts, somehow or another, revert to
Bürger's "Leonora." The wild midnight journey—the flying scenery—these combine, and
strike me with an odd sense of similarity; and
so I drop off to sleep again, murmuring,

"Hurra! the dead can swiftly ride!"

Then I dream that Théophile and the singer
are on before. Théophile is not only Théophile,
but Wilhelm. Wilhelm is not only Wilhelm,
but Death. He rides upon a shadowy steed,
and she clings to his waist in the likeness of
Leonora. This ghastly confusion of persons
fills me with inexplicable terror. I watch them
from the window (for it seems that I am following them in the post-chaise again). They
ride like the wind. Théophile looks round at
me; his face is that of a grinning skeleton, and
he points to Vogelsang sitting at my side. Horror! not Vogelsang now, but the livid corpse
of Fletcher is my companion in this frightful
chase!

I shriek for aid, and wake with the cry on my
lips—wake and find it gray dawn again, and
the towers of St. Denis showing dimly through
the mist. Beyond them, faint and yet distant,
lies the shadowy outline of a great city. Steeples, and house-tops, and shining cupolas grow
plainer with every instant of our progress—with
every fresh beam of early sunrise. Then glimpses of the broad bright Seine—of some grassy
earthworks stretching round the city—of the
hill, valley, and forest of Montmorency—of nestling country houses — of scattered suburbs—
streets—the walls of a station. We are arrived
at last, and it is a bright, fresh, sunny morning,
more like May than October.

Vogelsang is refreshed by a long sleep and
feels better, and we hire a voiture de place, desiring the driver to take us to the Hotel des
Etrangers in the Rue Duphot; for my companion has been here before, and knows where to go.

Oh, beautiful Paris! how fair and strange it
looks to me in the early morning! There are
no shops open, and but few people on foot.
The broad streets are silent and sunny; the
trees of the Boulevards have not yet lost all
their leaves; the gilded balconies of the hotels
and the white shutters of the lofty houses remind me of the City of the Caliph and the palaces of Granada. Now comes a graceful little
theatre—now a vista of glittering arcades—now
a glimpse of a broad street and a lofty iron column, with the statue of Napoleon crowning it
worthily—now a wide space planted round with
trees, and a white glorious temple in the midst
—a second Parthenon, classic, pillared, vast—

the church of the Madeleine. Far down toward
the left flits a vision of obelisk, and fountain, and
far palaces; but it is gone in an instant, and
we have turned aside into a narrow street, and
are pausing before the door of the Hotel des
Etrangers.

Now for an hour or two of rest and quiet ere
we search farther. We are shown to our rooms,
ordering breakfast in three hours, and desiring
the waiter to awake us at the time.

There is a sofa in my chamber, and I lie down
upon it in my clothes, preferring it to the bed,
and am soon sound asleep. The three hours
thus glide away like ten minutes, and it seems
to me that I have scarcely closed my eyes, when
the voice of the attendant outside my door informs me that it is already half past nine
o'clock, and that the breakfast is ready.

Can it all be true, or am I still dreaming?
Have I been pursuing Théophile and Thérèse,
with Vogelsang for my fellow-traveler? Have
I left Margaret and Belgium far away? Am I
in France, and is this really Paris?

CHAPTER XXXIV.

THE SHADOW OF DEATH.

"THE first thing to be done," says Vogelsang, "is to go to the prefecture of police, and
ascertain when they arrived."

To the prefecture of police we go accordingly, crossing the Seine, with a far prospect of the
stately river-palaces, and driving up a gloomy
court branching off from the Quai des Orfèvres.
The court is full of carriages, the dark passages
full of soldiers. In a long room surrounded by
clerks we next make our inquiries, and, after
meeting with many delays, and being referred
from desk to desk, are told at length that no
persons bearing such names have arrived in
Paris.

This is disappointing; yet we might almost
have expected it. It is hardly probable, after
all, that they would have traveled so unflag-
gingly as ourselves; and, in taking to the railway, it may be that we have even passed them
on the road. Well, it is but to wait another
day. They must be here to-morrow.

The morrow comes, and with the same result.
In the morning we are first at the prefecture.
In the afternoon we linger last. The officials
are very polite. They regret to disappoint
"messieurs" so often. "Messieurs'" friends
will be here to-morrow, sans doute.

And so the 19th of October passes, and they
have not yet been recorded. Oh, how dreary
and irritating is the rest of this second day!
How annoying to the heavy heart are these evidences of mirth and life—these open theatres
—these brilliant carriages—these pleasure-seek-
ers who crowd the dusk alleys of the Champs
Elysées, the booths, cafés, and concert-gardens!
How harsh is this music, and how hollow seems
the merriment of the gay city!

It is gorgeous—it is startling—it is utterly new and surprising to me; but its very splendor jars upon me now, and I could hate the people for being so happy!

Vogelsang, too, is a depressing companion—gloomy, reserved, abrupt; seldom speaking, and always absorbed in the one stern thought—revenge. He is much better now, but still very pale, and the livid mark upon his brow looks ghastly to the eye.

Night comes at last—night, and sleep, and troubled dreams, till the next day dawns.

Back then over the Seine—back in the early morning to the prefecture of police. The bureau is not yet opened—will not be opened for two hours more. Two dreary hours! What can we do for two hours?

"The Morgue is close at hand," says Vogelsang. "Let us go there."

The Morgue! I shuddered. I had often heard of the place. At any other time I should have refused to enter its dark precincts; but to-day it was in accordance with my morbid condition of mind, and I consented.

The morning was cold and bright, and the yellow Seine rushed in swift circling eddies through the arches of the Pont St. Michel, and rocked the floating baths beside the quays. I seem to remember every event of that hasty walk. There was a mountebank in a cart, dressed in motley, and vending his wares to the harsh music of a hand-organ. He had taken his stand where the carriage-way was broadest, and the surrounding crowd were laughing loudly at his jests. A troop of soldiers marched by, with ensign and band. Some children ran after me with cakes and chocolate for sale. All was hurry—gayety—life, and in the midst of it rose that one dark, melancholy building of the Marché Neuf. That low square pile, like a huge tomb, built with great blocks of stone, green and discolored from abutting on the water. Windowless, deathlike, dreary. There was a crowd of ouvriers, soldiers, women, and children gathered round the entrance. Many were going in, others coming out.

"What a pity!" said a young girl to her mother, as they passed close beside us, on leaving the place; "such a child, and so pretty!"

I looked at my companion, and drew back.

"I don't think I will go in, after all," I said.

He shrugged his shoulders and made no reply, but walked straight in, and so I followed him.

A fearful place indeed! There, on a black marble slab, exposed to the idle gaze of every eye, lay the body of a young fair boy, a mere child. His long bright hair fell in wet masses on the stone couch; his eyes and mouth were closed, and his pale lips were contracted into an expression of determined agony.

"Suicide!" murmured the people at the grating. "Suicide!"

I turned to a soldier standing by the door.

"Is it possible," I asked, "that this child can have purposely destroyed himself?"

"We can not tell, monsieur; but it is most likely. They often do."

I went back again, as if fascinated, and stood for a long time looking at him. There was another body lying at a little distance from him, but changed and frightful to look upon. I seem still to see that picture before me, with the long grating—the crowd of eager faces—the sad property of the dead, the wet and faded clothing hanging round the walls—the dim light coming from the roof—the trickling water flowing over the features of the drowned.

I could bear it no longer. I turned suddenly away, and hurried out into the street. I felt oppressed and shocked, and the blazing sunlight seemed unnaturally bold, and bright, and painful by the contrast.

Vogelsang follows me with a gloomy smile upon his harsh lips.

"You are not used to the sight of death, Monsieur Latour," he says, with a sarcastic accent.

"I have seen it but twice in my life before. Once when I was an infant, and my father died. Once again some few months since, while I was in Germany. Upon a battle-field it would not affect me thus; but upon the face of a young child—"

"Humph! Here we are in front of the prefecture of police. The two hours are nearly past."

Presently we go in again. Still the same reply.

"No strangers bearing such names upon their passports have yet been registered. We would recommend monsieur to call again in the afternoon, about four o'clock. By that time, perhaps, we may be able to afford him some information."

Will delays and disappointments never cease? It were vain to think of pleasure at a moment like this; yet how is the time to be employed? I have written to Seabrook, but it would be useless to seek letters at the post-office till to-morrow. Shall we go to the Louvre—to the Luxembourg—to Notre Dame—to Père la Chaise?

To the latter be it, then, for I am still sad and dispirited, and the face of that dead child is vividly present to my eyes.

How calm, and still, and melancholy it is here in the cemetery! The sunlight comes creeping through the leaves, and lying gently down along the graves, like a fond mourner; and we walk silently between the monuments, as in the streets of a dead city. Here are tombs like little chapels, with altar, and cross, and painted window; others like pyramids, or temples, or sharp granite obelisks. Some are carved into the semblance of a broken pillar—a draperied urn—an open volume lying on a desk, inscribed with holy and consoling words. A pleasant, tranquil place, dark with the pine and yew, planted by pious hands with every autumn flower, sacred to the Past and to the Future!

I am thinking of Margaret now, and I long

to be alone. Vogelsang has thrown himself upon the grass at the foot of a great tree, and is jotting some memoranda in his pocket-book; so I stroll away, and, finding a solitary high spot, with a view of the distant country and of the cemetery, sit down upon an humble grave, and suffer my thoughts to wander back to Brussels.

The dead are sleeping very peacefully at my feet and all around me, Margaret, and I am watching here among them with my human love beating at my heart, the only living thing in sight. It is very awful to think this; yet it fills me with a strange sort of gladness, and I feel that to have you sitting here beside me with your hand in mine, to lay my over-throbbing temples on your breast, and there die, would be a blessed rounding of my life, and happiness complete. Not in sorrow, Margaret, not even in weariness do I say it; but at this moment it seems to me that such a fate would be the fulfillment of love and life. My heart is heavy at the remembrance of all the miles that lie between us, and I can scarcely believe that you are so far distant from me. We are parted, and every parting is a form of death, as every reunion is a type of heaven.

It is well for me that I came hither to-day. The aspect of this garden grave-yard has soothed me—restored the balance of my mind. I was shocked erewhile by the sight of that fair child and his manner of death. Gloomy and terrible thoughts tormented and mocked me, as the pale Furies, Prometheus; but they are gone now, and to die seems beautiful. Death is not truly that brief pang with which we cease to live. It dates from the dark hour in which we first find that life has lost its charm; when fades the "glory from the grass, the splendor from the flower;" when all smiles are sad to us, and all tears indifferent; when, as with Hamlet, "man delights not us, nor woman either," and the very clouds and sunshine overhead look old and sorrowful.

But I did not intend to chant a requiem to thee, Margaret. I meant it for a love-song; and lo! my words are traitors to me—and mine eyes too, by this mist before them.

There is a little blue-eyed flower (a sickly, slender thing, that shivers in the cold autumnal breeze like a star in a frosty night) growing up beside the pathway at my feet. Stray child of the summer-time, I will gather thee in memory of this hour and its poetry!

And so I rise up and return to Vogelsang. My shadow has lengthened since I left him, and only the tree-tops catch the red sunlight now. His watch is in his hand. It is nearly four o'clock, and he is impatient to be gone.

Back, then, once more, to the prefecture of police. Out through the broad semicircular entrance, out into the stream of busy, careless life again, and on toward the accomplishment of our anxious task.

The clerk looks up and smiles as we approach his desk, in the long gloomy room, all lit with gas and crowded with people. He knows the errand on which we come, and begins rapidly turning over the leaves of a large volume. Presently he stops—reads some passages attentively—then, turning toward us,

"I am rejoiced to inform you, messieurs," he says, politely, "that your friends have arrived. Have the goodness to listen. 'On the evening of the 19th inst., Madame Thérèse Vogelsang; vocalist; Austrian subject; from Brussels. Also, Monsieur Alphonse Lemaire; proprietaire; French subject; from Brussels. *Description of person:* Tall; eyes, blue; nose, short; hair and beard, reddish-yellow. Residence, No. 30 Avenue ——, Champs Elysées.' Those, I believe, are the parties for whom you inquired?"

This is sufficient! The *fiacre* in which we came waits for us outside. We leap in, desire the driver to take us to the Champs Elysées, and are directly on the way.

Swiftly, swiftly along the quays and over the Pont Neuf—swiftly past the Louvre, and up to the Place de la Concorde, till we reach the central avenue leading to the Arc de l'Etoile. Here, although it is now almost dusk, the road is filled with carriages and the footways with promenaders. The long rows of bright lamps on either side look like illuminated chains stretching from end to end, and in among the trees is the gay perpetual fair of shows and mountebanks, and *cafés concerts.*

We move but slowly here, and as the Avenue —— lies up near the Jardin d'Hiver, it is long before we turn aside from the principal road to the quiet, retired spot, which, as our driver tells us, is the locality we named.

The houses are built as villas, and each is surrounded by a spacious garden. Many of them, says the *cocher,* are schools, boarding-houses, and *maisons de santé.* Within a few doors of No. 30 we pause and alight, for we are anxious not to attract the attention of the inmates, and so walk on and stop before the house.

It is built in the Italian style, surrounded by a wall and garden, and set round with lofty trees, on which few leaves remain. There are lights gleaming from some of the windows, and sometimes a passing shadow from within darkens on the blinds. By-and-by the sound of a piano is heard, and the tones of an enchanting voice linger, and rise, and fade upon the air. Then they cease—the outline of a woman's form flits along the curtain—all is still.

Observing thus, we wait and watch for full three quarters of an hour, and then turn silently away.

They are found now, and to-morrow shall see the work begun!

CHAPTER XXXV.

STRENGTH MEETS STRENGTH, AND CRAFT WITH CRAFT IS MATCHED.

It is bright morning again, and again I stand looking up at the house where my misguided brother and his mistress are dwelling. The air is chill; the blessed sun is shining as if there were nor sin nor sorrow in the world; the red and yellow leaves strew all the ground, and shower down with every gust of wind; the workmen are going to their daily labor; the little children are playing in the streets; all toil and pleasure is going on as usual, and I am standing there with a stern duty upon my hands, and a heart full of perplexity and trouble.

Looking down toward that point where the road branches off from the main avenue of the Champs Elysées, I see the figure of a man walking slowly to and fro. He pauses — he waves his hand impatiently. It is Vogelsang, and he is urging me to action. We judged it best that I should go in alone, and see my brother first, and he is waiting yonder till I return. Nay, I do not need urging; and in proof of it, I ring the bell beside the garden gate. It is answered by a servant in livery.

"Is Monsieur Lemaire at home?"

"He is breakfasting, monsieur."

"No matter. I will wait."

With these words I am shown in; and, following the man through the garden, am ushered up a broad flight of stairs, and into a small but elegant drawing-room.

"What name shall I say, monsieur?" asks the servant, lingering at the door.

"It is of no consequence. I am a stranger, and I come upon business."

Left alone in the room, I observe every thing with that peculiar susceptibility to trifles, that painfully acute power of seeing and reasoning, which, at times of great excitement or anxiety, seems to endue the senses with a twofold power.

The furniture of the *salon* is rich, but not new. One or two valuable paintings adorn the walls, and suspended in the most conspicuous situation hangs a superb full-length portrait of an officer under Napoleon. His breast is covered with orders; his weather-beaten face and white mustache tell of long service; he leans upon the neck of a bay charger, and a distant view of the sands and Pyramids of Egypt points to the scene of at least one of his campaigns. Crossing over to examine it more nearly, I see the name of DAVID in the corner.

The induction is easy. Théophile has hired the house for the season, while the owners are absent at their country seat or on their travels.

Some books lie on the table, and I examine one. It is the "History of the Consulate and the Empire," by Thiers; and under an engraved coat of arms pasted in the first fly-leaf, I see the name of De Montreuil—the name of the owners of the place, of course.

A grand piano-forte is placed close under the portrait. . It is open, and the candles which **were used** the night before are yet standing, half burnt down, on either side of the music-book. Near it, two chairs drawn close together seem to show me where they have been sitting side by side; and a man's hat is thrown carelessly upon a couch beside the window.

Strange that the veriest trifles should find a place in my attention at this moment; but I remember noticing that it was a white hat, and that I had never known Théophile wear a white hat before!

As I am thinking this, the door opens, the same servant appears, and I am requested to follow him.

Down stairs this time, through a broad hall and a spacious library, and into a pleasant parlor opening upon a conservatory and garden. There is breakfast on the table — a lady in a white morning robe leaning back in an easy-chair by the fireside, reading the newspaper—a gentleman with his back turned toward me, stooping over some flowers in the conservatory beyond.

She lays aside the paper as I enter, with an anxious glance at my face, and half rises from her chair.

She is most lovely to-day in that white robe. Her dark lustrous hair is gathered in massive rolls at the back of her head, and fastened by a single golden arrow; her beautiful arms are half hidden by the white lace sleeves; her attitude is that of a queen, graceful, indolent, dignified—like Cleopatra's in the golden galley.

"You wish to see Monsieur Lemaire," she says, courteously, and with the slightest foreign accent in the world. "He will be here immediately. Pray take a seat."

I bow profoundly, but remain standing, hat in hand.

"Laurent, request your master to step this way. A gentleman is waiting to **speak** with him."

The servant passes into the conservatory, and madame resumes the newspaper, but I can see that she does not read a single line.

Now the servant has reached **his** side — he pauses — turns — enters the room, and I recognize — not my brother — not Théophile, but a harsh, unprepossessing countenance, which I certainly remember to **have seen** and noticed lately, but where I can **not tell**!

"You have asked **for me**, monsieur? I am entirely at your service."

That sneering smile, that glance from beneath the drooping eyelids, that peculiar gesture, I could swear that I have—yes, by heaven! it is the **man** Lemaire himself—the real owner of the name—the lessee of the Brussels theatre!

"You have business with me, I believe. Pray, **is it** respecting theatrical matters?"

Still breathless, bewildered, utterly taken by surprise, I can only look at him. A crowd of ideas are flitting like lightning through my mind. Where is Théophile? Shall I ask for him? Shall I tell them who I am?"

"You have but to speak, monsieur I am waiting."

This is said somewhat impatiently, and with a surprised, suspicious glance from beneath the red eyelashes, which fills me with aversion, so foxlike is it, and so stealthy.

Madame drops the paper now, and fixes her dark eyes full upon my face.

"Perhaps," she observes haughtily, "if the gentleman will not state the purport of his visit, he will, at least, be so obliging as to inform us of his name."

My course is taken now. I return her gaze steadily, and the tone of my voice, as I reply, is measured, resonant, penetrating.

"My name, madame, could be of little importance to this gentleman. I came here this morning to meet a very different person. You, most probably, can guess whom I mean, and will, perhaps, favor me with some address by which I can find him."

She still looks at me fixedly, as before, for a few seconds. and the pupils of her eyes seem to dilate as if from some inner passion of anger, suspicion, or defiance. Then, finding that I sustain her scrutiny unwaveringly, she suddenly drops the lids, and leaning back with an affectation of proud indifference, turns to Monsieur Lemaire and says languidly,

"You see, Alphonse, it is a mistake altogether. This—this person is inquiring for the people to whom the house belongs. I think we can oblige him; for, if you remember, they left us a card by which we were to direct any letters that might arrive for Monsieur (what is his name?)—Monsieur de—de Montreuil. Will you have the kindness to pass me the paper-case? I am almost sure that the card is inside. We will not detain you, monsieur, many minutes. Ah! here it is—'Monsieur le Comte de Montreuil, Poste Restante, Baden-Baden, Germany.'"

"I thank you, madame," I reply, in the same tone, and without having once removed my eyes from her face, "but it was not to meet M. le Comte de Montreuil that I came here to-day."

"Indeed!" she exclaims quickly, looking up at me again with a sharp unquiet glance. "Pray whom else could you have thought to see here, in my house?"

"Monsieur Théophile Latour."

I have expected something of a start, an exclamation, a passing expression of surprise or shame; but no — she is calm, impassable, unmoved as a statue; only, on looking more closely, I fancy that the rich brunette tint upon her cheek is a shade paler, and that the delicate nostril quivers twice or thrice, but almost imperceptibly.

"You are in error, sir," she says, clearly and deliberately. "Monsieur Théophile Latour is not here. You had better direct your letters to Brussels. He is residing there, and they will be sure to find him."

"To Brussels, madame! But he has left Brussels!"

"Indeed? I was not aware of that."

So calm, so collected, so natural! I am almost thrown off my guard, and begin to doubt the evidences of the ball and the journey.

"Not aware of it, madame?"

"You echo my words strangely, sir. I repeat that I was 'not aware of it.' Are you contented?"

"But he traveled with you from Brussels!"

"Monsieur!"

She rises from her seat and draws herself to her full stature as she utters this one word so full of pride, anger, offended modesty. The flashing eyes—the indignant gesture—the imperious tone, baffle and confuse me. I hesitate—I pause.

"Have the goodness to repeat that assertion, monsieur."

"I—that is—Monsieur Latour—did he not travel from Brussels in your company?"

"Monsieur Lemaire was so obliging, sir, as to favor me with his escort from Brussels to Paris—Monsieur Lemaire, the impressario of the theatre in that city. I am but very slightly acquainted with Monsieur Latour, and though I do not feel myself called upon to account for my actions to any person (more particularly to an entire stranger), yet, rather than suffer such a report to become current, I must beg leave to observe that a step such as you have just named —a step so unusual, so equivocal, so open to observation and censure, would be utterly opposed to my principles, my inclinations, and the strictly reserved line of conduct to which I have adhered throughout the course of my professional life. Monsieur Lemaire, will you have the kindness to corroborate my words, and to show your passport to this—this very inquisitive and singular gentleman?"

I came here with the resolution of not exchanging one syllable, if possible, with this woman, and behold, she alone had taken upon herself the entire conversation! Her looks, her words, her very gestures were all - convincing, and wrought upon me with an irresistible power. Yet how reconcile this with Vogelsang's narrative—with my brother's disappearance—with the testimony of his note, now in my possession—with the cigar-case found in the carriage?

Monsieur Lemaire drew a folded paper from his pocket-book and handed it to me with his false smile.

"Monsieur may inspect my passport if he pleases," he said, shrugging his shoulders, "but really one might almost think that we were in a court of justice, or, at the least, passing through a frontier town!"

Yes. Here is the passport, and perfectly correct. "Monsieur Alphonse Lemaire; French subject. Tall; eyes, blue; nose, short; hair and beard, reddish-yellow." The same from which the entry was made in the books at the prefecture of police. I have nothing to say to this. I am almost ashamed of my own suspicions, and feel my situation more than embarrassing.

Happening to look up suddenly from the paper, I see a triumphant glance pass between

ll my former doubts.
madame turns to me,
small velvet case lying
s, even more haughtily

re, sir, if you choose to
en your curiosity is sat-
iew may be considered
red your intrusion and
ns, not because I felt
any law of politeness,
l it my duty to defend
the scandalous report
lacity to repeat to my
I can not imagine it to
urself, I fear must have
ent of my honor. It is
itradict that rumor, and
justice, you will not fail
ur, we fully understand

hat glance which I sur-
not have looked at her
that I should even have
gize for all that I had
, and dignity is there in
. As it is, however, I
the case from the man-
e along the document.
*gelsang; vocalist; Aus-
sels.*"

to this either. Every
le. I am defeated, but
hat I can do now is to

—I have even begun to
sudden thought flashes
ilation, and, taking the
re I had laid it upon the
gether.

*or Paris, October 17th,
au,*   E. LECROIX."

*or Paris, October 18th,
au,*   E. LECROIX."

upon my heart like a
elf grow pale, and the
d as I hold them up be-
ing upon the two sen-
xclaim hoarsely,
plain this? How could
madame, and yet pass
."

and downcast eye, and
es that mean? Is the

onsieur," interposes the
contempt at her silent
itless energy upon her
it. Monsieur Lemaire,
els at the same time,
ed to return when we
the frontier. He had
nt which demanded his
id he only rejoined me
the second day."

"Yes, yes," stammered the manager, "that was it! *Mon Dieu,* that was it, upon my honor!"

"And may I take the liberty of inquiring, madame, where you stopped to wait for the arrival of this gentleman?"

"It *is* a liberty, sir, yet I will answer you. It was at Douai."

At Douai—and we took the railway from Quievrain! Had we but pursued the journey as we began it for a few hours more, we should have overtaken her and known the truth of this story! Well, after all, it is useless to question or irritate her farther, and I feel that, as far as evidence goes, I am powerless. Best, then, to appear satisfied—to lull suspicion—to meet craft by craft—to *prove* all before I say more.

My face expresses, perhaps, something of the deliberations and doubts that are passing through my mind, for I find them both watching me narrowly. I make a strong effort to control voice and countenance, and, after a few moments' apparent reflection, assume a look of melancholy conviction, and sigh heavily.

"Then, madame, you can tell me positively nothing respecting M. Théophile, excepting that he has been in Brussels?"

"Excepting that he *is* in Brussels. I last saw him there, and I believe him to be still resident there. How do you know that he is gone?"

I meet her searching glance, and say quietly, "A friend of mine called at his house, madame, to endeavor to procure from him some money which I had lent to him not long since. They told my friend that he was gone nobody knew whither; but it was supposed (you will excuse me for repeating it)—it was supposed that he had accompanied you to Paris."

It is now her turn to suspect, to interrogate me. How stern and piercing is the steady, prolonged gaze of those dilating eyes!

"Then you have lent money to M. Latour?" she says, inquiringly.

I bow without speaking.

"How did you know my address?"

"I applied for it at the prefecture of police."

"And why did you ask for Monsieur Lemaire when it was Monsieur Latour you wished to see?".

"The entry stated that you were accompanied by Monsieur Lemaire. The description of his person tallied sufficiently with that of my —my debtor. I thought it possible that he might have assumed an incognito while traveling, especially if he be as deeply in debt to others as he is to me, and seeks to escape his creditors."

This explanation, and the manner in which I gave it, seems to satisfy her. She draws a long breath, and, for the first time since she rose from it in anger, sinks back into her chair.

"It appears to me, sir," she says, with her fascinating smile, "that we have misunderstood each other from beginning to end of this conversation. Had you told me at first that you were Monsieur Latour's creditor, and confided to me the motive of your visit, we need not have wasted so much time in useless discussion. I really regret that I can be of no service to you, and I hope that you may recover your money. I would advise you to send your letters to Brussels without delay, for if he were absent he has doubtless returned before this. I wish you a good-morning. Laurent, attend this gentleman to the door."

Thus saying, she inclines her head graciously, and resumes the newspaper. Lemaire stands scowling after me near the conservatory door, and I follow the servant back through the library and hall, across the garden, and out into the road.

"What news?" cries Vogelsang, eagerly, as I rejoin him in the Champs Elysées. "What news?"

And so I tell him all that has passed, word for word, as I have told it here, and when I conclude I ask him what he thinks of it.

But he shakes his head, and, looking downward with a troubled face, says,

"I don't know. Don't ask me. I don't know what to think—I don't know what to think!"

Then, silent and gloomy both, we walk on side by side till we reach the great post-office in the Rue Jean Jacques Rousseau, a long way from the Champs Elysées. Here I find one letter awaiting me, and the bold, careless superscription tells me that it is from Norman Seabrook. It is brief enough—scarce half a page in length—and I read it almost at a glance:

"Oct. 20, 18—

"I have only bad news for you, my dear friend. Hauteville is sold. The purchase-money was all paid in on the evening of the 15th, and we have every reason for believing that your brother has the entire sum in his possession. We know, of course, how and upon whom it will be spent! I have this from Monsieur Pascal, his lawyer. The amount was 500,000 francs. Madame L. bears it better than one could expect. I have no time for more at present, but will write again to-morrow.

"Yours ever,   N. S."

"Read this," I cry, thrusting the letter into Vogelsang's hand. "Read this! Mon Dieu! what is to be done? What has become of him? My dear, dear brother!"

Vogelsang reads it, and grows paler as he reads. Coming to the end, he crushes it in his hand and looks gloomily into my face.

"Foul play!" he says, in a low, deep voice. "Foul play somewhere! We must fathom this abyss: there is crime at the bottom of it, and my vengeance will be deeper yet—and sweeter!"

CHAPTER XXXVI.

REVELATIONS.

WE are on the road again! It is the evening of the 21st of October, about six or seven hours since I left the Avenue ——; and autumn's early sunset tints all the fields and house-tops of St. Denis with a red glow, as if we saw the landscape through a painted window.

On the road by which we came four days ago —that iron road which intersects France in a northward line from Paris to Brussels—flying forward, ever forward, while sunset fades into dusk, and dusk thickens into night!

We have a railway carriage to ourselves this time, for the sake of privacy and liberty of speech—this, chiefly, because we are no longer alone, and need to talk with our companion. He whom I style "our companion" is a small pale man, with green spectacles, and a particularly vacant countenance. He is dressed in a suit of threadbare black, wears a hat too large for his head, and a crumpled white neckcloth tied loosely round his throat. He looks more like a petty schoolmaster or peripatetic preacher than any thing else, and carries a large cotton umbrella between his knees. Neither beard nor mustache adorn his countenance. He looks not to the right nor to the left, and, when spoken to, turns upon you a large, dull, meaningless gray eye, in which no spark of intelligence is ever seen to quicken.

Certainly a more insignificant and utterly unpromising person could scarcely have been selected for a traveling associate; yet in that man's pocket are the only proofs we possess— the note and the cigar-case; and into his ear we are pouring all our doubts, adventures, discoveries, suspicions, and fears. Already he is in possession of all the leading facts, from the conversation which I overheard in the conservatory on the night of the soirée, down to my interview with Madame Vogelsang this morning, and to all this he listened with a face as absent and passionless as if he were counting the bricks in a dead wall.

Only now and then he asks some trifling question, or enters a brief note very slowly and methodically upon the leaves of a greasy pocket-book, and but for this we might almost fancy that he neither heard nor heeded a syllable of all that has been said.

His name is Pierre Corneille Barthelet. He is an agent of police, and one of the most sagacious of Parisian detectives.

Forward, always forward in the deep night— past the lighted stations with never a stop—past the up-train with a shock of vision, like the sensation of a sudden fall from some giddy height —forward, forward like the wind! It is an express train, bound for Brussels, and stopping only at Quievrain and Valenciennes by the way.

The whole scene, police agent and all, seems like some rushing terrible dream, and the tale we tell him a fantastic fiction.

"And now are you sure that I know all the circumstances?" he asks, carelessly, "because that is important."

"I believe that we have forgotten nothing."

"Humph! You made one very false move, gentlemen."

"When, and how?"

"In going to the house as you did. It must have put them on their guard."

"And they will escape us again!" cries Vogelsang, with a fierce oath. "Oh, I must go back—I must go back by the next train!"

"Indeed, they suspect nothing," I interpose. "Have I not already told you how I replied to her questions, how I satisfied her that I was but a creditor of Théophile's?"

"Yes, yes; but it is not enough! She only affects to believe you; she will escape before I can get back!"

"Be tranquil, monsieur," observes Barthelet, with calm indifference. "They are safe enough. I have provided for that, and set a watch upon the house. As it happens, no mischief has been done; but I objected to the way in which you entered. It was unprofessional."

So saying, Monsieur Barthelet looks at his watch by the light of the dim lamp above; observes that we have just three hours left; takes off his hat (brushing it carefully with his sleeve before he hangs it up), and, tying his pocket-handkerchief over his head, composes himself for a nap.

This nap lasts till we reach Quievrain, when he awakes, as if by magic, and follows us out of the carriage to the passport-office, where the elderly gentleman with the white head and the eye-glass is still sitting, as if he had never left his place since we last saw him.

He recognizes us the moment we enter, and the cunning smile hovers round his lips and in the corners of his eyes.

"Well, sir," he says, peering at Vogelsang from behind the top rails of his desk, "well, sir, have you found your wife?"

But, before my companion can frame a reply, Monsieur Barthelet has glided from behind us, and is standing beside the old gentleman's elbow. A whispered word—the sight of a written paper drawn from the greasy pocket-book, has worked wonders. The face of the *chef de bureau* has become suddenly grave and attentive. He requests us to be seated. He listens deferentially to the agent's hurried statement. He takes down the same great book, and again reads up every page, in the Hebrew fashion, only more quickly.

Suddenly the fore finger pauses in its course; the page is compared with one a little way before it; they look significantly into each other's faces, and we are called over to inspect the entries.

They stand thus:

"*Passed this day, Oct. 17th, 18—, between the hours of one and two P.M., Madame Thérèse Vogelsang; vocalist; Austrian subject. Going to Paris from Brussels. Seen at Quievrain, for Paris, Oct. 17, 18—.*

"*Chef de Bureau.*   E. LECROIX.*"

"*Passed this day, Oct. 17th, 18—, between the hours of one and two P.M., Monsieur Alphonse Lemaire; French subject; propriétaire. Going to Paris from Brussels. Description of person: Tall; blue eyes; auburn hair. Seen at Quievrain, for Paris, Oct. 17th, 18—.*

"*Chef de Bureau.*   E. LECROIX.*"

Then, a little farther on,

"*Passed this day, Oct. 18th, 18—, between the hours of four and five P.M., Monsieur Alphonse Lemaire; French subject. Tall; eyes blue; nose short; hair and beard reddish-yellow. Going to Paris from Brussels. Seen at Quievrain, for Paris, Oct. 18th, 18—.*

"*Chef de Bureau.*   E. LECROIX.*"

Two Monsieur Lemaires have passed the frontier!

CHAPTER XXXVII.

THE CHAIN IS BROKEN.

"AND it was from this point, gentlemen," says Barthelet, "that you took the rail in preference to the road?"

"From this point."

"Then, clearly, we must first find the post-house from which they had their next relay of horses. Thence we shall easily discover the road by which they traveled. *Tenez.*"

And Monsieur Barthelet takes a small volume from his pocket, and after referring backward and forward three or four times from the map to the letter-press, from the letter-press to the map, observes dryly that Quievrain has four *postes aux chevaux*, and that we must go from one to the other till we meet with the right.

This is dismal work, traversing the streets of Quievrain in the dark, three hours after midnight. It reminds me of the first step which we took upon the journey on leaving Brussels, only that it is infinitely more wretched; and over all we do, or think, or say, there hangs the "shadow of a fear"—sombre, chilling, undefined.

At the first post-house we have to wake the people from their sleep, and they reply to our questions surlily enough. They have no remembrance of any such carriage or travelers. What right have we to disturb folks for nothing? It is their business to furnish horses, not information. They have a great mind to give us over to the police; but they content themselves with slamming the door in our faces. At all of which Monsieur Barthelet smiles grimly, and, tapping the breast-pocket of his coat, says, with a tone of quiet power, that he has "a little paper there by which he could exact their civility —ay, and the civility of the gendarmes too, if he thought fit to produce it!"

At the second we fare no better; and at the third we find all hands busy, and every body up and stirring. It is now nearly half past four; the great lumbering diligence, swaying to and fro like a sleepy giant with a hood on, fills all the yard; horses are being harnessed; postilions are getting ready; luggage is being heaped on the roof; some early passengers are darting here and there, and getting in every body's way; and all this confusion by the light of glancing lanterns, with the black sky overhead.

Of course we can not get attended to in the hurry and bustle of the moment, so we wait till the diligence has departed, lurching and pitching, and still very sleepy, out of the yard, when Barthelet makes the old inquiry.

No one can remember any thing, whether of the carriage, the travelers, or their destination. This is the largest post-house in Quievrain; they keep the greatest number of horses—supply the most extensive circle of customers. It is hardly probable that they would recollect it, without something had occurred to render the journey remarkable. They are, however, very civil, and offer no objection when we request permission to interrogate the servants of the establishment. But from these we can obtain nothing, and are about to turn away in quest of the fourth and last post-house, when some one recollects that we have not yet spoken to the postillion, Van Comp, who, it appears, has not long come off a journey, and is now in bed.

Unwilling to lose any chance of success, we wait till Van Comp is awakened, and pass the time, weary as we are, in pacing up and down the yard, for the morning is bitterly cold, and there has been a frost.

At length Van Comp, a little, shrewd-looking man, with quick black eyes, makes his appearance, half dressed and shivering. So small, so puckered, so elfin is his *tout ensemble*, that I find myself at a loss to decide whether he be an active old man or a withered boy, which perplexity is increased when I hear the shrill treble of his voice replying to Barthelet's questions.

He speaks only Flemish, of which neither Vogelsang nor myself comprehend a syllable, and we watch the conference in silence. Barthelet, as usual, looks entirely unconcerned, and speaks occasionally in a low, drawling tone, to which the other responds with a torrent of volubility and a variety of lively gesticulations. This goes on for several minutes, when Barthelet seems to give some order—the ostlers run to the stables—a heavy post-chaise is brought out of a coach-house, and Van Comp, rushing over to a pump in a distant corner of the yard, proceeds to plunge his head and face twice or thrice into a bucket full of water, apparently as the first step toward completing his toilet.

"What now?" I exclaim, eagerly. "What does he say?"

"He remembers to have driven a lady and gentleman from here to Valenciennes about five or six days ago. All that he can be sure of is that the lady was very handsome, that her companion paid him in gold, and that it was about two or three o'clock in the afternoon. At Valenciennes they took fresh horses, and went on without delay. He can not tell where they went, but he knows the post-house to which he drove them, and he supposes that from the peo-

ple there we shall learn all we require. I have ordered a chaise to be got ready immediately, and he will drive us."

Monsieur Barthelet delivers this important news with about as much energy and emphasis as one might remark upon the state of the weather, or any other equally exciting subject, and then falls to consulting the map and the pocket-book.

And now we are on the road again.

It is still dark, and the bright carriage-lamps, illumining a narrow patch on either side, reveal brief glimpses of trees and gates, and show our little postillion jerking up and down before the front windows. Thus, in silence and gloom, we journey on to Valenciennes, where, with little difficulty, we recover the next clew, and so on, post by post, in the direction of Douai, which we enter between nine and ten o'clock in the morning, with the sun shining coldly overhead, and the white frost glittering like diamond dust on the ramparts and church towers.

We are driven to the Hôtel de Flandres, where we order breakfast, and request a few moments' conversation with the landlord—a lofty gentleman adorned with rings, pins, and chains, who listens to our inquiries with an indulgent air, and replies in an infinitely condescending manner.

Truly he has some recollection of the travelers to whom we allude, and he imagines that their stay at his house was not prolonged beyond a few hours. But madame keeps the books, and attends to all these little matters, and he thinks, upon the whole, that we had better mention the subject to her. Madame's little bureau lies to the right of the *salle à manger*. She is always there, and we may seek her when we are disposed.

And monsieur strolls out of the room, clinking the Napoleons in his pockets as he walks, as if to show us that he has plenty of them, and rather likes the sound.

To madame's room we repair accordingly. She is very gracious and has been handsome. She consults a large ledger, and presently discovers the following entry, which she permits us to read, and which Barthelet copies forthwith into the greasy pocket-book:

Monsieur and Madame—arrived October 17th, 18—.
Dinner for two...................14
Vin de Champagne......................20
Café for two............................4
Apartments and service...................16
Breakfast for two.........................10
Vin de Champagne at ditto..............10
                                        84

"And in what manner did this lady and gentleman leave?" I asked, eagerly. "Did they take a post-chaise from here?"

Madame shakes her head. Had they done so, there would be an entry of it in the ledger, which there certainly is not.

"Can madame remember at what hour they left the house?"

Madame thinks that it was immediately after

breakfast—about eleven o'clock; but perhaps the waiters can tell me this.

The waiters are called and questioned. They remember the lady and gentleman perfectly. "They arrived quite late the first day, and dined about eight o'clock in the evening. They went away the next morning after breakfast, about twelve or one in the day. They paid the bill, and walked out arm in arm. They never came back again."

"But their luggage?"

"They had no luggage, m'sieur."

"No luggage!"

"Not a single bag or box of any description. The gentleman had his great-coat upon his arm, and the lady carried a small velvet reticule." They were positive of this, because "down there in the *cuisine, là bas*, they had talked of it together, and, *mon Dieu!* what fun the cook made of it!"

And the waiters glanced at each other, and grinned behind their hands at the remembrance of this irresistible joke.

"Can you describe the lady?"

"No, m'sieur. They had the two rooms yonder on the *premier étage*, where the bedchamber opens off the *salon*, and there the lady retired whenever we were in attendance. At the dinner they would not suffer us to wait, but rang whenever they wished the courses removed; and then the lady sat with her veil down and her bonnet on. It was quite plain that she did not wish to be seen, and that made us try all the more to catch a glimpse of her face. But it was impossible, m'sieur—quite impossible. Her *finesse* was perfect."

"*Eh bien!* but the gentleman—what was he like?"

"The gentleman! Oh, he was tall and fair. Jeannette thought him handsome; but, at all events, he was very liberal—paid like a prince."

And this, question them as we will, is all the news that we can obtain. Barthelet, for the first time since we have been together, exhibits a faint emotion in his face, and looks less blank than usual. The emotion, unfortunately, is vexation.

He then dismisses the waiters, asks madame for our bill, and, when it is paid, strolls out into the street, whither we follow him.

"This matter grows difficult," he says moodily, as if thinking aloud. "We are thrown off the scent entirely now."

"Then all that we have to do is to find it again," interrupts Vogelsang, with a look of dogged resolution. "We must beat every bush in the neighborhood—try every petty village, inn, and farm-house all around, till we find the evidences of their track. Why, it must have been some time in the evening of the day they left this place when Lemaire joined them."

"Of course it was," replies Barthelet, referring to the pocket-book. "He passed the frontier between four and five. It takes about five hours by posting, and about one hour and forty minutes by rail, to travel from Quievrain to Douai. By whichever route, he would meet them that night. The time and place of that meeting once found, the object of our journey will be accomplished, or I am much mistaken."

And now, guided in every respect by our "professional" ally, we proceed upon the search. The first step, says he, is to make inquiry at every livery-stable in the town, though it should take us a week to do it. However, there are but three or four, and to these he pilots us through street, and market-place, and square, after a peculiar fashion of his own, wherein he leads without seeming to lead us, and by pointing out the road, gliding now before and now behind us, loitering, hastening, and doubling back upon his own footsteps, he dexterously contrives to make us always appear like the party in advance, while himself is strolling on carelessly in the rear, looking in at the shop-windows, or walking on the opposite side of the way with an utterly unconscious face, as if he had no acquaintances and no business in the world.

At no livery-stable or post-house in Douai had they been heard of or seen. The chain of evidence is completely broken, and to find the lost links seems now to be an almost hopeless task.

However, we hire a vehicle, and, taking the first road that presents itself, travel in a northerly direction, and after turning aside to many a little village, farm-house, and hamlet by the way, arrive toward dusk at the town of Orchies, where we dine and spend the night.

Alas! the seeking and waiting—

"All the hope, and the fear, and the sorrow—
All the aching of heart, the restless unsatisfied longing,
All the dull, deep pain, and constant anguish of patience!"

CHAPTER XXXVIII.

THE LOST LINKS.

NORTH, south, east, and west, in every direction for twenty miles round Douai, we sought them in vain. Had the earth opened beneath their feet when they went out arm in arm from the Hôtel de Flandres that morning of the 18th of October, they could not have disappeared more entirely till the period of their arrival in Paris. Northward as far as Lille and Tournay; southward to Cambray and Arras; eastward to Bethune, and westward over all the ground lying between Douai and Valenciennes, we searched diligently, and so passed four days more.

We began to despair. Even Monsieur Pierre Corneille Barthelet was heard to murmur occasionally, and Vogelsang became more morose and silent than ever.

It seemed really as if they must have taken the rail from Douai to Paris; yet, in that case, what had become of Théophile, and where had Thérèse been overtaken by Lemaire? The whole transaction remained a mystery, and suspense became torture.

Matters were in this position, and we were driving slowly along toward the evening of the fourth day, the 26th of October, when Vogelsang proposed suddenly that we should return to Paris.

"This hopeless wandering about is worse than useless," he said. "It will result in nothing. If you do not choose to go back, I will."

"I do not choose to go back," I replied warmly. "I will not be so easily baffled. I am determined to find my brother before I set foot in Paris again."

"Very well. I go to-morrow morning."

"You may do as you please, Herr Vogelsang. I remain."

"And what does Monsieur Barthelet intend doing?" asked Vogelsang, with a bitter smile. "Is he not yet weary of exploring this picturesque neighborhood?"

Monsieur Barthelet was looking out of the window, and appeared not to hear the question.

Vogelsang repeated it with emphasis.

"Sir," replied the police agent, still looking out of the window, "I have undertaken this case, and I have no intention of leaving it unfinished. My professional reputation is concerned in it. Hollo, you *garçon*, where does that lane lead to?"

He had let down the glasses now, and was addressing the post-boy.

"Over the fields somewhere, monsieur."

"Is there any village?"

"I don't know, monsieur. I think there are a few cottages."

"Well, drive up there."

"I can't, monsieur. The road is not wide enough for the wheels, and up yonder it gets narrower still."

"Then we will walk, and you may go back with the horses."

"But, monsieur—it is such a mean place—it is absolutely *au bout du monde*," remonstrates the post-boy. "Nobody ever goes there."

"No matter. *I* choose to go there; and if I can not be driven, I will walk."

So saying, Monsieur Barthelet alights and bids us discharge the carriage, wherein, as usual, we obey him implicitly; and so we set off on foot.

The first lane merges into a second, the second into a third, the third into a fourth, and so on, as if they would never end—long, green quiet lanes, all grass under foot, with holly and thorn bushes on either side, and long trailing boughs laden with blackberries lying across the path, and scant trees standing here and there, like lonely sentinels, at irregular distances.

The farther we go the farther we seem to wander from all human habitation. Before us stretch the lanes green and straight; behind us the sun is setting broad and red, on the very verge of the horizon. There is not a cottage or shed any where in sight.

Now we come upon two little children gathering wild berries under the hedge, but they can scarcely comprehend us, and the only reply we get is that the houses are farther on, "*tout droit.*"

So straight forward we go, and the night comes creeping up.

Suddenly the lane takes a curve—we see a column of white smoke above the trees—a faint light glimmering through the dusk—an open space of common, and a cluster of small cottages, with a wind-mill and a little mean auberge in the midst. The auberge is a wretched whitewashed building, with a dunghill before the door, and the words

HÔTEL DE NAMUR,
Ici on loge à pied et à cheval,

painted in large red letters across the front of the house.

Hotel, indeed! Miserable as it is, however, we must put up there for the night, for there is no other, and we have been on the road all day since dawn.

Tired, dusty, travel-worn as we are, it would seem that customers so well-dressed are seldom entertained at the Hôtel de Namur, for the landlady courtesies, and the landlord bows, and hovers round us, and dusts the chairs before he will suffer us to be seated, and is in an agony of bustling civility.

"Will messieurs please to dine or sup? Do messieurs intend to pass the night here? Shall a fire be lighted in one of the chambers, since we have not, I grieve to say, another *salon?*"

The "*salon*" in which we find ourselves is a long low apartment, with whitewashed walls and sanded floor, and the words *Salle à Manger* painted up over the door. A deal table, some benches and wooden chairs, and a stove, are all the furniture; and two peasants, with a jug of red wine between them, are sitting staring at us with open eyes and mouths in a far corner, near the window.

We decide upon dining up stairs, order the best dinner they can muster, and sit down by the stove in the public room till ours is prepared; whereupon landlord and landlady both disappear suddenly, before we can put a single question to either, and an immense confusion of heavy feet overhead and sharp voices in the kitchen is immediately begun. Presently the two rusties finish their wine and withdraw in bashful silence, and we are left with the place to ourselves.

Thus more than an hour passes away without interruption, save once, when a party of three or four men and women enter and call for the landlord; but, finding their custom unheeded and three gentlemen sitting round the stove in the dark room, they retire discontentedly, and return no more.

At length the door opens, and our host, with a napkin thrown over his arm and a candle in his hand, informs us that the chamber is ready and the table served. And really every thing is far more comfortable than we had anticipated. The bed has been wheeled on one side; the table-cloth and dishes are plain, but clean; a blazing wood fire is crackling on the hearth, and to travelers so weary matters wear a cheerful appearance.

The landlord will wait upon us himself, and the landlady too. They have provided soup for us, and omelettes, and fowls, and *bouilli*, and a dessert of cheese and apples, and three bottles of Macon wine, and a flask of *eau-de-vie*, which we are assured is "'*vielle de cognac*'—superb—equal to any we could procure in Douai, or even in Paris!"

So faint are we, and so tired, that for several minutes we can do nothing but eat in silence. At length Barthelet speaks.

"You have not many travelers come here, I suppose. Your chief custom is from those in the village, *n'est-ce-pas?*"

"Our *chief* custom, certainly, is in the village," says the landlord, with an emphasis on "chief;" "but we do entertain travelers sometimes—gentlemen, like yourselves, and even ladies."

"Yes, yes, even ladies," adds the hostess, with some pride. "For instance, messieurs, it is not many days since we lodged two gentlemen and a lady—people of the highest rank, messieurs, who did not care what they paid us!"

Ha! We all paused and involuntarily looked at each other. For some seconds nobody spoke, and then Barthelet resumed:

"Two gentlemen and a lady, you say, who did not care what they paid! They must have been rich, then!"

"Rich, indeed—yes! Monsieur should have seen the lady's beautiful ring and chains, and her cloak all of velvet and lace, fit for an empress! Ah! they *were* rich, and we should not care how many such guests came to the Hôtel de Namur!"

Barthelet was silent for some time, and went on with his dinner as if nothing had taken place. As for me, I could not eat another morsel, and even Vogelsang seemed perturbed and restless. Our hosts were in despair. Did not monsieur like the soup? Would monsieur try an omelette? The fowls were delicious—just a little wing? They were afraid that monsieur must be unwell!

I replied that I was too much fatigued to enjoy any thing, and finding that I could touch nothing else, I drank a glass of brandy, and tried to swallow a crust of bread that almost choked me.

So the meal draws to a close; the dessert is placed before us, and Barthelet, while leisurely peeling an apple, pursues his inquiries.

"I fancy, Monsieur Callot" (our host's name is Callot), "that your rich customers were friends of ours — friends of whom we are even now in search. Was not the lady very handsome, and the gentleman fair?"

"*Mon Dieu*, yes! The lady was beautiful as an angel, and the gentleman was fair. Both gentlemen, indeed, were fair, but the first was the handsomest. How astonishing that messieurs should know them! But it is charming!"

And both landlord and landlady rub their hands with delight, and then, finding that we do not respond to their congratulations, look surprised and uncomfortable, and full of curiosity.

"So, the first gentleman was the handsomest," says Barthelet, still occupied upon the apple. "Let me see: they must have arrived here about—about three o'clock in the day, did they not?"

"About four, I think, monsieur—about four."

"Just so—about four. And they dined here?"

"Yes, they dined here, but not till nearly eight o'clock in the evening. They waited, do you see, for the other gentleman!"

"Ah! true. They waited, of course. And he arrived in time?"

"Oh yes, he arrived by a little after seven."

"And they were delighted to see him?"

"Why, monsieur, really—I—that is, I don't think the handsome gentleman seemed very well pleased. He did not seem to be good friends with him at first; and, to tell the truth, my wife did overhear (quite by chance) a little conversation between the first gentleman and his lady that led us to think—Marie, tell the gentlemen what you heard them saying."

"Why, gentlemen, you see I was getting ready the table in this very apartment, and they were in there, in the second chamber, and I heard the lady say, 'He will soon be here now.' To which the gentleman replied, 'I am sorry for it. I did not want his company. I never liked him.' And then the lady said, 'But you know how necessary it is for us to be friends with him. And as matters are with us, it is very fortunate for us that he happens to be traveling our way. If there be any inquiries made, his absence will confirm every thing, and nobody will suspect your identity. Pray be civil to him, for my sake.' And the gentleman said, 'I would do any thing for your sake.' And that was all I heard."

"And then, I suppose, he did arrive. Had they any quarrel, these two gentlemen?"

"Quarrel! oh dear no, they got quite pleasant after the dinner, and when they parted at night they shook hands. They even took a little walk together in the morning before breakfast."

"Hum! that looked well, certainly. And after breakfast they all went away together?"

"The lady and the red-haired gentleman went away together, monsieur, and followed the handsome gentleman."

"Followed him! Do you mean to say that he started first, and without madame?"

"Yes, monsieur. He went on farther, when they took the little promenade before breakfast."

"And the other one came back alone?"

"Yes, monsieur."

"And what did he say when he came back alone?"

"He said that the gentleman had taken a fancy to go on in advance, and that he had desired madame to follow as soon as she had breakfasted and felt disposed to continue. *Ciel!* messieurs, what is the matter—you look so strange at me—what is the matter?"

"Murder is the matter," says Barthelet, rising from his seat, and suddenly casting off all his assumed indifference. "Murder is the matter. My name is Pierre Corneille Barthelet. I am a detective government agent, and I call upon all here present, in the name of the king and the state, to assist me in the discovery of this crime."

The landlady falls upon her knees with terror—the landlord trembles and turns pale—we have all risen, and are all agitated.

"Who saw them go out together?" asks Barthelet, taking pen, ink, and paper from a small case which he draws from his pocket. "Who saw them go out? I must take your deposition upon every circumstance."

"Oh, dear Virgin!" sobs the landlady. "I saw them go out."

"And what direction did they take?"

"I don't know, indeed, monsieur. I did not look after them."

"Did you, Monsieur Callot?"

"No, monsieur. I was in the kitchen at the time; but—but I think the *garçon* was outside, feeding the poultry. He might have seen them go."

"Let the *garçon* be called."

Barthelet is now writing briskly. The vacant look vanished from his face; he speaks with authority; and I am sitting, dumb and stupefied with horror, and my head leaning against the wall.

The *garçon*, a shambling, awkward fellow in sabots, comes into the room and is interrogated.

"What is your name?"

"Jean."

"Jean—and what else? You have some other name."

"No, m'sieur. I never remember to have had any other."

"It is true," interposes the landlord. "He is an *enfant trouvé*. We call him Jean."

"Good. Now, Jean, do you remember to have seen two gentlemen leave this house together early in the morning on the 19th day of this month?"

"I remember that the gentlemen went out together before breakfast, but I don't know what day of the month it was."

"Can you recollect in which direction they went?"

"*Plait-il?*"

"Can you recollect which road they went by—whether they turned off to the right or the left after they got outside?"

"They went right over across the common, toward the wood yonder."

"Then there is a wood yonder! Is it a large wood?"

"Oh no, m'sieur, quite a little place—about three or four times as big as the common."

"Can you show us the way there?"

"Yes, m'sieur—by daylight. One could not find one's way there in the night, it is such a deceitful kind of place."

"What do you mean by 'deceitful?'"

"He means, gentlemen," says the landlord, "that it is a troublesome place; and so it is, even in the daytime—full of bushes and holes, and scarcely passable in many parts."

"And is there no pathway through it?"

"There is a pathway, but it is very little used. All of us about these parts would rather go round than through it."

"And you think it would be dangerous to venture there to-night, even if we carried lanterns or torches?"

"I am sure, sir, that if you went, you could not take four steps without some accident."

"Did the gentlemen go into the wood together, Jean?"

"I can't tell, m'sieur. I did not watch them across the common; but they certainly crossed over that way."

"Do you think that either of them knew there was a wood over there?"

"One of them seemed as if he knew his way all about here, m'sieur, but I think he said, 'I've been in this place before, many years ago, and if you'll trust to my experience, I will lead the way.'"

"And which of the gentlemen said this?"

"The ugly one, m'sieur."

"And he led the way to the wood?"

"Yes, m'sieur. I would have warned him of the holes and bogs in it, only that he seemed so confident, and they walked away so fast."

"Is this all you know?"

"Yes, m'sieur."

"Enough, Jean, you may go."

And so Barthelet proceeds to record the testimony of the Callots, and defers all farther search to the morrow. The dreary night passes thus, in questioning and writing, and suspicions too dark for words, which merge rapidly into desolate certainties.

A dreary night indeed!

CHAPTER XXXIX.

THE DELL IN THE WOOD.

THE sad day dawns through tears, and a white fog hangs over the landscape as I look forth in the early morning. Barthelet and Vogelsang are sleeping in their chairs, worn out by excitement and long watching, and I alone have been unable to forget the terrible present.

"Oh, if it were but a dream!" I exclaim to myself, as I watch their closed eyelids—"oh, if it were but a dream, and there were no wood lying out there in the mist!"

The wood! I shuddered at the mere word, and roused them hastily. "Up! up and be doing! It is day."

Barthelet is awake and on his feet directly. He never seems to require a moment to regain his senses, but passes instantaneously from deep sleep to perfect consciousness, as daylight rushes upon darkness in the tropics.

"I am ready," he says quickly, taking his hat and glancing toward the window. "Let us call the people of the house. They must go with us as witnesses."

So he goes down and hastens them, while Vogelsang awakes with difficulty. Presently we have all assembled, and are proceeding in a body across the common.

The rain falls slowly, and the melancholy wind sighs over the far hills, and brings down the wet and withered leaves around our heads as we enter the bounds of the wood. It is a quiet, dreary place, dimmed by a half-twilight, and intersected by a labyrinth of tiny paths, like sheep-tracks, which are, however, all choked with brambles and heaps of rotting leaves. The ground is soft, treacherous, full of pits and ruts, and patches of black morass, and is covered, moreover, with moss and poison-weeds, and long rank grass that reaches to our knees, and drenches us with the dew and gathered moisture. The trees grow so low that we have to bend aside the branches as we go; the thorny bushes rend our hands and clothes; our feet slip, or sink ankle-deep in slough at every step; and the misting rain comes down, blurring the pale heavens, and wrapping us in a chill embrace.

Thus we force our way through, and emerge at last upon some fields at the farther side of the wood, without having arrived at any result. But we have traversed only one or two paths out of many, and so prepare to return, and take a footway that seems to branch off more toward the centre. Thus in dull silence, wet, weary, and cold, with sore hands and heavy hearts, we toil onward, and at last, for the sake of expedition, divide into three parties of two each—Callot and Jean taking one direction, Vogelsang and the woman another, Barthelet and myself a third.

In this way more than an hour passes, and I am almost ready to give up the search, when my companion stops suddenly, and, turning to me, says,

"Have any of us been along this path before?"

"I think none."

"Then look here"

I look, and see a fragment of cloth hanging to a bush at our right hand. Barthelet removes and examines it carefully.

"This shred is of fine Saxony cloth," he says, "and the color dark blue. Have any of our party a blue coat?"

"None that I can remember. The Herr Vogelsang, like myself, wears black, and the man Callot—"

"Has a gray blouse. This is important. Let us go on."

And Barthelet secures the piece of cloth in his pocket-book, and proceeds very slowly, noting each bush, and branch, and inch of the way.

Presently the path divides, and takes two op-

posite directions, the one tending toward the right, the other sloping downward by a deep curve, and leading to a dark dell, where the trees would seem to grow larger and thicker than elsewhere.

At this point the police agent pauses, and scans the ground narrowly; then, stooping low, proceeds to gather up the fallen leaves, and cast them on one side.

"See!" he says eagerly, but with an evident effort to maintain his old cool, indifferent manner, "see! there have been feet along this path lately. Here are the marks, half filled with water; the leaves lie deep above them, and have been falling for many days since the prints were made. They go down, you see, into the hollow; and here is a broken bough, where they forced a passage through the brambles. We have it now, sir! we have it now!"

Down, then, down the slippery steep path, and into the hollow all overgrown with bushes, and marshy as the basin of an empty pond—down to a spot where the mire is trampled over strangely.

"Don't stir a foot, sir," cries Barthelet, flushed and vehement, "don't stir a foot, or you will efface the trail! Look, look! here—where I stand: don't you see that dragging mark along the ground? Something heavy has been hauled all across! It goes right over to the foot of this alder, and is lost in the bushes! Now we must turn up every foot of ground in among these bushes, if we have to go back to the village for hatchets and cut them even with the earth."

Impelled by a feverish dreadful haste, trembling with anguish, yet conscious of a wild strength which I never possessed before, I seize the thorny bushes in my desperate grasp, and—Heavens! the first I touch comes away in my hand without an effort!

The next does the same, and the next, and that which Barthelet holds likewise. They have no root in the soil; their leaves are all yellow and drooping; they have been thrust in there as a blind—a screen—a mask!

And beyond them?

Beyond them, heaped over with more branches and brambles, lies something — something whereat I shudder and stand still, and from beside which a small black snake writhes away at our approach, and glides swiftly in among the gnarled roots of the surrounding trees.

Barthelet removes the branches in silence.

And there — yes there, with strength, and beauty, and desire struck into the dust, with his face pressed to the earth, and his yellow locks all dabbled in the mire—there, meaner in his abasement, oh God of mercy! than the meanest of Thy living creatures, lies the body of my brother Théophile!

CHAPTER XL.

THE WORK OF RETRIBUTION BEGINS.

It is night again—night for the second time since we discovered the body—the night of the 28th of October.

Our sorrowful duty to the dead has been accomplished as far as the law permits; the victim lies in his coffin at Douai, awaiting the inquest; and Vogelsang, Barthelet, and myself are traversing one of the least frequented avenues of the Champs Elysées in Paris, bound on an avenging errand.

Behind us, in silence and shadow, marches a company of gendarmes, with their officer at their head—breathless, statue-like, moving as one man, and heard only by the dull fall of their tread and the occasional clank of their swords.

Thus we move on in the darkness, and the distant clocks strike twelve.

Hush! we pause before the gate of that Italian villa where I entered some few days past, and the soldiers draw back out of sight, leaving me alone to summon the attendance of a servant. I ring—the gate is partially opened—the same footman looks out.

"Who is there?"

"The gentleman who called the other morning. I want to see Monsieur Lemaire on urgent business."

"Monsieur and madame are at supper. You can not see them to-night, sir. They receive no visitors so late in the evening."

"But my business, I tell you, is important."

"Well, sir, if you will give me your name and state your business, I will tell my master, but I am sure it will be useless."

"I do not choose to do either; I must see him."

"Then, monsieur, it is impossible. You must return in the morning."

So saying, the servant firmly, but respectfully, is about to close the gate, when it is wrenched suddenly back, and a gauntleted hand is closed upon his mouth.

"Not a word, or you are a dead man," says the officer, in a low, stern voice. "Your employers are charged with willful murder, and I call upon you to aid us in the discharge of our duty. Do you obey?"

The trembling varlet made a gesture of submission, and the officer, holding a pistol to his head, continues:

"Are they alone together?"

"Yes, mon capitaine."

"How many servants are there about the place?"

"Only myself and the cook, mon capitaine. The rest are all in bed."

"Where is the cook?"

"Down in the kitchen, mon capitaine."

"Can he give the alarm if he sees us?"

"Impossible, mon capitaine. The kitchen is at the back of the house, far enough from the salons."

"Lead the way, then—and mind! One syl-

lable of betrayal, and
lets through your brai

Scarce able to sup
footman proceeds onc
case and into the dr
the portrait by Davi
and the soldiers have
The room is but half

"They are at supp
guide, withdrawing a
the purpose of a door
apartment. "You w
salon at the end of th
don't compel me to go

"Leave the fellow
and go on," says Ba
make no noise, for yo

"Stay!" I exclaii
"let me go first. L
while I speak, come
voice will drown you

"And me with yo

"Oh, how I long to t
Barthelet shakes h
on Vogelsang's arm.

"No, no," he say
Monsieur Latour can
I don't recommend it

With this I pass t
a second room and fa
yond this lies a third,

The sound of voice
four lines of a wild o
loveliest of voices a
laughter—the chinl
these arrest my step
whom I seek are sep
few folds of drapery.

Looking back earn
I see some dark sha
curtain one after anc
by a magic lantern.
lost; I draw the har
surprise them—surpr
gies—surprise them
reveling in their blc
that pleasure-cup wh

The room blazes
laden with wines, anc
icacies served in glit
clines upon his brea
lips—

I stand before the
a moment they are c
less. Thérèse is the
she springs to her fee
ger; she draws herse
and confronts me.

"Who are you, si
upon my privacy?

"I am Paul Lato
my brother. Where

She quails before
blows, and catches a
mour for support. I
name, and turns a li

"Speak, woman. Where is my brother?"

Death-pale as she is, she bears a dauntless brow, and can reply haughtily.

"I know nothing of him nor of you. I have told you this before, and you have presumed to intrude here a second time. Be gone, sir, or my servants shall expel you."

"Summon your servants, if you choose; they will not come."

"Not come!"

She glares upon me like a tigress as she repeats these words, and Lemaire, stealing his hand along the edge of the table, strives to reach at a knife unperceived by me.

"Your anger can not move, or your words convince me. I stand here demanding from you news of the man who loved you—of the man who squandered his gold for your smiles —who staked his honor against your blandishments—whose gifts adorn your person—whose kisses are yet warm upon your lips! Speak, Delilah! Where is he? What have you done with him?"

"I know nothing of him—care nothing for him—nor for your threats either!"

Lemaire has grasped the knife now and got it down by his side, and all this time there are faint gleams, as of steel, crossing the gloom beyond the curtain, and ever drawing nearer.

"And if I have no need to ask—if I know all your depravity, all your falseness, all your crime—if I know how you fled with him, robbed him, connived at, planned, aided—ay! aided in his murder—"

The word is yet on my tongue when Lemaire springs at my throat!

There is a fierce struggle—a rush of many feet—a confusion of cries! The knife is wrenched from his hand; the deadly grasp torn forcibly away, and the miscreant lies felled and groveling on the floor, with half a dozen muskets at his breast!

The officer has his warrant in his hand.

"Are both prisoners arrested?" he asks, looking round at the faces that fill the room. "My orders are to secure the persons of Alphonse Lemaire and Thérèse Vogelsang. Where is the woman?"

"Where is she? Let me look at her—let me come near her!" cries a voice at the door —a voice trembling with suppressed hatred. "Where is this murderess—this adultress—this robber?"

We look in one another's faces and make no reply, while Vogelsang, forcing his way to where Lemaire lies prisoner, keeps repeating his savage questions.

No one can answer them. She was here but a moment since; I was speaking to her, standing within three feet of her, when Lemaire sprang at me with his knife! Has she sunk through the floor?

"Search the house!" says the officer, after a momentary pause of wondering silence. "She has slipped away in the scuffle. Search the house from top to bottom till you find her."

In vain. The house is ransacked thoroughly from attic to cellar; no cupboard, recess, wardrobe, or curtain is left untried; but Thérèse Vogelsang has utterly and mysteriously disappeared.

Her husband, balked of his vengeance, rages hither and thither like one frantic. He foams at the mouth; he offers unheard of rewards, which it is not in his power to redeem; he raves, curses, entreats, but all in vain—in vain! Search as we will from midnight to dawn, the task is hopeless, the fugitive not to be found.

And so, when three or four hours have been spent in useless investigations, we are fain to give it up. The officer then proceeds to affix his seal upon the furniture; the servants are compelled to leave the place in our custody; windows and doors are all fast closed and locked; the prisoner is placed in a coach, and removed to the Conciergerie in the Palais de Justice; and the house, as we look up at it from the road in the faint morning light, looks blank, melancholy, and deserted.

CHAPTER XLI.

OBITER DICTUM.

BEAUTIFUL and true is that passage in the Prose Edda of the wild Icelandic bard, Snorri Sturlason, wherein Har the Lofty relates how, after the Twilight of the Gods and the Destruction of the Universe, "there will arise out of the ocean another earth most lovely and verdant, with pleasant fields where the grain shall grow unsown." Thus it was when the Deluge swept over the world, and left it greener and holier; and thus it is that we stand in the pleasant fields of after-life, amid the harvest-plenty of our spring labors, looking back upon the anxieties and tribulations of the past.

How strange it is, this turning back to the contemplation of a great sorrow! Time has taken us by the hand and led us gently on since then. The dark shores of the dread land have faded in the distance. Ambitions, occupations, friends, all are changed with us. We feel ashamed that we can still be so happy, and would fain persuade ourselves that the golden sunbeams are less lovely in our eyes than the pale radiance of the lamp that lights the tomb. Vain self-reproaches and self-doubts! It was night, and the morning, according to Nature's inevitable succession, has followed on its path. Not always, perhaps, dawns so fair a day as the preceding. Some roses may have faded, some trees have fallen in the tempest that came and went with the stars. Yet, when the rain descended, it nurtured seeds that might elsewise have perished; and so, watered by the tears of our anguish, blossom the autumn flowers of life.

Writing thus, in the seclusion of my home, at peace with all men, surrounded by those who are nearest and dearest to my heart, and dwelling, moreover, in a gentle world of dreams and books, I recall with awe and **shuddering the** great tragedy of my youth.

Opposite the table where I sit in my quiet study hangs the portrait of a young man, of whom it might be said, as of Baldur the Beautiful, "so fair and dazzling is he in form and features that rays of light seem to issue from him." His lips are parted in a half smile; he leans indolently against the pedestal of a sculptured figure; his eye is bright and careless; his brow untouched by sorrow or study. Gazing **up at him** thus, his golden locks seem but to **need** the classic chaplet and the dropping perfumes of luxurious Greece. He might be Alcibiades—he was Théophile Latour.

Let me pause—let me pause for a moment amid the dark details of his errors and their punishment. Let me recall him in his beauty, irradiated as it now is by the light which streams down upon him through the brazen gates of eternity! He offended—he expiated. It is the old stern tale of heavenly compensation—the moral of the antique legend. Condemn him not, blame him not, judge him not too harshly, oh thou kind reader! This fair portrait is all that now remains of him—this checkered chronicle all the record of his deeds. Past art thou, my brother, like an errant and glowing meteor —past, and remembered only by the few who dare still to love and pity thee, although thou standest before the jasper throne, and we are "distant in humanity." The myrtles have blossomed and the daisies been mown down many times above thy grave since thou wert laid in the shadow of that old belfry-tower at Douai, sleeping, sleeping. Ever and anon, from the ways of busy life and the silent paths of thought, I turn aside and visit thy place of sepulture. Oftener still, as at this moment, I seem to hear the bells ringing solemnly, and the organ pealing, and the priests chanting their miserere, as once long since; and then I, too, lift up my voice in prayer and lamentation, and

"Bid thee rest,
And drink thy fill of pure immortal streams!"

One other thing have I to say. We all know that story of the painter of old, who, in representing the sacrifice of Iphigenia, depicted her father in an attitude of profound dejection, with his face buried in the folds of his mantle.

And he was right. There are griefs which transcend the skillfullest touches of the pencil or pen; and so, in imitation of a wise precedent, will I also draw a veil before the tearful countenances of some of the personages of this history. Too sacred—too sacred are thy sorrows, wife and mother! Enough if it be said that the writer of these pages took upon himself the heavy task of acquainting them with their bereavement; that he journeyed into Brussels, and thence on to the old chateau in pleasant Burgundy; that he wept with those who were desolate; that he returned, after an absence of little more than two days, compelled, by the stern call of the law, to be **present** at the examinations and trial; and, finally, that he passed through

the city where dwelt the gentle Margaret, without having it in his power to tarry by the way, though **never so briefly**.

This *en passant*, **reader, as an** *entre acte* in the pauses of the drama, while the scene is shifted and the players make ready with the mask and cothurnus; or, if thou likest it better, as the fragment of a requiem, **played** while the priests change their broidered vestments, and the congregation sit with their missals in their hands, listening dreamily to the music which breathes out from the golden organ-pipes, like the sighing of the evening air through the strings of an Æolian harp, sad, and whispering, and "softer than sleep."

But methinks I hear thee say, with Christofero Sly, "'Tis a very excellent piece of work—would 'twere done!" Patience, I beseech thee, during a few more pages. My story draws near to an end, and the curtain will fall and the lights be extinguished ere long.

"And therefore herkeneth what I shall say,
And let me tellen all my tale I pray."

CHAPTER XLII.

GUILTY OR NOT GUILTY.

IT is in the old justice hall of that antique city of Lille which Julius Cæsar founded. The morning is dark and raw. The privileged spectators are few, and there are some ladies in the galleries. The Procureur du Roi has not yet arrived; the president is deep in the pages of his note-book; the avocats are sorting their papers, and the jury shuffling their feet, and whispering together, and looking impatiently toward the clock over the president's chair. All is silent and heavy, and every now and then the opening of some outer door admits that uneasy, continuous, indescribable sound which proceeds from a multitude of persons.

Presently the clock strikes; the Procureur du Roi enters and takes his seat; there is a faint commotion at the farther end of the hall; every head is instantly turned, and a pale, cadaverous-looking man, scarce able to support himself, is brought forward by gendarmes and placed at the bar.

Strange alteration effected in so few days! Lemaire—that Lemaire whom I had surprised amid the lustiest enjoyments of life, with whom I had struggled, and whose strength I had but so lately experienced—is now humble as a beaten cur, and so weak as to be permitted to sit during his trial. His red hair and beard, unshorn **and neglected**, hang upon his face and downcast eyes; his shoulders are bent; his head droops **on his breast**; his hands hang listlessly on either side; his whole attitude and aspect **speak** dejection, cowardice, guilt.

The Procureur du Roi rises and reads the accusation.

The paper is long and **formal**; but the chief facts are these:

THE ASSASSINATION OF THÉOPHILE LATOUR.

It is now some months since Théophile Latour became intimate with a vocalist named Thérèse, or Thérèsa Vogelsang, an Austrian subject, then performing at Brussels. She is known to have encouraged his attentions, and to have carried on, at the same time, an intrigue with Alphonse Lemaire, a Frenchman, native of Paris, resident at Brussels, and then lessee of the Brussels theatre. The liberality of the deceased toward this woman was unbounded, and became the talk of all the city. Money and gifts were squandered hourly upon her, and the wealth thus obtained was shared between the receiver and her lover. At this stage of the affair, Heinrich Vogelsang, husband of Thérèse, made his appearance with an injunction granted by the Austrian government, which gave him full powers to remove, and, if necessary, arrest his wife above-named. To this end he consulted and entered into negotiations with Lemaire the manager, who, for his part, is supposed to have informed Madame Vogelsang upon every particular. The result was obvious, and the only remedy flight. Still acting the same double game, and interweaving it now with a darker purpose, she induced the deceased Théophile Latour to dispose of a valuable estate in Burgundy, to fly with her to Paris, and there to spend the proceeds of the sale in pleasures and excesses. They eloped accordingly on the evening of the 16th of October last—chose for their starting-point the masked ball held at the Opera House, and traveled unceasingly till they arrived at Douai on the evening of the 17th instant, where they rested for the night. They left their hotel the next morning, and when at a sufficient distance from the house, hired a fiacre which conveyed them as far as the opening of a certain narrow lane, on the western high road, where they alighted, and along which they proceeded. Toward three or four o'clock they reached a mean hamlet lying among the fields and lanes about seven miles west of the town, where they established themselves at an inn called the Hôtel de Namur, and were met some few hours later by the prisoner. The pretense on which this meeting was arranged concealed a deep and artful plot. Both deceased and prisoner had traveled under the name of Alphonse Lemaire, and, averse as the deceased appears always to have shown himself to the company of the prisoner, it seems that he submitted to it on this occasion for the purpose of a more skillful concealment. The ostensible plan was that Lemaire and Thérèse Vogelsang should, from this point, travel together into Paris, and be joined afterward by Latour, in order that, if inquiries were made, it might be established that they journeyed and arrived together, which deception would have been favored by the passports. The remote village was also chosen as affording a convenient place for the exchange of persons. All these, seen from this point of view, are clumsily contrived plans enough; feasible, however, to a man blinded by passion and hurried on by a will superior to his own. Viewed from the other side, unfortunately, its clumsiness vanishes, and gives place to a profoundly calculated scheme. The spot was known to the prisoner, eminently fitted for an assassination, and far removed from high road and town. All was preconcerted, down to the very copse where the murder was to be committed and the body concealed. All succeeded as it had been ordered. On the morning of the 19th instant the deceased and prisoner left the inn to take a walk before breakfast. The former never returned. A plausible excuse accounted for all, and in a few hours more the vocalist and the manager were on the road to Paris, where they arrived toward evening. A lengthened, tedious, and careful search, conducted by the detective agent, Pierre Corneille Barthelet, accompanied by the brother of the deceased and the before-mentioned husband of Thérèse Vogelsang, has been successful in bringing to light all the circumstances of this crime. The body was discovered concealed in a deep hollow toward the centre of a little wood bordering the hamlet. The deceased had been shot from behind, the ball having passed under the left shoulder-blade and penetrated to the heart. He must have expired instantaneously and without a struggle. The pistol with which the deed was effected has been discovered in a ditch not far from the spot.

Such are the leading facts which preceded and followed the crime imputed to Alphonse Lemaire and Thérèse Vogelsang, the latter of whom has escaped and not yet been apprehended. The accusation, therefore, impeaches both parties, namely, Alphonse Lemaire for having assassinated and murdered Théophile Latour, and Thérèse Vogelsang for aiding and abetting in the same.

Monsieur le Président then proceeded to interrogate the prisoner.

M. le Président. "Alphonse Lemaire, rise; state your age and profession."

He rose with difficulty, and almost immediately fell back in his chair, with an appearance of great weakness.

"He can not stand, so please you, M. le Président," said a soldier, stepping forward. "He has been very ill since his apprehension, and was brought up from Paris with difficulty."

The president appeared satisfied with this explanation, and the examination was resumed.

"Alphonse Lemaire, state your age and profession."

The prisoner continued to hang his head forward on his breast, and replied with a collected manner, and in a low but audible voice, that his age was thirty-seven, and his profession histrionic.

M. le Président. "How long have you held the management of the Opera House at Brussels?"

Prisoner. "About three years and a half."

M. le President. "You are a native of Paris?"

Prisoner. "I was born in the Rue St. Honoré, No. 85. My father was a manufacturer of bronze ornaments."

M. le President. "At what time did you engage the services of Thérèse Vogelsang for your theatre?"

Prisoner. "The negotiations were conducted by letter. She arrived in Brussels July 5th, and commenced her performances the next evening."

M. le President. "Were you cognizant of her connection with Monsieur Théophile Latour?"

Prisoner. "I knew that he admired her, and that she accepted gifts from him; but the world is so censorious, especially to ladies of her profession, that I attached no importance to the scandal of the green-room."

M. le President. "What were the propositions made to you by the Herr Vogelsang?"

Prisoner. "The Herr Vogelsang showed me a paper purporting to emanate from the Austrian authorities, by which he was empowered to remove his wife from the Brussels stage. He then proposed to me to suppress all knowledge of this paper from the lady and from Monsieur Latour, alleging as his reason that the family of that gentleman were anxious to separate him from her society, and to conceal from him where and by what means she had disappeared. To insure this the more effectually, I was to purchase the silence of all parties concerned in the affair, and to receive two thousand francs for my own co-operation."

M. le President. "And you agreed to this?"

Prisoner. "I agreed to it, M. le President, but only to lull their suspicions; for Madame Vogelsang had honored me with much of her confidence, and I was disposed to save her if I could."

M. le President. "And you betrayed all?"

Prisoner. "Yes, M. le President."

M. le President. "State the result."

Prisoner. "The communication was made to me only three days before the *bal masqué*, which I had fixed for the 16th of October. It was evident to us both that flight was the only resource, and equally evident that a better opportunity than the *fête* could not be chosen. We arranged, therefore, to leave Brussels on the evening of the 16th, and we did so, between twelve and one o'clock."

M. le President. "Do you mean to say that you accompanied Thérèse Vogelsang from Brussels?"

Prisoner. "I do. Though we had less than three days to prepare for the journey, I contrived to put all my affairs in order, to provide passports, and leave every thing under the management of a confidential secretary."

M. le President. "And in what manner did you travel?"

Prisoner. "We posted part of the way, and part we traveled by railway."

M. le President. "Do you deny that Monsieur Latour accompanied Thérèse Vogelsang to Douai?"

Prisoner. "I traveled with her all the way."

M. le President. "Did you spend one night at a little hamlet near Douai, and there meet M. Latour?"

Prisoner. "No, M. le President. We traveled without stopping any where. I never saw Monsieur Latour more than twice or thrice in my life."

M. le President. "This cigar-case, marked with the initials T. L., was found in the carriage abandoned on the road by Madame Vogelsang. How do you account for its discovery?"

Prisoner (hesitating). "That—that cigar-case, M. le President? It was left, I believe, by M. Latour at the house of madame. She gave it to me as a present."

M. le President. "And this note, directed to M. Latour, and dropped by Madame Vogelsang on leaving the ball, what do you say to that?"

The prisoner here asked to see the note, and read it attentively.

Prisoner. "I know nothing of it. I believe it to be a forgery."

M. le President. "Here is a fragment of blue cloth discovered clinging to a bramble in the wood where the body lay concealed. This fragment corresponds with a torn place in one of your coats found in Paris. Have you any thing to say respecting it?"

The prisoner shook his head, and declined making any farther replies.

M. le President. "Enough. Let the witnesses be called."

The first witness examined was Barthelet; the second, Heinrich Vogelsang; the third, myself. All that we knew is known already to the reader. Our statements coincided with each other word for word. Barthelet delivered his testimony concisely and unpretendingly; Vogelsang, with a sullen and subdued resentment breaking forth every now and then against his wife, sternly, briefly, comprehensively.

Ever since the night on which Lemaire had been apprehended and Thérèse had escaped, Vogelsang was an altered man. He spoke less than ever; wandered out for hours at a time, and returned to our hotel without saying where he had been; was frequently so absorbed in thought as to hear, see, and notice nothing; seemed to eat, even, as it were, mechanically, and more for the purpose of recruiting his physical strength than from any impulse of hunger or enjoyment. One would have said, on observing his settled gaze, the abstraction of his speech and attitudes, and the self-withdrawn inner look of his countenance, that he had some fixed idea upon which his thoughts fed continually—from which he could be roused only by an effort, and to which he returned the moment that his attention was released.

Yet there were occasions upon which a single inadvertent word, such as "flight," or "discovery," would rouse him as from a deep sleep, and then he was keen and watchful as a hare—all eye, and ear, and eager investigation. Sometimes I used to think that his dominant purpose was the patient searching after the missing criminal, and that he had resolved to devote life and energies to the working out of his darling vengeance. In this suspicion I was strengthened by the evident impatience with which he obeyed the business of the trial; the restless way in which he counted every day, and hour, and minute of his absence; the strong reluctance with which he left Paris, and the eager rapidity with which he hastened from Lille as soon as his share in the trial was concluded.

And this reminds me that I have wandered from my subject too long.

The examination of witnesses was tedious and minute. They were nearly a hundred in number, and comprised toll and post-house keepers, postillions, ostlers, inn-keepers, custom-house officers, and servants without end. This part of the trial lasted two days and a half.

I believe that I have not forgotten a syllable of the evidence, a glance or movement of the prisoner, or the merest incident of that terrible event. Yet, thank Heaven! I seldom think of it. When my attention is drawn to it, as in transcribing this narrative, it comes back to me clearly, circumstantially, and sharply defined, as if all had happened yesterday. Still, upon a subject so important, I will not trust the tablets of my memory. The subjoined *resumé* of some of the evidence elicited from the witnesses I copy from the leading journal of the day, preserved by my friend Seabrook, and by him lent to me for this purpose.

"THE TRAGEDY NEAR DOUAI—SECOND DAY.

"The most remarkable testimony, viz., that of Barthelet, Vogelsang, and Latour (*frère*), having been gone through yesterday, and given in our evening edition, we proceed to relate a portion of the facts obtained this morning from a host of minor witnesses, of whom there were too many called to be fully reported in our pages.

"*Jean-Simon Carpeaux*, and *Antoinette* his wife, depose that on the morning of the 17th inst. a carriage corresponding to the description previously given passed through the Porte d'Anderlecht, Brussels. Believe it to have been about one o'clock in the morning. Are sure that the carriage contained a lady and gentleman, and that they drove fast. On being asked if the gentleman in question and the prisoner were the same individual, Antoinette declared herself positive that they were not. Said that the gentleman whom she saw was fair and handsome. Husband not so certain.

"*Durand Stumph*, toll-keeper, deposes that a dark green chariot drove swiftly past before dawn. Is very deaf and old, and does not remember whether there was more than one person inside, or if it were a gentleman or lady.

"*Jerome Daunet* and *Amédée Coquart*, postillions, depose to having driven the fugitives. Are certain that prisoner is not the same man. The other was much better looking, and a gentleman every inch. The lady was very handsome. They talked some language, when speaking to each other, which witnesses could not understand. Are sure that it was neither French nor Flemish. Thought it might be German, by the sound. The gentleman, however, spoke French like a native.

"*Jacques Chappuy*, milk-salesman, deposes that he is in the habit of selling milk in the village of Jemappes. Was serving the post-master's wife while the dark green chariot was standing before the door. The lady expressed a wish for some of the milk, and on a glass being handed out to him from the house, he served it himself to her at the carriage-window. She was the handsomest woman he had ever seen. Lifted her veil to drink, and her hands were all over rings. Did not observe the gentleman particularly. Could not take his eyes off the lady, she was so beautiful. Can not be sure if prisoner be or be not the same person as her companion.

"*Félix Pradier*, post-master, deposes that the dark green chariot, now lying in his yard, was left there by a gentleman and lady a little after noon on the 17th of October. The wheels were torn to pieces by the roads. It often happens so with private carriages on the roads in Belgium. They seemed, both of them, very much annoyed, especially the lady. Were forced to take one of his (Félix Pradier's) post-carriages. They had no luggage with them. Witness searched the carriage carefully after they were gone, but found nothing in it except a bag with some biscuits, which he left there. Was surprised when the other gentleman found the cigar-case. Could not see the lady's face very plainly through her veil, but thought the gentleman handsome. The prisoner was certainly not the same man—nothing like him. The lady and gentleman, when conversing together, talked German. On being asked how he knew that it was German, he (Pradier) replied that his wife was a native of Kehl, and had taught him a little of the language—sufficient to convince him that they spoke it, but not sufficient to enable him to comprehend the sense of what they said.

"*Camille Dumont*, clerk in the passport office, Quievrain, deposes to having inspected both passports now produced. Did not remark that they bore the same name till his attention was drawn to the fact. Remembers nothing of the parties themselves. All was perfectly *en règle*, or he should remember something about it.

"*Edouard Lecroix*, *chef de bureau*, passport office, Quievrain, deposes that he inspected both passports, and countersigned the same. Took no notice of the first, or of the parties themselves. Grew interested, however, in the matter after his interview with Vogelsang and Latour (*frère*). Observed, and was surprised, when, on the afternoon of the second day, another passport bearing the name of Alphonse Lemaire was submitted to him for examination. Took particular notice of bearer. Is certain that the prisoner is the same person. Could identify him any where. Did not put any questions to prisoner. Thought it best, should there be any thing wrong, not to put him on his guard.

Had made an especial entry of the circumstance in his private note-book. (Witness here handed his note-book to the president.)

"*Philip van Comp*, post-boy, deposes that he drove a lady and gentleman from Quievrain to Valenciennes between two and three o'clock in the afternoon of the 17th of October. Is a native of Flanders. Not speaking French, was examined through an interpreter. The lady was very handsome, and the gentleman paid him in gold. Could not remember the latter with any distinctness, but is certain that prisoner is not the same.

"*Jacques Thayer, Henri Rude, Hippolyte Cogniet, Baptiste Fretté,* and several others, all postillions or post-masters, were next examined. They all deposed to having driven the fugitives, or supplied them with horses, from Valenciennes to Douai. No matters of especial interest distinguished this part of the *procès,* saving the complete establishment of every link in the chain of evidence. The case was then adjourned till the following day."

"THE TRAGEDY NEAR DOUAI—THIRD DAY.

"*The examination of witnesses resumed.*

"*François Roger,* hotel-keeper, Douai, deposes that two persons answering to the general description arrived at his establishment between six and seven o'clock on the evening of October 17th, dined and slept there, and left the next morning. Has very little recollection of the parties in question. Thinks the gentleman was fair. Is sure he never saw the prisoner before. Believes that the lady wore a veil. Remembers nothing farther, except that they drank a good deal of Champagne and paid liberally.

"*Claudine Roger,* wife of the above, deposes that the gentleman was very handsome—not in the least like the prisoner. In all respects corroborates the testimony of her husband.

"*Jeannette Thouret,* chambermaid, deposes that she conducted the said travelers to their apartments. Is a servant in the Hôtel de Flandres, kept by the couple Roger. Could not see the lady's face through her veil, which was very thick. She kept it down always. The gentleman was very handsome. She (Jeannette Thouret) had never seen a man so handsome. Could have looked at him for hours. Is certain that prisoner is not the man. Thinks the supposition absurd. This man is hideous in comparison. Only saw them twice, namely, on their arrival and departure. They left the house arm in arm together, and the gentleman gave her (Jeannette Thouret) a five-franc piece on the staircase.

"*Alexandre Thomas* and *Napoleon Barbet,* waiters, depose to having waited upon the travelers during their breakfast and dinner. The lady kept her veil always down; but her hands were covered with jewels. They tried to see her face, but could not. They (the travelers) would not suffer them (the waiters) to remain long in attendance, but rang when they wished the courses removed. Are sure that prisoner is

not the same person. The lady and gentleman spoke a foreign language to each other. Thought it was English from the intonation, or perhaps German. Are not acquainted with either language.

"*Etienne Blanchet,* hackney-coach-driver, deposes that he drove a lady and gentleman answering to the general description from close to the University as far as the opening of a narrow lane about two miles west of the town. They paid him more than his fare, and he saw them walk up the lane very slowly arm in arm. Is sure that prisoner is not the gentleman. The lady was very beautiful, and threw her veil up after they were clear of the town. Was surprised at the time to see them go by such a deserted path, but thought they might be lovers and liked to be alone. Asked them, under this persuasion, if he should wait to take them back; but the gentleman only shook his head and bade him (Etienne Blanchet) drive back again to Douai."

Here follows a detailed account of the examination of the host and hostess of the little Hôtel de Namur, and also of the boy Jean, all of which I omit, having already related it in my narrative. I resume the thread of the trial at the testimony of Achille Gaudin, the driver of a *fiacre,* whose vehicle they seem to have met on leaving the hamlet next day, and re-emerging upon the public road.

"*Achille Gaudin,* hackney-coach-driver, deposes that, as he was returning from Douai to Vitry, where he resides, he overtook a lady and gentleman upon the road, walking. They turned round and engaged him instantly. He drove them to the railway station at Vitry, where they entered, and where he saw them waiting before the ticket bureau. Can not be sure of the date, but thinks it must have been about the time stated. Is perfectly certain that prisoner is the same person. Knew him at once, and could have sworn to him any where. Can't say much for his liberality. He (the prisoner) bargained closely enough about the fare; and he (Achille Gaudin) afterward found that one of the francs in which he was paid was a counterfeit. The lady was handsome, but looked pale and ill. They scarcely spoke to each other at all, and when they did it was always in French. Does not remember to have heard them say any thing in particular.

"Here the examination of witnesses terminated. Monsieur Lebas, Procureur du Roi, supported the accusation. Messieurs Rebout and Fayot pleaded for the defense.

"After a long and able debate, sustained with equal learning and vigor on both sides, M. le President summed up an impartial and eloquent *resumé* of the entire case. The jury then retired into the *salle des délibérations.* The following question was submitted to their judgment on retiring from the hall:

"'Alphonse Lemaire, *ci-devant* manager of the Brussels Opera, is he or is he not guilty of having, on the 19th morning of October last,

18—, purposely and voluntarily murdered Théophile Latour, of Latour-sur-Creil, Burgundy?"

"At this exciting moment, the crowd outside, which had been gathering and increasing during the whole morning, poured suddenly and irresistibly into the hall. A great number of ladies (many more than had been present upon the two previous days) filled the galleries. The mass of expectants who had been prevented in time from following the rest, gave forth an impatient murmur, like the roaring of the sea; and the armed force, impossible as they had found it to exclude the public, were scarcely able to maintain any degree of order.

"The jury returned at a quarter past four o'clock P.M. and resumed their seats, when the foreman, on request of M. le President, rose, and placing his hands, according to custom, upon his heart, replied,

"'Upon my honor and my conscience, before God and before men, the declaration of the jury is—Yes; the accused is guilty.'

"The prisoner was then brought in, pale, almost insensible, his whole form drooping, motionless, and dejected, like that of a man without hope or fortitude.

"The decision of the jury was then read to him, and he was asked if he had any thing to say. He seemed neither to hear nor comprehend, and after a silence of several minutes the sentence of condemnation was passed, and this **terrible** sentence read aloud from the pages of **the Code** Penal:

"'All condemned to death are to be beheaded.'

"The commotion at this point was immense. A simultaneous cry, which might almost be designated as a yell of exultation, filled the hall, and, communicating itself to the mass beyond, effectually stopped the proceedings for several minutes.

"The wretched criminal heard all with the same apparent listlessness and indifference, but, on being removed from the dock, was found to have fainted, and was carried away by the guards in a condition of insensibility.

"And thus terminated one of the most remarkable trials which we remember to have recorded in our columns. Seldom has a crime been planned with more sagacity, or executed more craftily and remorselessly. No precaution that could have availed was omitted; and as it **was** conceived, so was this hideous drama enacted. The impression upon the public mind has been terrible and profound, and it is only to be regretted that the murderer's accomplice (a demon of beauty and sin, to the full as culpable as himself) should have escaped. We will trust, however, that the place of her retreat may be ere long discovered. The police are on the search in all directions, and it is confidently hoped that the ends of justice may not long be eluded.

"The execution, it is understood, will take place in about a fortnight, this crime having been the first upon the Assize-lists for the **present session**."

CHAPTER XLIII.

MISTS DISPERSING.

I MUST go back to the evening of the first day of the trial.

It was dark, and I sat, sadly enough, beside a blazing fire in a small sitting-room in the Hôtel de l'Europe, at Lille. A dull lamp stood by my elbow, and some untouched coffee upon the table. My thoughts were very gloomy—"deepe, darke, uneasy, dolefull, comfortlesse." The past was terrible and tragic; the future crossed and perplexed by many doubts.

To escape from the remembrance of all that had filled my mind for the last few weeks, I found myself turning with an irresistible tenderness toward the image of my gentle Margaret:

"O sweet pale Margaret,
O rare pale Margaret,
What lit your eyes with tearful power,
Like moonlight on a falling shower?
Who lent you, love, your mortal dower
Of pensive thought and aspect pale,
Your melancholy sweet and frail,
As perfume of the cuckoo-flower?"

I dwelt, with a satisfaction the more exquisite since it contrasted so strongly with the suffering through which I had lately passed, upon that singularly calm and lovely nature—that capacity of endurance and enjoyment—that patient courage—that love of knowledge—that rapidity and tenacity of apprehension — that childish self-abandonment to the full luxury of simple pleasures, all and each of which unfolded themselves by slow degrees from the outward reserve of her disposition.

It was as if her mind were some charmed volume, whose silver clasps resist the merely curious hand, but yield to the touch of lover or friend! Fair and pleasant are its pages within; inscribed with gracious thoughts and images, and pious hymns, and fragments of stories beautiful and wise; illuminated, moreover, with borderings of flowers, and pictures of the knightly Gothic times, and forms of saints and angels with folded hands and crowns of golden glory.

Dreaming thus, and watching the pictures in the fire, I suffered time to pass on unnoticed. It was so pleasant to think of her—to recall her words and gestures, and the memory of her face. Yet

"How, in thy twilight, Doubt, at each unknown
Dim shape, the superstitious Love will start;
How Hope itself will tremble at its own
Light shadow on the heart!
Ah! if she love me not!

"Well, I will know the worst, and leave the wind
To drift or drown the venture on the wave;
Life has two friends in grief itself most kind—
Remembrance and the Grave—
Mine, if she love me not!"

Alas! these doubts and weary changes, they overshadow life like a dark dream.

Suddenly a slow footfall on the stairs, and a **hand** upon the door, roused me sharply from my reverie. It was Vogelsang.

He looked more wretched and haggard than ever, and, walking up to the other side of the fireplace, sat down moodily without speech or greeting. He did not even remove his hat, but stared into the fire with a stern, sullen countenance, and sighed heavily.

I found myself in no humor to interrupt his strange mood or open the conversation, so I leaned back and looked at him.

What a singular face it was! Seen by the dim conflicting lights of fire and lamp, how pale, and worn, and prematurely old! There was a delicacy, too, in the outline of the features, and a certain stamp of youth yet lingering round the eyes and forehead that interested me—a settled purpose in the furrowed brow, the massive jaw, the square short chin, that riveted my attention, and told of strong will and passions. I wondered what might be the story of his past life—a remarkable story it must be, a story of storms, and trials, and endeavors, by the ravage of its progress through the years!

"I return to Paris to-morrow morning," he said at length, but musingly and to himself, as it were, with his eyes fixed on the fire.

"So soon? Will you not remain till this business is concluded?"

He shook his head.

"*Cui bono?* My evidence is given. I can be of no use. I must go back to—to my task."

"Uselessly. Where the police fail, how can you hope to succeed?"

He looked round sharply and suddenly; then, resuming his former attitude, but speaking in a slower and more resolute tone,

"I *must* find her," he said. "I have sworn it. It is all I live for now, and though I perish for it, body and soul, I will have my vengeance."

"Retribution is already at work," I replied, "and punishment is for the law."

He appeared not to hear me, and, after a pause, resumed his former subject.

"Yes," he said, "I return to-morrow; and in the fulfillment of one task, I leave others unaccomplished. How soon will this trial end?"

"In a few days, I suppose—perhaps three or four."

"And then what shall you do?"

"What shall I do? I—I can scarcely tell. Why do you ask me?"

"Shall you go back to Brussels?"

"Yes, I suppose so—on my way to Burgundy."

"Then you mean to live upon your estates again?"

"Perhaps."

Another long silence, which I interrupt by saying,

"It is strange, Herr Vogelsang, that you should make these inquiries. I never knew you interested in my proceedings before."

"True. So you will return through Belgium?"

I nodded.

Vogelsang rose abruptly, and took three or four turns up and down the room, like a man who weighs some subject in his mind and can arrive at no decision. Presently he stopped; his features assumed a look of resolve, and he turned toward me.

"I have a sister in Brussels," he said.

"Indeed!"

"The only creature I have to care for in the world—the only one who cares for me."

I became interested.

"I never heard that you had a sister," I said, kindly. "Tell me something about her. Can I do any thing for you in Brussels?"

"That is what I was about to ask you. I should wish some things told to her—something of this—this bad business. I could not write it down on paper, and she ought to know. And there is a portrait which I should like her to have." Here he took a small morocco case from his pocket and laid it down gently on the table. "It—it is our mother's."

There was a softness in his voice, a moisture in his eyes, that I had never seen there before. I felt touched.

"It shall be done as you desire," I said. "Tell me all that I have to say."

He sighed heavily, and covered his eyes with his hand.

"Tell her how all has ended. Something of the past she knows, but not all. I could not bring myself to relate to her the details of that degrading story. Do it as delicately as you can, and—and say that I don't think—I fear—that is, she may never see me again."

"What do you mean?"

"No matter. Will you do it?"

"I have promised."

"But I have not said all. There is something more—something which—which I can scarcely take the liberty of asking from you."

"Proceed."

He hesitated, seemed about to speak, yet checked himself more than once, and at length continued:

"My sister is younger than myself. We have been very much apart ever since our childhood. If I tell you something of our story, you will be better able to help me; at all events, you may be less likely to refuse what I am going to request."

"Pray do so. It is exactly what I would have asked you, if I had dared."

He passed his hand fondly over the portrait-case, turned toward the fire, and, resuming his former musing attitude, began:

"I will presume that you remember all I told you once before—on the night I first addressed you in Brussels. How I married in compliance with an old family agreement, being, at the time, little more than a boy. How I yielded to my father's entreaties—married, and, at last, loved her. How she wronged, robbed, fled me—left me poor, broken-hearted, and dishonored! Yes, you know all this—no use to dwell upon it. My mother was—was living at the time of my marriage, and, thank Heaven! she died before a year had passed (before I was made reckless and a wanderer), leaving my father broken-hearted for her loss, and one little girl just six years old. That was eleven years ago. She is now seventeen, and I am thirty. Thirty! Alas! I both feel and look many years older. When —when Thérèse became infamous, I left Vienna and my accursed home. I roamed from city to city, from land to land, in the vain search for a peace that was fled. From Germany to Italy, Switzerland, France, I wandered, and at last reached England, where I spent the last two years and a half. I procured a mean employment in a solicitor's office, and so contrived to eke out a subsistence, which, wretched though it was, occupied my time and thoughts, and rendered me a trifle less miserable than I had been since my—my voluntary separation from father, sister, and home. Besides, though I had no relatives there, and should not have known them if I had, England was my native country, and I liked—"

"Your native country, Herr Vogelsang!" I exclaimed. "Are you not a Viennese — an Austrian subject?"

He shook his head.

"She was Austrian, but my family is English."

"Yet your name?"

"The name," he said, "is one which she chose to assume on returning to the stage seven or eight months ago. It is not mine or hers."

"And, pardon me, she acted before you married her?"

"It was her profession—her innate vocation from childhood. My father and I were violin-players in the orchestra at the Royal Opera. We left England when I was scarcely ten years of age, before Margaret was born—"

"Margaret!"

I had sprung to my feet at the sound of that name: my heart beat wildly; I trembled from head to foot. Margaret!

He looked up, amazed at my agitation, and replied,

"Yes, Margaret—my sister."

It was all clear to me now; there could be no mistake about it; the mist was dissolving before my eyes, and I dared not trust myself to follow the chain of hopes and guesses that ran, like an electric current, through my mind.

"Your name is Fletcher!" I cried, scarce able to articulate. "Your name is Fletcher!"

He started.

"How did you know that?"

"Tell me—in pity tell me!"

"Yes, my name is Fletcher—Frank Fletcher."

"Thank God! thank God!" It was all that I could say.

I sank back, in my agitation, into the chair from whence I had risen. The tears thronged to my eyes. Oh, dear, dear Margaret!

My companion was almost dumb with surprise.

"What do you know of me—or of Margaret?" he asked.

I answered his question with another.

"Did not your father die at Ems—in the summer-time—of brain fever?"

Now he, too, was suddenly enlightened; a deep flush crossed his sallow cheek; he rose and extended his hand to me, for the first time.

"I know you now," he said, warmly. "I wish that I had known you from the first. You were my father's friend—you are Margaret's protector. I thank you."

He seemed quite overcome. Then, taking the portrait from the table, he opened and placed it in my hands.

"My mother and hers," he said, falteringly. "Do you think it like her?"

I could scarcely refrain from pressing it to my lips; but the presence of her brother, and a certain awe which I am unable to define, restrained me. It was Margaret herself, only a shade fairer and more blooming, and dressed in the fashion of some twenty years ago. The same calm forehead—the same sweet mouth—the same dark, thoughtful, earnest eyes!

There was a question trembling on my lips— a question which I longed, yet dared not to ask. At length, after many efforts, I ventured.

"You saw Margaret, of course, when you were in Brussels?"

"Only twice."

"Once at night—in the park?"

"Yes, once in the park, and once at the school. You know I kept out of sight, as much as possible, during the daytime."

"And in the park, that night, Margaret was speaking to you of me—you were urging her to concealment. Was it not so?"

"Yes—yes. How do you know this?"

"I overheard you. I was in the next walk, and only separated from you by a hedge. Oh! had I but known all this before, what a weight of grief it would have spared me!"

He looked up at me sharply and inquiringly, but made no reply.

"And you gave her a ring, did you not?" (I was determined to have it all cleared now.)

"Yes," he said, very gravely, "I gave her a hair ring which had been our mother's. That and the portrait were both mine, and I had always intended to give one of them to Margaret, when she was of an age to value the relic. I left her an infant—I found her a woman; and I performed my promise. She had but to look in her mirror for our mother's portrait; so I gave her the ring, and kept the miniature. She will have both now."

"But why do you part with the likeness?"

A dark shade passed over his countenance—his very voice changed.

"I have devoted myself," he said, gloomily, "to the execution of a task. I will have an eye for an eye, and a tooth for a tooth—justice, even justice, dispassionately weighed and measured. I shall not suffer vengeance to mislead me; but, once get her into my power, I will let her taste a cup to the full as bitter as that which she forced upon me. It shall be meted her, drop for drop, as it was meted to me. I will see her sufferings—I will be inflexible, pitiless, unwavering as time itself. In the working out of my plan, I bid adieu to the past and to the future.

Neither the pleasures nor pains that have been shall sway me one hair's breadth. I detach myself from life—from its ties—from its remembrances—from its hopes; and I go forth alone in the wide world, seeking but one living being, and seeking that one with a deep and deadly hate—which is all the more a hate, and a bitter one, in so far as it is yet leavened by an ineradicable wild passion of jealousy and love."

"And what, in mercy's name, do you purpose doing?"

"I know not. I have not fashioned it out yet myself. Be it, however, when and what it may, I feel that I shall not long survive it, if at all. For years I have borne within me the seeds of a disease which knows no cure; a sudden and violent excitement would probably be, at any moment, my death-warrant; and I know that the fulfillment of my revenge will herald in my closing scene of life. Till then I am resolved to live. But enough of this. I return to Paris by dawn to-morrow, and you will undertake to deliver this portrait (the only wealth that I possess) to my little Margaret in Brussels."

"Most faithfully. But there was something else which you were about to request from me, and of which we have since lost sight. What was it?"

A grim smile flitted over his face.

"It related," said he, "to yourself. I had no opportunity of seeing Margaret's unknown protector, and I felt desirous to know something more of his character and position. In fact, I was going to ask you to discover all this for me —to ascertain the particulars of his family connections, his age and prospects, and to sift his reputation to the bottom. I met Margaret, as I have told you, but twice, and both interviews were so brief, so anxious, so agitated, that I learned nothing more than that a Monsieur Paul had been a friend to our father, and had attended his death-bed; that Margaret had been recommended to his care; that he was very rich, and benevolent, and good; that he had made her position in the school more comfortable and independent; and that he was teaching her to draw. All this I heard in fewer words than I have repeated, and no more. To me you were Monsieur Paul, and I even believed that to be your surname. You see, I was about to request from you a troublesome and an important service."

"Nothing more than I would have done for you, Mr. Fletcher, were it not, fortunately, unnecessary. Of my family and rank you have heard sufficient upon the trial this day, and I rejoice to have it in my power to ask her brother's sanction before removing Margaret from the school where she is now placed, to my own residence in Burgundy. It is a step which I have long wished to take. My mother will receive her as if she were her own child; and I promise you, in her name and my own, that nothing which can add to her happiness, or her mental culture, shall be neglected."

Fletcher colored up again, and hesitated for several minutes before he made any reply.

"I appreciate your generosity, sir," he said, at length, "and I thank you for it. I could wish that my sister were—were less dependent on your bounty; but I have nothing, and my path lies far from her. It must be as you wish —it is to her advantage. I have, God knows! no right to mar her fortunes by my pride. I thank you, sir."

Hereupon he relapsed into his old stern, silent mood, and stared, as before, into the fire. Observing this, I hazarded one or two remarks, which he appeared not to hear or notice, but moved his lips now and then, as if speaking dumbly to himself, and shook his head mournfully in reply.

Thus a long time passed by, and the timepiece in the room struck ten o'clock. He started, rose hurriedly, and with the words "Goodnight, farewell," moved abruptly toward the door.

I seized him by the arm.

"You are not going thus?" I exclaimed. "Leave me, at least, some address by which a letter might find you, if necessary."

He looked at me with a sort of dreamy surprise.

"An address!" he replied. "An address! I am homeless. I shall wander till I find her, though it be to the ends of the earth. How can I give you an address?"

"Then, at least, you will promise to write?" He sighed and looked down irresolutely.

"For Margaret's sake! Stay! here is my card. I will write my own direction upon it— 'Château de Latour, Latour-sur-Creil, Burgundy.' This will always find me, and Margaret also. See, how easily you can do this! Surely, for your sister's sake, you will promise so small a thing."

He stretched out his hand for the card, but made no reply.

I glanced at his threadbare coat, his worn and haggard countenance, his thin, yellow hand—a rapid thought flashed across my mind—I turned aside and wrapped the card in a couple of banknotes before I gave it to him.

A peculiar expression passed over his face; he closed his hand over the card, and placed it in his waistcoat pocket; turned to leave the room—hesitated again—lingered—looked back —went out suddenly, and so parted from me without another word.

It struck me at the moment, and I have often wondered since, that he was aware of what I had done, and yet was too poor to refuse, and too proud to acknowledge the gift.

Poor Fletcher! I never saw him again.

<hr/>

CHAPTER XLIV.
COSMORAMAS.

As I left it in the gentle spring-time, so I find it in the still, bleak, sad November season. I stand in my own Gothic library again—stand with the lifted curtain in my hand, looking upon the shadowy Apostles ranged on either side—upon the recesses filled with books of poetry and learning—upon the silver lamp with its amethyst globe, swinging softly to and fro in the gloom, like a censer in an unseen hand.

There stands my chair, as though I had risen from it but an hour since—there my reading-desk and paper-case. The pen lies in the stand, but the ink has dried away, and the pen has rusted.

Slowly, almost doubtfully, I pass along between those colossal forms to the farthest end of the room, where I withdraw the heavy curtains, and look out into the night.

I have done this almost mechanically; yet, in one brief instant, a torrent of recollections rush over me—strange recollections of a warm passion, now cold and past—of a still, starry night in May, when the yellow moon hung low above the trees, and the nightingales recorded in the forest—of that almost forgotten moment when I first saw and loved Adrienne Lachapelle!

And now, how great the change! The moon is there, but her light is blue and cold; yonder black shadow is the leafless forest; the nightingales have fled long since; all is bare, and blank, and stern in the wide landscape.

And within? Ah me! the change within is yet greater.

Sighing, I drop the curtains and exclude the sullen view. Yonder lies my neglected atelier. Shall I enter? A feeling which is almost that of shame restrains me. I hesitate. At last I overcome it and go in.

There has been a gentle hand at work here also. I had half expected to find every thing as I had left it on the last terrible day, and it is a relief to me to see all traces of my fury disappeared. Easels, furniture, lay-figures, all are ranged about the room in unartistic order. My sketches have been pinned against the wall. Some of my finished paintings are framed, and hang in the best situations. Even the Medicean Venus, which I ruthlessly shattered in my unreasoning passion, has been replaced.

On yonder easel, however, a picture has been left, as if awaiting the last touches of my pencil. Half suspecting, half dreading what it may be, I compel myself to cross over and examine it. As I thought! Cathedral, and penitent, and shadowy aisles—the last and most significant of my labors! I gaze upon it long and very earnestly, and then, almost sadly, I turn the canvas to the wall and leave the room.

"Tis a dead past and a dead love; peace be to them! Forward, forward into the pleasant future, made beautiful by the vision of another and a dearer face.

I loved Adrienne—I love Margaret. How like the words, yet how unlike the feeling! My love for Adrienne was a trance, an intoxication, a delirium. Her wondrous beauty dazzled and subdued me. It haunted my sleep; it went beside me in forest and field; it glided betwixt me and the sunlight; it rose out from the pages of philosopher and poet; it usurped the place of reason and thought—I had almost said, of religion! It passed over my soul like a summer tempest, with lightning and thunder. In a word, it was the first deep, wild love of passionate manhood. Like a burning dream it came and went, and left, what such dreams leave—ashes and dust.

Not so, not so, my pale and patient Margaret, is this gentle affection which fills and satisfies my heart, and makes life holy. Thy fair calm face is ever with me, 'tis true, but it seems to read me a divine commentary on all that I do or think; it guides me, as the spirit of Beatrice guided the poet of old, from sphere to sphere of heavenly adoration. If in my sleep thou comest to me, it is in the likeness of a protecting angel, and only to think of thee is a prayer!

I can not remain apart from thee. An irresistible attraction draws me to thy side.' Farewell solitary library! There is another book, more enthralling in its pages than any volume here, which I must read to-night.

Three ladies are sitting silently together in the upper drawing-room. A blazing fire crackles and sparkles in the vast old-fashioned grate; the amber-damask draperies and antique mirrors throw back the bright reflection, and all, save the inmates, looks glowing and cheerful.

Pale and statue-like, with her deep mourning dress, sits my mother in her high-backed chair. The embroidery lies neglected on her lap; her thin white hands are pressed firmly together; her blue eyes, once so cold and frosty, are fixed upon the fire with a softened and melancholy expression that is infinitely touching. Her thoughts are with her youngest-born, wandering away, perhaps, to the time when he was an infant in her arms, or a bold and beautiful boy, reckless in the pursuit of pleasure and danger, foremost in the chase, and merriest at the vine-feast or the village fête.

Close beside her, with one hand resting on the arm of the high-backed chair, sits Adrienne, beautiful in her young widowhood, and clothed likewise in deepest sables. She too is thinking, and her eyes, bent toward the ground, are shaded by the drooping lids and long fringed lashes.

Farther back, shrinking into the shade like a little violet, sits my quiet Margaret. She holds a book in her hand, yet she is not reading. It is almost too dark in this recess to see her features distinctly, but her cheek rests on her palm, and her deep brown eyes glow through the dusk with an inner light of soul and earnest thought. She is lost in an absorbing reverie, and, from that musing smile that seems to hover round the delicate mouth, I should say the day-dream is far from sorrowful.

Hitherto my entrance has been unperceived, but, as I advance nearer to their circle, my mother looks up and extends her hand lovingly toward me; Margaret glances round with a pleased, shy smile; Adrienne alone remains motionless and unobserving.

Thus I glide into the shadow and take my

place by Margaret. We speak seldom, and then only in whispers; but our hearts are eloquent, and full of unuttered poetry.

By-and-by I imprison one little hand in mine, and draw still nearer toward those downcast eyes. Now I can hear the subdued fluttering of her breath; mine stirs the silken curl beside her check; the hand is not withdrawn; we are both happy—both silent.

> " Les anges amoureux se parlent sans paroles,
>   Comme les yeux aux yeux !"

It is winter, and the snow lies three feet deep in the court-yard. The trees look like great branches of white coral; the windows are covered with glittering traceries of feathers and frosted palm-trees; the vine-dressers' children have built up a colossal snow-man just outside the gate; the roads are blocked up from here to Chalons, and the post has not been in for nearly a-week.

> " Ah! bitter chill it was!
> The owl, for all his feathers, was a-cold;
> The hare limp'd trembling through the frozen grass,
> And silent was the flock in woolly fold."

We have done all that can be done to enliven the wintry solitude of Burgundy. Books, drawing, music, chess, and all indoor amusements are put in requisition. Sometimes I drive the ladies in my Russian sledge, and then we go flying over plains, and along the frozen rivers and snowy valleys, to the silver music of the jingling bells hung to the collars of the horses; sometimes we skate by torchlight on the little lake beyond the village; sometimes I sit apart in the recess of a bay window with my little Margaret, and give a drawing or Italian lesson.

Adrienne keeps much apart, and spends the greater part of every day writing or reading in her own apartment. One of her habits is to walk up and down the great oaken hall at the end of the north gallery, book in hand. This she will do for hours at a time, and we are careful not to interrupt these solitary moods. This hall was formerly the armory. Old helmets, and shields, and rusted falchions are yet suspended here and there against the wall, and the tattered banner at the upper end was taken from the English at the battle of Agincourt by our ancestor Louis Montmorency de la Tour, surnamed the Strong.

I have written to Seabrook entreating him to stay with us for a few weeks, but in vain. He is now resident in Antwerp, and studies severely. In a couple of months he will be prepared to pass his examination in England. He does not even say whether he shall be able to spare time for a flying farewell visit. His tone is affectionate and kindly as ever, but less frank. Of his ambition, of his prospects, he says nothing. An ill-concealed reserve clouds all his letter. I feel that there is more in this than he chooses to confide in me, and I am grieved by it.

And thus the winter passes.

Sitting alone in the library one bleak dull day in early April, when the sky, and trees, and earth look all one heavy gray, and even the fire loses half its glow, I find myself reviewing many things, revolving many plans in my own mind, and neglecting the open page before my eyes.

Not that the book lacks interest. Far from it; for it is Roger of Wendover's quaint old Chronicle, and I take all the delight of a true antiquary in the flavor of dust and vellum that hangs over the narrative. No, it is not this; it is a purely indolent, fanciful, dreaming reverie that wins me from it.

Yonder, too, lies the letter-bag, and here the key. I have not yet had the curiosity to open it, though it has been lying there for more than an hour. Come! I will rouse myself. Let us see what are the contents of the bag!

Three letters to-day—no more. Two of them are for Adrienne, and bear the English postmark. The third is for myself. I do not know this writing! I never saw it before, or I should remember it, so irregular, so blotted, so hasty and yet so tremulous is the superscription. The paper is of the coarsest and bluest description; the postmark is Philadelphia, U. S. America; it is fastened by a wafer, and is soiled by the transmission through many hands.

I know no one in America! How strange this is! I almost dread to read it; a presentiment of something unpleasant seems to stay my hand; at length I tear it open. It is this:

" I thought to live till my task was accomplished. I believed that hate was stronger than disease, and will stronger than destiny. It is not so; and, in compliance with your wish, I write these lines to tell you. I have sought her in many cities. I have followed the faint rumors of her flight even to the shores of the New World, and all vainly. I am dying. Before this can reach your hands I shall be at rest. They tell me that some six or eight days are all that remain to me in life. Be it so. Perhaps it is best. Vengeance is not to be mine, and I must prepare for eternity. My consolation is that the punishment must fall sooner or later, and that it passes, henceforward, into some other and surer hands. Break this gently to Margaret, and do not let her grieve for one who grieves not for himself. I have suffered but little. Farewell.   F. FLETCHER."

The rich autumn has come again. It is our holiday season in fair Burgundy—the merry vintage time. The purple grapes hang in heavy clusters toward the earth; the sunburnt laborers wade along the furrows, and bear away the fruit in long baskets; the wine-press is at work in the out-houses; and the peasant-girls sing like birds to the measured clicking of their shears. At night they have a supper spread for them in the hall, and afterward a dance under the lime-trees, to the droning music of a rustic musette, upon which the young men perform in turn. Then the stars come out, and the lovers, walking homeward by the light of the harvest moon, take the longest way, and go round by the river-side or the burnt mill. Truly a pleasant season is the vintage-time in Burgundy!

Pleasanter now than ever, for a dear friend has come down among us to witness the harvest of the grape, and to gladden our little circle with his genial face and joyous voice. Yes, it is Norman Seabrook whom I welcome to my old home—whose honest hand grasps mine—whose eyes beam with friendship, and whose cheery laughter rings along our shady silent rooms like a peal of wedding bells. He is paler and thinner, methinks, than when we first met in Heidelberg. London air and the study of the law hath left some traces—stolen some of the brightness from his smile and the roundness from his cheek. No matter! The soft air of our valleys and the breeze from our mountains, though his holiday last but six short weeks, shall work wonders, I promise him.

Now for excursions to the Fountain of Roses—now for long days of sporting in the forest—now for picnics and boating-parties, and drives to Chalons and Dijon, and railway trips even as far as Strasburg, for Seabrook must be shown all the beauties of our Eden!

My mother goes but little from home now. She takes no pleasure in it; but she welcomes us back at evening, and her chief delight is in preparing delicacies for our surprise at table. Hence all the exquisite creams, iced fruits, preserves, and quaint confectionery which, infinitely varied, succeed each other at our evening meals; hence the vases of fresh flowers in our sleeping-rooms; hence the boxes of chocolate bonbons which appear, as if by magic, on our dressing-tables. Her solicitous kindness meets us at every turn, and all her pleasure consists in making the happiness of others.

Thus we go out and revel, like children, by meadow-brook, and mountain torrent, and wild forest-path; and, somehow or another, Seabrook and Adrienne walk as slowly, and whisper as softly, and wander away together among the arching boughs after as pleasant and lover-like a fashion as Margaret and Paul!

> "So turtles pair
> That never mean to part!"

Winter came and went a second time, and then the Spring laughed out. Oh, beautiful Spring! Especial property of the lover and the poet! Fief, manor, and hereditary wealth of romancist and story-teller! Listen, most exquisite Spring, to the praises spoken of thee in the olden time by the worshipful and discerning author of that almost-forgotten volume, 'yclept "La Plaisante Histoire de Guerin de Monglave:"

"A l'issue de l'yver que le joly temps de primavère commence, et qu'on voit arbres verdoyer, fleurs espanouir, et qu'on oit les oisillons chanter en toute joie et doulceur, tant que les verts bocages retentissent de leur sons et que cœurs tristes, pensifs, y dolens s'en esjouissent, s'émeuvent à delaisser deuil et toute tristesse, et se parforcent à valoir mieux."

And it would seem that we mean to follow his advice down in this remote village of Latour-sur-Creil, for the bells of the chapel in the valley are ringing out peal after peal most "silver-sweet;" the servants and villagers are crowding to the porch in their holiday dresses; the church is one bower of roses and myrtle-boughs within; the rustic band of pipes, tabors, and musettes is waiting under the trees at a little distance, each performer carrying a gigantic bouquet in his button-hole and a bunch of ribbons in his hat; the good priest honors the day with a new gown, and two bridegrooms and two brides are standing at the altar!

Yes, the secret of Seabrook's industry is all told now. At first it was a panacea for a hopeless love; secondly, it was the window through which stole the first ray of sunlight; thirdly, it has become a means of great and perfect felicity. He has purchased a partnership, and can ask a wealthy lady's hand without shame. The saddest passage in this love-story is, to me, at least, that he and Adrienne must henceforth dwell in the great far city on the banks of the masted Thames!

I can not help sighing sometimes when I think of this; but then Margaret steals to my side, and, resting her cheek against my shoulder, whispers gently, "Shall I not be here, dearest?"

Even thus, reader. 'Tis a double wedding—

> "Bid the merry bells ring to thine ear!"

CHAPTER XLV.

THE CURTAIN FALLS.

It is not now many weeks since I visited England, being called thither by important business respecting the wine-produce of my estates, and being likewise desirous of passing a few days with the Seabrooks in London. I found them entirely happy, and surrounded by a little circle of intellectual and pleasant friends, artists, authors, musicians, and scientific men. Love has given to Seabrook's character all that it required of strength, and the influence of a professional career has added weight and practicability to his mind. With all his love of beauty, he is no longer a dreamer; with all his taste for enjoyment, he has learned to extract a higher pleasure from industry and honorable success. As for Adrienne, she adores him, and they quarrel on one point only, viz., as to which loves the other best. This, by the way, reminds me of Margaret and myself; but if I say that Norman and Adrienne are as happy as ourselves, I think that I have affirmed all, and more than all, that language can express.

But this is foreign to the purpose with which I have commenced this last chapter of my history. Loveless and joyless is what I must now relate, and the bell which gives the signal for the fall of the curtain is the passing bell of a guilty soul.

Returning one evening from a late interview

with some wine-merchants on the Southwark side of London Bridge, an adventure happened to me—an adventure so strange, that I have often wondered whether a presiding hand had not led me to that eventful spot at that eventful moment.

It was a wet wintry night, rent by stormful bursts of wind and rain, and pitch-dark overhead. The angry river, swollen by the tide, rocked the barges by the wharves; the furnaces along the banks shot up a hot fierce glare upon the sky; the dome of St. Paul's seemed, as it were, flickering in the blurred, uncertain distance, and the cabs and omnibuses rattled noisily past, splashing the foot-passengers as they went, and crowded within and without.

I was almost wet through, for I had forgotten to bring an umbrella, and I was shivering dismally. Cab after cab, omnibus after omnibus, had I hailed in vain. All were full, and not till I reached the Bank could I even hope to find any conveyance. The Bank was just half a mile distant, and I had the dreary bridge before me. After all, though, I could scarcely be more drenched, so I made up my mind to the evil, and took my fate leisurely.

Singularly strange, and cold, and dreary is the aspect of the city on a wet night from London Bridge! The shadowy steeples look warnful and ghostly, like tombs in a grave-yard, and the sleeping barges and steamers like river-hearses and mourning-coaches assembled for a funeral. How black the water looks down below, streaming through the arches—how black and deep, like the river of Lethe!

Musing thus as I go, my chain of thought is broken by the quavering tones of a woman's voice chanting the burden of a mournful ballad. Tremulous and shrill as the notes are, there is a something in them that arrests my attention irresistibly—a vibration, a fluency altogether superior to the style of the street ballad-singers of London. And surely—yes, the air is that sweet sad cavatina of the hapless Desdemona, "seated at the foot of a willow!"

Yonder stands the singer, a thin, pallid woman, wretchedly clad, and trembling with cold—a pitiable object. I place a shilling in her hand —it is all the change I have—and her large dark eyes, lifted suddenly to my face, look wild and hungry, and fill me with a kind of shuddering compassion.

Strange! though I have passed her, I can not refrain from looking back. Something in the glitter of those eyes has struck me with a feeling for which I can not account. It seems to me that I recognize, and yet am unfamiliar with their expression. Like the reflection of a face in water, broken, distorted, and uncertain, it hovers before me, and I strive in vain to analyze whether this be memory, or the vague promptings of some forgotten dream.

She is not singing now. She stands beneath the lamp where I left her, looking down at the coin in her hand, and shaking her head with a sad, despairing action, as though she would say, "It is not sufficient."

Not sufficient! for so I interpret the gesture. Not sufficient? Poor creature! she may have children and husband sick or starving at home —home! perhaps she has no home!

The thought is terrible. I stand back in the shadow, and take a sovereign from my purse. I will go back to her—I will question her—I will— But where is she? A moment since, and she was standing yonder by the lamp. Has she sunk into the earth, or, more probably, broken down by fatigue, stopped to rest upon one of the wet stone benches in the recesses on either side of the bridge?

Yes; as I thought, she is leaning against the wall yonder, and removing her bonnet. She must surely be ill. I hasten to her aid; she turns at the sound of my rapid steps—mounts suddenly upon the dizzy parapet—utters one piercing, wailing cry—wavers—leaps wildly forward—disappears, oh heaven, in the gulf below!

I have, even now, but an indistinct remembrance of what followed, save that with loud cries I summoned help; that, borne downward by a sudden crowd, I found myself standing presently upon a floating wharf, and watching with eager eyes the progress of a boat upon the murky river; that, amid a confusion of voices and lights, and terror-stricken faces, a wet and heavy burden was borne ashore, and carried, by the light of many lanterns, through the blank streets, stretched on a narrow plank, and covered by a fragment of sail-cloth.

Now we arrive at a building whence the curious by-standers are excluded, and which I alone, with the two boatmen, am permitted to enter. This is the police station; and here upon the narrow tressels she is laid, while the unmoved official at the desk questions me respectfully on what I have seen, and enters my replies in his ledger.

"Poor creetur!" says one of the boatmen, taking the dead hand pityingly in his own, and then laying it down gently by her side, "poor creetur! She warn't a bad looking one, neither, in her time. She have a forring look about her, too. Maybe she come from over sea, Jim!"

"Maybe," replied the other. "And she ain't old neither; but she looks half starved— she ain't nothing but skin and bone."

"It's a horrid death, poor creetur! but its surprisin' how they all seem to take to it. Poor creetur! Lord ha' mercy on her and on we, Jim!"

Their rough compassion touches me. I feel myself compelled to go back once more and look at her.

Her bonnet off—her long, wet hair, black as ebony, lying in clammy masses over her neck and arms—her white face so hushed, and still, and awful—Mysterious Providence, I recognize her now!

Thérèse Vogelsang!

THE END.

www.ingramcontent.com/pod-product-compliance
Lightning Source LLC
Chambersburg PA
CBHW060245030726
47493CB00025B/2607